Murder and Mendelssohn

Books by Kerry Greenwood

The Phryne Fisher Mysteries
Cocaine Blues
Flying too High
Murder on the Ballarat Train
Death at Victoria Dock
The Green Mill Murder
Blood and Circuses
Ruddy Gore
Urn Burial
Raisins and Almonds
Death Before Wicket
Away with the Fairies
Murder in Montparnasse
The Castlemaine Murders
Queen of the Flowers
Death by Water
Murder in the Dark
Murder on a Midsummer Night
Dead Man's Chest
Unnatural Habits
Murder and Mendelssohn

A Question of Death: An Illustrated Phryne Fisher Treasury
The Corinna Chapman Mysteries:
Earthly Delights
Heavenly Pleasures
Devil's Food
Trick or Treat
Forbidden Fruit
Cooking the Books

Murder and Mendelssohn

A Phryne Fisher Mystery

Kerry Greenwood

Poisoned Pen Press

Poisoned Pen Press
6962 E. First Ave., Ste. 103
Scottsdale, AZ 85251
www.poisonedpenpress.com
info@poisonedpenpress.com

Printed in the United States of America

This book is for Michael Warby,
peerless researcher, dear friend, il magnifico

Acknowledgments

With thanks to David Greagg (Duty Wombat and reason for existing); Ben Pryor, Shelley Robinson, Mark Pryor, Jade King, Patrizia di Biase, Themetrula Gardner, Helen Gordon-Clark, Mark Dolahenty, Patrick Burns, Vanessa Craigie, Cathy Collopy, Rita Battaglin, Daniel Barfoot, Winston B Todd, Tom Lane, Bill Collopy, Katie Purvis, Frank Mattea, Susan Tonkin, Woody, Marie Eleanor, Simon Johnson, Hugh Hunt and all my choral friends who sang rude pub songs with me and oratorios and masses and endless Christmas Carols and Laudate and "Wild Mountain Thyme"; my folk heroes Danny Spooner and Judy Small; and my mother, who sang my earliest song to me, to the percussion accompaniment of her heart.

Chapter One

As from the pow'r of Sacred Lays
The Spheres began to move;
And sung the great Creator's praise
To all the bless'd above;
So, when the last and dreadful Hour
This crumbling Pageant shall devour,
The TRUMPET shall be heard on high,
The dead shall live, the living die,
And MUSICK shall untune the Sky.

John Dryden
"A Song for St. Cecilia's Day"

It was a quiet St. Kilda morning in the summer of 1929. The Hon. Miss Phryne Fisher was sitting in her jasmine bower, drenched in scent. She was wearing a pale green silk gown embroidered with golden phoenixes, the symbol of the empress. Flaming pearls of longevity burned their way, comet-like, upon her fluttering sleeves. Her hair was as shiny as patent leather, cut in a neat bob which swung forward as she read. She was nibbling a croissant and drinking cafe au lait. With her pink cheeks and red lips and green eyes, she looked like a hand-coloured French fashion plate.

Sitting on the table in a pose made famous by Basht, goddess of cats, was her black cat Ember. He was waiting for the tidbits that her fellow break-faster would undoubtedly award such a beautiful cat who had not even ventured a paw toward that luscious stack of crispy bacon, though if a suitable offering wasn't made fairly soon, was contemplating preemptive action.

Phryne ought to have been reading *Vogue*, or perhaps some yellow-backed scandalous French novel, occasionally making arch comments to her lover, who would be exhausted from a night of passion. Instead, to ruin the picture, she was reading an autopsy report, and her companion was a tired-out police detective, eating one of Mrs. Butler's break-fasts and absorbing very strong tea as a corrective to not getting any sleep.

Dot, Phryne's companion, was embroidering waratahs on her hope chest table linen. She fully intended to marry Detective Sergeant Hugh Collins in due course, and had no wish to be found unprepared for that happy event. Tinker and Jane were playing chess in the arbour. Ruth was in the kitchen with Mrs. Butler, cook to the household, shelling peas and discussing ways to cook pineapple. The black and white sheepdog Molly was lying under the table with her head on the inspector's foot, confident that he would drop bacon rind before his toes went numb. This trick had always worked for Molly, and if it didn't on this occasion, she had a way of laying her head confidingly in a male lap with just a hint of teeth that invariably produced results.

A steady hum of useful activity serenaded Mr. Butler as he sat down on his comfortable chair and sipped his after-breakfast cup of coffee. Fortunately, he could not hear the topic of conversation.

"All right," said Phryne, putting down the report and pouring her favourite policeman another cup of the stewed licorice black tea. Just the way he liked it: enough tannic acid to dye a cauldron full of stockings. To which he then added milk and three lumps of sugar. Generations of tea aficionados rolled in their graves. "I've read it. Someone has stifled an orchestral conductor with really quite a lot of sheets of Mendelssohn's *Elijah* stuffed down his throat."

"Right," said the detective inspector.

"Seems excessive, even as musical criticism," commented Phryne. "Your doctor has done a competent examination. Taken samples of blood, urine, and stomach contents. Noted no signs of struggle, no scratches or bruises except those on his shoulders, which seem to mean that the murderer knelt on him while suffocating him. I think those are kneecap marks. And he didn't struggle because he had a tummy full of—" her eyebrows lifted "—enough opiates to knock out a smallish rhinoceros. In fact, enough to kill him, which makes the added sheet music supererogatory. Baroque, verging on rococo. A flamboyant murderer, Jack dear, with a point to prove."

"Yes," said Jack. "But what point? I don't know anything about music. And I don't know anything about these…these sort of people. I thought…" His voice trailed off and he took a strengthening gulp of the tar-water tea.

Phryne smiled. She knew how much Jack Robinson hated asking for her unofficial and potentially world-shattering help. She volunteered.

"I have always liked Mendelssohn," she told him. "Who is performing it?"

"The Melbourne Harmony Choir, with the Occasional Orchestra. Amateurs but with professional soloists and a professional conductor," Jack read from his notebook. "The dead man was called Hedley Tregennis. Forty-five, born in Richmond, separated from his wife, no children. Bit of a reputation for being loud, insulting, and impatient."

"That applies to most conductors," said Phryne.

"See? I don't know all this stuff. They're having a rehearsal tonight at the Scots Church Assembly Hall, just before the lantern lecture. Can you come along with me? You're sure to notice things that I won't. Just as long," added Jack Robinson anxiously, noticing the bright interest in those green eyes, "you don't get the idea that it's your case, or anything silly like that."

"Of course not," cooed Phryne. "What time? Can I pick you up?"

"Mr. Butler driving?" asked Jack Robinson. Miss Fisher drove like a demon and he had to keep his eyes shut the whole journey, in case he saw how many breaches of the traffic laws she committed, and closing his eyes in a moving car made him queasy.

"Yes, there will be nowhere to leave the car on Collins Street."

"Right, then, five thirty at the police station," he told her.

"What's the lantern lecture?" she asked, as he dropped bacon rinds to Molly, fed Ember a large piece of the same, and wiped his mouth preparatory to facing the world again.

"Some bloke called Rupert Sheffield," he said. "On the science of deduction. Ought to ask him to help," he added, and left, thanking Mrs. Butler on the way out through the kitchen.

Phryne was unexpectedly stung. Science of deduction? What did any man called Rupert know about deduction that the Hon. Miss Phryne Fisher didn't know?

Ridiculous. She shook herself into order like an affronted cat and ate the rest of her croissant with a sharp snap of her white teeth.

"We got a case, Guv?" asked Tinker. A Queenscliff fisher boy, he had attached himself at heel, like a small scruffy terrier, and Phryne had decided that he might be useful. As well as being endearingly intelligent. And devoted to Sexton Blake. He had fitted in well. Phryne's adopted daughter Jane found him clever and was teaching him chess. Her other adopted daughter Ruth liked his appetite, which was reliably voracious, even for cooking experiments which had slightly failed. Mr. and Mrs. Butler appreciated the supply of fresh fish and Dot liked having someone sleeping in the back garden, which made her feel more secure. Molly liked accompanying him on fishing expeditions. Ember tolerated him with his usual amused disdain. Ember was utterly uninterested in any other humans apart from his own family (Phryne, Ruth, and Jane), whom he considered to be under his protecting paw. Others might be awarded some passing notice if they came bearing food. Possibly. Tinker was bearable, and pleasantly free with his fish.

That meant that Tinker was enveloped in a glow of approval from the entire household, which in turn had meant that Tinker could be easy in their company. He adored Phryne with his whole heart. And, together with Dot, he worried about her. She was far too bold for someone who was only five-foot-two and weighed in at about seven stone in a wringing wet army overcoat.

However, he thought, as he returned to Phryne's briefing on this odd murder, even the Guv'nor couldn't get into too much trouble at a choir rehearsal and a lantern lecture.

Could she?

As he often did, Tinker felt uneasy, and shared a glance with Dot. She was concerned, too.

"Any ideas?" Phryne asked her household.

"Must be very angry," offered Jane.

"Why angry?"

"Didn't just want Mr. Tregennis dead," said Jane, who was destined to be a doctor. "He would have died with that overdose. He was dying, in fact, wasn't he, when the music was stuffed into his mouth?"

"Probably," agreed Phryne.

"If the murderer just wanted to get rid of the bloke, then the morphine would have done the trick," said Tinker, with the callousness of fourteen. "But that wasn't enough."

"And if the murderer wanted him to suffer, he went the wrong way about it," said Dot. "The poor man can't have felt a thing."

"Yes, and isn't that odd?" commented Phryne. "The music stuffed into the mouth is, as my learned colleague says, an act of rage. But the method of death, as my other learned colleague observes, is peaceful and painless. Not a mark on him, no struggle, no bruises. And from this we can surmise…"

"Well," said Jane, "either the murderer is mad, a person of moods…"

"Yes," said Phryne. "Or?"

"Or the murderer is two people," said Dot. "One who just wants him dead and one who's real furious at him."

"Yes," said Phryne, "or…?"

"The murderer's weak," said Tinker. "Not strong enough to hold the bloke down and suffocate him without drugging him first."

Phryne continued, reading from her notes. Jack had rather meanly taken his file with him. "Now, stomach contents disclose that he had eaten a rather expensive snack just before he died. Half a dozen fresh oysters, a slice or two of smoked salmon, a small piece of stilton, and water biscuits."

"Expensive is right," commented Ruth.

"Stilton has to be specially imported, oysters are really unsafe to eat unless you buy the ones from select fishmongers, and smoked salmon comes from Scotland."

"Correct. As last meals go, it is a rather lavish one. He seems to have drunk…"

"Champagne?" suggested Ruth, who knew which wines were appropriate for shellfish. Mr. Butler was a mine of information on the subject.

"No, oddly enough, a sweet dessert wine. Muscat, perhaps, or Imperial Tokay," replied Phryne. "Which is costly, but in my opinion has a tawdry taste and is far too sugary."

"But I bet it would cover up the taste of the poison," said Dot. "Like putting bitter medicine into syrup."

"Never fooled me," said Phryne, brooding darkly on the cough medicines of her youth. She particularly had it in for Buckley's Canadiol Mixture, which tasted like rendered-down pine trees. "But a good notion, Dot dear. Presumably Mr. Tregennis had a sweet tooth, his poisoner knew that, and instead of providing a light dry sparkling wine with his after-rehearsal amuse-bouche, gave him a glass of some noxious wine which would hide the poison. Morphine is extremely bitter. Only other way to hide it would be in a naturally bitter drink or food. Keep that in mind next time you are contemplating murder."

"Six months ago, Miss, I would have been shocked at that comment," said Dot.

Phryne beamed at her. "See how you've been coming along, Dot dear? Well done!"

Dot was not sure whether this was a sign of growing sophistication or an indication of moral degeneracy, and decided to confess it to her local priest in due course. He was an old priest. He would cope.

"The body was found on the floor of the conductor's room. He had been dead for some time. The cleaning lady found him when she came in to sweep at six this morning. He was last seen—by everyone else—retreating there and slamming the door after an unusually fraught rehearsal. He seems to have been a short-tempered bully, and one wonders if the entire choir—or perhaps only the basses—decided to remove him."

She looked up to see if the joke had registered. No one smiled. She decided that she really must see to the musical education of her minions, and went on.

"No sign of any plates, glasses, or cutlery," she told them. "Whoever brought the food took all evidence away with them. The usual police search found no suicide note, no useful calling cards, matchbooks, foreign coins, obscure words written on the walls, or scales of rare venomous reptiles."

"Oh." Tinker was disappointed.

"The choir departed in a body and caught the tram into Carlton, where they went to a sly-grog pub and sang very rude songs until at least three in the morning."

"But they can't have been in full view all the time," objected Dot. "Some of them must have, you know, visited the conveniences, gone out for a breath of air—any one of them could have come back to poison Mr. Tregennis."

"Yes, Dot, true," said Phryne. "That is why Jack wanted me to come and look at his choristers. In case something leaps to mind."

"Where did the food come from?" asked Ruth, who had been thinking deeply. "That's not ordinary pie cart stuff, that's expensive hotel food."

"Another thing which the overworked constabulary are even now trying to ascertain." Phryne leafed through her notes. "Questions?"

"Any sign that he had…been with a lady?" asked Dot, even more convinced of her eventual destination. "No lipstick marks, things like that?"

"I am not going to harrow your innocent ears with the ghastly details, Dot, but he certainly hadn't had any close communion with anyone for some days, and only Jane can ask me how I know that, and only if she looks up the anatomy text first on seminal vesicles. And asks me in private. No lipstick, greasepaint, love bites, or other indelicate things, but long blonde hairs on his coat. Blondes are being asked pointed questions as we speak."

"Because it is the sort of intimate supper they describe in *Larousse Gastronomique*," added Ruth. "Oysters, smoked salmon, wine. Even though it's the wrong wine." Ruth was aggrieved. Anyone who could afford smoked salmon ought to know that it went with champagne.

"It might have been a love affair gone wrong," said Jane.

"Then why stuff music down the poor bloke's throat?" asked Tinker.

Phryne patted his shoulder.

"We need, as Sherlock Holmes would say, more data. So I shall go out this evening and get some, and I would rather go alone, darlings. Then I shall come back and we shall discuss it. All right?"

"If you say so, Guv," said Tinker, on behalf of them all.

"Good. Very good, all of you." Phryne smiled general approval. "You have all done very well. Science of deduction, indeed," she added, and swept into the house to bathe and dress.

"It's just a choir rehearsal," said Jane to Tinker.

"How much trouble can she get into at a choir rehearsal?"

"She's Miss Phryne," said Dot. "She could get into trouble in heaven. God forgive me," she added, and crossed herself.

Chapter Two

All things shall perish from under the sky,
Music alone shall live, music alone shall live,
Music alone shall live, never to die.

—Traditional round

Phryne remembered the stairs up to the Scots Church Assembly Hall. She put on a low-heeled pair of shoes, as she had slightly sprained her ankles dancing the Charleston two nights before. Not wishing to overawe the choir, she dressed in a decently quiet turquoise dress, jacket, and hat and took a large handbag. As usual her petticoat pocket contained emergency requisites: a spare lighter, a banknote, cigarettes, a pearl-handled .22 Beretta. One never knew what the exigencies of rehearsal might entail. Mr. Butler drove Phryne and her policeman with calm and dignity into the city, left them at the corner of Collins and Russell streets, and took the car to the garage where it had been built. He had instructions to come back at nine. Phryne had decided to watch the lantern lecture. It might even be instructive.

She was making suggestions to Jack Robinson as she felt her way, a little gingerly, up the stairs. Hugh Collins waited at the door.

"You need to find out who brought that food, Jack dear, and I suggest you start with the hotel just across the road. That was, as Ruth pointed out, expensive provender, not available from just any soup kitchen. Then you need to find the conductor's lover."

"His lover?" asked Jack.

"Well, yes, that aphrodisiac little supper was an invitation of sorts. Then you need to talk to the choir's librarian."

"Why?" asked Jack.

At that moment someone caught Phryne around the waist and dragged her into a close embrace. He never knew how close he was to a knee where it would not have been appreciated because, fortunately for him, Phryne recognised him and flung her arms around his neck.

"John!" she exclaimed. "John Wilson, how can you possibly be here? One moment." She turned in his arms and said to Jack Robinson, "The librarian has all the scores, numbered. Get her to call them all in. That music had to come from somewhere. I'll be in directly."

Jack Robinson shook his head, collected his detective sergeant, and entered the hall. John Wilson chuckled.

"Still the same Phryne, eh?" he asked. "And it's Dr. John, now."

"Oh, excellent, so you went back after… afterwards?"

John Wilson had been a medical student in 1918 when he had been dragged from his residency and dropped into the Battle of the Somme. He had run a forward casualty-clearing station, dipped deep in blood and death. Horrified, shell-shocked and twenty-two years old, he had met Phryne, bringing in the wounded. There, in her ambulance, under bombardment, he and Phryne had mutually ripped the clothes off each other and mated fiercely, deaf from shelling, desperate to find a warm living body to hang on to while the world bled and fractured and blew up around them. Thereafter Phryne had invited him into her ambulance frequently. He had always been delighted to accept her invitation, alone of the women in the world, for John Wilson's heart was given to men. Phryne seemed to be in a different category. He had often puzzled about it. However, she was exceptional.

And then, near the end of the war, in

November, for God's sake, a sniper had been amusing himself shooting at the red cross on John's tent, and only Phryne jamming her ambulance into gear, forcing it up and over a trench and covering him, meant that he got a bullet in the leg, not a number of them in head and heart. He had been standing just behind the red cross. He had been carried off by his own stretcher-bearers, and somehow he had never seen Phryne again.

She looked just the same, a little plumper than the starveling he had known, still the same black hair, red lips, and green eyes that cut through all pretence. She smelt bewitchingly of clean hair and Jicky. She was waiting for his reassurance so he gave it.

"It was just my leg, dear girl, not my hands. And it isn't too bad. I can get along. And if it hadn't been for you—" he tightened his embrace "—it wouldn't be anything at all."

Phryne kissed him on the cheek. He smelt the same as he had when she had last kissed him. Coffee, pipe tobacco, his own warm, earthy scent. No faint overscent of ether; not practising medicine, then. His kindly blue eyes were still the same, his skin more weathered, his military haircut greying a little at the temples. His body, under her hands, was muscular and stocky. She would not at all mind hauling John Wilson into her ambulance again—and this time she had a house and a comfortable bed. Definitely today's Good Thought.

"What are you doing here, John darling?" she asked. "Can you dine with me?"

He smiled gently. He had always smiled at her like that. As though her energy amused him. He had always been quiet and kind, a stalwart presence, as the young soldiers died under his hands and he and Phryne wept in each other's arms over the death of hope and innocence, kisses tainted with high-explosive smoke. How had she lost touch with this admirable John? He had gone back to university and she had stayed in Paris. She had heard that he was living with his young man, what was his name…Galahad? Lancelot? Something like that. And she had assumed he was happy. From the sad shadows under his eyes, she had been wrong. She patted his cheek with one scented hand. He took this as a cue.

"Do you mean here in Australia, Phryne love, or here on the steps of the assembly hall, where we are making exhibitions of ourselves?"

"I always liked your voice," she said. "So deep and pleasant, it made the poor boys feel better just to hear you. Here in all senses, please."

"I came to Australia with Rupert Sheffield, who was a code-breaker and mathematician. Did something very hush-hush. In Greece, you know.

He's a dear fellow but a tad accident-prone. We had barely arrived in your fine country when a whole net of cargo just missed flattening us. Careless. We are in Melbourne for him to give his mathematical wisdom to the masses. I'm here on the steps because he is giving a lecture tonight and wanted me to test the apparatus. It flickered too much last night."

"Sheffield the Science of Deduction man? Oh, and are you and he…?"

"No," he said quickly. "Not at all."

"And Arthur?" She had remembered the name.

"Arthur died," he said steadily. "A long time ago. Heart failure. Never knew he had anything wrong with him and even I didn't diagnose it."

"John dear," she said softly. He leaned his forehead into her shoulder a moment, then she felt his spine straighten, the military manner reassumed like a coat. Or a mask.

"Now, I must go and see about that projector," he said. "Are you helping the police with their enquiries, Phryne?"

"Oh, yes, just with the choir. My policeman doesn't know anything about "these sorts of people" and I do."

"Madame." He bowed her through the door.

"And dinner? Dr. MacMillan is here, too. She'd be delighted to see you again."

"I'd love to, Phryne, but I'd have to find out what Sheffield…"

"All right, I see," said Phryne, who knew a case of raging unrequited love when she saw it, even if John ignored his own clinical indications. "I'll stay for the show, and you can talk to me afterwards."

"Thanks," he murmured, and kissed her cheek.

Phryne went toward what sounded like a full-scale choral riot in a mixed frame of mind. On the one hand, her old friend Dr. Wilson was in Melbourne. On the other hand, her chances of resuming their former relations seemed increasingly unlikely.

"Drat," she murmured, and plunged into the fray.

◇◇◇

Approximately thirty singers were gathered around approximately one librarian, who was trying to order her scores by their accession numbers. She was not assisted by the voices, which were explaining that they'd left their score 1) at home, 2) in the dressing room, 3) on the bus, or 4) had never had one to begin with, despite that signature in the book; yes, it was their signature, but they couldn't remember being issued a score and had been looking over Matt's shoulder. Phryne had sung in many a chorus and saw this as situation normal, but Jack

Robinson was disconcerted. Disconcerted police-men have a tendency to shout.

"Silence!" he bellowed, in tones which had frozen spines in darkest Little Lon and compelled instant obedience from Fitzroy hooligans. The choir didn't precisely fall silent, as any choir has been yelled at by experts, but the squabbling abated enough for him to make himself heard.

"Hedley Tregennis has been murdered," he announced. "Show some respect. I need to talk to all of you. Who wants to be first?"

There was a noticeable lack of volunteers. Phryne had taken a seat on stage and was scanning faces in her usual manner. She nodded toward a stocky lad with blond hair and blue eyes. That was the leader of this group. The collection of singers were all keeping him in sight. Jack beckoned and he came forward, tripping over a piece of string and having to be helped to his feet by a large economy-size bass.

"Name?" barked the policeman.

"Smith," he said. "Matthew. Tenor."

"Collins, are you writing this down?" demanded Robinson.

Hugh licked his indelible pencil and nodded.

"When was the last time you saw Hedley Tregennis?"

"Last night," said Matthew Smith. "He

slammed off stage in a filthy temper and told us to bugger off and not come back until today, so—" he shrugged "—we buggered off as requested."

"Where did you go from here?"

"Most of us went to the pub," the young man answered. "I went home. They stayed until quite late at the pub."

"More like early morning," observed the large bass. "I didn't get home till four. My landlady had locked me out and I had to sleep in the laundry. Lucky it's summer."

"I got home at three thirty, but I live in Carlton; you must have had to walk home," commented another bass.

"Well, yes, Tom, I spent all my money at the Cr—" said the bass, and shut up abruptly as a small fierce alto slapped a hand across his mouth.

"I am not interested in sly grog," said Jack Robinson with deteriorating patience. "I am interested in the last time you saw Hedley Tregennis. And if you don't tell me everything you know about it, I shall arrange a raid on the Criterion and you will have nowhere to drink. Line up and give names, addresses, and the time you last saw Hedley Tregennis to the constable at the table over there. Anyone who has something particular to say, talk to my sergeant. I'm going to sit over there and wait until someone tells me something interesting."

He found a seat. Phryne stayed where she was, watching. Robinson admired the way she did not seem to watch; inspecting her nails, running a finger up her calf as though to check for a run in her stocking, fussing with her hair. She looked perfectly harmless, unless you caught her eye, in which case you felt that you were stripped down to component molecules, weighed in the balance, and found wanting. She examined the choir as they returned from giving their details and lined up on stage, beginning to sing rounds as a warm-up as soon as there were more than four of them. Led by Tom, the bass, they started the charming and absurd "Life is But a Melancholy Flower" to the tune of "Frère Jacques" and sang along quite tunefully until a soprano clutched her hands dramatically to her bosom and wailed, "We shouldn't be doing this!" in a voice trained to carry. The singing died down.

"Why not, Julia?" asked Matthew Smith. "We're a choir and we're stuck here and the concert's on in two weeks."

"But we should have some respect, like the policeman said," she declaimed.

"Why?" asked a tall, affected tenor with sleek brown hair and a determined pair of spectacles. "He didn't have any respect for us. Or for the work.

Poor old Mendelssohn, taken at a breakneck gallop like that."

"What about the poor old dead man?" asked a redheaded alto.

"It's all right for you, you're a med student, Bones," protested Julia, who unlike the stereotype was thin, dark, and would be scraggy when she was forty. "You're used to dead people. He was just lying on the floor like a bundle of old…old music. That's upsetting!"

"Dead people are dead," said Bones, shrugging again.

"You're disgusting!" protested Julia.

The interaction was interesting. Phryne listened carefully, then cut Julia out as she lined up for a cup of the choir's thin tea.

"Talk to me," she said politely.

Julia bridled. The temperament, however, was canonical. "Why?"

"Me or the cop," said Phryne.

Julia tried a half-hearted flounce. Phryne had seen flounces before. She raised an eyebrow. Julia surrendered.

"Oh, all right, who are you?"

"I'm Phryne Fisher," said Phryne. "Come and sit down over here. Now, tell me how you knew what the deceased Hedley Tregennis looked like."

"I was guessing," said Julia.

"Like a bundle of old music," persisted Phryne. "He could have been flat on his back or on his front or sitting in a chair, but he was, as it happens, lying curled up and there was music involved. How did you know that?"

Julia looked around wildly for rescue. No one interrupted.

"Woman's intuition?" she ventured.

Phryne chuckled. "Have a heart. When did you see the body?"

"Oh, all right," said Julia crossly. "I wasn't going to the pub, I was going home, then when I was halfway there I remembered I had left my score behind. I knew the caretaker wouldn't lock up until after ten because of the lantern lecture so I came back and went backstage to the conductor's room."

"Why there?" asked Phryne.

"It has a lock; the librarian stashes the scores there when someone leaves one behind. Scores are expensive. That's why she carries on so much if someone loses one."

"Then how were you intending to retrieve your score?" asked Phryne. "Do you have a key?"

"No, but there's one hung up in the locker. In case we forget. No one knows it's there."

"Except thirty singers, their friends and hangers-on, and the pianist," observed Phryne. Julia bit her lip.

"Oh, yes, them. Us. I suppose. I unlocked the door and he was lying on the floor all dead and I was so scared I just ran away."

"Locking the door behind you," said Phryne evenly.

"Yes," said Julia.

"And taking your score."

"Yes, well, it was just on the desk—I didn't have to step over him or anything," explained Julia. "And I needed to rehearse. I've got a quartet. It's "Holy, Holy, Holy." Everyone says I'm ready to sing it."

"Right," said Phryne. Singers. She had forgotten what they were like. "I'm sure you'll be good. Now, I want you to close your eyes. Think for me. You're back in the conductor's office. You're not looking at the dead man. You're looking at the room. Are you there?"

"Yes," breathed Julia, who would have been an ideal hypnotic subject.

"Look around. What can you see?" prompted Phryne in a soft, gentle voice.

"Desk, chair, scores on the desk, teapot, teacup. Coat hung behind the door. Wastepaper basket full of torn-up paper."

"Music paper?" asked Phryne.

"No, just writing paper, white, with black ink on it. That's all, really. Dead man on the floor. Mr. Tregennis. Horrible man."

"Why was he horrible?" Phryne enquired, taking advantage of Julia's trance.

"Hands," said Julia. "All over us. Any girl. He'd pinch and poke and grab. Like an octopus. Nasty hot hands. And he'd yell and stamp and call us all tarts and whores if we sang a note wrong. I'm not sorry he's dead," said Julia, coming out of her fugue state. "What have I been saying?"

"Nothing at all worrying," said Phryne. "Tell me, did Mr. Tregennis have a girlfriend in the choir? Someone special?"

The pink mouth made a creditable moue of distaste.

"Not us," she said loudly. "None of us would go within arm's reach of him."

"Right," agreed the redheaded alto. She held out a hand.

"Annie," she said. "You're Phryne Fisher, aren't you? Seen you before. Detecting?"

"Just here to help my favourite policeman arrest the right person."

"Good, because it wasn't us. Not that we're weeping buckets," confessed Annie. "Because we aren't. He was a pig. And that's being unkind to pigs. But you want to tell your policeman to look for the mystery woman."

Her voice had a portentous tone with an edge of irony.

Phryne grinned. "And who would this mystery woman be?"

"I don't know," said Annie crossly. "If we knew that she wouldn't be a mystery woman. She always came to see him after a rehearsal in this hall. Tommy said he saw her but he's not a reliable person. Loves practical jokes. Leg pulls. You know. You could ask him," she said, suddenly smiling at some wicked thought.

"Do you think he will try to pull my leg?" asked Phryne.

"No, probably not, but it would be nice to watch when you demolish him," said Annie. "Tommy's been getting on our nerves lately."

"You do me too much credit," murmured Phryne. "I shall sic my policeman on him. That ought to be sufficient."

"Thank you," said Annie.

"Now, Julia, you left the hall with your score and went home—at what time?" asked Phryne.

"Must have been about nine," said Julia. "Was it really awful of me to leave him there?" she asked pathetically.

"Nothing could have done him the slightest good at that point," Phryne reassured her. Annie took Julia back to the tea queue and Phryne drifted over to Jack Robinson.

"He was dead by about nine, and the tray was

gone as well," she told him. "Rehearsal finished at eight when the lantern lecture started and most of the choir were out of the hall by eight thirty. Some would have gone to the facilities and some stayed to wait for those who had done so, but apart from the caretaker and one soprano the place would have been empty of this choir by eight thirty. The lantern lecture finished at nine and Tregennis was dead by then."

"I'm not even going to ask how you know that," Jack Robinson replied.

"Good, because I'm not going to tell you. I suggest that you have a word with that big dark-haired bruiser over there. Name of Tommy. Practical joker. If he found Tregennis dead, he might have thought it amusing to stuff music down his throat."

"Might he?" asked Robinson. "Sense of humour, eh? And he's a big bloke, he could have done it."

Phryne nodded. "Anything interesting from the interviews?"

"The ones who didn't go to the pub went blamelessly home, some to their doting parents in South Ybarra and some to their digs in Carlton," said Robinson. "The piano bloke lives in Collins Street at eighty-eight, so just had to totter. Must have been a good piano player before the grog got him, though. Says he played with Beecham. Called Tregennis a butcher."

"Only musically, Jack dear, just an expression. Right, you get Tommy, and we'd better clear these people backstage—it's time for the lantern lecture on the science of deduction."

"That sounds like it might be useful," said Jack Robinson, and went off to apprehend the bass. Phryne snorted. Deduction was not a science. It was an art, and she was very good at it.

◇◇◇

Phryne slid out into the auditorium and slipped into a seat at the back. The hall was half full, not bad for a summer weekend, when most people would be at the beach. But the Melbourne craze for self-improvement apparently continued. She could see the solid, comfortable outline of Wilson sitting next to the lantern slide projector. And she could hear the speaker. A beautiful voice. A voice that was English, educated without being shrill, deep, rich, and perfectly pitched. A voice which could only be compared to Irish coffee with chocolate on top.

She looked at the speaker.

Oh, my.

He was tall and slender. He moved with the assurance of a dancer, occasionally flinging out a hand for emphasis or to point out an equation on the lantern slide. He had a mop of dark curls and a long, pale, sculptured face. Greek? If so, Ancient

Greek. Strong. Disdainful, as though he knew that his audience couldn't possibly be bright enough to really appreciate him. And the oddest eyes that Phryne had ever seen. Liquid, quick, set at a cat-like angle, chillingly observant and, Phryne could swear, in some lights, lavender or silver.

John Wilson's devotion was instantly explained. Not so the lecture. Phryne knew that she had one flaw (she admitted to one, apart from an occasional nostalgic plunge into the foods of her youth, such as dried apricots): she had no head for mathematics. Smitten young physicists had poured explanations into her ears, and she had or had not seduced them, but she had never understood any physics or mathematics except the Newtonian, because they were the ones which got you shot. Words were being used, concepts explained, that she did not even begin to comprehend.

"When estimating the interpolation error, carefully select the interpolative points and use Tchebyshev polynomials."

The lecture ended with the last slide. The lights came up. The audience rose, stretched, filtered out. Phryne went to the projector to stand beside John as the lecturer leapt lightly down off the stage and walked forward.

He moves like a cat, she thought. A big cat.

Panther, perhaps. Phryne put a hand on John's arm. "Introduce me?" she asked.

He smiled at her. "Of course. This is Rupert Sheffield. The Hon. Miss Phryne Fisher," he said. "An old friend of mine whom I have not seen since the war."

"Delighted," said Rupert, taking Phryne's hand and bowing a little.

"As am I," she replied.

"Apart from the fact that you are wealthy, have a black cat in the house, use Jicky, and have slightly sprained your ankles dancing, I know little about you," he told her.

Tit for tat, Phryne thought, and you started it. She smiled up into the amazing lavender—they really were lavender—eyes and said, "And apart from the fact that you went to Winchester and Cambridge, spent the war breaking codes, have your shoes made by Loeb and your suits in Savile Row—and I think that tie is from Westford's in Soho—use coconut dressing on your hair, are right-handed, and a friend of my dear John Wilson, I know very little about *you*."

John chuckled.

Rupert stiffened and touched his tie. "Halogen's," he corrected.

"My mistake," said Phryne amiably.

"My dear," said John, "you have always been exceptional."

"In many ways," agreed Phryne. "What I don't know is whether you would like to come to dinner tomorrow night?"

"You may have John," conceded the beautiful man, "since you have a prior claim. I shall be busy. Thinking," he threw in, as he paced off down the aisle like a panther to whom an indecent suggestion has been made by a gutter cat of no breeding.

"Right," said Phryne, desperately trying not to laugh. "It is offended, see, it stalks away," she added. The outer door slammed and she giggled helplessly.

"He's a good fellow really," rumbled John. "You shouldn't tease him, Phryne."

"He started it," Phryne reminded him.

"Phryne, you were in Intelligence, weren't you? After the war?" he asked.

"Yes, for a while. Why?"

"I don't like these…accidents. Someone may wish to harm Rupert. Could you…ask around?"

"Of course," said Phryne, patting his cheek. "Seven, at my house? Here's my card. Try to soothe the poor dear. I don't want to steal you from him, John."

"You don't…no, Phryne, you've got it wrong," he called after her receding figure.

"Wouldn't be the first time," she answered, her hand on the backstage door. "Must go, I've got choristers to grill."

And then she was gone. John packed up his lantern slides with the slight breathlessness that close contact with Phryne had always given him. It occurred to him that, for the very first time in his life, Rupert Sheffield might have met his match.

Then he chuckled, too.

◇〉◇〉

Jack Robinson was not managing the massed choir very well. They milled about. They talked all the time. They wanted to go home. They fretted.

"Herding cats, Jack dear." Phryne patted him on the arm. "Watch."

She stood on a chair with a fine flourish of silk-clad legs, which riveted all the male eyes, and clapped her hands twice. More or less instant silence fell.

"Everyone who went to the pub, take the hand of a person that you know was in the pub with you and walk to the right. Only a person whom you know accompanied you to the pub. To the tune of "Life is But a Melancholy Flower" divided by sop, alto, tenor, and bass," she said, and they began to sing and move like little lambkins.

"*Life is but a, life is but a,*" sang the basses.

"*Melancholy flower, Melancholy flower,*" sang the tenors.

"*Life is butter melon, life is butter melon,*" sang the altos.

"*Cauliflower, cauliflower,*" sang the sopranos.

Silly sort of song, reflected Jack, but it was working. Most of the choir were grouped together, still singing their nonsensical round. Eleven of them remained, those who had gone blamelessly home. Apart from the ineffable Julia, they named themselves as Jenny Leaper, soprano; Helen Burke, alto; and one Tabitha Willis, a vibrant young woman with black curls who exuded such an air of health and well-being that Phryne found herself smiling at her. You could cure a migraine just by leaning on her shoulder. She, of course, was also an alto. The other soprano was Chloe McMahon, who had the heft and force of a woman destined for Wagner, an armoured brassiere and a horned helmet. Formidable. The others were all male, the pianist, tenors, and basses. Which rather cut down their chances of being the mystery woman, although Miss Fisher knew some very strange people. Mr. Tregennis was probably not a candidate for one of Krafft-Ebing's studies, as he had been molesting the female choir members exclusively. She led them away in a group to allow Detective Inspector Robinson to question the ladies. He shot her a resentful look. She blew him a kiss.

"Well," she said, perching on a table and again displaying silk stockings, "what can you tell me about this regrettable occurrence?"

"Define regrettable," said a skinny young man with overlong hair and a handful of written notes.

"Oh, do shut up, Len," said Matthew, the placid blond with the beginnings of a beard. When he grew up he was definitely going to play Father Christmas with conviction and no need for padding. Tasty. Phryne's mind was rather running to men with a certain embonpoint. If only as a contrast to the beautiful Lin Chung, away in Hong Kong on business, drat it all. She restrained herself, as Jack would not look kindly on her seducing the suspects.

"Introduce yourselves," she told them, and shook hands with, successively, Leonard, tenor and nuisance, he of the notes; Oliver, another economy-size bass, with red hair and a gorgeous smile; a tall and rather languid medical student called Bones; and a palpable gigolo called Luigi. He lingered over her hand, bent to kiss it, and gave her his practised flash of white teeth and a waft of bay rum. She awarded him a glance which smouldered. He preened. That was quite enough of that, she thought.

"Tell me about the conductor," she said.

"Why are you just talking to us?" demanded Len suspiciously.

"Because, my pet, you have no alibi. You could have doubled back and…caused his death. Show me your scores."

They were produced from bags and satchels. Phryne flicked through them. Every one was complete.

"Good. Now, you were saying?"

"He wasn't a very nice man," said Matthew.

"He was a pig," riposted Oliver, blushing with annoyance. "He couldn't keep his hands off the ladies of the choir. Some of them were threatening to leave."

"I was in favour of speaking very severely to him," said Matthew. "But the others wouldn't let me."

"Because he came cheap, you see," said Bones the medical student. "We're only semi-professional, we haven't got a lot to spend on conductors when we have to pay the orchestra."

"Tell me," said Phryne to him, "do you work in a hospital?"

"Not yet, they aren't going to lose us on the wards, not even in a free clinic," he replied. "Why?"

"Drugs," said Phryne mysteriously.

"Oh," exclaimed Oliver. "He was poisoned?"

"Among other things. Anyone drug in your choir?"

"Us? How could we afford drugs? And they affect the voice," Matthew told her. "We might drink a bit much sometimes…"

"Most times…" said Oliver.

"When we have a chance…" put in Leonard.

"Or when someone else is buying…" agreed Bones.

"But we don't take drugs," concluded Matthew. Fugues, thought Phryne; they were obviously contagious. Like singing in harmony. The main choir was still buttering melons.

"And what about this mystery woman?" she asked.

"Tommy said he saw her," said Matthew.

"But you don't altogether believe him," said Phryne.

They gazed at her, astonished.

"How did you know that? No, never mind, let's get on—I want to get home before morning or I'll be sleeping in the back garden again," grumbled Len. "No, we don't. We were curious about her. I even hung about one night hoping to catch sight of her. But I didn't. Can we go home now?"

"Who's taking over as concert master until you get a new conductor?" asked Phryne.

"Me," said Matthew. "I'll do, in a pinch."

"You don't want to be a conductor?" asked Phryne.

"No," said Matthew. "I want to be a diplomat. Languages."

"My card," said Phryne, handing them out. "Telephone if you remember anything you don't quite want to tell a policeman without a little… filtering."

She gave them a comprehensive smile, and wandered over to join the ladies. Who were reducing Robinson to spluttering fury. They seemed incapable of speaking one at a time or keeping to a subject.

"This way, ladies." Phryne led Chloe away by one smooth, pearly, dimpled hand and the others followed as if towed. She formed them into a neat half-circle and scanned every face.

"All right, you have ten minutes to tell me about the mystery woman, one at a time, or I'll give you back to that poor detective inspector and he can lock you up for the night. He's about three, perhaps two and a half inches from the end of his tether. Right? Then we all get to go home."

"Right," said the alto Tabitha, shaking her dark curls. "The mystery woman wasn't one of us."

"Very well," said Phryne, who knew how interconnected choirs were, and how impossible it was to keep a secret among them. "Who is she?"

"Not sure," said Chloe in her creamy voice. "Tommy said he saw her but…"

"You don't believe Tommy, yes, I know. Any more clues?"

"She was tall," offered Julia. "I heard her walking down the corridor and she had flat shoes on."

"And that makes her tall?" questioned Tabitha.

"Yes, Tab, because you know how he hated any woman being taller than him and you know how he loved high heels," explained Julia. Phryne thought about it. It made a certain kind of sense. Julia sense, in fact.

"She brought him food," said Helen. "When I went into the conductor's room the next day, I could always smell food. Expensive food. My mother is a very good cook."

"Hotel food," said Jenny, who was small and dynamic. "He didn't offer to share it with us!"

"And he was secretive about her," said Chloe.

"I think she might have been a musician," said Tabitha.

"Why?" asked Phryne.

"The orchestral score was always open on the desk when she had been there the night before," said Tabitha, thinking about it. "If she had been a singer it would have been the score for voice."

"And Tommy said she had black hair," said Chloe, "but we don't—"

"All right. Scores."

They were produced. Phryne flicked through them. No pages missing but some rather good cartoons of a pig in a suit, waving a conductor's baton. That would be Miss Willis. Phryne checked the name pencilled in the front. Right. She glanced at Miss Willis and she grinned.

"Cards." Phryne distributed them. "Call me if you remember anything which you need to tell the cops without attribution. Clear?" She scanned the faces again. They nodded.

Phryne dismissed them. The rest of the choir was sent out, singing a new round. "*London's burning, London's burning…*"

"The mystery woman," Phryne told Jack, "probably has black hair or blonde hair, is probably taller than the conductor, might be a musician, and always brings him food. Best I could do, Jack dear."

"Better than I did," snarled Jack. "You going home?"

"And that right speedily," agreed Phryne, and wafted out to Collins Street, where Mr. Butler was patiently awaiting her.

"Did you have an agreeable evening, Miss Fisher?" he asked, putting the Hispano-Suiza into gear.

"Most intriguing," said Phryne, leaning back into the butter-soft upholstery. "I met an old friend, heard an incomprehensible lecture, and talked to a lot of singers."

"And a nice murder," said Mr. Butler comfortably. "Cocktails when you get home."

"Mr. Butler, you are an ornament to your profession," commented Phryne, and smiled.

Chapter Three

What Passion cannot Musicke raise and quell?

John Dryden
"A Song for St. Cecilia's Day"

Phryne had related all the details she had gleaned about the case of the murdered conductor to her family at a late supper. They all liked supper, because they had been given a high tea at five o'clock to prevent hunger—Mrs. Butler abhorred hunger and would not have it in her house—so they were only peckish by nine thirty. Nevertheless, it was fine to sit up late, and grown-up, though by half past ten they were all yawning.

"To bed," announced Dot.

"Miss Phryne? Can I go and see that mathematical lantern lecture?" asked Jane.

"Certainly. Tomorrow, if you like. Do you want to take Ruth?"

"No," said Jane. "She'd be bored. Tink, you want to come?"

"If you like," said Tinker. He enjoyed being an escort. It made him feel brave. Not that Phryne's children would be in any danger from the actual villains in the city. News like Phryne got around. The fate of previous unwise attackers had also been quite the topic of conversation in Little Lon. It was whispered that certain sharks had a well-fed look and would come to her hand for tidbits of dissected enemy. But there were always larrikins and dolts and drunks. And a young girl on her own was, by default, prey. Not with Sir Edward the Brave in attendance. Tinker had been a small thin boy in a very tough seaside town. What he didn't know about dirty fighting, gouging, biting, kicking, and squirrel grips wasn't worth knowing. And this lecture might be interesting. He had discovered a fine natural talent for mathematics. Another way of looking at the world. Anyway, the Guv'nor was having a private dinner with her old friends, and he would have been eating in the kitchen anyway. This way he and Jane could go to Little Bourke Street for a Chinese meal—Lin Chong's family owned several restaurants—go to the lecture and come home in a taxi in the dark. Tinker had never got over being able to just summon up a cab and ride home in luxury. Jane loved them, too. Ruth would like having Mrs. Butler to herself, to talk endlessly about food, free of Jane and Tinker imploring them to find another topic of conversation. Good-o all round, he thought.

◇◇◇

Phryne slept soundly all night, dreaming of Mendelssohn. GBS had been rude about him, and he did tend to write the musical equivalent of fairy floss, but some of the choruses in *Elijah* were superb. "He Shall Give His Angels Charge Over Thee," for instance. She was singing "*Take all the prophets of Baal, let none of them escape you*" as she came downstairs.

"Good morning, Dot, lovely day—where is everyone?" she asked. The house seemed strangely quiet. Only Ember and Dot sat in the parlour, Dot embroidering and Ember watching for a chance to stitch himself into the pattern.

"They've gone swimming and taken that dratted dog with them," said Dot. "Imagine, she barked at poor Ember!"

"What did Ember do to her?" asked Phryne, speaking from long experience.

"I don't know—it was all over by the time we got to the kitchen," Dot told her. Phryne inspected Ember. Even for a male black cat, he looked smug.

"I shouldn't be concerned, Dot, I expect that

Ember started it. He usually does. Now, I have to send a telegram—anything you want in town?"

"You can just telephone, Miss," said Dot.

"Not this sort of telegram," said Phryne. "I have to send it from the GPO. Fancy a little walk?"

"Oh, yes, please."

"And we can have lunch in Coles, if you like," said Phryne generously. For the impoverished Dot, Coles Cafeteria was the height of luxury, and even after having been introduced to raspberry and champagne sorbet made with, as it might be, real fruit, she preferred lime green jelly with artificial cream on top. A concoction which can never have seen an actual lime. Or a real cow. But Phryne could take a few smooths with the rough, and a lunch at Coles would really make her appreciate the delicate cuisine which Mrs. Butler had planned for her dinner with Dr. MacMillan and Dr. Wilson. She could smell the leeks and potatoes cooking. Vichyssoise. Delicious. Since Phryne had encountered both of her guests in France, Mrs. Butler had decided on a French menu. Could not be better.

Phryne dressed in a violet suit and dove grey blouse—those eyes, those strange eyes of that annoying man! She had never known that eyes could be that colour. She wondered what they might be like, close, gazing into her own.

That was beyond unlikely. If Phryne was

any judge of men, and she was, having intimately encountered many, he was frigid. Probably a virgin. Uninterested in women; probably uninterested in sex. And, thus, uninterested in poor John Wilson, sterling fellow as he undoubtedly was.

Phryne tutted, tilted her shady hat at an attractive angle, took up her bag and gloves and her draft coded message, and left the house. Mr. Butler drove Dot and Phryne decorously into the city and left them at the General Post Office, which was the only place in Melbourne where one could send a coded telegram.

The GPO had been erected in Marvellous Melbourne days, when if it wasn't huge, turreted and requiring the same amount of stone as Mycerinus' pyramid, it wasn't a state building. Phryne had always liked it. It was so shiny, so clean, smelling of beeswax and paste, always hurrying to get the mail out on time, to send those vital messages to and from. Commerce, romance, sad news, good news. Testaments and sonnets and love letters and news about the sinking of ships and the landing of cargos; good terms and bad debts and secrets scribbled in darkness. Long wooden counters lined one wall. Rows of cubicles were opposite, and one of them was marked in severe lettering CODING CLERK. In keeping with the opulence of the building, however, the lettering was in gold leaf.

"Coding clerk?" asked Dot. She was a little out of breath after all those steps.

"I am concerned about the company my old friend John is keeping," said Phryne. "Rupert Sheffield was in Intelligence in Greece, therefore he was under the command of my friend Compton Mackenzie. Amazing man. An actor from a whole lineage of actors. Has only one subject, which is himself, but an excellent section head and as sharp as a needle. He retired and bought an island in the Hebrides. I am going to ask him about—"

"Mr. Sheffield. Is he dangerous? Should we have kept Jane and Tinker away from him?" asked Dot, worried.

"No, I don't think he's dangerous," said Phryne, trying to analyse her reaction to Sheffield. "But he might attract danger. I don't know, Dot, but it does no harm to enquire. John Wilson asked me. He is uneasy. So I will. And I can't just send a telegram to Compton in clear. Not if there is something covert going on. I just hope he remembers that alphanumeric. It must be out of date by now."

"I see," said Dot. She suppressed a shiver and wandered over to look at a display of postage stamps of all nations. They were very pretty. She wondered where Magyar Posta was.

"Destination, please?" asked the coding clerk, a thin young man who appeared to have been carved out of soap. Phryne wondered if he ever left the building and went into the sun. Perhaps coding clerks were required to live in the cellars, existing on post office glue and old stamps and lost parcels. That explained all those lost Christmas cakes…

"The Island of Barra, Outer Hebrides, Scotland, United Kingdom," said Phryne, sitting down.

He shoved a form across the desk for her to fill in, which she did with commendable patience. He blotted it thoroughly. Then he read it through, stamped one side, turned it over and counterstamped the other side, and put out his hand for her draft.

"Mr. Compton Mackenzie?" he asked.

"The very same," agreed Phryne, and tried smiling at him. It had no effect. Another impervious young man! Was she losing her charm?

"And you are the Hon. Miss Phryne Fisher?" he asked.

"Indeed," said Phryne, handing over her passport. He inspected it carefully and eyed her and the picture narrowly. A very careful young man. Fairly soon Phryne would lose her fight to contain the impulse to swipe him with that elaborate *Post Office Guide* with the red cover. She wondered if the King's monogram would be embossed on his cheek.

Just in time to prevent a breach of regulations, the young man handed back Phryne's passport.

"Two shillings and sixpence," said the coding clerk, and Phryne paid.

With a twiddle of the fingers, the young man sent the message. His hands were very deft and expressive, unlike the rest of him. In a trice or two, the telegram was off across the world. Phryne wondered what Compton would make of hearing from her after all these years. The answer should be interesting.

Now for a little wander through the city. Dot usually wanted to go to Georges, although she never bought anything there. And, of course, the promised lunch at Coles Cafeteria.

Georges would be amusing, anyway.

◇◇◇

Phryne and Dot returned home with an armload of bags (Phryne), a small packet of embroidery silk (Dot), a sense of a good morning's work (Dot) and a mild case of heartburn (Phryne, who did not like lunching on one slice of orange, one slice of tomato, one slice of canned beetroot, one slice of onion, one transparent slice of ham, a leaf of lettuce and salad cream). Next time, thought Phryne, I shall miss the lunch and just drink the tea, which was very good. That salad cream would kill slugs. Hasn't done me any good, either. And it really is getting hot. Me for a soothing cool swim and then a soothing cool, scented bath and I fancy lounging around for the rest of the day reading those library books, which will be overdue soon.

Though Phryne was neither mouse nor man, her plan went agley as soon as she walked inside and found that she had visitors. Three choristers, Mr. Butler informed her, were waiting for her in the smaller parlour, where they were drinking lemonade and picking out tunes on the piano.

"Leave them to it for a while, Mr. Butler; I need a bath and a change of clothes and some milk of magnesia."

"I will bring a draught up directly, Miss Fisher," he told her, and she ascended to her own apartments, where she drew and wallowed in a cool, scented bath. She dressed in a loose silken purple gown patterned with dragons, drank her milk of magnesia ("Coles lunch, Miss Fisher?" sympathised Mr. Butler) and sailed down to the smaller parlour, where three voices were extemporising on a Sanctus, as there weren't enough people to sing four-part harmony.

"*Sa-a-a-a-an-ctus,*" sang a bass.

"*S-a-a-a-anctus,*" sang a tenor.

"*S-a-a-a-anctus,*" sang an alto.

"*Dominus Deus Sabaoth,*" concluded Phryne as she walked in. "I do like plainchant. A considering cocktail, Mr. Butler, if you please. Would you like a drink?" she asked them.

"What a silly question," said the tenor, the Father Christmas Matthew.

"Foolish indeed," said the black-haired alto, Tabitha.

"But extremely generous," said the large economy-sized redhead, Oliver. "Thank you!"

Mr. Butler provided gins and tonics all round. Phryne waited until they had all sipped and then asked, "Is there a reason for this musical visit?"

"Yes," said Matthew. He was appreciating Phryne's gown and her delicate bare feet in her sandals. Phryne felt relieved. She hadn't lost "it," after all. She was gratified, and the young man had a mouth which just needed to be kissed, but she wasn't supposed to be seduced by the suspects, either.

"And that would be?" asked Phryne.

"The mystery woman," said Tabitha. "I pinned that idiot Julia down and made her tell me everything she remembered about seeing Mr. Tregennis dead. He had sheets of music stuffed down his throat, didn't he?" she demanded.

"He did," said Phryne. Today's considering cocktail was lemony and sharp, flecked with shaved ice. Delicious.

"Which is why that cop thinks it's us," said Oliver in his deep rumble.

"Got it in one," said Phryne.

"The cop called in all the scores," said Tabitha.

"His name," Phryne reminded her, "is Detective Inspector Robinson, and he didn't detain the lot of you last night, so it might be sensible to be polite. Also, he is a friend of mine."

"Sorry," Tabitha said conventionally. "We're a bit upset. Anyway, there are two scores missing. Two choral scores, that is. Was it choral music in his…er…mouth?"

"I shall find out," said Phryne. "Do you know if he was writing anything? A journal, perhaps, a lot of letters? His wastepaper basket was full of torn paper when your Julia saw it. It was empty when he was found."

"No idea." Tabitha consulted her colleagues and received head shakes all round.

"She saw a teapot and cup. They were also gone," said Phryne. "Any ideas?"

"He always had a teapot and cup," said Matthew. "Insisted on not drinking our tea, which is fair enough, that urn leaves a copper deposit on the teeth. I've tried to scour it but it really needs sandblasting. Or mining. It was an institution teapot, made of stainless steel, and his cup was a Coles china cup, thick, with a blue ring around the edge. It's missing?"

"It is," said Phryne.

"Odd," said Matthew.

Tabitha retrieved the conversation.

"Anyway, the missing scores belong to Oliver and Chloe. And we didn't do it."

"No?" asked Phryne.

"No, really not," Matthew assured her. "He was a nasty man and definitely deserved a thump or two, but not death. Not for being grabby with sopranos and unpleasant to the tenors. That's not uncommon. Chloe really only cares about music. She wants to sing the Ring Cycle, and she might. She never even listened to what Tregennis was saying about the sopranos. She knows how good she is. And he didn't grab her much."

"All right, where were the scores left?" asked Phryne.

"Last I saw mine I left it on the piano," rumbled Oliver. "Then I had to rush off to my father's office, and I forgot it. That was two weeks ago. Haven't been able to find it since."

"Did you tell the librarian?" asked Phryne.

"No, because she'd fine me and I haven't even so much as a split pea until next week," confessed Oliver, blushing red to match his hair.

"And Chloe put hers down on a chair. She put her straw hat on top," Tabitha told her. "When she came back, the hat was there but the score was gone. She didn't think anything of it, because scores get mixed up. We're not supposed to permanently mark them so someone who ripped pages out of theirs might have taken hers and rubbed out the pencilling and substituted their own."

"So they might, but that assumes that the score stealer is a chorister, and the chorister is also the murderer. We really don't know that. Besides, you told me that the choir didn't do it. It is a capital mistake," quoted Phryne from Conan Doyle—her mind really was running on the Science of Deduction lately, for some reason—"to theorise ahead of one's data. All we know is that someone pinched your scores. Tell me what you have gleaned about the mystery woman."

"We don't think she's a singer. She might be a violinist. Jenny remembered seeing a bow in the conductor's room—more than once."

"How well do you know your orchestra?" asked Phryne.

"They don't mix with us," said Matthew. "Professionals, you know, where we're just amateurs."

"And your répétiteur?" asked Phryne. Eyes widened.

"Professor Szabo?" boomed Oliver. "He's an old darling. Was a great pianist once."

"Before the grog got him?" asked Phryne. They boggled at her acumen.

"Yes, poor old man. But he likes us and he

plays well enough for a rehearsal. He lives in one room in that seedy apartment house and likes to get out occasionally."

Matthew clearly had a soft spot for Professor Szabo. Possibly he had a soft spot for anything weak or damaged. He definitely had a house full of ailing kittens and three-legged dogs and probably lame ducks, too.

"Tell me about yourselves. Are you all students?"

"Yes," said Tabitha. "I'm vet sci. That means I get to fix all of Matthew's wretched pets. Matt's arts and languages. Oliver's commerce. His father's a capitalist. Not that you'd know from Oliver. He's as poor as a church mouse."

"I say, Tab," murmured Oliver.

"And his brother's a famous actor," added Tabitha. "Oliver lives with his father in Kew. I live with my family in Yarraville. Matthew lives with his aged evil grandmother in Carlton. We all attend the University of Melbourne. Is that enough for you?" she demanded.

"Oh, no," cooed Phryne. "Not nearly enough—but enough for now."

Mr. Butler entered. "Detective Inspector Robinson, Miss Fisher."

"Oh, help," said Tabitha.

"Very well, Mr. Butler, I shall be there directly.

Could you put him in the parlour, and then take these young persons out through the kitchen? After they have written their names and addresses on this piece of paper. Drink up, darlings," said Phryne. "I decline to get involved in a French farce. Mr., while you're in the kitchen, I suspect Mr. Robinson would like a few sandwiches, if there are some left over from your lunch, which must have been better than mine. Au revoir," said Phryne, and floated out after the butler.

The choristers exchanged glances.

"Strewth," said Oliver.

They all agreed.

◇◇◇

"Jack dear, you look hot," she observed, as she sat down near the sweat-drenched policeman who was wiping his forehead with his handkerchief.

"More Science of Deduction, eh?" snarled Robinson. Phryne was taken aback. Jack did not usually snarl at her without a reason.

"Whatever is wrong?" she asked, patting the hand not holding the handkerchief.

"I'm so sorry, Phryne," he said, grasping her hand. "I shouldn't snap at you when all I want to do is deck that snobby Englishman."

"Oh, Rupert Sheffield has been helping you, has he?" asked Phryne maliciously. Jack had clearly brought this dreadful fate upon himself.

"Helping! Stalking around making observations! Telling us that we were idiots!"

"Ah," said Phryne, pleased. "The very intelligent quite often have no manners. And no tact," she added. "Come, here's Mr. Butler with a pint of iced soda water, a nice bottle of beer, and a selection of dainties, as I expect that you have not had lunch."

"Thanks, and sorry," said Robinson, grabbing the soda water and draining it in a draught, then starting on the beer and sandwiches as though he was starving. With his mouth full, he directed Phryne's attention to a file on the table, and she took it up and leafed through it as he methodically cleared the tray of anything edible in a manner made famous by the Sunshine Harvester Factory's best-selling machine. Mr. Butler, almost raising one eyebrow, took the tray away and brought it back, reloaded. That American Refrigerating Machine kept leftovers nice and cool and moist, but if this demand continued he might have to wake Mrs. B from her after-lunch nap and request more food, and that would not be conducive to domestic harmony. Mrs. Butler valued her rest, having earned it.

Fortunately, halfway through the replenished sandwiches, Jack Robinson was slowing down.

"So, no breakfast, either?" asked Phryne.

"Y'know, we don't appreciate you," said Robinson, fingers hovering over the selection of sandwiches. Egg next, or perhaps ham? He took both. He was not up to complex decisions at the moment. The presence of Rupert Sheffield had left bruises on his amour-propre.

"You don't?" asked Phryne, collecting a potted shrimp sandwich for herself. Her insides had quite settled.

"No," said Jack. "You could do the same as that…bloke. You're as clever as him. Cleverer, probably. You could make me feel like a dolt, easy. But you don't."

"No, because I like you, and you are not and have never been a dolt. Dismiss the thought from your mind," said Phryne, making a fluttering motion with her fingers which mimed the thought flying off like a butterfly. "And do not let some up-jumped overeducated mannequin tell you otherwise. What did he see that we didn't see?"

"Made the point about the scores," said Jack. "About the missing teapot and cup, the missing tray, the mystery woman."

"Nothing new really," said Robinson. "It was just the way he said it all."

"Good. Now drink your beer and we'll summarise. The music in the conductor's mouth was indeed from a choral score of Mendelssohn's *Elijah*. That is on open sale. Easy to find. Might not have anything to do with the actual Harmony Choir.

There are two scores missing, one belonging to Chloe McMahon and the other to that large red-haired chap, Oliver. Neither seem to have a reason to kill the conductor. They are not romantically involved and, in any case, Miss McMahon was only occasionally the subject of the conductor's unwelcome attentions. Matthew, their friend, professed a desire to thump the victim, but by the sound of him that would not be a rare impulse."

"Yes," said Robinson, bolstered by the beer, the food, and Miss Fisher's decorative and comforting company. "I always like cases when the victim's been practically begging to be killed. It means I don't have to be sorry for him."

"Oh, I do know what you mean, Jack dear." Phryne beamed on her favourite policeman. For the first time since Rupert Sheffield had entered his life, Jack Robinson smiled. Phryne went on.

"The scribbled pages have been collected by a cardboard manufacturer and you don't think that there's a chance of finding them—and neither do I. You have very sensibly secured the conductor's residence. When it is searched I think you will find love letters—I think that is what he was writing. Either a love letter, or a letter breaking off the relationship. Attempts to write those sort of letters tend to fill the wastepaper basket with failed drafts. Not letters to banks or creditors. This feels like a personal murder, Jack dear, does it not? A domestic murder."

"With added music," Jack reminded her.

"Might be an afterthought. Might even be a different person."

"Don't," groaned Robinson.

"Do we know where the food came from?" Phryne reminded him.

"Still asking," said Jack, heaving himself to his feet.

"And did anyone happen to look out of their window and notice a woman walk into the hall? Any person, in fact. The mystery woman was supposed to be black-haired, but there are blonde hairs on his coat."

"We got that one," he said. "The victim tried to…embrace Miss Chloe. He grabbed her and some of her hair got on his coat. She kicked herself free, which explains the bruise on the victim's shin."

"Odious man," commented Phryne.

"Too right," said Jack. "Thanks," he said, taking her hand. "You've been…kind. And we really do appreciate you. Thanks," he said again, and Mr. Butler let him out.

Phryne sat down and requested another cocktail. Jack had quite forgotten that he had left the file on Phryne's table. She would read it again before he remembered and sent someone to fetch it. Things like files and scores did get misplaced, she thought. Now for a nice drink, and a nap. She had guests to dinner, and as they were old friends, it might be a long night. Phryne accepted her drink, carried it and the file upstairs to her boudoir, and lay down on her sumptuous couch, sipping and reading, until she was sleepy enough to close her eyes and rest.

Chapter Four

There must be spirits willing to be driven
To that immeasurable blackness, or
To those old landscapes, endlessly regiven,
Whence Hell and Heaven itself were both
begotten.

Wallace Stevens
"For an Old Woman in a Wig"

Ruth had seen Jane and Tinker off to catch the train into the city and had returned to the kitchen, where Mrs. Butler was perfecting her French dinner. It was a lovely menu, delicate and light, as befitted the close, humid weather. Cold leek and potato soup. Little pastry boats filled with minced chicken or fish in a white sauce. A large green salad, a tomato and spring onion salad, a cold roast of beef with horseradish or port wine jelly to taste, cold roasted chickens with sage and onion stuffing, with a variety of crisp cold vegetables, each with their proper sauces. Fruit salad. A marmalade-filled roulade with slices of sugared oranges and crème Chantilly which was even now rolling in its damp tea towel as though there were no such things as culinary accidents in the world. Cheeses and fruits and coffee or tea. Ember had been fed, and was now licking leftover whipped cream off Ruth's finger. Molly had been fed and shut out in the back garden, where she would not get underfoot. Molly was of the opinion that a sufficiently distracted cook dropped things. This was true. She had caught a pastry bateau, a scrap of chicken skin, and a lump of codfish roe. But the last one had been an empty saucepan which had narrowly missed her head, so she had been gagged with a large bone and sent out to recover her wits in peace. Mrs. Butler directed Ruth to slice the rye bread which would accompany the soup. Ruth dipped the big carving knife in hot water and sliced with extreme concentration.

"Good," said the cook, stretching and massaging the small of her back. "You've been a real help, dear. I reckon that's all done. Just fill the coffee percolator for me, will you? And have a bateau. I'm not sure about that pastry in this dratted weather."

Ruth nibbled. "Flaky, light, and crisp," she reported. "As if it would dare to be anything else."

"That American Refrigerating Machine is so useful," admitted Mrs. Butler. "Not only nice cold drinks but proper butter pastry—at this temperature! Now, how about a glass of something cold and a nice sit-down? I shall ask Mr. Butler to make us a shandy."

Feeling very grown up, Ruth took off her apron, pulled off her scarf, and accompanied Mrs. Butler into the garden. The orchids were doing well, and the scent of jasmine was almost a taste. Presently Mr. Butler brought out a tray on which reposed three tall glasses, frosty with cold, in which a delightful golden liquid tinkled. Dot put down her library book.

"Oh, lovely," she said, taking a glass. "Thank you so much. It's just getting hotter," she added.

"And your aspirin, Mrs. B," said Mr. Butler.

"Thunderstorms give me a headache," said Mrs. Butler, taking the tablets and swallowing them with the first sip of her shandy.

"Going to storm," said Dot. "We'll know as soon as poor Ember dives for the wardrobe."

"He just can't stand thunderstorms, can you, my darling?" asked Ruth in a besotted voice. Ember, who was sitting on the wrought-iron table, allowed her to stroke his whiskers, which were quivering unpleasantly. Fairly soon it would be time to seek the safe haven of a good thick mahogany wardrobe between him and the weather.

"I hope Jane will be all right," said Ruth.

"She's got Tinker with her," said Mrs. Butler comfortably. "He's reliable. And he knows that Mr. Lines' people will be keeping an eye out. They seem to think it's their duty, God bless them. Tinker knows the way home. He's smart. And he's probably really nasty to get hold of in a fight. They've got the money for a taxi. All they can get tonight is bored and wet."

"Of course," said Dot.

"And this is a buffet dinner, so we can lay it out and then we can all sit down to a nice supper in the kitchen, just us," said Ruth. She was very fond of Jane and she liked Tinker, but it was nice to have a small gathering. And Dot was interested in food, too.

Ruth sipped at her very first grown-up shandy with contentment in her heart and flour on her plaits.

◇◇◇

Phryne woke in good time to bathe again, put on an even more silky costume, and take the autopsy report downstairs with her. After all, she had two doctors to dinner. Mr. Butler showed her the buffet, covered for the moment with a muslin cloth. He poured her a champagne cocktail. Perfect. Just the right combination of sour and sweet.

"The bottles of Glen Sporran are on the

sideboard, Miss, with the ice bucket and the soda. What will the gentleman drink?"

"Good, my dear Dr. MacMillan doesn't really drink anything else. And I don't know what John Wilson prefers to drink."

"You do not know the gentleman well, Miss Fisher?"

"I know him very well. But on a battlefield you drink what you can get. Including a dreadful pastis made, I swear, out of licorice allsorts soaked in medicinal alcohol. And British Army brandy, than which there is none worse."

She paused, seeing that she was shocking Mr. Butler. He shuddered lightly.

"Whatever the gentleman would actually prefer, Miss Fisher, we have it. From very good red wine or white wine or sweet wine or dry wine or sparkling wine to beer or brandy, indeed, though not that British Army liquid, which I have tasted."

"You have?" Phryne was surprised. She hadn't known that Mr. Butler was interested in the mortification of the flesh. He gave a small butlerine wince.

"And it gave me no pleasure. Indeed, I do not think it could actually be called brandy. I would call it rectified spirit with a spoonful of molasses in every bottle. But we have nothing made of licorice.

Though he might like real pastis? I shall bring in a bottle in case."

"Your cellar does you credit, Mr. Butler," Phryne told him. Ah, champagne. There were few situations which the divine drink could not improve. "In victory, one requires champagne," a short dark corporal with dreams of empire had declared. "In defeat, one needs it."

"*J'ai besoin de toi*," thought Phryne. John Wilson had said that to her, one freezing lice-ridden night on the Western Front. "I have need of you." In that case, it was to stop the both of them from dying of hypothermia. They were both alive in the morning. A lot of soldiers weren't, had frozen where they lay, curled up like embryos, sunk back into the Great Mother's womb. She recalled the first bath she took, after she left the front, in the Hotel Splendide in Paris. It had taken one scalding disinfectant bath just to kill the lice, body lice and head lice, and another to soothe the myriad bites on her white skin. And a third, highly scented, to take the stench of dead men and high explosive and mud out of her nostrils.

Phryne drank more champagne. It was fine to be alive. And in Australia, where such things did not come.

Dr. MacMillan was shown into the parlour and proceeded to shed clothes. Phryne watched, fascinated, wondering how far this naturist urge would go. She stopped at shirt and trousers and bare feet.

"Would you like to change into a gown, Elizabeth?" asked Phryne. "I've got lots. Silk? Cotton?"

"No, my hinny, just get me a lot of soda water and a triple whisky," said the doctor. "I've had the devil of a walk in air that feels like the tropics and the thunder is itching in my head."

Mr. Butler materialised at her side with a miraculous pint of water, a triple whisky on ice, and a paper of aspirins. Dr. MacMillan stared at him in amazement.

"Thank you," she said, taking all three. "You are a remarkable man."

"Mrs. Butler gets thunderstorm headaches," he said, explaining his deductions. "I always have some aspirin in my pocket in this weather. Perhaps a refill?" he asked, as the whisky had unaccountably vanished.

"Indeed," said Dr. MacMillan. She added in Gaelic, "*Moran taing agus beannachdan leat*," and sipped at her second drink.

"What's been happening with you, my dear doctor?" asked Phryne.

"Oh, women trying to die, staff falling sick, outbreak of measles—the usual things," said the doctor. "But your mention of John Wilson has caused me to recall…many things which I thought I had forgotten."

"Me, too," said Phryne. "The Somme has been in my mind ever since I met him again."

"Ach, weel," said Elizabeth. "I wonder if he will still call me Lisbet? He said his mother was called Elizabeth and he didn't see me as a Liz. He was a very good man." She sipped again. "Like this is very good whisky. I never asked you," she said, changing the subject, "where does it come from?"

"Specially made to a secret recipe on the island of Mull," said Phryne. "They only make it for me and the Gentlemen's Studio in Carnaby Street."

"I can taste the peat," said Dr. MacMillan.

"That's how I found Compton Mackenzie again," explained Phryne. "He's moved to Barra and is a Highland laird."

Elizabeth chuckled. "I did not know him, but they say he puts his whole heart intae whatever the man is being," she said.

"He does indeed, and I expect he is the most Scottish of all possible Scots, even though he was born in West Hartlepool. I've just sent him a coded telegram."

"You have, hinny? Why?"

"He was head of Intelligence in Athens, and a very strange man, who is now accompanying our John Wilson, was also there. I wanted to ask about him."

"His name?"

"Rupert Sheffield. He detested me on sight."

"And the feeling was returned in full measure?" Dr. MacMillan knew Phryne very well.

"I'm not at all sure," said Phryne slowly, holding out her glass and receiving another champagne cocktail from the attentive Mr. Butler. "He is very beautiful, but alien, an angel or a demon."

"Fey?" Elizabeth MacMillan was from the highlands, herself.

"Yes, that's what's worrying me. That neck-or-nothing, tare-an'-hounds drawling Cambridge courage which is a cover for despair. The ones who rush into the frontlines and win medals for bravery because they don't care if they live or die. And some not only die, but they are the cause of death in others. I don't like it. He's here doing a lantern show on the Science of Deduction. Ostensibly. And he's insulted my favourite policeman."

"The good Jack Robinson?" clucked Elizabeth.

"The same."

"I've never heard of the man," said the doctor. "But I stayed in France and then went home to Scotland and I didn't meet you, m'dear, until the flu epidemic. But I knew John Wilson. He wasn't even a doctor then—did he qualify?" Phryne nodded.

"Well, iphm, I would have expected it. I received the patients from his clearing station—ay, and they were well cared for, held together, stitched in lantern light, even emergency amputations. Most of them lived, which argues skill, and most of them thanked him, which argues compassion. I myself plugged up the hole in his leg when they brought him back to me, thankful that he had a Blighty wound, after some Hun sniper had targeted his Red Cross tent."

"And I only got to you, Lisbet, my dear, because Phryne drove her ambulance between me and said Hun," said a voice from the door. "At serious risk of her irreplaceable life, might I add."

"John Wilson," exclaimed Elizabeth Mac-Millan, rising to her feet and embracing him. "I wondered how you got on, my hinny! You never wrote. I feared that…I was feared. But here you are."

"Here I am," he said, and kissed her on the cheek. "And you look just the same, short hair and trousers, just as you were."

"Did that bad girrl really drive her ambulance in front of a sniper?" asked Elizabeth.

"She did. Ruined his day and saved my skin."

"You still got shot," Phryne pointed out. "It didn't work. And I stripped the gears, such as they were. You were wounded."

"But not shot dead," said John, dragging her

into his arms. She kissed him cordially on the mouth. He tasted tired and discouraged.

"She's always been a wild child," said Elizabeth. "Wait till I tell you about her landing a plane on a Hebridean beach during the flu epidemic. Now, sit, man, what will you drink?"

"What have you got?" asked John, limping toward a solid chair and leaning his cane against it. He tried to conceal his sigh of relief when he sat down and the weight was off his wounded leg.

"Knowing the admirable Mr. Butler, my man, anything your heart desires," said Elizabeth.

"Really anything?" asked John. He was in pain, Phryne noticed, chronic pain, the little wrinkles around the eyes, the careful movements. Stoic, that was John. I bet he arrived at Elizabeth's field hospital making the stretcher-bearers laugh at his jokes. He needs amusement and distraction. We can do that.

"Really," Phryne assured him. "I would trust Mr. Butler's cellar against any request. Wine? Beer? Cider? Brandy? Gin? Dr. Mac's Glen Sporran whisky? Name your poison, my dear. I'm drinking a champagne cocktail and about to venture on a glass or two of wine to go with the cold supper."

"Pastis?" asked John hopefully.

Mr. Butler unbent enough to smile. "Sir," he

said, and produced the bottle, a glass of ice, and a little jug of water.

"Amazing," said John. He poured and diluted the spirit until it was as white as milk. He sipped. It tasted much better than ethanol and liquorice allsorts. "I've been thinking about France all day," he confessed, and Phryne and Dr. Mac laughed.

"So have we," said Phryne. "Ever since I saw you again. And we have a French dinner. Mrs. Butler is a gem amongst cooks. Another drink, or are you hungry?"

"Starved," he said.

"Ravenous," said Dr. Mac.

"Then we shall dine," said Phryne. "Here are comestibles of the best; do you remember that Gascon who sold cakes? He used to say that."

"Very superior comestibles," said John. "Much better than those sawdust brioche he used to sell, the rascal."

"Sit, and I shall serve you," said Phryne. When John protested, Mr. Butler murmured in his ear, "If you would indicate your preference, sir, it would be my pleasure to serve you."

"A bit of everything, especially roast beef with jelly," said John helplessly. He was staying in a good hotel but this was a lavish feast even by hotel standards. Mr. Butler brought him a small bowl of *vichyssoise*, and a plate laden with a selection of the available food. It looked lovely and he was very hungry. Sheffield never had time for lunch. It was a meal to which John was rather attached. The pastis had sharpened his appetite and it didn't actually need sharpening.

"Some hae meat and cannae eat," began Elizabeth, "and some can eat and want it: but we hae meat and we can eat and so the Lord be thankit."

"Amen," said John, and picked up his cutlery. He drank his *vichyssoise* first, and it was very good, and then attacked a mound of rare roast beef of such quality that he tried not to whimper in gratitude. Phryne ate *petits bateaux* and talked amusingly about her home and her family and her profession. He gathered that she was a private detective, had three adopted children and some connection with Chinatown which he could not quite fathom. One piece of news made him swallow and attempt to speak.

"Good gracious, Phryne, your sister Eliza is in Australia?"

"All of the outsiders end up exiled to Australia," she told him airily. "She's a Sapphic and her beloved came here. Actually, it was rather exciting for a while. It was just like one of Ruth's romances with more sacks and guns and fewer roses. And a mummified man from a funfair. And they went on to do Fabian good works in St. Kilda. Father isn't speaking to either of us, thank God."

"I am never going to get this straight," said John, not at all cast down. He ate some more roast beef and handed his plate to Mr. Butler for a refill.

Really, thought that admirable functionary, Miss Fisher's friends have all been starving today. Luckily it is a generous house. There is no lack, thought Mr. Butler complacently, and supplied John with more rare beef and potato salad. The doctor's preferred drink, apart from pastis, was a robust red wine. Very suitable. Mr. Butler refilled his glass. This friend of Miss Fisher's was a war hero. He should have the best that the Fisher ménage had to offer. Who knew how many young men lived because of Dr. John Wilson? And nearly at the cost of himself. It was like Miss Fisher to think of a solution to a sniper in time to save a friend's life. Bold but not really reckless. Those ambulances had armoured sides.

Mr. Butler decided he should create another cocktail for her on the morrow. He would call it "Phryne." Sour, certainly, with a lime juice base, perhaps, and…Cointreau? Cherry brandy? Noyau? This would require study.

Meanwhile, there was dinner to serve. The doctor was underfed. This would be remedied.

"Wonderful food," said Dr. MacMillan. "What's in that little pastry thing?"

"Minced cooked chicken with *sauce blanc* and chives," Phryne replied. "Have another."

"I shall," said Dr. MacMillan, and did. John tried the roast chicken. He tried the carrots in Vichy water. He nibbled at celery with cream cheese. It was all delicious.

"I feel like a python who has been given his very own water buffalo," he said, finally laying down his knife and fork. "No, Mr. Butler, I couldn't eat another bite. Thank you very kindly."

Mr. Butler bowed and withdrew. Dessert and coffee were all prepared. Now he could go to the kitchen, loosen his braces, take off his shoes, and dine lavishly on extras and have a few glasses of that red, which was really very palatable. There were at least ten more bottles of it in the cellar.

"John dear, you were famished," commented Phryne. "What have you been doing all day?"

"Had to go along with Sheffield to see some people, and he walks very fast on those long shanks; it's hard for him to remember that I'm an old crock. Then he got into an argument with a policeman. Then more visits to various people. I missed lunch."

"There's a lot of that about," said Phryne. Walks too fast for a war-damaged man, *un mutilé de guerre*, to keep up, does he? The hound. Rupert was going down in her estimation like a rock in seawater.

"I've got an interesting case from that same policeman," she said lightly. "I'll ask you about it after dessert."

"Oh, yes, you're a private eye, aren't you? How very enterprising of you, Phryne," said John. He felt contented. That had been a very good dinner and here were two people who unaffectedly liked and approved of him. It was a change from his usual company. He relaxed and his scarred leg began to hurt less. Both women noticed this and resolved to keep him in that condition.

"This weather," grumbled Dr. MacMillan. "How anyone knows what to expect is beyond me. This very week it has been hot, cold, wet, windy, and sunny."

"And that was only Wednesday," laughed Phryne. "You'll become accustomed, Elizabeth. You'll know that you've settled in when you reach for your umbrella and your sunhat together."

"It's better than London," said John. "Rain, cold, more rain, occasional bursts of spring so beautiful that it breaks the heart, and then—for a change—rain."

"And then days when it is so hot that you swelter, just in time to catch pneumonia because the weather changes and you're out in a storm in insufficient clothing," agreed Phryne. "How about a little more wine?"

"A little more," said John. His kindly blue eyes surveyed Phryne and Elizabeth sitting side by side on the sofa, looking innocuous, which was not like them at all, either of them. It would be very pleasant to allow them to continue being considerate of his feelings. It had been a long time since anyone had worried about what he felt. A very long time since he had sat in a comfortable parlour with two people who knew him from the war and still liked him. But it would not do. He straightened up a little.

"All right, lovely ladies," he said, and smiled. "Ask me whatever you like, and I'll tell you. And I'll ask whatever I like, and you will tell me. Deal?"

"Are you sure, sweetheart?" asked Phryne.

"I am," he told her. She leaned forward and patted his shoulder.

"I put on the tourniquet and got you loaded up," said Phryne. "We were all shocked. Young Ginger was crying."

"You kissed me," he said.

"Of course I did," responded Phryne. "Then they took you off and there was a bombardment. Almost the last one of the war. You arrived at Elizabeth's hospital. Go on from there."

"Lisbet knows better than I," he told her. "I only remember the jolting of the stretcher. I heard someone shout, "The docks copped it!" My leg burned like fire. Then I woke up, days later."

"I took out the bullet," reported Elizabeth, "but it had done a good deal of damage. Missed the main arterial structure, but smashed the femur and ripped through muscle and tendon. I put him back together again as best I could, dealt with the inevitable fever, and—"

"You used to sit by my bed," he said to her, tenderly. "You held my hand. Once you even fell asleep, your head on my arm. I remember the nurses tiptoeing around you. They said you'd been awake and operating for forty-nine hours. You were absolutely soaked in blood."

"And none of it mine." Elizabeth wiped her eyes. "Lord, yes, I recall those two days; they brought in four transports, one after another. I couldnae tell them to bring no more, with them dyin' in heaps. And I thought I had a hard day today." She laughed briefly.

"I've always wondered," said John. "With the femur in that condition, and a reasonable stump left, why didn't you amputate?"

"Because it was you, my mannie." Elizabeth wiped her eyes with the back of her hand. "I thought, if I could save one, if I could only save one limb, it would be yours. Outsiders must stick together. I wanted you to go home to your young man with both legs."

"I never knew that," John told her. "Thank you."

"It almost didn't work. You seemed obstinately set on dyin'."

"But you wouldn't let me," he said gently.

"I would not. When we discharged you to the convalescent home you were expecting to go back to university and finish your degree. Was your young man not waiting for you?"

John smiled sadly. "Oh, yes, he was. We got digs together and never slept apart one night for three years. Art was a sweet, gentle boy. And then he died, and I couldn't seem to care about anyone else. I qualified and worked in the Royal Free in London. In Accident and Emergency."

"But that wasn't enough," hinted Phryne.

"No," said John. He drank more wine. "I was quite comfortable, had my room in the doctors' lodgings, but I was slowly going mad. Dreams. Nightmares. And this confounded leg. Working on the wards always aggravated it. I decided that I would emigrate, to New Zealand, perhaps—that was far enough away from my memories. Then I thought, no, that's foolish, the memories were part of me, I couldn't escape them by running away. So I went looking for a service flat, found that Rupert

Sheffield had a very good two-bedroom place, and needed a fellow lodger. That's when Sheffield came into my life."

"Ah," said Phryne. "So you live together?"

"Yes, but not like that, Phryne."

"I understand," she replied. "I know the sort. The body is just a machine to support the mind."

"The mind/brain hypothesis is very interesting," said Elizabeth, picking at her marmalade roulade. It was superb.

"He needs someone to look after him," said Phryne relentlessly. "To make sure he eats and sleeps occasionally. To soothe people after he has insulted them. He needs you, though I bet he hasn't noticed that he does, or thanks you for your care."

"No, he hasn't," said John, reddening a little. "But I wouldn't have expected him to notice."

"And you, my mannie, need someone to look after," said Elizabeth. "I can comprehend that."

"And he is gorgeous," said Phryne.

"And blazingly intelligent," said John. "He really can do some of the things which Sherlock Holmes could do. After all, Sherlock was based on Dr. Joseph Bell, Conan Doyle's mentor at Edinburgh Medical School."

"And still a legend when I was there." Elizabeth felt that she could possibly manage just one more mouthful of roulade.

"Was he, Lisbet?" asked John.

"Och, yes. The professors all told stories about him. Observation, that was his watchword. "You must see everything, or why did the good Lord give you eyes?" He used to run diagnosis classes— they still do. A person comes in and sits down and the students are allowed to look as much as they like, but not to ask questions. So my own Professor McIver, as a student, diagnosed the subject as an alcoholic. Bell challenged him, and he said, alcoholic skin, tremor, unfocused eyes, and so on, and Bell told him he was right, very good, "You see but you do not observe," and directed him to look at the man's coat pocket. Which contained a half-empty bottle of cheap whisky."

John and Phryne laughed.

"What do you know about Rupert, then?" asked Phryne. "Family? Background?"

"Oh, Winchester, his father's a life peer."

"Oh, good," said Phryne. "I outrank him."

"Phryne!" exclaimed Elizabeth.

"Sorry," said Phryne unconvincingly. Usually she never thought her father's title to a minor and unimportant barony at all significant. But it was pleasant to have something which Rupert Sheffield, for all his aristocratic airs, didn't have.

"He volunteered for Intelligence, he was finishing a maths degree at Cambridge, and went out to Greece to break codes. He's never talked much about it."

"That is as it should be," said Phryne. "I did a little Intelligence work too, as you know, but I have never spoken of it. Besides, it was messy."

"When you say messy, my dear, are you referring to…" Phryne waited for the end of Elizabeth's question. "On second thought, do not answer that. Even if I ask again, I must beg you never to tell me what you meant. As you say, it should not be spoken of."

Phryne nodded. "You know, the war did terrible things to us," she said, toying with her glass of wine.

"Ay, it did," said Elizabeth. "I learned the meaning of despair, and I have never forgotten it."

"It made me, at least, quite ruthless and willing to kill," said Phryne.

"Indeed," agreed John. "I saw you shoot that trench raider with a smile on your lips. I would have done it, too, but you had my Webley."

"You wouldn't have reacted fast enough," Phryne replied. "You are essentially a very good man and you are a doctor: doctors don't want to kill things. Whereas I…don't mind. If I have to, to prevent injury to the people I am protecting."

"And how did you get my Webley, anyway?" asked John. "I was so relieved, I never thought to ask."

"I picked your holster," answered Phryne. "If that is the right term. I gave it back," she protested. "Ginger found me one a couple of days later. There was no shortage of abandoned weapons at your place, John dear."

"That's true," he said, remembering.

"And the Webley Mark VI is a good solid weapon, though heavy, getting on for three pounds; I had to use two hands to hold the thing. And a large calibre at .455. Now my little Beretta is only a .22, but has quite enough punch for anything I might need it for. Threats, mostly," said Phryne.

"Even your Detective Inspector Robinson might find it hard to ignore you shooting someone in Melbourne, Phryne," said Elizabeth.

"Yes, so I shall try very hard not to do that. Poor man is harrowed enough. Your Sheffield gave him the rounds of the assembly hall and called him an idiot."

"I know. I was there. I'm so sorry," said John dotingly. "He really has no manners at all."

"And yet 'manners makyth man,' that's the motto of his school," Phryne told him.

"The only things from school that seem to have stuck are quadratic equations and a very acute clothes sense," said John. "Now you, Lisbet, how did you come to this far-flung place?"

"I was restless and bored and Europe was

ruined," Elizabeth replied. "There was an appeal for female doctors from the Queen Victoria Hospital. I got passage on a ship and there was Phryne. She was coming here to investigate a suspected poisoning. Then I went to work, and now I have a little house, a friend, and a lot of roses."

"A friend? Or a lover?" asked John.

"Both," Elizabeth smiled. "Her name is Marie, she's Scots from Inverness, and she just wants to stay home and keep house, which is why I had to get a house. But I do like growing roses."

"Not a sane one amongst the three of us," murmured John.

Phryne laughed and kissed him. "We shall be happy lunatics," she told him. "Sanity is overrated. Let's move into the parlour. There are liqueurs and coffee and tea and things like that. I am having… let me see."

They did not assist John in rising, finding his cane, or moving to another room, for which he was very grateful. He sank down onto a soft aquamarine leather sofa in a cool green and blue room. A life-size nude painting of Phryne pouring water from an amphora riveted his attention.

"You were an artist's model, Phryne?" he asked.

"Certainly. It's called *La Source*. Isn't she beautiful?"

"Too thin," said Dr. MacMillan. "You were all bones at that age, girl, I can count them."

"But that's how I remember you," said John, accepting a small glass of the whisky. "Just like that. Smudgier, perhaps, dirtier. We were always grimy."

"You too, darling; the only clean things about you were your hands," teased Phryne.

"But you always smelt lovely," said John. "Now I come to think of it, how on earth did you manage that? I remember burying my face in your neck and smelling that spicy, flowery, utterly unlikely scent."

"The only cosmetics I took with me to war were cold cream and a large flask of Stephanotis. Still one of my favourites. Here," said Phryne, perching on the arm of the sofa and allowing his head to incline into her neck, under the swinging hair.

John took a deep breath, and was flooded with obscene reminiscences.

"So you do," he stammered. "Delightful."

Phryne released him and took her own chair. She had a glass of ice, in which a very small amount of green chartreuse puddled. He wondered if she had chosen the drink to match the room. Phryne was wearing evening pyjamas of pearly, undersea silk. She might easily have had some mermaid in her ancestry. He suspected as much. She could probably swim like a fish.

The conversation roved over Australia

(extraordinary), international affairs (ghastly as ever), and medical practice (innovations in infection control). John and Elizabeth talked about Edinburgh and John talked about Rupert Sheffield's remarkable intelligence. They both read the autopsy report on the late Hedley Tregennis.

"It's a toss-up, Phryne," Elizabeth told her. "The opiates would have killed him, anyway."

"But there might have been two murderers, the poisoner and the music stuffer," said Phryne. "I need a cause of death."

"Och, I see the difficulty. What do you think, John?"

John had been thinking how extraordinarily foolish he had been not to find Phryne earlier. She was so beautiful she hurt his eyes. He recalled his wits.

"Petechial haemorrhages in the eyes, Lisbet, swollen trachea—I think he actually died of suffocation, though you are correct that a massive dose like that would have killed anyone. So that makes the second person the killer."

"Not legally," said Phryne. "The first one left the victim in a state which allowed the second one to kill him. If they knew each other it's a felony murder. If they didn't it will be one serve of attempted murder and one serve of actual murder. Oh, well, thank you for your expert opinions—that will be very helpful."

Finally the hand-painted art deco Lamia clock chimed eleven.

"Well, it's been fine to see you again, John," said Elizabeth, levering herself to her feet. "I'll be asking Mr. Butler to call me a taxi, I'm thinking. I've babies to deliver tomorrow. Will I see you again? Can I show you my roses?"

"Of course—we're here for another week," said John. "So good to see you again, Lisbet dear."

Mr. Butler summoned a cab, and Phryne and John saw her off with her bundle of discarded clothes. The air was thick with heat; there were ominous grumblings in the east. John took Phryne's hand. Strong hands, he remembered.

"I suppose I should be going too," said John Wilson with absolutely no sense of urgency.

"Not unless you wish to, in which case Mr. Butler will call you a car. It's too hot to walk anywhere tonight and the hot weather makes the local criminals positively cranky. Your choice, darling. I'm not dragging you into my ambulance anymore."

"What if I ask really nicely to be dragged?" he said, and Phryne kissed him on the mouth. John Wilson's fate was, at that point, sealed.

Chapter Five

There must be spirits wandering in the valleys
And on green-planed hills, that find forgotten
Beggars of earth intent
On maids with aprons lifted up to carry
Red-purples home—beggars that cry out sallies
Of half-remembered songs...sing "Tarry,
Tarry, are you gone?"...*Such spirits are the fellows.*
In heaven, of those whom hell's illusions harry.

Wallace Stevens
"For an Old Woman in a Wig"

Tinker liked Chinese food. It was tasty, if a bit unidentifiable. A child of semi-starvation, he could eat anything that wasn't actively poisonous, and didn't even blench when the chicken soup with the actual chicken's feet sticking out of the bowl had been put before him. Actually it had been really good chicken soup. Mrs. Hoong of the Golden Lotus cafe liked feeding these western children who seemed to appreciate her cuisine. And they were of the inner chamber of Miss Fisher, concubine to the master of the Lin family, Lin Chung. She would, of course, never let them pay, but they always left a tip, sixpence under the teapot. Mrs. Hoong thought that was an indication of very good breeding.

If she had been aware of Jane and Tinker's actual breeding, it would not have changed her views. Tinker liked the Golden Lotus because the Chinese tarts who inhabited it between transactions were so beautiful and so strange. When they caught him looking at them, they would smile and blow him kisses.

Jane just adored lacquered duck, steamed pork buns, and a uniquely glutinous rice cake wrapped in banana leaf. It had black sesame seeds in it. Only Mrs. Hoong knew how to make it. Jane was picking up quite a lot of Cantonese, just by hearing it spoken, and could thank Mrs. Hoong fittingly for her excellent dinner.

"*Do jeh, Ayi,*" Jane said, putting her hands together politely.

"What does *ayi* mean?" asked Tinker, also making the correct gesture.

"Aunty," Jane replied. "A title of affectionate respect."

"*Ng-sai ng-goi, biu jie mui.* Very welcome, little cousins," said Mrs. Hoong, and they left their sixpence and went out into the dark of Little Bourke Street, which was electric with noises, quarrels, laughter, and scents. Familiar and really exotic, thought Jane, taking a deep sniff of rice wine, roasting meat, exhaust smoke, asafoetida, pork fat frying, melon tea, starch from the big laundry and the sweet, pervasive underlay of the opium pipes that some of the old men still smoked.

A couple of intoxicated Chinese sailors almost jostled them off the pavement into the path of an oncoming truck. Tinker seized Jane and they scrambled back to safety. Ahead they saw that the mariners had been hustled into Celestial Way by a couple of blue-clad men who were addressing them in very strong tones.

"Jang jang dei jou ng-ho chung chong Lum-gar ching-fu Phryne geh siu pun yau."

"It is unwise to jostle, hustle, or otherwise endanger the children of the Lin concubine Phryne's house," translated Jane.

"I didn't know you spoke that much Chinese," commented Tinker, as the two blue-clad men elevated the sailors by their collars and banged their heads together.

"I don't, I just speak Mr. Lin," said Jane. "Come along, we don't want to be late for the lecture."

They paused to bow courteously to their avengers, then went up Little Bourke Street, were stunned briefly by a wave of cooking from the Imperial Hotel on the corner, then turned into Collins Street and walked down to the Scots Church Assembly Hall. This was the long way, of course. Tinker and Jane could have got to their destination in three minutes by ducking down alleys. But Jane loved walking in the city after dark, and Tinker distrusted alleys and lanes, even when he knew that he had guardians. By daylight he was happy to explore. By night, he preferred to stick to streets with streetlights. And, even though it pained him to admit it, strolling policemen.

It was a hot night, pregnant with storms. Tinker was pleased that they had an umbrella. He was carrying it and the satchel with a notebook and several pencils. If Tinker did not have charge of it, Jane would leave it behind when she became engrossed in her own theories. Retracing her own steps had become something of a specialty of Jane's until Tinker had arrived. He seemed to be able to find anything. Perhaps he had learned this valuable skill scavenging along the beaches and docks in Queenscliff. He didn't mind accompanying Jane. She liked him. Anyway, Jane always wanted to go to interesting places. The Medical Museum at the University of Melbourne, for instance. And because she was terribly clever, she had no room in her head for unimportant information, which was why Tinker and Ruth often had to remind her of the way home and the location of her other shoe, and the fact that it was dinner time.

The lecture room was about half full, good attendance for such a hot night in the middle of the week. The speaker was introduced by a small, old professor of mathematics from the university of Cambridge. Jane wondered how much esoteric knowledge was hidden under that bald scalp. Tinker wondered why he had come. The introduction was close to inaudible but Jane got the idea that Rupert Sheffield was a prodigy, a coming man, an amazing mathematician of whom great things were expected in his field. Which was what such persons always, to Jane's knowledge, said.

But Rupert Sheffield was another thing altogether. He was tall and graceful and extremely well dressed. Jane had not tried to acquire any knowledge about clothes while in Miss Phryne's house, but some of her visitors had worn suits like that, and she had heard them described by such terms as handmade, Savile Row, and (by the charming old tailor Mr. Rosenberg, who always had a pocket full of barley sugar for good children) as high-class schmutter. The suit was dark grey, the shirt pale blue, the tie from some public school (she would ask Miss Phryne when she got home) and he moved like a dancer. Very smooth.

His voice made the audience fall in love with him. Rich, educated, seductive. Jane thought that he could read out the phone book in that voice and they would all sit there riveted. He began by talking about deduction, a process of rendering the world predictable and understandable by observation. "If this, then this." That was easy enough; everyone did that, to some degree. But Sheffield explained that by using various mathematical methods, he could give a value to every piece of information, greater or less depending on importance, and discover patterns, parallels, and connections not noticeable to the ordinary person.

He was a magician, thought Jane, instantly suspicious. He was like the man at the Tivoli who made the lady disappear and then reappear, who made flowers fall out of the air, who poured milk into the bowl and revealed swimming goldfish.

Tinker felt the same. "I reckon this bloke's got a bridge to sell," he whispered.

Jane nodded, and gestured for her notebook and pencil. Rupert was beginning to expound his deductive method.

Tinker parted company with the lecture at the mention of "non-linear integrals." There followed by Tchebyshev polynomials, roots, nodes, and one sentence which went "points in range in which error converges to zero"—at which the speaker flung out a triumphant hand in a very graceful gesture, Jane scribbled furiously, and Tinker wondered if they were handing out tea at this bunfight. Probably not.

Instead, he examined the other people in the hall. Tinker would have bet the cuppa for which his soul longed that most of the crowd didn't understand this maths gibberish any more than Tinker did. Jane might, of course. She was now frowning and biting the end of her pencil. If not fed at intervals by her doting sister, Jane might subsist entirely on tea and pencils. And all that graphite couldn't be good for her.

The speaker continued, speaking of lattices. Not the sort you grow roses on, but some strange way of looking at facts. Tinker realised that this was not maths, it was philosophy. He cheered up immediately. He was a sailor's son from Queenscliff. No one would expect him to understand philosophy. And this had to be over soon.

At last, the speaker concluded his remarks, the projector was turned off, and Jane shut her notebook. She was in that euphoric state which Tinker had last seen when she discovered simultaneous equations. He picked up the umbrella, shoved both notebooks into the satchel and took Jane's hand. He slid it into the crook of his elbow and guided her out of the hall, down the steps and into the hot night.

Thereafter, all the way home in the taxi, she didn't say a word. By the time they were both in the kitchen and Ruth was making tea, Jane had calmed down enough to babble about variants and reflexives. Ruth looked at Tinker. He shrugged.

"I dunno. We had dinner at Mrs. Hoong's, then this bloke with a voice like red velvet started talking, and that's the last I understood."

"Oh," said Ruth. "That's all right, you did well. It's just a state. She gets into them. She'll come out of it. Tea, Janey," she said into her sister's ear. "Orange biscuits. Eat. Drink. Now."

Jane did as requested. A blessed silence fell in which the word "deduction" was not mentioned, which was all right with Tinker. He drank his second cup of tea and grabbed another orange bikkie. And one more for Molly. It was late, he was tired. He went to his bachelor quarters to read Sexton Blake.

Numbers, concepts, they spun in her head in a fascinating cloud. Ruth put Jane and herself to bed.

"Better in the morning, Jane," she said, and returned to her romance. Jane closed her eyes, the better to appreciate the glories of the lattice.

◇◇◇

John Wilson managed the stairs to Phryne's boudoir quite well. Of course, he had incentive. He could smell Phryne's scent, taste her mouth, and largely forgot about his damaged leg as she moved up before him, her rear elevation almost as enchanting as her front view. And blessing of blessings, her bedroom was not only provided with green silk sheets and a drinks trolley, but an arrangement comprising an electric fan and a block of ice which cooled the air to liveable temperature. He sat down and almost groaned with relief.

"Oh, lovely," he said. Phryne looked at his honest kindly face and his beautiful blue eyes. There were plenty of pretty men—indeed, she rather had a penchant for them—but this was an old friend, as precious as a childhood teddy bear. Phryne still had Lambie, her childhood stuffed toy. She did not mind that Lambie was partially bald and more than a little battered. This man needed to be loved and cosseted and soothed, and Phryne was in the mood for those things and also in the mood for a different body in her arms.

Therefore, time to extract the doctor from his clothes. She knelt down and removed his shoes, peeled off his socks, unbuttoned his shirt. Ember, who was expecting thunder and appreciated cool air, left his post on the bed. He knew from experience that once Phryne started undressing gentlemen, it would be no place for a cat of delicate sensibilities. Besides, his wardrobe called. The thunder was getting close.

"Hello, cat," said John. Ember gave him a dismissive sniff and walked to the wardrobe. Phryne opened the door and he jumped inside.

"Why does he do that?" asked John, removing his own shirt and beginning on his trousers.

"He was abandoned in a thunderstorm when he was just a slip of a kitten," Phryne told him, allowing the top of her pyjamas to fall to the floor. She loosed the drawstrings and kicked off her trousers. "We think he was shell-shocked. Come here," she purred, extending her arms.

John slid forward into her embrace. She smelt bewitching and his lips found the hollow in the base of her throat, the cleft between her breasts, the slight curve of a belly which had always been concave. He liked her with more flesh on her bones. More Phryne was definitely an improvement. Satiny, smooth, warm flesh, in the cool wash of scented air. And so profoundly unlike his own desire that she was alien and marvellous. He found names for her; Circe, mermaid, nymph.

She assessed his state of health quickly. That scarred thigh would possibly not take his weight, but, then, it didn't have to. She gently pushed him down onto his back and slipped between his legs, rubbing like an amorous beast, while he shivered under her touch, and found all those pleasure points which he remembered Phryne to have; since she was the only woman he had ever lain with, he recalled them perfectly. She murmured his name, John sweetheart, John darling, as his fingers found the right places and he felt her convulse above him. Then she straddled his hips, taking care not to touch the scar. He was embraced in a wet heat which belied the icy air, and he dissolved in fire, an orgasm so strong that he nearly fainted.

"Phryne," he murmured.

"Oh, that was *so* nice," she said, disentangling herself and then sitting up a little so that he could rest his head upon her breast. "And it's better when no one is shooting at us, isn't it?"

"Infinitely," he agreed. A small breast was under his cheek. Strange feeling, reminding him of no one else, for his mother had been a cushiony, comfortable sort of woman, and Phryne was his only other female lover. She was thin but not as skinny as she had been, the smoke-stained scarecrow hauling stretchers out of that wretched ambulance with surprising strength. "*Point d"appui,*" she had explained. "It's just finding the balance. Then every-thing slides into place." She had found John's point of balance, all right. When first seized and kissed by that fierce mouth, he had briefly thought of trying to explain that actually he was "so," a player on the other team and uninterested in her gender, but then decided not to, because 1) she wouldn't have listened, and in any case, 2) it suddenly wasn't true. He had seesawed down into heterosexuality, to his great astonishment. And here he was again, while the object of his profound adoration slept—if he slept—in his room at the Windsor and had probably not noticed that John had not come back.

"You really do love him, don't you?" asked Phryne. It was not an interrogation, she was affectionately curious, so he answered.

"Yes," said John.

She stroked his hair. "And he doesn't love you?" she asked.

"He doesn't love anyone," explained John. "He doesn't have any idea of the concept. He's all mind. All intellect."

"Nothing is all intellect," said Phryne. "Unless he is supernatural. I agree that he is as beautiful as a succubus, no, incubus, but he is made of flesh."

"He detests the flesh," said John. "I have to make him sleep, remind him to eat. When he's not thinking, he enjoys gourmet foods and fine wine. Then he doesn't eat for days. If he didn't have me to mind him…"

"He would have burned out by now," concluded Phryne crossly. She had seen this before. The tyranny of weakness. The means by which the heartless gained all that they wanted without giving one solitary kiss in return. "But what would happen to him without me?" was the cry of many an abused spouse, sister, mother about husbands and widowed mothers and frightful siblings. And Rupert Sheffield had managed it without any emotional involvement. Without the concurrent statement from the bruised wife: "He really does love me." Ingenious. He might just be as intelligent as John thinks he is, damn him.

"It's not his fault," said John, sensing tension in the breast upon which he was reposing.

That was the third thing they always said.

"So what do you get out of this...partnership?" she asked. "Just the right to stare at his gorgeous face all day?"

"No, he needs me," said John. "He relies on me to watch his back. People dislike him, there have been attempts to silence him, when he knows something about people, and he says it—he always says it. And I was so bored, Phryne, after Arthur died. I was sinking down into grey fog, and then Sheffield came along and it was all sparkling and bright again."

"I see," said Phryne. She did. Regrettably. A nectar trap, like those of the sundew or the pitcher plant. Brilliant in conception, beautiful to the sight, ruthless in execution, and the fly gets digested alive all the same. Nice petals, though.

"As it is here," John continued, drawing a

callused finger down her thigh. "Here, with you. All sparkling."

He kissed the breast he was lying on, then down Phryne's body, lingering over her belly, licking with interest at her navel, into which it might be nice to pour wine. It was amazing some passing sultan hadn't offered her an emerald or a ruby for that navel. His clever mouth moved down until he found the sweet spot and Phryne arched her back. He forgot his damaged leg as he moved above her and inside her, belly to belly.

Phryne was pleased, assuaged and holding him around the neck while he shuddered into another climax.

He recovered his breath, realised that his leg was registering a complaint, and lay on his back, panting. Phryne fetched a cool wet cloth and washed him with precise licks, like that of a mother cat. Then she stretched out beside him and sighed a sated sigh.

"I should go," John murmured. Storms gave him bad dreams. It would be the height of ill manners to scream and cry and remember the war in a lady's bed.

"Why?" asked Phryne.

"I…" he began.

She suppressed his attempt to rise with a firm hand on his chest. "He won't notice you have gone," she told him. "And it might do him some good to know that you aren't always there. Lie down, it's going to storm. I…would like some company. Thunderstorms make me remember…"

"Oh, God, Phryne, and me. Of course I'll stay."

"All right. If I have a nightmare, you wake me, and I'll do the same for you. Deal?"

He took her hand and kissed it.

"Deal," he said.

◇◇◇

John fell asleep like a man falling down a well. Phryne considered him as his features relaxed. You could tell a lot about a person if you watched them as they slept. The face they wore for the world was gone; the face they actually owned was on display, vulnerable and soft. John was sad, even in sleep. Unloved since Arthur died, she guessed. That scent of wormwood had been strong. He was still a young man. The semen of young men was lightly scented. He had been without a lover, possibly without even release, for a long time. That could be remedied, at least while he was in Melbourne. He was a considerate and comfortable lover. Not exciting, but Phryne could always find excitement. Excitement, indeed, had a way of finding her.

She snuggled down beside him in the wash of the cool air and tried not to listen to the noise of the electric fan, which emitted an intensely irritating "cluck" every seven minutes.

The storm hit at three am. From inside his wardrobe, Ember wailed his discomfort and outrage. Molly gave the thunder her usual remedy for anything strange: a good solid barking. Phryne heard big guns and smelt the reek of trenches. She was endeavouring to coax another m.p.h out of her baulky ambulance, trying to outrun the creeping barrage. Her patients in the back moaned and screamed and young Audrey beside her was praying. Every bounce of the ambulance brought a massed shriek of agony. She'd done this before, grimy hands white-knuckled on the wheel, trying by main force to shove the gears into place, hearing the explosions coming nearer. But this time she was not going to get out of range. She struggled, stamping and slapping the engine into a lower gear as it shuddered and whined. But this time, they were all going to die…

John Wilson, not even yet a doctor, despaired. He was standing in a pool of fresh blood. The last patient had bled to death in his hands as he tried to staunch too many wounds with too few swabs, with no disinfectant and no morphine and no help. The creeping barrage was coming closer, and suddenly he laid his head down on the ruined chest of the dead soldier and waited, almost happy, almost peaceful, thinking that it would be all right to die now, because it would take away the pain…

And felt hands flailing, a voice screaming. His dead man wasn't quite dead. He closed his arms around the soldier, clasping him in a close embrace, and soothed him. "There, there, I'm here," he told the corpse. "I won't leave you, and it will all be better soon. We'll all be safely dead soon."

"John?" asked the dead man, and he found he was awake and pinning Phryne Fisher down. He had flung himself across her as he had during an artillery bombardment, to protect her from shrapnel with his own body.

"Get off," she squeaked, poking him in the ribs. "You're heavy."

"I was dreaming," he explained, rolling aside and gathering her into his arms.

"So was I," she told him. Her eyes in the actinic light were huge, dilated black with shock. She was shivering. "Creeping barrage?" he asked.

"Yes. I used to outrun them. But this time, I…didn't."

"I had just watched one too many lads die," said John, tears running down his face and dripping onto Phryne's shoulder. "Just the one too many. I despaired. I always knew that there would be one too many deaths."

"And then you'd lie down and die too?" asked Phryne, recovering her courage.

"Yes," he said simply.

"I didn't let you then, and neither did Elizabeth, and I won't let you now," said Phryne. "Sweetheart," she added, kissing him soundly. He tasted bitterly of tears.

"I'm cold," said John, releasing her as she got up to turn off the fan and pull on her pyjamas and robe. She rummaged and threw him an extravagant red silk gentleman's dressing gown. He put it on, still shaking, wiping his wet cheeks.

"Downstairs, my dearest John, there is cocoa made with your actual chocolate, and that's where my household will be. Come along," she said, and preceded him out the door. John found his cane and followed. Perhaps he really was still dreaming.

But in a spacious kitchen, he was introduced to Mrs. Butler, who nodded affably, and Jane, Ruth, and Tinker, who shook hands like good children. Dot smiled at him. Molly, who was bouncing up and down, was the picture of a Good Dog, sure that she had seen that presumptuous storm off all by herself.

There was indeed cocoa. It was made with fresh creamy milk, demerara sugar, and chocolate from a tin with a Dutch lady on it, and it was sweet, hot, and heartening.

"Miss Phryne's got shell shock," Jane informed him, as he sat for the first time in his life in a warm kitchen surrounded by accepting faces, wearing some other gentleman's gown. It was a splendid one, agreed, but it wasn't something in which retired army doctor John would normally be seen dead. He stroked it appreciatively. It had padded lapels and golden dragons on it.

"Indeed?" he asked. He was not used to children. This blonde one had eyes like a hawk. She knew all about John, she also knew what he had been doing in Miss Fisher's bed, and was not remotely bothered by any fact. She disconcerted him.

"And so have you," Jane continued. "We always have cocoa on thundery nights. Cocoa feels more real than tea."

"So it does," agreed John.

"The Guv'nor always puts rum in hers," suggested Tinker, hefting a bottle of Queensland OP. "You want some too?"

John extended his mug. Tinker was generous with his rum. The sip went right down into John's memories and warmed them to the cockles. Ruth offered him his own pipe and tobacco. Phryne must have sent her upstairs by another stair. She thought of everything.

"Miss Phryne thinks you need a smoke," she explained. "She'll be back soon. She's in the garden."

"Then I shall join her," said John, and took his cup and his smoking materials and went into the small garden, where Phryne stood under the verandah and scanned the sky.

"Looking for Very lights?" he asked. She did not jump but leaned back into his side, as though he was a tree. He found this extremely touching.

"Yes," she answered. He put his mug of cocoa down on the small table and began to fill his pipe. Phryne found a gasper, lit it, and offered him her box of matches.

"Three lights from one match will draw a sniper," she said.

"I know," he told her.

They smoked companionably. Phryne had scanned the whole horizon. There were no Very lights, sent up to guide a barrage or an assault. In fact, there were few lights of any kind. In the silence, the sea made itself heard. John smelt rain-battered jasmine flowers and cocoa. He puffed. The fear began to subside. He could feel his heart slowing down, his respiration improving. Phryne, leaning against him, was drawing in long breaths of sweet air.

"We'll never really forget, will we?" she asked him.

"No," he said. "But it's better with company. You dragged me out of my dream, Phryne dear. I was quite happy to die in it. One day, I'll die in it for real."

"No, you won't," she said fiercely. "A solution will be found," she told him.

"If anyone can find it," he replied, "it would be you."

Presently they went back to bed. Tinker, it seemed, lived in a shed in the garden. He took Molly with him, saying that he was going fishing early. "Fish rise after a storm," he told John. "It's the fresh water."

The household took its leave. Phryne dissuaded Jane from attempting to interrogate John about his injured leg, and led him back up the stairs, which had roughly doubled in height and gradient.

Usually after one of those dreams he felt utterly exhausted. This one, dreamed in company, had had a reduced effect. Another thing for which he had to thank Phryne Fisher.

"Pyjamas," she said, throwing him a pair of flannelette garments in his size. "Let's get warm," she added, leaping into bed and drawing up the blanket and comforter. "I will never get used to this weather. You can get sunburn and frostbite on the same day, while not moving so much as an inch. Come along, John," she chided. He took off the dressing gown. He put on the pyjamas. He got into bed and was embraced. And he fell asleep again.

It really had been an astonishing night.

Chapter Six

Of the milk within the saltiest spurge, heard, then,
The sea unfolding in the sunken clouds?
Oh! C'était mon extase et mon amour.

Wallace Stevens
"Sea Surface Full of Clouds"

Dr. John Wilson woke in luxury. Green silk sheets. Cool morning light. The Hon. Miss Phryne Fisher curled up beside him, snuggled into the curve of his arm. And a black tomcat seated on his chest, tail wrapped around paws, staring censoriously into his eyes. He was just withdrawing the paw which he had used to pat John's cheek. John got the impression that if he did not respond he could find himself short an eye. An extremely male fellow mammal was making a claim to Miss Fisher. What that paw on Phryne's shoulder said was *mine!*

"Very well, old chap," murmured John. His

body felt lax and full of ease. He leaned down and kissed Phryne on the forehead.

"Mmm?" she asked.

"It's dawn and your cat seems to be suggesting breakfast," he told her. Phryne never woke up easily. She shut her eyes again and replaced herself in his embrace, snuggling emphatically. Ember waited until she had settled and then patted John's cheek again.

"I'm sorry, old chap, but ladies will be ladies," John told him. "You of all creatures ought to know that."

Ember thought about clawing him, glanced at Phryne again, then got down off John's chest and curled up beside Phryne, putting nose on paws.

"That's a sensible cat," John told him, and went back to sleep.

◇ ◇ ◇

When he woke again it was full light, Phryne was sitting up in bed, and she directed him to the bathroom because it was breakfast time and she wanted to feed him properly.

"When are you due back at the hotel?" she asked.

"Not until eleven," he said.

"Good. I shall escort you down," said Phryne, in defiance of all custom, and went into the lavish bathroom—a malachite bath, he had never even heard of such a thing—to bathe and dress. John had only the clothes in which he had gone to dinner last night. He felt quite raffish. He started to wonder why Phryne owned a pair of striped flannelette pyjamas in just his size, and who owned the splendid red dressing gown, and then stopped wondering about it. She had her mysteries. And at this hour he might not be able to cope with the answers. If at all.

If breakfast at Miss Phryne's had been the last meal of a condemned man, he would have gone to his execution whistling. Phryne bade him return whenever he wished. Would tonight be too soon? he wondered. After the lantern lecture?

Phryne kissed him and consented.

Regretfully, he took his leave. He passed the telegraph boy on his bike at the gate.

As Phryne received the telegram and paid the boy his penny from a jar kept on the hall table, the phone rang and she answered it.

"Your appointment with Dr. Fanshawe is for two o'clock this afternoon," said a nasal female voice.

"Have you got the right number?" Phryne was extremely healthy.

"Miss Phryne Fisher, *chatte noire*, two o'clock, Dr. Fanshawe, 123 Collins Street," intoned the female voice.

"Oh, very well," replied Phryne. Black Cat. That had been her code name when she had done a little light espionage for Compton, many years ago. He must have telegraphed the local branch of MI6. Must be about Rupert Sheffield. Could be interesting. "I'll be there."

The phone went dead without further comment. Phryne opened her telegram. In code, of course.

"I'll be a little while," she called to her family, ascending the stairs again.

Ten minutes work and she had decoded the flimsy. She laughed as she read it. She had sent "who is Rupert Sheffield query" and the reply had come back, recalling Compton's voice and his signalling eyebrows, "Idiot Savant stop Emphasis savant stop Emphasis idiot stop regards C."

She could just hear him saying it. She laughed again.

"Miss?" Dot's voice. Telegrams worried her, and all her generation. Mostly they came to announce the death of another brother, son, lover.

Intelligence habits are not easily abandoned. Phryne tore her ciphering across and shoved it into her fireplace along with the telegram, set a match to it and watched it burn to ash. Then she crushed the ash with the poker.

"Best thing to do with them," agreed Dot. "Bad news, Miss?"

"No, just confusing. Well, I haven't anything to do until this afternoon, when I have to go into the city again. Have we heard from Jack Robinson?"

Dot blushed. "He's sent Hugh with the choral people's statements, and he wants him to stay here until you've read them all, because he can't just lend them to you."

"Well, you can entertain Hugh and I can read the file—that ought to take up the time until my doctor's appointment."

"Oh, Miss—you aren't feeling well?" Dot clasped her hands to her bosom.

"I feel in top form, Dot dear. What did you make of Dr. Wilson?"

"Seemed a nice man. The girls liked him. Jane says he's sad."

"She is very acute," commented Phryne. "Hand me those shoes, will you? The glacé kid. Ember's been chewing my slippers, the naughty puss."

She cast a reproachful glance at Ember. He turned his head elegantly, shedding all reproof. They were of an interesting texture. He liked chewing them. No further correspondence would be entered into.

"I thought he was sad too," said Dot. "But he's

sad and kind, not sad and bitter. What happened to him?"

"His lover died of a heart attack after only three years," Phryne told her truthfully, not mentioning the gender of the lover because this could only get more confusing. "And he had a bad war."

"Mr. Butler said you saved his life."

"I did, and Dr. MacMillan saved his leg. But we couldn't save his heart, Dot dear."

"You're on the way to patching it up again, then, Miss. That's a good deed," said Dot, who had clear views on the Cardinal Virtue of Charity. It took strange forms. Especially when Miss Phryne was dispensing it.

Meanwhile, there was Hugh Collins sitting in the garden, sipping a shandy and guarding the file. Dot felt that her embroidery needed to be inspected in sunlight to make sure that the colours balanced, and went with it to keep it company.

Jane was in the parlour, attempting to improve her understanding of a sentence which began, "The conditioning of problems: perturbations in input data can have large changes in output. If this is not so, the problem is well conditioned. If it is so, the problem is ill conditioned."

She had almost understood that. The next heading was "Homoscedasticity." She started to read about multiple regression models. She blinked.

She rubbed her temples. Ruth took the book firmly out of her hands and shut it with a slap. *Pure Mathematics* was placed on the table. Jane was hauled to her feet.

"We're going swimming," stated Ruth. "But first, a nice glass of lemonade and an aspirin."

Jane went quietly.

◇◇◇

Phryne spread the statements out over the dining table. She compared all of the available manuscripts to the master list of choristers which Jack had provided. There seemed to have been nine sopranos, twelve altos, four tenors, six basses, and the répétiteur, Professor Arnold Szabo, present at the fatal rehearsal. Phryne decided to sort them by first names and by presence or absence after rehearsal was finished, as every statement insisted that the unlamented and very late Tregennis had been offensively present until he had stormed off to the conductor's room and bidden them all begone at about eight. She made two lists.

At The Pub In Each Other's Company

Were sopranos Millicent, Miriam, Caterina, Isabelle, Calliope, and Josephine. Of the tenors only Daniel Smith had managed the journey. Almost all of the altos, comprising Annie, Irene, Maisie, Lydia, Mary, Emmeline,

Lobelia, Alison, Geneva, and Ophelia were there. And basses: Tom, David, Aaron, and Luke.

UNACCOUNTED FOR

Julia, left hall at nine, by her account, soprano.

Jenny Leaper went on to her job in a bakery, soprano.

Helen Burke went home to mind her little sisters, alto.

Tabitha Willis went home to finish an essay on distemper (duly handed in), alto.

Chloe McMahon went home to wash her hair, (Wagnerian) soprano. Score missing.

Leonard Match went home and has now got on a train to Albury to visit relatives and is still there, bass.

Matthew, the Father Christmas blond, went home to his grandmother and cooked a late dinner, tenor.

Mike aka Bones, the languid medical student, went to a cramming session on anatomy with two others, tenor.

Luigi had an assignation with a lady whom he

would not name [of course he did, thought Phryne], tenor.

Oliver went to work filing in his father's office, bass. Score missing.

Professor Szabo went home to his room in 88 Collins Street, drank the rest of his bottle of ruby port, and fell asleep. The poor old man.

It looked all very organised set out like that, of course, but it didn't really help much. Phryne, with the help of a considering cocktail, read rapidly through all the statements, collating times and places (as far as could be dredged up from multiple inebriated reminiscences) and decided, after two hours, that she was amply provided with information and completely clueless about the murder.

The doctors Wilson and MacMillan had agreed that the actual cause of death was choking. He must have died between eight and nine, when Julia saw the corpse complete with music, and although Julia was vague about anything which did not involve singing, Phryne had scared her and, thought Phryne, she had told the truth. As she saw it. Therefore, the conductor barrels his way out of the hall, flinging epithets at the choir, and stomps into his room at about eight. There someone brings him sweet poisoned wine and an intimate little supper. They find him writing something incriminating—a love letter? Worse, a letter dismissing a lover? But surely whoever brought those exquisite little suppers wouldn't ask him to drink Tokay. As Ruth said, it didn't match. And Hedley Tregennis was an unpleasant man, but no one had accused him of lack of taste. Perhaps she needed to look at this another way.

Phryne pulled a clean sheet of paper and wrote a time line which did not rely on any assumptions.

1. Eight o'clock. Tregennis is in his room. Writing and tearing up letters.

2. Someone—mystery woman?—brings him supper and the correct glass of champagne. She goes or is sent away, taking the tray or basket with her. At this point Tregennis is alive and well fed.

3. Another person brings him tea in his teapot, and a glass of Imperial Tokay improved with morphine. This person may just wait to see him drink it, and then leave.

4. He collapses to the floor. He is dying. A third person enters, stuffs music down his throat (thus killing him) and departs.

5. Nine o'clock. Julia enters, picks up her

score, and leaves again, locking the door behind her and not mentioning it to anyone.

6. Someone removes the wastepaper and the crockery.

So far, so good. This schematic made sense of all the information. She estimated that a small supper such as the one Tregennis had eaten would only occupy fifteen minutes, even if he lingered over the smoked salmon. And it was possible that the papers, the teapot and the cup had been removed by the assembly hall staff collecting dishes for washing, though he or she would surely have noticed a dead conductor on the floor. Then again, caretakers were underpaid and overworked, also under-appreciated. The caretaker might have thought that it wasn't any of their business if the choir slaughtered the conductor. Or might not have noticed the body on the floor.

She searched through the statements. One from Mrs. Elsie Cook, caretaker. Yes, she had removed the teapot and the cup. And the paper. And she had not observed any corpse. Observing corpses wasn't her job. For which she didn't get paid enough anyway.

Well, then, that paper was gone. The tea things had been washed. Other clues must be considered.

It had been choral music stuffed into Tregennis' mouth. So it could have come from Oliver's score, abandoned on the piano, or from Chloe's score, pinched one rehearsal from under her summer hat. Or even bought for the purpose. *Elijah* was a popular oratorio and often performed; the music would be readily available. She giggled as she remembered a list of scores for sale. And the Lord Gave Mendelssohn fourpence.

Well, this had all been illuminating, but she needed to go and see the local representative of MI6 as personified by one Dr. Fanshawe, and she decided to lunch in town.

She returned the file to Hugh Collins' custody, elaborately did not notice that he had actually put his blue-clad arm around Dot's virgin waist, and sauntered out into the sunshine.

◇◇◇

The nearest hotel with a reputation for haute cuisine to the Scots Church was probably the Imperial Hotel. It stood right across from Parliament House, in Spring Street. It was a plush hostelry, catering as it did for patrons with very high standards: politicians and prostitutes. The Ladies of the Night needed sustenance and it wasn't going to come from the pie cart, not if someone else was paying for the pleasure of their company.

The verandahs had been removed, Phryne knew, by a censorious city council, because said ladies were sheltering under them while plying their trade. This had not driven the ladies further away than the very comfortable precincts of the Maj theatre. Which also sold chocolates. The Imperial was still a notorious place, but its ladies' lounge had twice the acreage of the average drinking hole.

Phryne strolled in and found a seat at the bar. She bought a gin and tonic and then remembered that unaccompanied ladies could not lunch at the Imperial. She smiled at the barman, a middle-aged man with world-weary eyes and thinning hair. "Just mind my drink for a moment, will you? I've got to go and get a man."

"Plenty on offer," he said, grinning. "I can introduce you, if you like. No pollies, it's holidays."

"That's a mercy," commented Phryne.

"Well, there's cops in that corner," said the barman, laying out his wares like a showman. "Tarts over there, theatre people over there, and that bunch I'm not too sure about. Hanging round here more than a bit. Had to throw 'em out last Tuesday for singing. Or there's me." He waved a bar towel at himself. "I'm yours, anytime. I get off work at six."

"So kind, but I can't wait, I want some lunch," Phryne told him, blowing him a kiss.

She carried her drink over to two choristers.

"But Aunty is coming soon," Oliver was protesting. "And that friend of his, Gawain, isn't that his name? You know how cross he gets when the choir isn't up to speed."

"Well, we'll just have to tell Aunty it wasn't our fault that our conductor got murdered, and it wasn't us, so we'll just have to get on with it," stated Matthew.

"Hello." Phryne subsided into a chair. "Might I ask you both to lunch with me?"

"Miss Fisher!" gasped Oliver, blushing a pretty pink which clashed with his hair. "We'd be delighted. But…We'd be…"

"Honoured," said Matthew. "But we just about afforded a beer…"

"Each," concluded Oliver.

Phryne fleetingly wondered if choristers were always fugual, and in which circumstances this could be really intriguing. She slapped her imagination down. It really was most indelicate, bless it.

"My treat. I want to lunch here but I can't without a gentleman, and I have always been a fan of excess, so I shall greedily help myself to two."

They went quietly.

Phryne looked at the folio-sized menu and said to the maître d', "Shucked oysters, six, if you please, with lemon juice. A little smoked salmon. Then something light—a cheese soufflé would be perfect. Later we can talk about dessert. Gentlemen?"

Matthew was fighting down the urge to say, "One of each, please," but ordered soup and roast beef, and Oliver ordered soup and roast chicken, one of his favourite dishes. Phryne ordered wine for all of them.

"This is very kind of you, Miss Fisher," Matthew began. "Is there anything that we can…er… do for you?"

Phryne could think of lots of things, but was supposed to be 1) solving a murder, and 2) engaging in espionage, and 3) seducing an old army friend, and decided with regret that her life had enough divertissements at present. Matthew would probably keep. Therefore she gave him a wicked smile and said, "Talk to me about the choir, about Mendelssohn's *Elijah*, and any other thing which enters your heads."

"Matt, don't turn round," said Oliver urgently. "It's that deduction bloke. The Pommy."

"Is anyone with him?" asked Phryne, seeing Rupert Sheffield in the pub mirror, artfully angled so that diners could catch sight of avenging wives, angry constituents, and process servers and have time to escape out the back way. Phryne could not see John Wilson in attendance.

"How do you feel about lunching with him?" asked Phryne.

"Ponce," said Oliver. "He was real rude. To everyone."

"Yes, that does seem to be his trademark," answered Phryne. She raised a finger and a waiter was instantly at her side. She beckoned him to lean down, whispered in his ear, and dropped a ten-shilling note on his tray. He nodded soberly, trousered the note, and flickered away—clearly another graduate of the Mr. Butler school of evanescence.

"Do either of you speak French?" asked Phryne.

"No," said Oliver.

"Yes," said Matthew.

Of course, he was going to be a diplomat. Phryne smiled at him. He really was very attractive.

"In that case, Matthew, I must ask you to stay silent about anything you hear—and for the purposes of this conversation, you don't speak a word of French, right? *Tais-toi*," she said, and tapped him on the lips with one forefinger. He nodded mutely.

"Miss Fisher?" asked Rupert Sheffield, alone and without his minder. The waiter stood to one side, eyes averted, waiting for orders. Sheffield really could move like Ember. She had not heard his approach.

"*Bonjour*," said Phryne. "*Tu es venu à propos du petit souper?*" You are here about the little supper?

"*Bien sûr. C'était clair.*" Of course. It is obvious.

"*Il est venu de cette cuisine,*" said Phryne. It came from this kitchen.

"*Évidemment, tout le monde pourrait le voir.*" He snapped. Clearly, anyone could see that.

"*Alors, ça va rendre l'Inspecteur principal Robinson très heureux,*" Phryne told him. So that will make Detective Inspector Robinson very happy.

"*Tant pis,*" said Rupert. Too bad.

Rupert was still standing, looming over Phryne, who had a limited tolerance for being loomed over. The waiter delivered the first course, and she invited him to sit with an imperious wave. Reluctantly, he obeyed. The waiter brought him a glass of wine. Phryne gave him an oyster fork and pushed over the plate.

"*Je pense qu'elles sont très bonnes,*" she said. I believe they're very good.

Ungraciously, Rupert took up a shell and drank down an oyster.

"*Assez passable,*" he said. Quite passable. "*Vous avez appris le français à l'école, puis vous avez vécu à Paris.*" You learned your French at school, then you lived in Paris.

"*Et tu l'as appris d'une nurse francophone, ou bien, peut-être de ta mère,*" Phryne replied—And you learned yours from a French-speaking nanny, or maybe, yes, your mother—eating an oyster. It was very good, creamy and tasting of the sea.

"*Ma mère*," confirmed Sheffield.

"*Tu parles un français soigné et correct,*" said Phryne, tu-toi-ing him shamelessly. You speak very formal and correct French.

"*Et vous parlez un français pitoyable de les rues de Montparnasse,*" snapped Sheffield. And you speak Parisian French from the gutters of Montparnasse.

"*Comme de juste, Auguste,*" agreed Phryne, with a cheeky grin. "*Dis donc, ce n'est pas la peine de t'en prendre à moi. Je vais parler à la femme aux cheveux noir, et je dirai à mon policier que tu m'as tout expliqué,*" she said condescendingly. But let us not become too personal. I shall speak to the woman with black hair, and I shall tell my policeman that you explained it all to me.

Sheffield glared at her.

It was a very good glare, she thought, dark, brooding, very Heathcliff. Phryne had been glared at by angry people before, and on one occasion an affronted tiger. This was about five on the "I'll skin you alive, gnaw your beating heart and dance on your bones" ten-stage Glare Scale. Though a ten was only briefly seen before a necromancer sacrificed you to the demon Astrophel. Phryne smiled sunnily.

Sheffield was nervous. He shifted in his chair, his long, elegant fingers drummed the white-clothed table. He caught the eyes of both singers, who looked away. At least the glare worked on them, thought Sheffield. The detestable Miss Fisher seemed immune to glares as well as all decency. Phryne did not speak further, though she offered him another oyster. Finally, he could not stand it any longer. He had to know what she had done with him.

"*Où est Jean Wilson?*" he demanded. Where is John Wilson?

"*Jl'ai renvoyé chez lui il y a trois heures,*" I sent him home about three hours ago, said Phryne. "*Tu ne le mérites pas, tu sais.*" You do not deserve him, you know.

Rupert gave her a sudden, piercing flick of his violet eyes, said "*Je sais,*" I know, and left with hardly a whisk of his beautiful suit.

"*Nom de dieu! En effet, merde!*" said Phryne, and fanned herself. Bloody hell.

"*Le souper?*" Supper? asked Matthew. "*Tu veux dire que la femme mystère l'a acheté ici?*" You mean that the mystery woman got it from here?

"*Oui, et je suis sur le point de la retrouver. Mange.*" Yes, and I'm about to find her. Keep eating, Phryne told Matthew, and beckoned the waiter again. He bent, she whispered, a note flickered in the air.

"Have an oyster?" Phryne asked Oliver. "So

rude of us to speak another language. I'm sure that Matthew won't tell you all about it later. How is the soup?"

"Wonderful," said Oliver. He could see a trolley with a whole baron of beef on it, accompanied by every possible vegetable. This morning he had scraped up the threepence for one pot of beer and had been expecting not to eat again until supper. He didn't care what French plotting had taken place over his head, though from the stunned expression on Matt's face, it had been juicy stuff.

He ate the oyster. It was very good.

As the choristers were ploughing into amazing quantities of roasted beasts and Phryne ate her cheese soufflé with delicate licks of her fork, an aproned woman was escorted in by the waiter and sat down beside her. Phryne ordered wine with the crook of an eyebrow.

"I'm so sorry," Phryne told her.

Reddened eyes looked into hers. The woman scraped back her long black hair, which she had tugged out of its bun.

"He wasn't a good man," she whispered.

"I have never found that that makes the slightest difference," said Phryne.

"No," said the woman.

"You'll have to tell the cops you were there,"

Phryne said gently. "You haven't done anything wrong."

"But was it the oysters?" The question burst out of the scratched throat in a fierce whisper. "Was it my food that killed him?"

"If I thought it was, would I be eating them?" asked Phryne, exhibiting six empty oyster shells.

The woman with black hair was on the verge of tears of relief. Phryne gave her a napkin and bade her drink her wine.

"It was someone else," Phryne told her. "You brought him his little supper and a glass of what—champagne?"

"Yes, of course, what else would you drink with smoked salmon?" asked the cook, outraged.

"What is your name? I'm Phryne Fisher." Phryne offered her hand and the waiter poured more wine at her signal.

"Genevieve Upton," replied the woman, sipping at her second glass. "How do you know it wasn't…"

"Because someone came along afterwards and gave him a glass of something really sweet—probably Imperial Tokay—which was poisoned," said Phryne.

"Tokay? We don't keep it here," said Genevieve.

"Good thing too, it's ghastly, like white port with sugar in it. How long did you know Tregennis?"

Genevieve raked her hands through her hair again. She sniffed.

"Oh, it's been four months. Came in here and I thought he was..."

"Quite," said Phryne.

Matthew and Oliver were listening with their ears flapping, but that hadn't hindered their consumption of a truly heroic number of calories. The ghostly waiter had refilled their plates several times. Ah, to be young again, he thought, rubbing his ulcer.

"I took him his basket at eight as usual," Genevieve said. "I stayed while he ate. He said he'd see me that night, but he never came....He never came."

"When did you leave the assembly hall?"

"About twenty past eight. I had to get back here—there was a private party."

"And you were at work all that evening?"

"Oh, yes, Miss. With about twenty witnesses."

"Then you just need to go and tell your tale to Detective Inspector Robinson, who is a very nice man. He will understand why you fibbed to him. Your work is your livelihood. You were terrified that it was your food that had killed him. He'll comprehend. Then it will be all over," said Phryne, and patted Genevieve's work-hardened hand.

Dark eyes looked into Phryne's green ones.

Then Genevieve emptied her glass in one gulp, got up, straightened her apron, and went out.

"So she's the mystery woman!" marvelled Matthew.

"She is, but she isn't the murderer," Phryne told them.

"Good," said Oliver. "I liked her."

"So did I," said Phryne. "Now, how about some dessert? And you need to tell me about Mendelssohn's *Elijah*. About your choir. And many other beautiful things."

Dessert was a trifle so rich, so creamy, so fruity, that Matthew groaned.

"We're going to have to go home and sleep off this lunch," he told Phryne. "Can we talk to you again?"

"Of course," said Phryne indulgently. "Telephone my house when you have recovered. Thank you for your company," she said, dropped some notes on the ever-present waiter's tray, and sailed out.

"All right," said Oliver. "I want you to tell me everything they said."

"It's printed on my eardrums," said Matthew, and began to recount it.

Chapter Seven

Let the wind blow high, let the wind blow low
Through the streets in me kilt I go
All the lasses say "Hello!
Donald, where's your troosers?"

Folk song,
sung to the tune of "Johnnie Cope"

So this was 123 Collins Street. What an excellent place for an intelligence cell, thought Phryne. A hairdresser's establishment, a pharmacy with bow windows, each one exhibiting the curved jeroboam of coloured liquid which had fascinated her as a child, a flower shop and doctor's offices. She would bet that the three-storey red-brick buildings backed onto Flinders Lane, a quick exit into a world of buttons, braid, and schmutter, always busy at any hour, as fine tailoring waits for no man. It looked ultimately respectable. And a café which served little cakes and rather good coffee, by the scent.

What could be more comfortable? It reminded her of Paris.

Phryne consulted brass plates and opened the heavy wooden door of number 123 into a small atrium with a staircase and a modern lift, without attendant. There were also stairs. Dr. Fanshawe was on the second floor. Phryne did not like lifts, so she climbed the stairs. There was no one around. Her heels clicked on wooden boards. The place smelt of coffee and brass polish. She was wondering if this might be a trap, and had her little gun under her hand as she continued. After all, her telegram had not mentioned this Fanshawe. Rupert Sheffield might have brought all manner of enemies—the man had a positive genius for making them, after all—and one of them might decide that Phryne was part of his ménage. Not while she was still breathing, but John might be in danger. Therefore she kept going.

The second floor showed her a row of doors, all firmly shut. She searched for and found Fanshawe, went in, and was greeted by a plump motherly receptionist, who was knitting a tiny pale blue garment, probably for a grandson. A cup of tea steamed at her elbow.

"Hello, dear," she said. "Miss Fisher?"

"That's me," said Phryne, hand still on gun. One never knew.

"Go right in, dear, Mr. Fanshawe's waiting for you." As Phryne drew near to her desk, she whispered, "He's a bit put out, to be honest. That loathsome man was here yesterday and upset him. See if you can cheer him up a bit."

"Let me make a wild guess—would that be Rupert Sheffield?" asked Phryne sotto voce.

The plump woman's face crumpled into a grimace.

"That's him. Beautiful as a devil. My gran always said the devil was beautiful. In you go, dear," she added, waving her knitting at the door into the inner office.

Phryne knocked on the glass and was bidden to enter. A youngish, baldish man stood up from behind a desk stacked with files. He had a sharp face and bright eyes. He beckoned Phryne to a seat, said, "Excuse me for a moment, Miss Fisher," and started rummaging for his notes.

Phryne looked around. Public school. Cricket trophies on the shelves. Textbooks, Glaister on Toxicology, *Gray's Anatomy*. Journals. Doctor's bag. Drugs in a locked cabinet. Medical background, so he could convincingly imitate a doctor if he had to do so. No framed degree, so he probably wasn't an actual doctor, at least under the name Fanshawe. Pictures of a good-looking wife and two good-looking children. Nice office, with the sun streaming in the window. Local. Army. Had a photo of a graduating class for officers—now, could she pick him out? Too difficult from where she was sitting. With an "Aha!" Mr. Fanshawe found what he was looking for.

"I've a set of questions to ask," he said. "You know the drill, Miss Fisher."

"I just hope I remember the answers," said Phryne. "It's been a long time since I did this. All right, fire away."

"What was your name?" asked Mr. Fanshawe.

"*Chatte Noire. Je suis la chatte*," said Phryne.

He inclined his head. "In England, who was your contact?"

"Major Russell."

"In France?"

"Georges Santain."

"Is there no help for…"

"The widow's son?" asked Phryne. "I always thought that unwise. I can hardly be a Master Mason."

"Er, possibly. I believe that they don't say that now. I might be out of date. I mean, we are out in the colonies, you know, Miss Fisher."

"I like it here," declared Phryne. Mr. Fanshawe had that bruised, harried look Phryne was beginning to recognise. Victim of Rupert Sheffield. She seemed fated to follow him around, trying to glue his subjects back together with food and praise. Phryne was intending, if the occasion offered, to take this out of Rupert Sheffield's very decorative hide. She could think of lots of ways in which he could compensate her.

"Is that it?" she asked.

Mr. Fanshawe consulted his paper. "What was your first coding phrase?"

"Precious stone set in a silver sea."

"And the second?"

"Earth hath not anything to show more fair."

"What phrase meant 'Come at once'?"

"It wasn't a phrase. It was a word. Lucknow."

"Right. I'm Peter Fanshawe. Nice to meet you, Miss Fisher." He stood up and shook her hand. Phryne wondered what he would have done if she had failed to remember her code words. She refrained from scanning those innocent walls for hidden machine guns.

"And nice to meet you. Now, what can I do for you? I've been entirely out of any Intelligence work for years and years."

"Mr. Compton Mackenzie sent a special telegram," said Mr. Fanshawe. He had a pleasant voice, definitely a local, and Phryne could just see his children rushing up to hug him as he came home. He was bright and quick, and essentially nice. How could Sheffield have ballyragged him?

"How is good old Compton? Apparently he's quite the laird these days," said Phryne warmly.

The young man blushed a little. "I've never met him," he confessed. "We're not important here, Miss Fisher, as has recently been pointed out."

"Might I make a broad intuitive leap and tell you that whatever Rupert Sheffield said to you is to be completely ignored? Just cut him out of your remembrance."

"Miss Fisher!" exclaimed Fanshawe. "Are you another mathematician?" Two of you, he managed to convey, would be too much for one lifetime.

Phryne patted his hand. "No, no, I'm not going to lecture you on the Science of Deduction, I've just been meeting his victims a lot lately. So let me apply some balm to your feelings because I would like this to be a pleasant meeting and I really need you to trust me. Right?"

Fanshawe nodded. "Mr. Compton Mackenzie said to trust you."

"This is how it went: he swanned in here, sneered lightly, pinned you with his violet eyes, told you that Australia was the end of the universe and any attempts at espionage here must be utterly pitiful. Right?"

Fanshawe nodded.

"He then told you that only fools played cricket, as he had seen your trophies. He insulted your school, as even though you went to Melbourne Grammar and were in the First Eleven, that would not compare to Eton, Harrow, or Winchester."

"Right."

"He sneered at your suit, though it is a bespoke, hand-finished one from…probably Mr. Merrydale—he favours those slightly wider lapels—in Flinders Lane, and entirely as good as anything from Savile Row."

"Right again."

"Then he told you that he had no intention of allowing you to know what he was doing in Australia. Then he swept out. Right?"

"Yes," said Fanshawe.

Phryne jumped up and began to pace. Fanshawe watched. She was small but she was exceedingly fierce. Mr. Compton Mackenzie had told him not to underestimate Phryne. He wouldn't.

"The person who was waiting for him outside your door was an old and dear friend of mine called Dr. John Wilson, and this Sheffield is such an idiot that if he is doing anything odd in Australia, he might get John Wilson killed. And I do not—emphatically do not—care about Rupert, but I really do care about John. Someone has already tried to kill him. Hence my telegram to Compton, and your summons to me. Right?"

"Right," murmured Fanshawe. He felt immediately better. He tapped a bell and sent Mrs. Thomas for tea and cakes.

"Did you really make one hundred and sixty-seven against the Scotch oafs?" she asked, looking at the trophy. "That must have been a long day."

"It was," said Fanshawe. "I was so tired that I stumbled and was run out on the one hundred and sixty-seventh. But we won."

"Yes, cricket matches between Scotch and Grammar are always something of a tribal feud," she said. "Now, let's have a nice cup of tea and you can tell me what you want of me."

"Right-o, Miss Fisher," said Peter Fanshawe. "Head Office has sent names, everyone that Sheffield might have offended. He was quite a good agent, you know, brilliant code-breaker. He did a little fieldwork. He was in a group that broke up a gun-running ring. He located some missing children. He did a few police-type things."

"By deduction," said Phryne dryly.

Fanshawe grinned at her tone. "Yes—he's a pig, but he's awfully good at deduction."

"So am I," Phryne told him, "and I am not a pig. All right. Any of them likely to be here?"

"I really can't find anyone at present," said Peter Fanshawe. "Most of the gun-runners are still in jail, except the ones whom the Albanians shot."

"Those Albanians," sighed Phryne. "So hot-tempered."

"And the Turks shot some of the others," continued Fanshawe.

"Ditto," said Phryne.

"There was a man called Mitchell, an Englishman, who they never could lay hands on. Still trying to trace him. No record of him entering Australia. And the rest of the files are still on their way. We have a dedicated telegraph but it all has to be decoded."

"All right," said Phryne. "I'll look out for stray gun-runners. Meanwhile, I shall keep an eye on the repulsive Rupert for you. And—" she leaned closer to him "—if I need help, if I need a few agents and some firepower, can you command it?"

"Yes, Miss Fisher," said Peter Fanshawe. "Here's the telephone number. There will be someone at the end of that line at any time, day or night. Just say your name and state your wish. You shall have everything I've got."

"Wonderful. Of course, perhaps Sheffield is just as he seems," said Phryne. "Accident-prone. But I like to be careful."

With this patently untrue statement, she allowed Mrs. Thomas to pour her a cup of tea and began to talk to Peter Fanshawe about his children.

"Little Alice is such a sweet girl," said Peter.

"And Norman is going to be a good athlete. Right reflexes."

"You still play with the Grammar Old Boys, don't you?" asked Phryne. "Do you take Norman to your games?"

"Of course…how did you know?" he asked nervously. Deduction was going to make this poor man jumpy for a good while, Phryne thought.

"You dote on your children and you still have batting calluses on your right hand," said Phryne. "Sorry, didn't mean to sound like Sheffield."

"Not in one million years could you ever sound like that…person," said Mrs. Thomas. "Well, I'd better get on with my decoding." She went out.

"She's your code-breaker?" asked Phryne, chuckling.

Peter Fanshawe grinned. The grin lit up his whole face. "Yes. She's brilliant. Never guess from looking at her, would you?" he asked, delighted. "It's the knitting, I think."

"Great cover," agreed Phryne. "And Rupert didn't deduce it?"

"No, just told her that her grandchild was going to be a girl. Which he isn't, because he is already born. How I disliked that man! Now, Miss Fisher, let me show you the way out. You can't come in the front door if you're pursued," he told her, as he led the way downstairs. "But if you need to sneak in, then the Flinders Lane entrance is your best bet. This way."

The offices had been modified. The red-brick buildings actually shared internal walls. One of these had been holed and a door installed, masked by a hanging curtain. This led to a narrow stairwell, down into what seemed to be a tailor's shop. Phryne smelt steam and starch and tweed. Peter turned a handle on a blank bit of wall, and Phryne emerged into a changing room.

"When you come in, just pull on this clothing hook and turn it to the left," explained Peter Fanshawe, smiling at her. "This way."

"Very pretty," said Phryne. The tailor's shop was busy. Several ladies worked there. They gave Phryne an uninterested once-over and went back to their tasks, sewing on buttons and neatening seams.

"And here you are in Flinders Lane." Peter waved as though to make a present of the scene. Phryne took his hand again, shook it, and left. Nice. A good little niche, excellent organisation, and Mrs. Thomas to break the codes. Rupert Sheffield had altogether missed the intelligence in Mrs. Thomas' eyes. He had a huge—in fact, a bloody enormous—blind spot. Women.

That could be useful, thought Phryne. Her

diabolical grin caused a lounging gentleman to choke on his afternoon beer.

◇◇◇

When she got home she found the household peaceful. Jane, having been dragged out for a swim and aware that no more exertion would be demanded of her, was placidly playing chess with Tinker. He had brought in the fish for dinner and was feeling gratified by Mrs. Butler's praise. It was not every passing fisher boy who could haul in a snapper on a cheap, light rig. Tinker had done it. Mrs. Butler was already talking about roast *poisson a Nivelles*. Tinker was sure it would taste fine.

"So, what did you make of Mr. Sheffield's lecture?" asked Phryne, as Tinker sadly tipped his king onto its side.

"Not a thing, Guv," confessed Tinker. "I was lost after he said 'the science of deduction.'"

"I was too," said Phryne. "Jane?"

"The mathematics are beyond me," said Jane, biting her forefinger. "At least, at present. I think they might be sound enough. The problem is that giving each element of a situation a value is not a mathematical judgment, but a personal one."

Phryne and Tinker looked at each other. Tinker shrugged.

"I mean," said Jane, "say there is a crime scene

at which there is a flannel soaked in ether and a pelican. You have to give a value to the flannel and the pelican. So you believe that the anaesthetic is more important than the pelican, so you give the pelican a one and the flannel a six."

"I begin to see what you mean," said Phryne.

"Yes, Miss Phryne, because what if it turns out—"

"That the rag was being used to clean stains off an overcoat, and the pelican was the key to all of it?" asked Ruth, coming in from the kitchen bearing a plate. "Would anyone like to try some slightly-not-quite-right gingerbread? It's made with treacle," she added. "Which is probably why it hasn't quite worked."

"So," said Jane, "if it's a pelican-smuggling ring, or the pelican has swallowed the gold watch that proves who the murderer is, then giving them numbers just confuses things."

"Interesting," said Phryne, trying a corner of the treacly gingerbread. It was good, but heavy. This was not a gingerbread to drop on your foot. But it would probably feed the poor for weeks. "And giving them values is not a matter of logic or scientific reasoning. It's up to the detective to say, this is important, this isn't, for no better reason than his own experience."

"Yes," said Jane.

"Or intuition," said Phryne. "Which is another way of saying a good informed guess."

They all laughed.

◇◇◇

Phryne was roused from a decadent afternoon snooze by Dot, coming in with an armload of ironed garments and the news that choristers had been visited upon her. Six of them, it appeared. Phryne brushed her hair and washed her face and went down to the garden, where Mr. Butler had corralled them and supplied them with drinks.

They seemed perfectly happy to sit and sing and drink for the foreseeable future. Phryne was greeted with a shout of welcome by Oliver and Matthew. Tabitha smiled at her and raised a glass. A stunningly beautiful young woman, with a rope of chestnut hair and eyes like agate, turned a perfect profile to her.

"Caterina," she introduced herself. "Soprano."

"And are you a soprano, too?" Phryne asked the remaining woman.

"Of course," she replied. "Calliope, they call me Cally." Calliope had the sort of bosom on which one could repose with perfect confidence. She was born to nurture.

And another bass, presumably. This one appeared to be called Tommy and was very big.

Probably a rugby player, employed for crushing opposing wings to death. And he was clumsy. Phryne saw Mr. Butler's point. Loose Tommy in a drawing room and there would be breakage. Sooner introduce a buffalo into a china shop. Even now he was struggling to subdue a perfectly solid wrought-iron chair.

"Oh, do stop it," said Matthew wearily. "Just sit down and fold your hands in your lap, Tommy, like a good boy. We've got enough trouble without you going five rounds with the garden furniture."

Tommy sat down with a thump. He folded his hands. Matthew, it seemed, had some sort of moral suasion over these people. That could be very useful.

"All right," said Phryne. "To what do I owe the honour of this visit?"

"You found the mystery woman," Matthew said. "She didn't kill him."

"No," said Phryne. "And you weren't supposed to tell anyone about that, Matthew."

"Oh, but I didn't think you meant *us*," protested Matthew.

Choristers, thought Phryne. "All right, I forgive you, as long as only the choir knows. What brings you here?"

"You wanted to talk about Mendelssohn," said Matthew, "and choirs and conductors and so on.

I brought Tommy and Cally and Tab and Cat and Oliver. We know a lot about *Elijah*. Cat's brother is a famous pianist. And Tab has sung *Elijah* eight times."

"Right," said Phryne. "I appreciate your expertise. Tell me all."

"That might take awhile," said Caterina, "and I have to be home by seven."

"Start telling me all," said Phryne. "I, too, have company coming tonight." She smiled at the thought. More John Wilson, yum. "We can continue this conversation at another time if needs be. But first, who is Aunty? You were talking about her at lunch."

They all giggled, except the deeper voices, who chortled.

Tabitha explained. "He's Mark Henty, a very good soloist with the Sydney Opera company. Known as Aunty Mark for reasons which—"

"Are apparent," said Phryne.

"He's going to sing the role of Elijah for us," explained Tabitha. "He's bringing Gawain, his accompanist. But he is going to go mental at the state of readiness of the chorus. You have to get Mendelssohn right, you see. You can fudge the edges with really strong composers, and everyone gets lost sooner or later in Bach, but Mendelssohn's so delicate and light, a blurry sound ruins him. And when Aunty Mark is cross, we all smart for it."

"Especially me," said Matthew ruefully. "Because I'm choirmaster now. I've called extra rehearsals. We're not far off getting it right. Not really all that far off," he said hopefully.

"Possibly," said Tabitha. "At least Leonard is in Albury and will be missing for a couple of days. One day I'm going to slaughter him when he stands up with two pages of notes and cross-questions the conductor."

"Now if it had been good old Len who was poisoned, we would all be suspects," agreed Calliope. "But as it happened, it wasn't." She sounded regretful.

"What was wrong with Tregennis as a conductor?" asked Phryne.

"Hard to know where to start," said Matthew.

"Oh, I know where to start," said Caterina through clenched (white) teeth. "I could show you the bruises."

"Would you, Cat?" begged Tommy.

"No," she said, quite without malice. "Cali's seen them. He pinched."

"And he groped," said Calliope. "Horrible man."

"And not only that," protested Oliver. "I mean, sorry, ladies, but just being a disgusting old lecher isn't too uncommon. But he was rude to everyone. He hated sopranos—well, that isn't that uncommon, either…" He ducked as Caterina clipped at his ears. "They mostly carry the tune, and you can really hear it when they are flat." Oliver became aware that even the delightful Calliope was glaring at him and coughed himself into silence.

"But, as my tragically tactless colleague is trying to say," put in Matthew hastily, "Tregennis also screamed at the altos, yelled at the basses, and was exceptionally nasty to the tenors. Instead of making us go back and trying over a whole chunk again, he would concentrate on a few notes, and after awhile you can't sing six notes correctly without the rest of the piece. Then he would swell up, scream at the accompanist, and reduce everyone to tears or impotent fury."

"That sounds like a very bad way to get the best out of a choir," said Phryne.

"Oh, it was," agreed Tabitha. "The sops were scared to sing out, the basses growled, the tenors lost their places, and the altos all wanted to kill him."

"And then someone did. Or several someones," Phryne reminded them.

"I spent an hour trying to talk Professor Szabo out of leaving, poor old man," said Calliope. "He was so distressed. All he would say is that Tregennis was a butcher and that when he played with

Beecham, Mendelssohn sounded like Mendelssohn would have wanted." Of course, one would apply Calliope to the wounded souls. She was an emollient, like cream. But in defence of the weak and the oppressed, Phryne felt that Calliope could surprise the oppressors.

"Poor old prof," said Tommy. "He did play with Beecham, you know. He's still got the concert programs. Showed them to me when I carried him up all those creaky old steps one night."

"That was nice of you," said Caterina.

"Oh, he wasn't heavy," said Tommy.

"Of course not," agreed Caterina. "Not for you."

Tommy glowed.

"What should Mendelssohn sound like?" asked Phryne.

"He's called flimsy," said Tabitha. "I've sung *Elijah* a lot, it's very popular. I prefer Handel's *Messiah*, actually, lots of big strong fugues, solid music. But this is a bit fugitive if badly conducted. His recits are extremely boring if they aren't well sung, and they're usually not, because the soloists are used to opera."

"And the old Felix was a conductor himself. I wish they'd had recording back in 1846. First performance was in Birmingham and it's been a favourite ever since," said Matthew. "He's a romantic, his works are poetic. Not a hammer, hammer, hammer on the majors like your Handel."

"He's not my Handel," protested Tabitha. "I just like singing him. As do you."

Matthew conceded that this was so.

"Did you say someones?" asked Oliver. "More than one person killed him?"

"Yes, at least two of them," replied Phryne. "The mystery woman brought him his supper. He ate it and she took away the basket. She was gone in twenty minutes. Then someone brought in his teacup and pot. And a glass of poisoned wine. And someone else stuffed music in his mouth while he was dying."

"Erk," said Caterina, summing up the feelings of the gathering.

"Then the caretaker collected the crockery and took away the wastepaper. Can any of you tell me what he might have been writing? He was scrawling a draft, screwing it up and throwing it away and starting on another," said Phryne.

They all looked blank.

"That sounds like love letters," offered Calliope.

"I thought so too," said Tommy. "The bl— dratted things are so hard to write. A man might go through a hundred sheets of paper and still not get it right."

Phryne had no doubt as to the intended recipient of Tommy's love letters. Neither had the others. The only one who wasn't grinning was Caterina.

"You're wrong about the number of some-ones," stated Calliope.

"Oh?" asked Phryne. "Why?"

"Because Tregennis used to make poor Professor Szabo bring him his tea," said Calliope, her voice warm with sympathy. "I tried to take over a couple of times, but Tregennis told me that women couldn't prepare tea properly and it was Szabo's duty, and he made such a fuss that it was doing more harm than good, so I stopped. So the prof brought in the tea, and then someone else brought in the poisoned wine."

"Why not Professor Szabo?" asked Phryne.

"If there was any wine around," said Calliope sadly, "he would have drunk it. He's a soak, the poor old dear."

"No, couldn't trust him with a glass of any-thing, up to and including battery acid," agreed Tommy.

"In any case, didn't you say that the poisoned wine was Imperial Tokay?" asked Matthew.

"What, in that conversation you weren't sup-posed to be quoting?" asked Phryne. He blushed. "But, yes, it was something like that."

"Then it couldn't be the prof. Where would

he get his hands on expensive wine? He can just about afford cheap port."

"Well, there we are. When is your next rehearsal?" asked Phryne.

"Thursday," said Matthew. "Do come along. Can you sing?"

"I've sung this before," Phryne informed him. "See you then, thank you for visiting." She ushered the young people out of the garden and shut the back gate on them.

"Very nice young people," observed Mr. Butler, gathering glasses.

"Indeed, and I do hope one of them isn't a murderer," said Phryne.

◇◇◇

The evening was quiet, as Jane was attempting to understand higher mathematics, Dot was at the pictures with Hugh Collins, Tinker had gone out for a spot of twilight fishing and Ruth was reading her favourite recipe book. The roast fish had been delicious.

Phryne took her glass up to her boudoir and stared out her window at the sea. Very comforting, a seascape. It was eternal, and completely unaffected by humans and human wars and human cruelty. She could see Tinker on the pier. Molly was lying next to him, paws in the air, tail stretched out to trip passing anglers. Darkness was creeping over the bay.

Australia did not have the long, delicious twilights of Europe. Nor the fast passing of light to dark of the tropics. Phryne had always enjoyed twilight, the gentle transition from being able to see to being in the dark. The thud with which the night fell in the equatorial bits of the world she found disconcerting.

But with the darkening of the sky came John Wilson limping valiantly up the stairs. Mr. Butler shimmered up behind him, carrying a tray of drinks. Both of them seemed a little out of breath when they arrived.

John sank down into a plush armchair, panting a little.

Mr. Butler set down the tray. "A telephone message from Inspector Robinson, Miss," he announced.

"Indeed? And what does Jack have to say?" asked Phryne, still staring out the window.

"The mystery woman is confirmed to be innocent of any wrongdoing, Miss."

"Good."

"And he has a mass of papers which he would like you to inspect, Miss Fisher. He suggests tomorrow morning?"

"Yes, tell him to bring it all here at about ten.

Also tell him that the person with the tea and the person with the wine are two different people."

"As you wish, Miss Fisher. Will there be anything else?"

Phryne looked at John, who shook his head.

"No, thank you, Mr. Butler."

Mr. Butler vanished in his usual way.

"John dear, have a drink. Whatever is wrong?" she asked. He took the whisky, gulped it down, and held out his glass for a refill.

"Sheffield," he gasped.

"What's happened to him?" asked Phryne, hoping that it might be humiliating or at least involve loss of underwear.

"Nearly run down by a car," said John. "Just now, as we were leaving the assembly hall. Big black car, fast."

"In Collins Street?" asked Phryne. Usually that street was far too busy to get up any speed. She should know. She had tried.

"Came out of one of the lanes like a bat out of hell. Just when Sheffield stepped off the kerb. I barely managed to drag him back."

"Which hasn't done your leg any good," diagnosed Phryne.

"Just gave my knee a bit of a bang," he said dismissively. "No lasting damage. Not asking you to nurse me, Phryne."

"Spiffy, because I am not going to," she said. "However, you are dusty and grimy and in need of a bath, so I shall run one in my new malachite bath, and I shall watch you take it, and I shall sit on the edge and amuse you. Does that sound good?"

"Good? It sounds wonderful," he replied.

She rumpled his greying fair hair. "And if you merit it, I might join you," she told him, and went to run the bath. "If you get out of that suit, I shall have someone brush it."

He got out of the suit, putting on that same beautiful dragon-emblazoned dressing gown. Phryne spoke on the house telephone. Presently Dot arrived, smiled at him, and picked up the clothes. She was so patently a Good Girl that he felt less uncomfortable about the way that Phryne had wrapped her establishment around him like a greatcoat around a chilled soldier.

"Hello, Miss Williams," he said. "Sorry to be a trouble."

"No trouble," said Dot. "Miss Phryne says you nearly got run over!"

"Yes, but I'm not hurt, just a bit shocked," he said, as her beautiful brown eyes beamed compassion at him.

"Nasty things," said Dot, "motor cars. I always keep my eyes closed when Miss Phryne's driving."

"Oh, so did I," John told her.

Dot examined him. "What was she like when she was driving that ambulance?" she asked quietly.

"Skinny and fierce," John told her. "Wild. Feral, perhaps. Always untamed and unfazed."

"Just like now, then," said Dot. "I'll have to get the oil stains on these out with petrol," she told him, "and leave them out to air until the morning. Did you take all your things out of your pockets?" John nodded. "Good night, then," she said, and went out.

"Well, now you're here for the night," said Phryne, emerging from the bathroom. "I have your trousers hostage. Always a position of strength. And you will allow me to assist you into the bath," she told him.

Since she had removed most of her clothes in order to do so, John felt it was only fair to allow himself to be helped. Besides, that knee was developing a really impressive bruise. It hurt. Also, he was still shaking. That metal monster had come so close to Sheffield, it had brushed the front of his coat. So close to obliterating John Wilson's reason for living.

And, just for that moment, he had grappled Sheffield in his arms, his face against Sheffield's neck; he had inhaled that expensive cologne, that scent of honeysuckle. That keen, strange herbal smell of his skin. Just for a moment. And Sheffield, to keep his balance, had embraced John. Just for a moment.

No wonder John was still shaking.

Phryne, losing patience with his slowness, had stripped him and was conducting him to a massive bath, fully large enough for two. There were steps up and steps down and he managed them with care. Then he lay down, slowly, in green pine-smelling water, just this side of too hot. Phryne lowered his head to rest on a little rubber travelling pillow and he closed his eyes.

"And since it is inadvisable to fall asleep in a bath, I shall tell you all about a strange case in which I am involved. You've seen some of it already." Phryne's voice was close. He opened his eyes. She was sitting on the edge of the bath, quite naked, with her feet in the water. Phryne was more comfortable without a stitch on than many people John knew who were wearing a full bathing costume.

"The dead conductor?" asked John. The hot water was soothing his nerves. His knee, however, was enpurpling a treat. It would be his bad leg that took the knock. "Rupert thought it was the woman who brought the food."

"It wasn't," Phryne assured him, a little smugly. "I found her. Just before Rupert did. Cook at the Imperial Hotel."

"Oh dear," said John, stirring a little to get

the bad knee underwater. "He wouldn't have liked that."

"No, he didn't. We had a brief but blistering conversation, fortunately in French. I don't think he likes me," said Phryne. "He speaks beautiful French, though. It was worth being insulted to hear such a lovely accent."

"His mother was French," John murmured. "Pity she didn't like him."

"Oh?" asked Phryne.

"No, she hated his father," John responded. "So she hated her son, too. He was fobbed off on nannies as a child, then sent to school as soon as he was old enough. And he must have had a bad time there, too."

"Indeed?" insinuated Phryne. "Know thine enemy" had always been her watchword.

"Yes. He's very clever. But he tells people that he's very clever. He can't see that a little modesty might be a good idea. At least Winchester didn't have fags, didn't beat him too badly, because he was so bright and willing to learn. He wanted, he says, to know everything. So they could characterise him as a swot and leave him alone. He had a maths master who understood him, and he was always very good at languages."

"I could hear that," agreed Phryne. She splashed the water with her toes.

"When they took him out of Cambridge, like they took me out of medical school, he was too young to cope with a war."

"Yes, darling," said Phryne, picking up one of John's hands and stroking it. "We were all too young."

"They sent him to Athens. I think that they were fairly kind to him. He broke codes, he's a shark at codes. And he learned Turkish and Greek and so on, just by being around speakers. I don't know if he ever left Athens, he's never said. He read the Koran in a Turkish translation. Just to practise his Turkish."

"Not religious, then?" coaxed Phryne.

"No, poor chap. I always found faith a great comfort. Otherwise it is too much, Phryne. Too cruel. To think that all the lads, all those boys, were just gone, blown out like candles. Don't you agree?"

"I do," said Phryne. "I like to think of them sitting down with all their mates to a serious drinking session, washed clean of mud and stench, all shiny and jolly. And if that doesn't constitute heaven, I'm not going; though, of course, I might not have the option."

"Don't be silly," murmured John. "All of those dead boys and quite a lot of the living ones will petition the deity for your presence. And me too," he added, kissing the hand which lingered over his.

"Very kind," she said. "And your voice ought to be heard; you are one of the truly good people I know. Not a long list, either."

"Don't be silly, Phryne, I'm an—"

"Invert?" said Phryne. "Of course you are." She said this as though he had just claimed to have blue eyes, as something utterly ordinary.

"And that means," John persisted, "that I am a sinner."

"Rubbish," said Phryne sharply. "No one can help whom they love. I am positive that your God doesn't care a fig."

"This from a woman who isn't going to heaven," said John, and chuckled.

"Not for that reason," Phryne replied. "I can prove it to you."

"You can prove that Leviticus isn't God's word?" asked John.

"Certainly. Leviticus was a series of rules for a nomadic desert-dwelling culture, where it was sensible not to eat bacteria-enhanced shellfish or terrine of unclean creeping things, where you needed to isolate people who might have leprosy, granted. But consider: if you wish to condemn yourself to hell for Leviticus 18:22, then you need to carry out all the rest of the laws—stoning blasphemers, buying foreign slaves, killing witches, making burnt offerings, and slaying those who twist thread of two types, which means you have to rise from this bath and slaughter Dot, who uses twined cotton and silk thread to embroider her hope chest table linen."

"I have never had scripture explained to me by a naked woman before," said John, somewhat startled.

"All the better to concentrate your attention," said Phryne, reaching down and taking a handful of his attention and squeezing gently.

"I'm listening," he assured her. Fervently.

"It's not Christ's law," she said. "I would draw your attention to Galatians, where my absolutely least-favourite saint—and it hurts me to admit this—made the point. The Apostle Paul—he of the "women should shut up in church and obey their husbands," *that* Apostle Paul—says that Christ redeemed us from the laws. We are no longer under Old Testament law. Galatians, in fact, chapter three. Look it up, though not immediately."

Her fingers stroked a little. John, who had thought himself exhausted, found that he wasn't. Not really.

"And do you know what your Christ thought of male lovers?" asked Phryne.

"No," breathed John.

"Read Luke. I like the Book of Luke, he's a good writer and he wrote in Greek, so it went through fewer translations. In Luke a centurion called Longinus comes to Jesus and asks him to heal his boy who is dear to him. The Greek word is *pais*. That means lover. Not servant, not slave. He tells Jesus he doesn't even need to come to his house, just to—"

"Speak the word only, and he is healed," remembered John.

"Quite."

"But, Phryne, Christ healed lepers, he ate with tax gatherers, and talked to prostitutes."

"Your point?" asked Phryne. "He liked stimulating company? Those pharisees must have been extremely boring, even at dinner."

"No, he was merciful to the sinners," said John, aware that he was on shaky theological ground. He remembered Longinus, a Roman, going to a Jewish faith healer on behalf of a "boy who was dear to him." He had wondered at the time. It seemed like extreme action for a Roman to take on behalf of a slave.

The hand under the water became a little more insistent.

"So, if the reason that you are not leaping on Sheffield is because you do not want to drag him into your sin, dismiss it," urged Phryne.

"All right, all right, I'm convinced." John grinned at her. "You have remarkably effective debating methods, Phryne! Where did you learn all this theology, anyway?"

"When I was at school they made me sit for hours in a freezing church and listen to sermons which were the epitome of the word 'tedious,'" she explained. "So I read the nearest book, which was the Bible. I found it fascinating. But occasionally contradictory."

"But doesn't Saint Paul say something about homosexuality being wicked?" asked John, as lessons came back to him.

"Yes, but there he is being an idiot," rejoined Phryne.

"You must have been a frightful child," commented John, sliding a wet hand down her thigh.

"Oh, I was," said Phryne proudly.

"But the other reason I am not leaping on Sheffield is that he doesn't want me," explained John.

"Ah," said Phryne, sliding down into the bath beside him. "But I do."

Henceforward, John found that making love in a warm bath put no strain whatsoever on his injured leg. And he would emerge cleaner than one whose sins had been scarlet, but now were washed as white as wool.

◇◇◇

He woke at about dawn and looked out across the

sea from Phryne's bed. The sun was rising, the darkness lifting. Phryne was asleep beside him, snuggled into his side. She slept like a cat sleeps, neat and elegant, making every place a subtle background to the picture of utter relaxation. No nightmares tonight, he thought, and lay back down, closing his eyes. Even if he wanted to slip away, his trousers were still unransomed.

Striving and failing to force down a smug smile, John Wilson went back to sleep.

Chapter Eight

But joy incessant palls the sense
And love unchanged will cloy
And she became a bore intense unto her
*   love-sick boy.*
With fitful glimmer burned my flame and
*   I grew cold and coy.*
At last one morning I became
Another's love-sick boy!

Gilbert and Sullivan, *Trial By Jury*

Phryne woke, slid out from under John Wilson's embrace as a cat slides out of an importunate grasp, and went to dress. Dot knocked at the boudoir door with her coffee and croissant.

"Nice day, Miss. Detective Inspector Robinson is coming at ten."

"Then we had better give John back his clothes," said Phryne, sipping. "All well?"

"Yes, Miss. Tinker got knocked into the sea by

one of those horrible old men, but no harm done, he can swim."

"Then why are you looking so worried?" asked Phryne, nibbling her croissant.

"Because Molly bit the old man and Tinker thinks he's coming to complain," said Dot, shifting from foot to foot. "He might complain about her and get her shot."

"No, that won't happen," said Phryne. "Every dog is allowed one bite, and we didn't know that Molly bit people before, did we?"

Dot looked down and tugged the end of her plait. "Well, actually, Miss, we did, because—"

"No, we didn't," said Phryne firmly. "Suppress your incurable honesty, Dot. If the old child-beater has the nerve to come here, escort him in to see me. Anything else?"

"No, Miss." Dot was delighted. She was very fond of Molly.

"Though you might rinse poor Molly's mouth—she might have caught something, biting such bitter flesh. Right, I'd better get dressed."

"I brought the doctor's suit," said Dot.

Phryne dropped it quietly on the end of her bed, where John Wilson was sleeping like a child, and donned suitable clothing to inspect documents. While Dot informed Tinker that he didn't have to spirit Molly away, Phryne sat down in her parlour with her policeman and a large cardboard box full of Hedley Tregennis' papers.

"Tip them all out on the table, Jack dear, and we shall sort. Bills here, correspondence here, all the rest of the stuff here. He was quite well off," she said, looking at a passbook. "More than a hundred quid in the bank. Cheques mostly drawn to cash, took out ten quid a week for usual expenses. No large withdrawals, nothing odd that I can see. Some sort of salary paid in every month."

"His rent was paid up until the end of the month," said Jack.

"He favoured French food; this is a menu from Le Perroquet in Prahran. Expensive."

"He was negotiating for a conducting job with the Sydney Opera chorus," said Jack. "They didn't seem to want him, even though he reduced his usual fee."

"Choristers gossip," said Phryne. "Almost as much as policemen. Someone would have asked about him, and whole fistfuls of black balls would have gone into the hat. More bills, all docketed, all paid. A neat life, so far. Right. What about all this crumpled, scribbled, and torn stuff? What do you have there, Jack?"

The detective inspector's eyebrows were rising toward his hair.

"Love letters," he said faintly. "Should be handled with tongs."

Phryne read a few smouldering sentences and giggled. "I shall have Mr. Butler fetch you a set of oven gloves. Speaking of which, here is the very man. Yes, Mr.?"

Mr. Butler's utter lack of expression indicated extreme displeasure.

"A Mr. Brown, Miss Fisher. A person from the pier, I believe. Come to complain about—"

"Send him in, and send in Tinker, too. I'm so glad you're here, Jack dear. I may need some official backing."

Jack Robinson felt uneasy. He would have to support Phryne, no matter what she did. He hoped it wouldn't mean his badge, or the infliction of serious injuries. On anyone. By anyone.

Mr. Butler ushered in a crabbed, shabby old man who stank so strongly of old fish that Mr. Butler took it upon himself to open the parlour window.

Mr. Brown, failing to remove his cap in the presence of a lady, stared at Phryne and snarled, "That mongrel of yours bit me. I want it shot."

"Then want must be your master, I'm afraid," said Phryne. "I had no notion that she would bite. Suppose you tell the detective inspector what you were doing to make the previously friendly dog bite you?"

"Jeez," said Mr. Brown. "Cops?"

"I'm Detective Inspector Robinson," snapped Jack, who didn't like the look of this old reprobate. He also had a soft spot for Molly. "Well? What happened?"

"I was just sitting there fishing and the mongrel bit me," protested Mr. Brown. "See? Here. Look, there's blood."

Robinson inspected an undoubted dog bite on his insanitary calf. He hoped Molly hadn't been poisoned.

"All right, I see there's blood. Now, why did the dog bite you?"

Greater criminals than Mr. Brown had broken down and confessed under Jack Robinson's relentless regard.

"I might'a, I say I might'a given the young bloke a bit of a shove with me foot," he stammered.

"Tinker?" asked Jack Robinson.

Tinker peeled back his shirt to show the clear mark of a boot sole. He had been kicked off the pier into the water.

"You're lucky you didn't break his ribs," said Robinson. "You want to charge him with assault and battery, Tinker?"

Tinker shook his head. "As long as Molly's all right," he bargained.

Robinson favoured Mr. Brown with a long, slow, considering stare, as though he was memorising his features and would know him if he saw him again.

"Get out, and if I hear of you abusing boys again, I'll have you. All right?" he said very quietly. Mr. Brown looked as though shortly Mr. Butler might have to call someone to scrub the carpet.

"Yair, all right, boss, don't go crook."

Mr. Butler escorted the cringing Mr. Brown out of the room and subsequently out of the house. Tinker grinned at him. Molly, from where she was tethered in the back garden, gave him a valedictory snarl.

"Better watch out for him in future, Tink, I don't think he likes you," said the policeman.

"I catch more fish than him. I can stay out of his way," said Tinker, who had never got used to having allies. It was a strange and intoxicating sensation. And Molly was safe. How had she known that Brown was in the house? Musta smelt the old bastard, thought Tinker. Good old Molly. Just wanted another go at him, despite the way he must have tasted.

"All right, Tink, ask Mrs. B for some arnica

and get Jane to put it on," Phryne ordered. "That's going to be a nasty bruise."

"Can I help with the paperwork, Guv?" asked Tinker.

"No fear," said Robinson. "I don't think *I'm* old enough to read these letters, much less you. Arnica and a bandage, and you can play hero for the rest of the day."

"Grouse," said Tinker.

He left to be attended by his female house-mates. Jane was very good at first aid. Her hands were sure and she was not crippled by Ruth's empathy with the pain of the sufferer. Phryne remembered poor John Wilson and his damaged leg. She would attend to him when he woke up. They read in silence for some time.

"All right, the person who signs herself "Aspasia" is clearly besotted with Hedley Tregennis," said Phryne. "And we know she's not Genevieve Upton because of the dates. Aspasia's been with Tregennis for three years."

"A woman of strong feelings…" said Robinson.

"And no taste whatsoever," concluded Phryne, fanning herself with a handful of inflammatory correspondence. "Interesting epistolary style, though. Could write erotica for a living. Anaïs Nin would be intrigued. She seems to have been a musician. Jenny saw a violin bow in the conductor's room on one occasion."

"Right, female violinists of the orchestra," said Jack, rummaging for his file.

Mr. Butler had returned with Jane. Jane looked excited and smelt strongly of rubbing liniment.

"Miss Phryne, can I go and put arnica on the doctor's knee? He's up now. I've already got arnica on my hands. And I can look at his leg," said Jane. "Might make it easier for him to get down the stairs, poor man," she added, belatedly remembering that doctors were supposed to be compassionate. She was trying to acquire this skill.

"Take Dot with you to preserve the poor man's modesty, Jane dear, and try not to hurt him," said Phryne absently.

"I don't want to hurt him," Jane told her. "I want to make him feel better."

"So do we all," agreed Phryne, reading a few more lines of Aspasia's impassioned prose. My, my, Hedley Tregennis must have had hidden talents. The writer was describing something which Phryne had not only never tried but never even thought of, which was a vanishingly small number of things…

She heard Jane and Dot go up the stairs. Jack ran a finger down the list of musicians and found the female violinists.

"No Aspasia, of course. There's an Anne,"

offered Robinson. "So you're…looking after that doctor bloke?" he asked abruptly.

"He's a very old friend of mine, Jack; he incurred a back full of shrapnel on my account, and I am very fond of him," said Phryne. "Would you like to see the scars?" She dragged up her blouse and showed him her smooth side, pitted with small scars. "Creeping barrage got us. I would have been eviscerated if not for John Wilson."

"I owe him a thank you, then," said Jack, trying not to touch that soft skin. "I thought, because he was with that Sheffield…"

"Sheffield is not John's fault," stated Phryne. "And yesterday someone nearly ran him down."

"I can understand that," said Robinson, and grinned.

"Oh, so can I. Fortunately I have an alibi, so it wasn't me. But poor John saved Sheffield's life, and I bet he never even noticed. And John's banged his already injured leg, which is why Jane has gone to apply arnica to him. And to get a good look at the scar—she loves scars. Dot will make sure that John doesn't feel like an anatomy specimen."

"Well, poor bloke just stood there and looked embarrassed when that Sheffield was mouthing off at us," said Robinson. "I reckon you're right, Sheffield isn't his doing. All right, and it was nice of him to save your life, too. Makes a bit of a habit of it."

"So he does," agreed Phryne. "Have you got descriptions of the female violinists?"

"I have. Why?"

"From some of her letters, it is clear that Tregennis called her the Queen of Sheba, who is popularly pictured as dark-skinned. At another point she mentions that he adores her dark eyes. So you want a dark-complexioned woman, rather tending to the embonpoint. Plump," said Phryne. "She rather goes on about how much he likes pillowing his head on her…never mind. Dark. Plump."

"Only one," said Jack. "Mrs. Horace Reagan. Given name Alice."

"Ah," said Phryne. "Right, mark her down and let's look at all the rubbish."

She placed the love letters in a pile with a snow globe on top, which might cool their ardour, and began straightening out and laying flat the screwed-up pages.

"Oh dear," said Robinson, fitting together two ripped pieces.

"Yes, I've got the same thing," said Phryne.

"*I never want to see you again, you traitorous bitch*?" asked Jack.

"I hope that's a quote," said Phryne, a little taken aback.

"Of course it's a quote." Jack touched the back of her hand. "What have you got?"

"And I quote, *get out of my life you…*well, *bitch* is the nicest thing he says. I don't know why he threw these away; they all seem to be variants on a theme. Surely there are only so many ways of calling a woman names that begin with a "c"?" asked Phryne.

"You'd think so, wouldn't you?" murmured Jack. "Oh, wait one moment. Here's one that isn't just abuse. *'How is Horry going to feel when I show him the letters?'* Now there's a nice motive for murder."

"Nifty," said Phryne. "I wonder if he was blackmailing her, as well? I am having the greatest difficulty feeling sorry for this murder victim, Jack."

"Me too," said Jack. "But a policeman's lot is not a happy one, you know."

Phryne smiled at him with great affection. There was a discreet cough (Butler's Instruction Manual lesson 7: attracting attention without causing offence).

"Yes, Mr. Butler?" asked Phryne.

"Mr. Rupert Sheffield, Miss Fisher."

"Show him in," said Phryne.

"He is just enquiring for Dr. Wilson, Miss Fisher," said the butler.

"Send him up to the boudoir, then. I don't need to speak to him. Jane should be almost finished with her ministrations by now," said Phryne, and turned back to Jack, hearing feet pacing up her staircase. She hid a private smile. Making Rupert jealous in a good cause was too diverting. Another reason why Phryne would not be entering heaven. There were already far too many, but she was not sorry about any of them. And that trench raider had really merited it.

◇◇◇

Rupert Sheffield paused at the door to Phryne's boudoir. It was a beautiful room in the art deco style. Miss Fisher liked green and purple, clearly; there was even a vase of irises on her table. He caught sight of his own face in an elaborate mirror with pinkish glass, wreathed in ceramic vine leaves. Anyone invited into this room was invited to a bacchanal, that was plain.

He looked ivory-pale and alien in all that luxury, and the vine leaves crowned a face which might have belonged to Apollo in one of his world-shattering, plague-spreading moods, but not Pan or even Dionysus.

He was looking at John Wilson sitting with his trouser leg rolled up almost to the hip. His bare foot was on a hassock and a blonde girl was kneeling by his side. A sharp scent of arnica hit Rupert's nose. Not a scent common in Miss Fisher's boudoir, he was sure. A plain young woman was seated in the other chair, hands folded over a rolled bandage, a safety pin stuck into her cardigan.

Miss Fisher does not even attend John herself, thought Sheffield, but orders a servant to look after him. She did not deserve him either. The girl was talking to John, and John was replying.

"Yes, shattered the femur," he told the girl, who was massaging liniment into a red bruise on John's knee and shin. Recent. Must have been sustained when he pushed Sheffield out of the way of that car. Unnecessary. Sheffield had been in no danger at all. He would have been able to leap back to the kerb. John had injured himself without reason. Illogical reaction. "My surgeon wouldn't take the leg off, fought to save it. I was picking slivers of bone out of the scar for weeks."

"But the bone must have regrown," observed the girl. "And at least some of the muscles and tendons reattached. Otherwise you would not be able to walk and you walk quite well."

"Yes, the human body has remarkable regenerative qualities," John agreed.

She was too bold to be a servant. Must be a daughter of the house. And the plain woman would be Miss Fisher's companion, who would cast a cloak of respectability over her mistress' affairs. She did look very respectable. By the crucifix, a Catholic, too. She loved all the shades of autumn; her dress was beige and her cardigan dark brown. Good but subdued clothes, sensible house shoes, clean hands with pinpricks in one forefinger—an embroiderer, then. Long hair in a plait, no cosmetics, scent of roses—an old-fashioned person. No rings on the hands. But she was easy in the presence of a strange man in a boudoir, therefore was probably engaged. Then again, the girl was comfortable in her situation, and she rewarded Rupert's interest.

Her hands were assured and skilled. Her massage was firm but John was not in pain. She knew where the bones and muscles attached, where the pressure points were, and how to produce the right effect. And the questions she was asking John were very intelligent. Her accent was educated young female Australian. She was dressed in a blue linen shift, covered with an oversized gardening smock, so as not to get liniment on her clothes. Her hair was clipped short. She was not interested in her appearance, though the person who had chosen the dress had done so because she had quite unusual dark blue eyes. She had raised them, summed up Sheffield with a long glance, then had dismissed him as of no importance to her task at hand and returned her attention to John. She had extended her massage from the bruise to the complex scar on John's thigh. She seemed to find it fascinating. So did Rupert, who had never seen it before. The bullet had shattered the bone and mangled the flesh, and the medical attendant had only been able to reorder it as best he could, extract the missile, and stitch the remnants together in a purse-string suture, open to allow drainage of the inevitable infection.

"Why didn't Dr. MacMillan amputate?" the girl asked in her clear, dispassionate voice.

The plain young woman exclaimed, "Jane! Miss Phryne told you not to hurt the doctor, and that includes his feelings!"

"No, no," soothed John. "She's gathering information. I'm familiar with that look. Sort of sharpens the face…"

Where could he have seen such a look before? Rupert asked himself. Oh, of course. Me. Do I look like that?

"There's enough thigh to make a suitable stump," said Jane, shaking off the plain woman's objection.

"Yes, but she said she wanted to send me home to my…to my…to someone who was waiting for me, with both legs," explained John. "And here I am, still bipedal, you see. That feels very nice," he added, as the tight scar tissue eased under Jane's fingers.

"So, wasn't your lover waiting for you?" asked Jane.

The plain woman was about to object again,

but John raised a hand. "Yes, but it's not a story with a happy ending, Jane. I don't want to talk about it, if you don't mind."

"All right," said Jane equably. There were many other interesting things about Dr. Wilson which she could explore instead. "The car hit you here," she observed, putting a finger on the centre of the bruise. "That's the round boss of a hub cap. You must have been right beside it. Did Mr. Sheffield thank you for saving his life?" she asked, and Sheffield was aware that Jane knew he was watching.

"Didn't need to," said John valiantly.

"That will do for now," said Jane. "I can bandage it again tomorrow morning if you are here."

"Thank you, Jane, you are very kind," responded John.

She took the bandage from the plain woman, wound it and secured it expertly, and then pulled the hem of the trouser down. Then she put on a sock and John's shoe, tying the laces neatly.

"Up you come," said Jane, offering a hand. The contrast of the small girl and tall, stocky John was piquant.

Rupert stepped into the room. The plain woman jumped. Jane assessed him coldly.

"Might I be of assistance?" he asked.

John flushed red. But he took Rupert's hand

and was lifted to his feet. Jane held out his stick. Rupert took it.

"I believe I should thank you for saving my life," said Rupert. John flicked him an amazed upward glance which for some reason made Rupert feel briefly ashamed.

"No trouble, my dear chap," said John.

"But it would only be polite to thank you. After all, you were injured. I didn't realise that it was significant. Can I give you an arm down the stairs?" asked Rupert, his voice at full Irish coffee with extra cream and chocolate liqueur.

Greatly wondering, John leaned his full weight on Sheffield's arm and they went down the marble stairs together. Phryne, catching sight of them from her parlour, suppressed a chortle and came out to bid farewell to her guests.

"Thank you for lending me Jane," John said to her. "And for everything else."

Phryne leaned across Rupert's immaculate chest to kiss John on the cheek. "Pleasure, in every sense," she said. "Can't you stay for breakfast?"

"He's breakfasting with me," said Sheffield flatly. "Good morning, Miss Fisher."

Phryne waited until the door was safely shut before she collapsed into helpless laughter. Jane, going back to the kitchen to replace her smock, gave her a piercing look just as she was calming down and set her off again.

"What was all that about?" asked Jack Robinson. "No, on second thought, don't tell me. Come back here, Miss Phryne Fisher. We've got a murder to solve and we are finally getting somewhere."

"As you wish," murmured Phryne, and returned to the Case of the Vengeful Violinist.

Presently, Jack took his evidence and went to interview the epistolatory Mrs. Horace Reagan. Phryne had nothing to do and was full of energy. She called to Molly, put on her lead, and took her for a brisk walk along the foreshore. There was always a chance she would meet Mr. Brown, and get another chance to remonstrate with him for kicking Tinker.

The picture of John leaning on Sheffield's arm with a look of schoolgirl adoration, however, worried Phryne as much as it amused her. She had better not get this wrong.

Therefore, she wouldn't. It was as simple as that.

And now it must be time for lunch. She turned for home. Molly romped beside her, full of the consciousness of being a Good Dog. Phryne shared it.

◇◇◇

Phryne was engaged in a fitting for a new dress,

which was trying. That was because it was for Jane, and Jane thought that clothes were tedious and being fitted for them even more tedious. She did not wriggle, precisely, but she was never still. Madame Fleuri's best fitter was getting cross. Cross fitters have ways to punish annoying subjects.

"If you talked to me, Miss Phryne, I wouldn't feel like I had pins and needles," she said.

The fitter, Mlle Galle, sent Phryne a look of heartfelt pleading. This was going to be a very nice little dress but it had to drape correctly, and she had another child to fit before she got that cup of tea that Mrs. Butler always made her. Phryne did not want to see Jane perforated.

"Fine. Your topic?" asked Phryne, perching on the arm of a chair.

"Will you answer anything?" asked Jane cunningly.

"Probably," said Phryne, who was never an easy touch.

"Why are you trying to drive Dr. Wilson into that unpleasant Mr. Sheffield's arms?" asked Jane.

Occasionally Jane's questions dropped onto the listener with the approximate weight and impact of a falling piano. Phryne blinked.

"Your perspicacity never ceases to astound me," Phryne told her. "Because that's where he wants to be, Jane dear. I am not forcing John into

Sheffield's arms. I want Sheffield to recognise John's devotion."

"But I really do not like Mr. Sheffield," Jane told her. "He is rude and I don't think he cares for anyone. Isn't that an unkind thing to do to nice Dr. Wilson?"

"No, because that is nice Dr. Wilson's dearest wish."

"People," sighed Jane. "I'll never understand them."

"They are not logical," agreed Phryne.

Mlle Galle patted Jane's shoulder and unpinned the marked basque. Jane sped off down the stairs. Ruth stood up in her sensible undergarments. Mademoiselle smiled at her. This one would be no trouble at all. And then there would be *thé anglaise*, for which she had acquired a passion.

◇◇◇

Four o'clock brought a very pleased Jack Robinson.

"Got her," he said. "She stole the morphine out of her husband's medical bag, and the Tokay out of his wine cellar. You know what he was angriest about? Not the affair—apparently she has lots of them. It was the wine. "I don't know why she had to use my Tokay," he grumbled. "I've only got three bottles left." Thank you for all the help," said the policeman.

"My pleasure, Jack dear." Phryne hugged him briefly. "But…"

"Yair, I know. Cause of death is choking, and we still don't know who choked him."

"I might be able to assist," said Phryne, steering him to a chair. Jack Robinson sat. Phryne was about to land something frightful upon him, and he liked to be sitting when she did so. It was hard to stagger while sitting down.

"How?" he asked, really wanting to know.

"I might join the choir," she told him.

"That sounds like it might be all right," he said, on a breath of relief.

"I have sung *Elijah* before," she told him. "Choirs can always do with a new soprano. The person who stuffs music into a dying man's mouth isn't bold or dangerous. I won't be in any peril."

"You create your own peril," grumbled Jack. "All right, that sounds good."

"Excellent—there's a rehearsal tonight, I'm going to volunteer."

Jack Robinson had to say it, even though he knew it would be useless. Phryne defined "precipitate."

"Just don't get into…don't put yourself…" He stumbled over his warnings. Phryne had heard them all before, anyway, and had never taken a blind bit of notice.

She smiled at him brightly. "I won't," she said. He didn't believe a word of it.

◇◇◇

Bidding Mr. Butler to return for her later, Phryne climbed the Scots Church Assembly Hall steps one more time and found a gaggle of choristers just inside the door.

"Scores," announced the librarian.

Phryne smiled at Matthew, who was looking rather harried, and at the embraceable Calliope and the elegant Caterina. She signed for a score with her flamboyant pen and looked around for fellow sopranos. Julia was there, already mouthing over her quartet. So was the Wagnerian Chloe.

"Come along," urged Matthew, waving his arms in broad, shooing gestures, as if he was herding goats. "Think of what Aunty Mark is going to say to us if we can't get through "Oh Lord Thou Hast Overthrown" without getting lost again."

"Ouch," commented Oliver. "That's the entry to his big recit."

"Right," agreed Daniel grimly.

They flurried and moved, shedding hats, until they were lined up in the proper order. A small man, bald, shabby, muttering, confronted Phryne as she stood in the front row.

"You're new. Who are you?" he demanded in a thick Mittel-European accent.

"I am Phryne Fisher," she said with a beaming smile, as though he was a favourite uncle. "And you?"

"Just a poor strummer of keys," he muttered. "When I was with Beecham…"

Phryne could smell the cheap port on his breath, see the damage that the alcohol had done: reddened eyes, jaundiced skin, tremor, chapped lips. He might have been a good-looking man once, before, as the policeman had said, the grog got him. Tommy, who seemed to have a sympathy for the old man, led him away from Phryne, patting him on the shoulder. Poor creature. Not likely to last much longer. But his hands, as he laid them on the keys, were as steady as a rock.

The choir began to sing scales and exercises. Voices eased, high or low notes were reached without strain. They sang the absurd lament that life was but a melancholy flower to warm up.

"Basses and altos," said Matthew. "From A, if you please."

"*Open the heavens,*" boomed the basses, "*and send us relief.*"

"Sops and tenors," said Matthew. His beat was clear. This was a relief. Phryne had sung with conductors who waved their arms around as though they were flinging away armloads of rotten fish. She had sung with ones whose delicacy and economy of movement had been called "mouse-milking." Both were equally hard to follow and both would scream at the choir for not following the unfollowable. Then there were the ones who forgot that the choir did not speak, as it were, Hungarian, and who roared at them for not following instructions in a foreign tongue. At least Matthew wouldn't do that. He pushed his wheat-coloured hair back from his brow. Phryne reminded herself he was off limits, drat it all.

However, she could not imagine him stuffing music into anyone's mouth, unless they asked very nicely. But he was still a suspect and she was in the middle of a murder investigation, so she told her libido to lie down and tackled her notes again. The piece was almost correct but colourless and lacklustre.

"No, look," pleaded Matthew. "There's a drought, you're begging for rain, you're representing the people—put some emotion into it! Imagine your children dying." The choir looked at him. He made a wild gesture. "All right, imagine your favourite sheep dying! Now put your backs into it. Boy, you ready?"

"Ready," said Caterina. Anyone less like a boy would be hard to imagine.

They sang it again. Matthew seemed pleased.

"Right, that was all right, we'll run on. Tommy, you do Elijah. Some passion, please!" demanded Matthew, and raised his hands again.

Just as the prophet Tommy was asking his boy if there was a cloud in the sky, the door banged open. A large man whisked inside and stood with his hands on his hips. He listened for a moment. Then he sang a challenge, in a baritone voice with a tenor quality clear as a bell and rich as plum pudding.

"*I am a Pirate King!*" he sang, and the whole choir forgot Mendelssohn.

"*Hurrah, hurrah, hurrah for the Pirate King!*" they chorused. He walked down the aisle, a big man with a bony face and closely cropped brown hair. He had immense presence.

"*It is, it is, a glorious thing to be a Pirate King!*" he sang.

Everyone seemed to agree. They flocked offstage to embrace him. Phryne caught his eye, and he took her hand to kiss it.

"Hello, Miss Fisher!" he exclaimed.

"Hello," replied Phryne. Up close, he was a bit intimidating, being so very large and strong and totally immune to her charms. She was never wrong about the team for which any person played. And Aunty Mark's was not Phryne's, though they probably had a lot of friends in common. His lips were warm and soft. No wonder several male persons were staring at him as though they had been recently gaffed. He was very attractive. He really needed the ruffled shirt. Or a cloak. Or a feathered hat. Or all of the above.

"Do I know you?" she asked. She was sure that she hadn't seen him before. He had a way of being noticed.

"You were kind to a friend of mine and got him out of trouble," he replied, and leaned close to whisper a name. Phryne nodded. A simple matter of paying off a blackmailer, following him home and burgling his house, stealing a whole safe full of secrets and, more importantly, the photographic plates which would have ruined Gawain's life.

She had also given him back all of his money. Phryne liked neat solutions. Which was why she had burned the personal secrets of the innocent and given all the politicians' dreadful transgressions to Jack Robinson, who had prosecuted with a certain decently suppressed glee.

She had lost touch with Gawain, but there he was, following this magnificent presence up the aisle, grabbing her hand and squeezing it.

"So you moved to Sydney?" asked Phryne.

"It seemed best," he replied. He was not much taller than Phryne, with pale blue eyes, and he was already losing his hair, but the look which the Pirate

King directed at him was very affectionate. "Fell on my feet," he murmured.

"You call that Mendelssohn?" Aunty Mark was demanding. "You're praying for rain from a parched land, not asking someone to pass you the sugar!"

"Sorry," said Matthew. "But our conductor got murdered."

"Really? Do tell!" He intercepted Matthew's wounded look. "No, sorry, Matt—your rehearsal. Suppose I just take over Elijah, and you get on?"

"All right," conceded Matthew, and the choristers moved back to their places. The tempo picked up, the voices quickened. Aunty Mark was listening. Mourning for their dying children or perhaps sheep, the people sang, "*Open the heavens and send us relief,*" as though they meant it. "*Help thy servant now, O God.*"

"*Go up now, child, and look toward the sea,*" sang Mark, and Caterina replied in a boyish pipe which belied her womanly stature, "*There is nothing. The heavens are as brass.*"

Australians would know what that looked like, Phryne thought. Nowhere in Europe could one see those bleached skies, that coppery, shining, unbearable light. Elijah enjoined the choir to pray and confess and sent the child up again to look for a cloud.

"*There is nothing. The earth is iron under me.*"

Matthew waved at Caterina to skip to the end of her piece. She obediently sang, "...*the storm rushes louder and louder.*"

"*Thanks be to God for all his mercies,*" sang the people.

Phryne had sung this before, but now began to realise how tense the situation was. Elijah had boasted that his god was the best. The prophets of Baal had been bested (and horribly executed). But then Elijah had to make good on his promise. In the Bible he sent the boy to the mountain seven—or was it nine?—times. Here it was only thrice, but the music rang with strain. Elijah was trusting in the Lord, and so was everyone else, but what if it didn't work?

He'd be down there on the bank of the brook Cherith minus a head, of course. In company with the prophets of Baal. When she had been a child, Phryne had relished the violent bits of the Old Testament. As a grown woman, she was beginning to think that gentleness had something going for it.

A brief discussion broke out about the next piece, and Phryne had leisure to inspect the choir. It was fairly easy to pick out the couples. It was even easier to identify the one-mind-one-body-one-heart couple, who appeared to be called DavidandLobelia. They were alto and bass, and David had moved through the tenors to be near his beloved. They were presently entwined in an embrace so close that fairly soon David would be wearing Lobelia's dark blue dress. Every choir had one of them. The established couples just kept an eye on each other. The rest were circling, considering, snatching glances. Caterina was the cynosure of at least four sets of eyes, the most ox-like being Tommy. The giraffe boy Daniel was intercepting and apparently failing to notice ardent passion being directed at him from the sops. Tiny dark Josephine clearly thought he was gorgeous, perhaps hoping to breed some legs back into her bloodline. He, on the other hand, was gazing at tall, fair, and dismissive Isabelle, who was a legal secretary and not interested in anyone at present.

Any chorus is a hotbed of emotion, of course, but Phryne had previously sung with older people, who were more experienced at hiding their reactions. This was at white-heat, dangerous and visible on the surface for all to see who could. There might be any number of reasons for any of these people to thrust music down their conductor's throat.

Matthew raised his hands again, the choir ruffled and settled, and then began ensuring that Ahab would perish, by singing "*he shall perish*" a great number of times.

Phryne stopped analysing and started singing.

Chapter Nine

If once a man indulges himself in murder, very soon he comes to think little of robbing: and from robbing he comes next to drinking, and Sabbath-breaking, and from that to incivility and procrastination.

Thomas De Quincey
"On Murder Considered as One of the Fine Arts"

The rehearsal ended with a resolutely cheerful Matthew telling them that they had tried really hard, which was not, as the alert noticed, the same as saying that they had produced anything good. Aunty Mark gathered his acolytes and prepared to take them back to the Windsor, where he was staying. As were John Wilson and Rupert Sheffield, who met the group at the door.

Thinking that this ought to be an interesting encounter, Phryne hung back far enough to clearly see each face. John, a good fellow, merely nodded, smiled, and passed on to the lantern projector. Rupert stared straight into Mark's eyes. Both of them were very tall. Mark was muscular and Sheffield was slim. Phryne was just about to comment when the rest of the choir came up beside her.

"My money's on Aunty Mark," whispered Calliope.

"Every time," agreed Tabitha. "I've just been reading about male displays of dominance and aggression."

"And you are looking at one right now," murmured Oliver. "Who will crack first?"

"I really can't tell," answered Phryne. They were both very dominant personalities.

"If it's the Pommy bloke, you pay for dinner," said Matthew to Phryne.

"That presupposes that I will dine with you," Phryne returned.

Someone laughed. The tension began to grow. Silence fell.

"If they were roosters, they'd be pecking by now," Tabitha informed the group. "If they were lions, they'd be biting the throat or belly."

"With Aunty, that's not out of the question," murmured someone behind Phryne.

"Sheffield," called John. "Can you see if these slides are in order?"

Sheffield, summoned away, lowered his eyes. The choir let out their held breath.

"I still think Aunty would have won," said Matthew.

"You know," said Phryne, impressed, "I agree with you. Therefore, dinner is on me. Just wait a moment, I need to speak to someone."

She moved down the hall to linger near the projector. John looked up and smiled at her. Sheffield finished leafing through slides to glare.

"Hello, m'dear," said John. "So, they're all right, Sheffield?" he asked.

"Of course. They were in perfect order, as you should have known," snapped Sheffield, and flounced off.

"He really does a wonderful flounce," sighed Phryne. "He could give lessons."

"Good dancer, too," said John. "You're a singer, Phryne?"

"Just for this *Elijah*. Are you dining with me tonight?"

"No, m'dear, Sheffield and I have an engagement in St. Kilda. The mayor."

"Can I give you a lift?" she offered.

"Thank you—at about nine, then? Are you driving?"

"Mr. Butler is coming back for me," Phryne assured him.

"Oh, good." John tried not to sound too relieved.

"Right, see you then," Phryne told him, and went back to the group at the door.

"Sorry, can't dine tonight," she said. "Are you going to the Windsor with Aunty?"

"No, we'd love to, but he always insists on paying, and we feel…" said Oliver, blushing.

"Oh, I see. Well, off you go, here's a retainer for your help with Mendelssohn; drink one for me and I wish I was coming with you."

She allowed herself to rumple Matthew's golden hair, which felt like Lin Chung's best silk, and stuffed some money into his hand. She waved away his protest.

"I will find a manner in which you can repay me," she told him.

His eyes widened. He smiled.

The choristers went to the door and Phryne went backstage. A little snooping would definitely while away the time more pleasurably than listening to the science of deduction again. Like Tinker, she had got lost at "The Science of Deduction."

Snooping yielded little new data. A member of the choir had a taste for barley sugar. Someone else read Sexton Blake and had left their copy behind. There was also a lost hat and a score. Phryne unlocked the conductor's room and left the score, marked Chloe in pencil, on the desk. The desk bore three blunt pencils in a cup, a clutter of ink nibs and a pen, a clean new blotter, some slide fasteners in a chain and some old tram tickets. And a lot of dust. Which also cloaked the back of the chair and a coat hung behind the door. Twopence and some cough lollies in the pockets. Probably belonged to a singer.

Nothing of interest. A burst of applause indicated that Sheffield had finished and Phryne locked the door, replaced the key in its absurd hiding place, and went out into the auditorium.

John was waiting at the door and limped ahead, down to the kerb where Mr. Butler awaited in the Hispano-Suiza. Sheffield was already there, examining the hub cap. It might have occurred to him as to just how close he had come to falling under that big black car the other night.

In any case, he did not make any comment, but got in next to the doctor. Phryne accepted John's hand and climbed in.

"Do you need to change into evening clothes, gentlemen? We can wait for you," she offered.

"No, my dear. His Worship said quite informal, and Rupert is always well dressed," replied John.

Did Phryne see a faint tinge of rose on that porcelain cheek? Vain as a girl, thought Phryne. Well, vain as this girl.

"He is a poem in summer-weight worsted," she agreed. Yes, that was definitely a blush. Hmm. "More Keats than Wordsworth," she added. John looked confused. Sheffield turned his face away but not before she saw his smile. "A thing of beauty is a joy forever."

"I have no idea what you are talking about," said John. "But never mind."

"Yes, off we go, Mr., if you would be so kind. St. Kilda, ho!"

"Indeed, Miss Fisher," said the chauffeur.

He allowed the big car to slide into the roadway. Collins Street was always busy, and trucks and motorbikes jostled for space with bicycles and even horses. Not to mention the pedestrians, who at this hour were rare, endangered, and outnumbered. Mr. Butler drove very well, smoothly, without stops and starts which might jar the elegant machine's feelings. They were held up on the corner of Spring Street when Phryne felt a sharp tug at the brim of her hat, registered that a shot had been fired, and stamped on Mr. Butler's accelerator foot.

The Hispano-Suiza screamed in protest but leapt away, narrowly missing a truck, a couple of pedestrians and a traffic policeman. She had registered the *putt-putt* of a motorbike, though this one sounded more like *potato-potato*. The rider, disguised in flying helmet and goggles, dragged his machine upright and hared off down a lane.

"We'll never catch him," said Phryne. "So sorry, Mr.—I hope I didn't hurt your foot. John? All right?"

John had flattened Sheffield beneath him and now was struggling to sit up. Mr. Butler pulled the car off the road. Phryne leapt into the back seat, grabbed John by the back of his coat and hauled him into her arms.

"You've been making a regular habit of flinging yourself in front of bullets," she remarked amiably. "It's really not a good custom. Curb this tendency to self-immolation. Hurt?"

"Felt it pluck my shoulder," John gasped.

The ruffled Sheffield seated himself again, smoothing down his suit, reshaping his elegant hat.

"Was that necessary?" he snapped. "Really, John, you do panic."

Phryne's voice approached absolute zero.

"Oh, panic, was it? Examine this." She snatched off her hat. There was a neat hole in the brim.

Rupert touched it. "A large calibre," he remarked. "Probably a .45."

"And if you would care to look at the fortunately padded shoulder of your friend's suit?" she demanded.

Sheffield turned John toward him, gently.

There was another hole. Large calibre. It had carved a furrow through the shoulder padding of John's old-fashioned suit. Phryne saw Rupert calculate angles, sines, and cosines, basic ballistics, the height of the shooter, and where he had been before John had thrown him out of the line of fire. He swallowed abruptly.

"That shot," Phryne told Rupert, "would have gone straight through your pretty head. Now, thank the man nicely for saving your life, again, and decide if you need new clothes. The Windsor or St. Kilda? John has had a shock. He needs hot sweet tea, a bit of mending, and a little rest."

"What about you?" snarled Sheffield.

"Oh, I'm used to it," said Phryne brightly. "I'm always just very happy that my assassins have such poor marksmanship. And you?"

"I was in no danger," said Sheffield. "John? Are you coming with me?"

"You go on," said John. "Don't worry about me. I'll be all right after a bit of a rest. I'll join you later."

"Right," said Rupert. He left the car and strode away.

"Home, Mr.," ordered Phryne. "Dot can mend your suit, John, and I can spring you for a cab to the Mayor's."

"Thanks," gasped John Wilson, reflecting that

his life already contained far too many instances of close encounters with missiles. It wasn't as though he was looking for trouble. But somehow it always found him. "And you seem to have developed a habit of gluing me together again," he commented to Phryne.

"And I'll stop doing it the very moment you no longer need paste, stitches, or arnica," promised Phryne.

"Agreed," said John Wilson.

Phryne occupied the journey home by considering the many really satisfying ways by which she could murder Rupert Sheffield without a trace. She had reached thirty-five—cyanide distilled from apple pips, and there were plenty more on the list—when they arrived, and Phryne escorted John Wilson inside for some repairs to his health, spirits, and attire.

She sat him down in the parlour. Dot selected matching threads to repair his coat, Jane asked about the damage to his leg occasioned by sudden movement, Mrs. Butler brought him hot tea and passionfruit biscuits, and Phryne fumed. Sheffield was a callous beast with not an iota of gratitude in him. John was hopelessly devoted to the creature, and kept saving his life at risk of his own. And her hat was ruined. It was a smart bleached straw with raffia asters in it. And now it had a bullet hole in the brim. She had really liked that hat.

Presently, John professed himself recovered, Mr. Butler rang him a taxi, and he limped away.

Phryne asked for a very large emergency cocktail and went to the telephone. Fanshawe had told her that there would be someone at this number at all times. That shooting had been a direct and unequivocal attempt on the loathsome Sheffield's life, and needed to be reported. What appalling enmity had the little tick dragged after him all the way from Europe to Australia?

The phone was answered by Fanshawe himself. He sounded delighted to hear from her.

"Is this line secure?" asked Phryne, using her identifying phrases.

"It is," replied the calm public school voice. "What's happened?"

"Two more attempts on Sheffield's life," said Phryne, and outlined the facts quickly and clearly. "I am concerned for my friend John. Can you put a guard on that mathematical automaton?"

"No," said Fanshawe. "He's seen us. He'd remember. He's very acute."

"I know," said Phryne. "Any joy from your knitting decrypter?"

"She's still working. Looks like he really annoyed that gun-running ring. The remainder threatened him with all manner of deaths. Two missing: a man called Mitchell, an Englishman—we never caught him or even had a clear idea of what he looked like. Supposed to have retired to Australia. And an Italian, Guido Calvi. Very nasty piece of work. We're trying to trace him now. So far no sign of him. Anything more you can tell me about the shooting?"

"Large calibre—in fact, one bullet may even now be buried in my precious coachwork. I'll have it dug out. Probably a .45. War souvenir, perhaps; there are a lot of them around. The rider was slight but strong. No idea of colouring because of the helmet and goggles. But the bike made an unusual noise. Instead of 'putt-putt' it had a broken rhythm, more like 'potato-potato.'"

"Harley," said Fanshawe. "Only Harley-Davidsons sound like that. Expensive bike. We might have a brief trawl around the Elizabeth Street motorbike shops. But they hang together pretty well, those chaps."

"Well, do the best you can," encouraged Phryne. "I'll try to keep John alive until you catch someone."

"You mean Sheffield," said Peter Fanshawe. "Keep Sheffield alive."

"Do I?" asked Phryne, and hung up.

◇◇◇

Phryne occupied the evening following Beecham's *Elijah* with her score. Excerpts had been released on disc. Tinker appointed himself her record changer and winder. He seemed to like the music.

"You like this stuff, Tink?" she asked.

"Never heard anything like it before, Guv," he replied. "Angel music."

"So it is," Phryne agreed.

"Guv?" he asked, in the interval between taking off one record and putting on another.

"Mmm?" asked Phryne, musing on angels.

Tinker looked worried. "Guv, you got shot at. Who's after this Sheffield bloke?"

"That I don't know," said Phryne. "But I'm beginning to think it is time I found out. John ought to be safe enough tonight. Tomorrow, I am going to make some enquiries."

"Who with?" asked Tinker.

"Everyone," replied Phryne. "Part two, please," she said, and he wound the gramophone again and placed the needle very carefully.

More of them angel voices. Grouse.

◇◇◇

The morning brought Jack Robinson, traffic summons in hand and face lined with care and woe.

"Someone shot at you!" he exclaimed.

"Yes, I noticed," Phryne returned. "Tea?"

"*Shot* at *you* from a *motorbike* in *Collins Street*!" elaborated Jack Robinson.

"Not at me, I think," said Phryne soothingly. "I suspect it was aimed at the very annoying Rupert. And in any case, he missed."

"Only because his bike slid on a patch of oil," said Robinson. He mopped his brow. He drank tea. "And you almost ran down five members of the public and a traffic officer, plus nearly colliding with a truck."

"There were only two people, I missed the truck and the policeman, and I thought we came out of it rather well. Except for my poor car. She has an appointment at the garage to have her bullet removed this morning, poor girl. And if I catch who did this they also owe me compensation for the ruin of a rather nice hat."

"Is this connected with the murder of the conductor?" asked Jack, drinking more tea in a fraught manner.

"No, it's connected with Sheffield, who seems to have brought his enemies with him," said Phryne, settling down to a cosy gossip. "I am absolutely not allowed to tell you any of this, Jack, so I'd better only tell you all about it once. And you really can't tell anyone else. Are you willing to hear it within those constraints?"

"Yes," said Jack.

"All right, then. Rupert Sheffield was a code-breaker in the Great War. Stationed in Greece. I happen to know the man who was in charge of that section, and I sent him a telegram asking about our Rupert."

"How do you happen to know the head of Intelligence in Athens?" asked Jack.

"Another story for another time. Or ask Tinker to lend you some Sexton Blake stories. Suffice it to say that I was never bored when acquainted with the man—I'll call him C."

"I can just see you as Mata Hari," chuckled Jack.

"Don't be ridiculous. I was nothing like Mata Hari," said Phryne, insulted.

Jack backtracked and apologised. "No, of course not, I didn't mean…" He faltered.

"She got caught," Phryne told him. "Anyway, C told me that Sheffield had done some fieldwork, and would let me know about people who might prefer him to be titled Rupert Sheffield, deceased. Apparently there is a list."

"Not as if we didn't have enough criminals of our own," said Jack wearily. "Some Pommy bastard has to import more."

"Yes, I know, coals to Newcastle, eh? I do not care about Sheffield, though apparently he is a fine mathematician, but we really can't have spy versus spy enacted in our nice clean streets."

"Or even in the filthy ones," said Jack. "What can I do to help?"

"I need to find—so far—a man called Guido Calvi and another called Mitchell, who must have retired here, who might be connected with crime—after all, it is their speciality. They were gun-runners, but that's rather a dying trade at the moment."

"Not a big market," agreed Jack. "So what would they be doing instead?"

"Import/export covers a multitude of sins," suggested Phryne.

"I'll get on to a bloke I know," said Jack. "And you'll get on to your two red-raggers?"

"Of course," said Phryne. "I'm expecting them any moment."

"Good-o. Better stay off the phone, then?"

"You pick things up very quickly," said Phryne in admiration.

"I have to, just in order to keep up with you," said Jack Robinson. He kissed her hand gallantly, and was escorted out by Mr. Butler. The detective inspector noted that Mr. Butler was limping slightly, and assumed it was rheumatism.

◇◇◇

Bert and Cec came into the house through the

kitchen as was their custom. That way they got a taste of whatever Mrs. Butler was baking, a brief summary of Phryne's problem, and could collect beer without bothering Mr. Butler. That worthy was, most unusually, sitting down with one bare foot on a chair. Jane was rubbing arnica into a bruise on his instep.

"Jeez, mate, what happened to your plate?" asked Cec, tall and concerned.

"Miss Phryne stood on his foot," said Jane.

"She's no more than a featherweight," responded Bert, short and scowling. "She musta landed on you from a height."

"She stamped," said Mr. Butler.

"You really musta annoyed her." Cec rumpled his blond Scandinavian hair.

"It was a rather difficult situation," said Mr. Butler. "Beer in the refrigerator, gentlemen."

"She's dived into the soup again," said Bert resignedly. "Don't move, Mr., we're soldiers, we can always carry our own beer."

"And these cheese crisps," said Mrs. Butler approvingly. "And ask Miss Fisher if she would like a drink."

"Never known her when she didn't," responded Bert. "All right, Cec, you grab the ice bucket and I'll take the beer and bikkies, and we're set. You're doin' good work there, Janey."

"I just can't imagine how she managed to bruise his Achilles tendon," worried Jane.

"I bet she's got a kick like a horse. Come on, Cec."

"Right," said Cec.

They found Phryne reading through a long list and grimacing.

"Gidday," said Bert. "C'n I interest you in a cheese bikkie, a couple of wharfies, and a strong drink?"

"Always," said Phryne, not looking up.

Cec mixed the drink, Bert opened the beer bottles, and they both sat down.

One of the things Phryne really liked about Bert and Cec, who had managed a whole war and an eventful career on the wharves without undue damage, was their patience. It was probably a function of having been snipers. Snipers had to still their excitement, slow their reactions, never take their eye off their target, and fire between breaths. That took immense self-control. The two of them were gulping beer and munching cheese crisps and talking quietly about Cec's intended and how they could organise some fine linen for her hope chest. Admittedly, "organise" meant "steal." Phryne didn't expect them to be angels. But if a threat eventuated, that moment, in that parlour, they would be on their feet and reacting sensibly before the second shot shattered the window.

Phryne did not wonder where her images were coming from. She really did not like being shot at. She put down the list and handed Cec her ruined hat. Bert poked a finger into the hole in the brim.

"It's a .45," said Bert. "Eh, Cec?"

"Too right," agreed Cec. "Pity, it's a nice hat."

"I thought so too," said Phryne. "And the head inside it is also nice and I'd like to keep it that way."

"So, who's after you?" Bert leaned forward, fists on knees. "Anyone we know?"

"No," said Phryne. "Someone's after Rupert Sheffield, and that someone is probably connected with his past." She outlined as much as she knew of Rupert's intelligence work.

"It's no use," said Cec slowly, "asking you to stay away from this doomed bloke? I mean, just asking."

"No," said Phryne.

"Thought so. Right, we're looking for import/export of the dicey kind—or are we talking real bad?"

"Probably real bad," said Phryne. "It took a lot of daring, shooting at a car in Collins Street."

"Did you get a squiz at the gunnie?" asked Bert.

"No—overall, helmet and goggles, with

matching Harley-Davidson," said Phryne, taking a sip of her drink. Cec evidently believed that half a pint of gin was needed to soothe her nerves. He might be right, at that. Two of Cec's offerings and she would be soothed into unconsciousness.

"Harley," said Bert.

"Yes, the engine made this odd noise, and I was told that only Harleys sounded like that."

"So they do," said Bert in a voice of lead.

"What?" asked Phryne, putting a hand on his arm. Bert looked concerned, which was a very bad portent.

"There's a bloke…" Bert drank a long gulp of beer. "Bad bastard."

"Very bad bastard," agreed Cec.

"He uses blokes on Harleys. Good way to kill someone. Fast."

"Yes, it was," said Phryne. "If the bike hadn't hit a patch of oil and spilled the rider, he would have been gone and someone would have been dead. And he zoomed off down the lane. Melbourne's full of lanes, though I'm betting he ended up in the bike shops in Elizabeth Street. Ride into the workshop, ditch the disguise, warehouse is full of bikes anyway. And out into the street as an innocent citizen."

"Yair," said Bert.

"Bert, you sound unhappy."

"This bloke…" he began.

"The bad bastard?" asked Phryne. Cec was resembling a Viking who had just been told of an enemy fleet in sight. Keyed up. If he was a dog, his hackles would have been rising.

"Yair, him. Name's not Mitchell, but. And he isn't a dago. English. Got that lah-di-dah voice what makes you want to belt him with a brick. You know?" asked Bert.

"Oh, I do," agreed Phryne.

"If he's after this Pommy pal of yours, then he's got a big problem."

"Yes? Cec, why don't you ring for some more beer?"

"I'll go get it, save poor old Mr. B's plates of meat," offered Cec. "Bert can tell you about Ratcliffe."

"All right, Bert, tell me about Ratcliffe."

"Why did you stamp on Mr. B's foot, anyway?" asked Bert.

"It was between me and the accelerator. As I informed Jack, I also missed the two pedestrians, the truck, and the traffic policeman. I had to get us out of the immediate vicinity of the shooting."

"Always a bonzer idea." Bert rubbed his eyes. "Look, we don't know much about this Ratcliffe, and some of it's probably furphys, right? But he's got phizz-gigs on the docks telling him which cargos he wants to pinch, and somehow they always go missing. Cec reckons one of the gangs worked for him, all of the blokes in that gang. But now there's the strike he must be working out of Willi and not Port. That means he's come up against Maginnis, and he owns Willi."

"Oh," said Phryne. She sipped her drink. "That's…really not good. Mr. Maginnis is notably touchy when it comes to his territory."

"Yair. One of Ratcliffe's main blokes was pushed under a train last week. Then day before yesterday one of Maginnis' blokes fell into a crushing machine."

"Oh, wonderful. A criminal feud. And throw the pestilential Rupert into the mix with a revenger's tragedy and you get…"

"Boom," said Bert.

"Well, there it is," said Phryne. "We'll just try not to get slaughtered."

"Always been my ambition," said Cec. "Beer," he added, shoving a cold opened bottle into his mate's hands. "You starting a war, Miss?"

"No, I'm trying to extract someone out of a war. All right. Don't do anything for the present; just keep an ear to the ground and let me know if you hear any whispers about Rupert Sheffield."

"What's he to you?" asked Bert.

"Less than nothing," admitted Phryne. "If this

had happened in another country I wouldn't have said a word or lifted a finger. But it's here and now and my dear friend John Wilson is likely to be shot for being an innocent bystander."

"Oh," said Bert. "Yair, well, that's always been a dangerous occupation. You give your D the office?"

"Yes, so keep any delicate operations out of his way. And don't use the phone. Leave a message with the household if I'm not here."

"Yessir," said Cec. He put down his beer bottle and saluted.

◇◇◇

Dot came into the parlour to gather up the beer bottles after the wharfies had gone home. She found Phryne staring at a piece of paper in what looked like wild excitement.

"I shouldn't have said that this wasn't about the conductor's murder, Dot," she said.

"Why not?" asked Dot. "I don't like this, Miss Phryne, shots fired and nice hats ruined and all."

"No, I don't like it either," Phryne said absently.

"Though I reckon Miss Ellen can fix the hat—curl up the brim and sew on another aster."

"That would be pretty. Look at this, Dot."

Dot looked. It was a list of singers. Phryne's forefinger had landed on one name.

"Luigi Calvi," read Dot.

"Precisely," said Phryne. "It could be his father who is trying to kill Sheffield." Her eyes sparkled as other women's eyes shone when contemplating their sleeping firstborn or the prospect of a dance and a new dress.

Dot wondered, as she did occasionally, what her life might have been like if she had not met Miss Phryne.

Probably very tedious, she reflected. But sometimes tedious was pleasant.

Chapter Ten

Mathematics possesses not only truth, but supreme beauty—a beauty cold and austere, like that of sculpture.

Bertrand Russell
"Mysticism and Logic"

Phryne reported the presence of someone who might be related to Guido Calvi to Mr. Fanshawe. Then she put herself resolutely to bed for an after-lunch nap. Tonight's rehearsal might be testing, in more ways than just musically.

◇ ◇ ◇

Rupert Sheffield sat in the smaller bar at the Windsor Hotel. The larger one was filled with choristers, even at this hour of the morning. None of them appeared to have been to bed at all—not to sleep, at least. The Cricketers was loud with trained voices singing very rude songs for the most part.

Occasionally they would segue seamlessly from "Charlotte the Harlot" in four-part harmony—which he had never heard before, admittedly—to achingly beautiful plainchant. Or a folk song.

Sheffield was considering the problem of John Wilson. He had never asked John what he had done in the Great War. Now it seemed that he had been a frontline casualty-clearing medical officer, at only twenty-two years old. He had been brave. He had, indeed, been a hero. And he was scarred in the way that many old soldiers were. He had injuries. He had nightmares.

Sheffield had seen the limp, had heard his friend scream himself awake in the next room. Why, then, would he voluntarily stay with Sheffield, when there was a chance of being shot again? Why hadn't he left for nice, safe London the moment that whoever it was had tried to kill Sheffield? Why had he thrown himself across Sheffield to protect him? His behaviour made no sense. Sheffield could not stand things that made no sense.

He sketched out the equations in a notebook. His pencil flew over the page. John lived with Sheffield. John was a hero. John was willing to risk his own life to save Sheffield, even though he knew what it was to be shot. John had sustained bruises pushing Sheffield out of the way of that car. John never asked for anything from Sheffield, except his occasional attention. John looked at him.

Hard to work out what loading he could give to the way that John Wilson looked at him. Not dotingly or anything sticky like that. Affectionately. In a kindly manner. John tried to save Sheffield's face, even when he didn't care what effect he had on other people. John stood between Sheffield and a considerable number of annoying humans with their annoying emotions. John had caught an enraged fist and twisted the owner's arm behind his back with remarkable speed and skill when one of the university's more effervescent associate professors had objected to Sheffield's annihilation of his ridiculous theory. And perfectly justified criticism of his pretensions to knowledge. John saw Sheffield as someone in need of his protection. Insufferable! High-handed! Outrageous!

Sheffield looked at the way his Venn diagrams were coming out. They were resolving to an unacceptable conclusion.

He tore out the page, screwed it up, and started again.

By the time John was due to join him for lunch, he had completed the equations three times. Each time, he had seen the same conclusion revealed by his very own system, which had utterly betrayed him. Sheffield drained his glass of soda and wished that he drank alcohol.

Now what was he going to do?

He sat quite still for some moments. John came in and saw him sitting there, looking like a marble statue of Saint Sebastian on receipt of the fourteenth arrow. When he caught sight of John, he grabbed his notebook and began scribbling again.

John went to order himself a drink. Mark sang "*Au fond du temple saint*" with his accompanist so beautifully that Sheffield could almost forgive him for challenging him. John sat down opposite him. Ordinary, pedestrian, unimaginative John. Strong, blunt hands, pleasant enough features, undistinguished blue eyes, greying hair. Nothing surprising about Dr. John Wilson at all. But he occupied an unduly large part of Sheffield's world…

Sheffield, mind whirling, sought for a new mathematics to describe his new universe.

◇◇◇

Phryne woke, went downstairs and dealt with her household problems (one sock lost in the laundry and Tinker's destruction of a good pair of trousers by falling off his bike). She ordered the purchase of more socks and a new pair of trousers, asked Dot to mend the old ones for disguise, inspected Tinker's healing skinned knee, admirably cared for by Jane, and went in to lunch with a feeling that she almost knew what she was doing, which was a refreshing change. Not enough to give her a damaging sense of complacency, of course. But better than "utterly at sea," her previous option. If the bad men were in Australia, a combination of Fanshawe, Jack Robinson and Bert and Cec would find them. She did not look forward to any contact with Maginnis, a vile creature with nasty henchmen. Or with this challenger, Ratcliffe. Bandit gangs became more marked in their attentions and flamboyant in their demonstrations when they felt threatened.

What had Sheffield done to threaten them? Was this revenge? Or had he actually taken some action in Australia which had drawn attention to himself—and John? It was no use asking Sheffield. He would definitely not confide in Miss Fisher. He was, though he did not seem to recognise the emotion, jealous, or possibly envious, of Phryne. And by the way poor Fanshawe had flinched when recollecting Rupert's visit, Sheffield would not tell the representative of MI6 in Melbourne, who might be able to help him. So who would he tell? Should she sic Jack Robinson on him? Not after Rupert had scorned him. She had already involved him, informally, in matters which he ought not to know. If pressed, he might protect Rupert by trying to deport him. A nice idea, but that would not protect John, if he persisted in bone-headedly flinging himself between that gorgeous creature and danger, as though his own life was not a good deal more precious.

He might tell John, if John asked. That looked like Phryne's best bet, unless her own enquiries bore fruit. Meanwhile, there was tea and a soothing afternoon watching Tinker play chess with Jane, watching Dot embroider waratahs, watching Ruth read her cookbook as though dreaming of amazing dishes.

Phryne had books which needed to go back to the library, so she settled down with a glass of wine—poor Mr. Butler would be back at his shaker soon, but Jane wouldn't let him walk around much yet—and read her latest. If only the real world conformed to Hercule Poirot's rules. It would be so nice. She would love to gather all the suspects together and state, on the authority of the little grey cells, exactly how each one could have been the murderer but wasn't, until she reached the last person, who was, and who always confessed instantly.

That must be so convenient.

However, back in 221B the Esplanade, St. Kilda, matters were extremely complex.

Just before five, Bert arrived at the kitchen

door with urgent news. Phryne then rang Detective Inspector Robinson and arranged a few trifling matters. Then she called a friend in the country. Tomorrow ought to be intriguing.

◇◇◇

Phryne took her score and went to rehearsal. The choir gathered, flocking to the stage. Rupert and John had not arrived. Phryne found herself cornered by the old pianist, Professor Szabo. He had lunched and probably breakfasted on ruby port, and was trying to tell her about Beecham and about the airy lightness with which Mendelssohn had to be conducted. She agreed with him. It was always politic to agree with passionate alcoholics.

But now there was a new conductor. Phryne took her place next to Chloe and examined him carefully.

Mr. Henry James. Stout; nice corporation beneath that flamboyant waistcoat, dark, thick black hair, brooding stare. Trying to look like Beethoven, she diagnosed. Quite a good imitation, except he didn't look Germanic enough. The face was weak, the curves soft and undistinguished, the mouth small. Did Melbourne specialise in the dark, swarthy, and brooding? The choir already had Luigi Calvi, who was trying to be Rudolph Valentino, and there was also Rupert Sheffield, whose hair was as black as a raven's wing. Phryne did not mind embonpoint in men; they were huggable, like Matthew. Making love to Rupert, a concept which she was not entertaining for one moment, definitely not, would lead to bruises from those sharp hip bones and elbows and knees. And while she had treasured bruises acquired in a good cause, pleasure being a very good cause, those wouldn't be. Really.

Anyway, the new conductor surveyed the choir without any expression, raised his baton, and they began the usual warm-up exercises. His beat was reliable. He had a habit of raising one hand and smoothing back his shock of hair, which Phryne could tell was going to get on her nerves fairly soon. He also licked one finger to turn the pages of the score. Very insanitary. This, too, might well begin to annoy after a while. Phryne gave it about ten minutes.

"We'll begin with part one. The chorus is "Help, Lord. Wilt thou quite destroy us?" Much better in German as *"Hilf Herr! Willst du gavertil gen?"* But since we are singing for a monoglot Melbourne audience, English it is. Pay attention to the dynamics. This isn't hard. If you can't do this, you shouldn't be singing Mendelssohn. I don't even know why you chose Elijah. Inferior to the *Messiah* in every way. But there it is. Sing!"

There was a murmur of protest, quelled by the descending beat. "*Help, Lord!*" sang the sopranos. "*Help, Lord!*" sang the altos. "*Help, Lord!*" echoed the tenors and basses. "*Wilt thou quite destroy us?*"

The baton cut them off. "You shouldn't be singing Mendelssohn," Mr. James snarled. "You shouldn't be singing "Baa Baa, Black Sheep." Revolting. Sops, you are sharp. Tenors, you are off-key. Basses, you sound like mud. And as for the altos…" He stroked back the magisterial hair in a manner which made Phryne long for a serviceable hedge cutter. "Again."

"*Help, Lord,*" sang the choir, this time with an edge which almost resembled prayer.

"Terrible," snapped Mr. James, cutting them short again. "Those of you who can actually read music should endeavour to do so. The rest, try to keep up. Right, this time we are going all the way through."

"We haven't learned the notes yet," said Matthew, putting up a hand. "We'll need to note-bash before we can sing this one all through."

"Nonsense," said Mr. James, glaring at Matthew. "I thought you were a semi-professional choir, or I would never have taken this position. All the way through, please," he said, and they tried.

By the time James called a halt, Mendelssohn was revolving in his grave and the chorus was totally lost. The basses had taken the wrong cue and were more than half a bar ahead. They finished first.

"We won!" said Tommy triumphantly.

James glared at him. Tommy stared back. He, too, had been glared at by experts.

"Répétiteur," ordered James. "The soprano line, if you can manage it."

Professor Szabo, his hands as steady as a rock though the rest of his body was trembling with indignation, played the soprano line. Then the tenor line, the alto line, the bass line.

The errors in the next attempt at "Help, Lord" were pardonable. Mr. James did not pardon them. He castigated the whole choir and sent them off to their tea break indignant, tearful or depressed, according to personal character.

"Where did we get this bloke from?" asked Oliver, blushing with indignation. "And can we throw him back? That's what I always do with slimy horrible fish."

"We need a conductor and he was the only one who was willing to do it for that money," said Tabitha. "Unfortunately."

"Why can't we just declare Matthew the conductor and get shot of this overbearing bastard?" asked Chloe, about to don breastplate and helmet and mount her white horse.

"He's got a following," explained Tommy. "People pay to see him."

"I wouldn't," muttered Caterina. "That hair!"

"Just makes you long for a pair of secateurs, doesn't it?" asked Phryne. "I wonder what he uses on it?"

"Axle grease," declared Tabitha. "And I'm not touching any score he's been spitting on."

"Can't we find someone else? Aunty's not going to like this one," protested Daniel.

"He called us eunuchs," said Luigi, who had insinuated himself close to Phryne and spoke into her hair. She could feel his hot breath on her nape.

"That could never be said about you," she replied, leaning back a little into his body. Unmistakable proof that Luigi was not a eunuch pressed into her hip. Oh dear, thought Phryne. This is not a subtle Valentino. He just keeps trying it on until someone succumbs. And it isn't going to be me. Such a seducer has a hide of brass. People keep rejecting him until some poor weak-willed or distracted girl accepts, and then wonders what on earth she was thinking of. Thus his success.

"*Ciao*," she said to him, fairly confident that no one else—except the polyglot Matthew, perhaps, or Caterina, and they were both out of earshot—spoke Italian.

"*Bellissima*," he breathed into her ear.

"*Sei un bel ragazzo*," said Phryne, calling him a beautiful boy.

"*Non bello com sei.*" He was close now, almost embracing her. No one else would hear this conversation.

"*Forse, potrei venirlo a contatta in seguito, se te lo meriti*," she whispered, suggesting a later meeting.

"*A zia Marco*, Windsor," he promised.

Phryne drew herself away. She turned to look at him, smiled wickedly, and went to get some tea. Flirtation without attraction was very tiring. But if finding Guido meant flirting with Luigi, she could do it. The deceased Mata Hari should have taken lessons from Phryne. Especially in how not to get caught.

"I say, you ought to be careful of him," Tabitha warned. "He's a bad man."

"I know what I am doing," said Phryne, and sipped tea. "And I've met bad men before." She did not mention what she had done to them.

The second half of the rehearsal was as bad, if not worse, than the first. Mr. James not only went in for blanket condemnation—"You are a pack of talentless amateurs"—but also specific—"Which soprano is flat? You, sing the note. No, not you. You, sing the note…" until he had found Millicent, the soprano who sang flat, and unceremoniously ejected her from the choir.

Phryne left with her and caught up with

her backstage. Millicent was at the point of tears, flushed and humiliated.

"And he doesn't even like Mendelssohn!" she exclaimed.

"He's a pig," said Phryne, offering her a cigarette. "Right up there with the worst. Have a hankie," she said, handing her one. Millicent sniffed and blew.

"What am I going to do? My boy is in this chorus! I don't want to leave it without him! And he really wants to sing this!"

"Then come back tomorrow," advised Phryne. "Mr. Henry James doesn't look at faces. He's totally self-involved. I promise, if you come back next rehearsal he won't know that you were the one he threw out. Trust me," she said, and Millicent nodded.

"All right," she agreed. "Are you going to Aunty Mark's soiree tonight?"

"Probably," said Phryne. "He's at the Windsor, yes?"

"Royal Suite," said Millicent. "He always takes the Royal Suite when he's here. The bath has gold taps. It's very…well, very suitable."

"He really ought to have ivory, apes, and peacocks," agreed Phryne.

Rehearsal dragged to an acrimonious conclusion, Mr. James stalked off to the conductor's room, and the choir grumbled their way into the street.

"Coming?" asked Millicent.

"I'll just wait awhile," said Phryne. "I'll see you there."

She was, in fact, making sure that Mr. Henry James snarled his way into his outer garments and left the assembly hall. The Scots Church wouldn't tolerate any more corpses on their nice clean floors, and the choir needed somewhere to rehearse.

She saw Professor Szabo leave, en route to the Windsor. She watched the choir join up into their groups and couples and pass through the main entrance as Rupert and John came in.

"Hello, hello!" said John, sweeping her into an embrace. "Come to keep me company, my dear?"

"Alas, no," said Phryne, with genuine regret. "I have a party to attend, but it is at your hotel. The Royal Suite—shall I see you there?"

"Am I invited?" asked John.

"Of course," said Phryne, and kissed him soundly.

There was a hiss behind her, such as is produced by a cat on whose delicate tail someone has just placed a chair.

"Miss Fisher," said Rupert Sheffield. His beautiful face could have been carved out of ivory by someone wishing for a talisman against humanity.

"Delighted as ever," said Phryne. She failed to take his hand. She stood on tiptoe and kissed his cheek, then sauntered out of the assembly hall without a word or a backward glance.

"She…" protested Sheffield to John. He raised a hand to his cheek. He could feel her mouth, as though she had branded him. He felt oddly helpless. John took out his handkerchief and wiped the lipstick off.

"Always been an enthusiastic girl," rumbled John. "She didn't mean any harm, my dear chap."

Phryne walked on, aware that she had just kissed what was in all probability an entirely virgin cheek. Leaving aside his mother, nanny, or favourite dog. None of which she could imagine Rupert Sheffield actually owning or tolerating.

She giggled. Privately.

No one tried to kill her as she crossed the road, which was nice, and the Windsor was just as it always was. Plush, confident, and luxurious. Phryne loved it. She had lived at the Windsor when she first arrived in Australia. It was flexible, in the manner of the great hotels. With courtesy and aplomb it coped with exigent guests, including the actress with the leopard cub, the drunken rugby players, the visiting politicians with their mistresses and demands for entertainment and eccentric food preferences, and the tantrums of spoilt princesses. It had even coped with Phryne nearly being arrested on the premises for drug-dealing. Though the manager had reproved her, gently, at that point.

She had never been to the Royal Suite. It occupied fully half of the top floor and reminded Phryne of the setting of a romance novel. Everything which was not scarlet plush was specially woven, taffeta, mahogany, gilt-edged, or marble. The bathroom taps, in the spacious chamber, were gold. As advertised.

The parlour was draped with silk velvet. It included a dinner setting. On this was a selection of cocktail savouries. Next to it was a full-sized bar with its own cocktail waiter, whose strained smile indicated that he had not been at the Windsor long. He was engaged in pouring Pol Roget into, of all things, a punchbowl, which was a wicked thing to do to such a venerable wine. Phryne claimed a glass as it was poured. The '97. Superb. If Aunty Mark was intending to adulterate this champagne, she would report him to the authorities for Cruelty to Wine.

Mark himself was dressed in a luxurious costume, somewhat recalling the Turkish: loose trousers, blouson silk shirt, and colourful waistcoat. He was so forceful that the clothes looked fitting on him, and not in the least feminine. He caught Phryne's eye and winked.

"*Salut.*" She raised her glass. "Very good champagne."

"Nothing but the best for all my chums," he replied. "Once a year I stop being respectable. I come to another city, and then it's celebrate, sing, celebrate, sing, celebrate, concert until—I have to go home and be respectable again." He made a sad face and Phryne laughed.

"Your liver will last longer that way," she said unsympathetically. "Tell me, is this going to turn into an actual orgy? I made no preparations, even assuming I would be welcome."

"No, no, dear, just a little fun. Risqué, perhaps, but not obscene. Not until the company has thinned rather a lot to invitation-only. Tell me, who was that gorgeous piece I met at the door yesterday? The one with the witch-finder's eye and the face of an angel?"

"That would be Rupert Sheffield," said Phryne. "Mathematician and unwise acquaintance."

"Oh, I could tell that, dear," said Mark.

"Inadvisable doesn't mean undesirable, I know," said Phryne. "But I would say he was not sexed."

"Not in your playing field, dear Miss Fisher, but probably in mine. But I have no taste for such creatures. I prefer them short, blond, and cuddly."

"There is a lot to be said for blond and cuddly,

I agree. Will you have a party every night until the concert?"

"Mostly," replied Mark, pouring her another glass of champagne. "Unless I feel like a cosy night in, with room service and…"

"Cuddly company?"

He smiled a wide, gleeful smile. Phryne liked him enormously. This was a man with relish and zest in a shabby, exhausted age.

"Just so, Miss Fisher," he agreed.

"And your view of Henry James?"

Mark's face screwed up into a frightful grimace.

"No, really, they've got him? How perfectly dreadful. You won't have any trouble finding out who killed Henry."

"No? He isn't killed yet, by the way."

"The hour will produce the man," prophesied Mark. "And the answer will be—he will be stoned to death by the whole choir, though the altos and the basses will probably do the most damage. They're generally more muscular. Of course, it depends on the size of the stones."

"He's that frightful?" asked Phryne.

"Oh, yes," said Mark. "Have another drink to take the taste out of your mouth and let me introduce you to my friends."

Phryne had an agreeable half-hour meeting the rest of the choir, all of whom were mopping up free drinks with alacrity. She was discussing Mendelssohn versus Handel when someone eased through the throng to stand far too close behind her and press his enthusiasm into her back. It could be no one else.

"Luigi, *caro*," she murmured.

"*Si, Principessa*," he agreed.

"*Vieni con me*," she told him, and led him by the hand to a secluded nook, of which the room had many. They sank down onto a loveseat, which ought to keep his manhood on his side of the sofa. Phryne had chosen this chair on purpose. Not only did it preclude having to knee Luigi, but it meant that she could watch his face as the door opened and allowed, with any luck, John and Rupert into the room. If Luigi Calvi was Guido's relative, then he would have to react. His face was responsive, dark eyes and mobile mouth. If he did react, Phryne would see it.

Just as she was getting very tired of fending off his advances, John came in. But no Rupert followed. Drat. Sheffield must be tucked up in bed with his nice glass of hot milk and his equations to keep him warm. Luigi looked at John with complete indifference. Experiment over.

"*Ciao,* Luigi," said Phryne, leaping up and moving out of grabbing range. She took John's hand. He smiled down at her, a little disconcerted.

"Hello, my dear, this is a crush!"

"Have a glass of this champagne, it's superb, and allow me to introduce you to our host. A very fine baritone."

"Oh yes, indeed—Mr. Henty, my dear fellow, how very nice to meet you!" exclaimed John. "Heard you sing in Sydney."

"This is John Wilson, a dear friend of mine," said Phryne.

"And with excellent taste in music," beamed Mark. "Have another drink!"

A glance passed between John and Mark. Like knows like. Phryne wondered if Mark was going to invite John to stay on afterwards, when the choristers had gone home.

"I heard you this morning," said John. "In the Cricketers bar. That was you singing *Au fond du temple Saint*, wasn't it?"

"It was indeed. Are you here alone?"

"No, I am travelling with Rupert Sheffield, the mathematician."

"We've met," said Mark flatly.

"He's a good fellow, really," said John.

Phryne actually saw the moment that Mark put all the salient facts together. He gave John Wilson a sympathetic, manly pat on the shoulder, and moved along.

Phryne found her choristers and they took to

John immediately. The languid medical student Bones shed his indifference and hung on his every word. John looked comfortable talking to the young. Phryne could leave him and circulate, meeting the rest of Aunty Mark's broad acquaintance and talking to the balance of the guests.

It was an interesting party. It included firemen, a few doctors, a plumber, a principal dancer from the Ballets Russes, and a lot of singers. She asked about the new conductor.

The general choral opinion was that Henry James was a blighter, a bounder or a bloody bastard (Tommy, whose rugby days coloured his vocabulary). He had favourites, though he did not prey on the sopranos. Or any other voice. He seemed to hate altos, for some reason. As to his musicality, opinion was divided. Some thought that he was skilled and had a good ear; others conceded the good ear but protested that he made all composers sound alike, and an attempt to make Mendelssohn sound like Handel was doomed to be frightful.

"Not that the audience will notice," commented Matthew. "They come to see oratorios like they go to church: to be bored in a holy cause."

"Tsk," said Calliope, slapping his wrist.

"There must be good conductors," said Phryne. "I sang with one in England who was a darling. Preferred coaxing to abuse. We sang like a heavenly choir for him."

"Oh yes, we know one," said Matthew. "But he's conducting in Ballarat. Patrick Bell. Good old Pat. It is such a pity he's busy. He never shouts, always praises, and after a while you sing your heart out because you can't stand the pained look on his face when you get it wrong."

"But for the present, we've got good old Henry," said Tabitha. "And we're going to have to make the best of him."

"How do you do that?" asked Phryne.

"Don't take anything he says personally," Tabitha advised. "I always imagine him the moment after his trousers and undergarments fall off in full view of the audience. Makes me feel much better."

"Excellent idea," said Calliope.

"Still, erk," Caterina pointed out.

"In your imagination, just concentrate on his mortified face," said Phryne. Caterina brightened. Her agate eyes softened with delight. She clasped her hands. A delicate flush appeared on her peach-blossom cheek.

"Oh, lovely," she crooned.

Tommy gulped a lot of his drink at once and choked. Calliope pounded him on the back.

"I do wish you'd rein that in a bit," remarked

Tabitha. "You know what an effect you have on him."

"Sorry," said Caterina. "Wasn't thinking. Would it help if I kissed him better?"

"Yes!" choked Tommy.

Caterina drifted over to his side, kissed him very gently on the forehead, and wafted away again. Phryne laughed. She went over to the bar to get another drink and was instantly claimed by Leonard, eyes burning, who demanded, "They've actually employed Henry James for this concert!"

"Yes," said Phryne, directing her gaze to the hand which was clutching her arm.

Leonard looked down. He let her go abruptly.

"Sorry, I wasn't at rehearsal. I just heard, thought it couldn't be. I mean, Henry James!"

"Instead of, as it might be, you?" asked Phryne.

"Yes!" he almost shouted. "Well, yes, of course, me—I've been studying the piece for months, I know all about Mendelssohn, why not me?"

"I don't know," said Phryne, inspecting him. Sweating, almost panting, reddened eyes, chewed lips, chewed fingernails, this one was a boiling-over bouillabaisse of emotions. A nice potential murderer, if he desperately wanted to be conductor. Could he have removed Tregennis, then had to go away to Albury and had thus not succeeded in getting his appointment? Would he now try to kill

Henry James in order to take his place? Interesting. Leonard would bear watching. "Why do you think Henry James got the job?"

"Influence," growled Leonard, leaning closer than Phryne would consider pleasant. "He's commercial. He's bribed all the newspaper critics. He's successful. He steals all the best singers from the church choirs, promises them roles, solos, anything. Then he just uses them as chorus. They can't go back. Anyone who's gone with James is a traitor. He's clever." Leonard's voice sank to a whisper. "He's got spies everywhere."

"I see," said Phryne, who did. "Even here?"

"Of course," affirmed Leonard.

"Point one out?" asked Phryne.

"I don't know," said Leonard. "If I knew them they wouldn't be spies."

"Of course. Well, must go, it's been very diverting." She moved through the crowd, looking for John Wilson. He was still with the choristers, discussing the superiority of Vaughan Williams over Elgar.

"Oh, dear, Len got you, didn't he?" asked Calliope with warm sympathy.

"How badly does he want to be a conductor?" asked Phryne.

Matthew was fastest on the uptake. His eyes widened with shock and then narrowed with calculation. He looked a little sickened by his conclusion. "You don't think…"

"Ah, but I do," she said, sipping the drink. She really must lay in some more champagne of this quality. "There is nothing which is, per se, unthinkable," she told him.

"But wasn't he somewhere else?"

"Something I shall be ascertaining when I get home and look at my notes."

"Look, he's always had a bee in his bonnet about being a great conductor," explained Matthew, now seriously worried. "But he wouldn't…"

"Wouldn't he?" asked Phryne.

Matthew did not reply. The choristers looked at each other with what Keats would have described as a wild surmise.

"Oh, goody, it's Len," said Tabitha. "Now if he can only get rid of Henry James, it will be a better, brighter world."

"Tab!" exclaimed Calliope.

"You've forgotten something," Phryne reminded them.

"What?" asked Tabitha, who liked her reasons for optimism.

"If he does that, you get Leonard for a conductor," said Phryne.

There was a general groan.

"Count your blessings, one by one," said Caterina.

"Must go," said Phryne. "It's been such fun. John, are you coming or staying?"

"When you say "coming" do you mean coming back to your house with you?" he asked.

"I do," said Phryne, smiling.

"I'm with you," he said.

"Half your luck," muttered Matthew.

Chapter Eleven

Camerado! I give you my hand.
I give you my love more precious than money,
I give you myself before preaching or law;
Will you give me yourself? Will you come travel
with me?
Shall we stick by each other as long as we live?

Walt Whitman
"Song of the Open Road"

John Wilson reclined in Phryne's bed. She was curled up beside him. It was a loud night in St. Kilda. Drunks were shouting, policemen were whistling for assistance, even ships navigating the channel were blowing sirens and foghorns.

Inside it was quiet and dark. Phryne was not sleepy. Making love seldom made her drowsy. John seemed to be thinking about something. His free hand was clenched on her breast. Phryne took it in both of her own.

"All right," she said. "What is it? Having second thoughts about me?"

"What?" He was startled entirely awake. "No! I mean, of course not. No, it's about Sheffield."

Of course it is, Phryne didn't say. "Tell me all."

"I do go on about him," muttered John.

"No, I'm fascinated—please."

"If you're sure…" He hesitated.

Phryne knew a demand bid when she heard one, even though she refused to clutter her mind with the rules of bridge.

"I'm sure. Go on." Phryne rearranged herself so she was sitting up. John put his head in her lap and she stroked his hair.

"I had the strangest conversation with him today," John reported. "I was just ordering a little lunch in the smaller dining room—you know, the one with the deco murals of the sunbathers?"

"I know the room," said Phryne, who was not going to let him digress too far.

"And he came in and, without even sitting down, he demanded, "Why do you stay with me? It makes no logical sense." And I didn't know how to answer, so I told him that I was his friend. I also made him sit down. You know how tall he is, he looms and the rest of the diners were all looking."

"I can imagine." Phryne suppressed a chuckle.

"And my soup arrived, and he took my spoon

and tasted it, as he always does, and then he said, "But you were in danger," and that's interesting, Phryne, because he's been telling me that there was no peril—not with the car, not with bullets—and my actions were quite unnecessary."

"Yes, I heard him," said Phryne, repressing "that little tick."

"So then he said, "I have no friends," and I told him, no, you have at least one, and that is me. And friends do not allow their friends to get shot if they can prevent it. He thought about that for a while."

"While eating your soup?"

"Yes, he seemed to quite like it. Mushroom, very good. They do a very fine lunch table at the—"

"You were saying about Rupert," Phryne reminded him.

"Yes, the conversation got stranger. He asked me if I was your friend. I said yes, we had been friends for many years. Then he wanted to know how we could be friends when we hadn't seen each other for ten years, and I had to explain that distance in time and place doesn't affect a deep friendship such as ours." He turned his head to plant an affectionate kiss on Phryne's navel. He really liked that navel. It really ought to have a ruby. Or possibly a star sapphire. That would contrast beautifully with her skin.

"And how did he react?" asked Phryne, very

interested. Her campaign might have just taken a giant leap forward.

"He asked me if I had a lot of friends, and I said I had been remarkably lucky and had several. I said…" He faltered. "I said I hoped that I could count him as my friend, as well."

"And what did he say to that?"

"I swear, Phryne, he blushed. Then he muttered, 'Of course,' and stalked off. What do you make of it?"

"I suspect that Rupert is realising how much you mean to him."

"Really?" asked John. Hope was stirring in his voice.

Phryne put a quelling hand on his chest. "Yes, but we must make haste slowly. A grab-and-kiss-him-senseless would not be the way to manage this situation; it is extremely delicate."

"Why?" asked John.

"Because the object of your profound affection is an idiot," Phryne told him. "You must go on as you are; try touching him gently, patting his shoulder, that sort of thing, very manly. And you must leave the rest to me."

"Phryne," said John, extremely worried, "if your plan should go wrong…"

"I understand what is being risked," she assured him. "Leave the matter confidently in my hands, and I shall have him in your arms in—oh, a couple of weeks."

John shivered. Phryne hauled him up into her embrace.

"It will be all right, I promise," she said firmly. "Trust me."

"I do," he said. Then he repeated more firmly, "I do. You must have been a very dangerous spy."

"I was," she said. "How did you know I was a spy?"

"Sheffield told me. Someone from the Athens office—nice girl, apparently, Mlle Jeanne? Was your dresser? She told Sheffield how wonderful you were."

"So she was, excellent seamstress and loose-tongued as ever. And I bet she failed to seduce Sheffield."

"He has no interest in the flesh," said John, evidently quoting Rupert.

Phryne laughed. "We shall see," she said. "Now, would you like to have another drink, or get dressed and go home or back to Aunty Mark's party, or for me to do something mildly obscene to you to distract your mind?"

"Oh, only *mildly* obscene?" asked John. "I was holding out for banned by the Lord Chamberlain, utterly filthy."

"We can manage that," Phryne assured him,

laying him out flat. "The Lord Chamberlain—" she kissed his shoulder "—is very—" she kissed his nipple "—easily shocked."

Her mouth continued downwards. John Wilson's mind was comprehensively distracted.

◇◇◇

At breakfast, in her boudoir, Phryne received a coded message which had been handed in at the door by a messenger who did not stay for an answer. She allowed John to feed her nibbles of her croissant while she sipped her coffee. Her pencil flew across the sheet, transposing numbers and letters.

"I see," she said, as John kissed the last crumb from her cheek. "Right. John dear, I have several things to tell you. But I shall wait until you finish that plate of breakfast—my, tomatoes and sausages and eggs and bacon and mushrooms."

"For some reason, sleeping with you gives me a real appetite," said John, and Phryne screwed up message and translation and flipped them into the fireplace, lighting the ball of paper and crushing the ashes.

Then she went to her malachite bathroom for a wash. She dressed with her customary speed in an elegant purple cotton dress. With it she wore an extravagant Spanish shawl, embroidered to within an inch of thread tolerance with parrots and hibiscus. Her hat was broad, shady and loaded with bright orange hibiscus flowers. On Phryne, nothing appeared to be overstated. John thought of her dressed entirely in cloth of gold, crowned and hung with Byzantine gems. She would still be essentially Phryne, black hair, green eyes, personality vastly greater than someone of five-two ought to command. Phryne could lead armies, and would do a damn sight better job than General Haig.

"You look tropical," said John.

"It's the weather," Phryne replied. "How was breakfast?"

"Excellent," said John, buttering his last piece of toast, pausing, then marmalading it too. "What news?"

"It appears that your Rupert's most persistent enemies are called Calvi and Mitchell. Mitchell is thought to have come to Australia. They are not on record as entering Australia, but then, they wouldn't be. No one has had even a sniff of them in Europe. They were not, regrettably, shot by either the Turks or the Albanians, and they are not in jail in Greece, or in England."

"Drat," said John, crunching.

"I have a description of Guido Calvi which is so generic it could be anyone, and no description at all of Mr. Mitchell."

"Ditto," said John. "Excellent marmalade, this."

"Made by Mrs. Butler's sister. Have some more tea to wash it down. However, it seems possible that this Mitchell character is a new man in the local criminal arena. His name is Ratcliffe. Heard the name?"

"Apart from the Ratcliffe Highway and the Ratcliffe Highway Murders, no."

"All right, but keep an ear out. If anyone called Ratcliffe writes to or talks to or calls on or telephones your Rupert, then stick with him. Especially if he hares off like the worst sort of Gothick heroine, burning the assignation in the candle and going out to the abandoned castle after dark in her nightdress."

"Right," said John, chuckling at the image presented to him. Rupert Sheffield would look amazing in a long lace nightgown.

"And you do still have that Webley, don't you?" asked Phryne. "I remember giving it back to you."

"Yes," said John.

"Then I should take it along with me," she advised soberly. "I suspect things will be hotting up any time now. Two attempts have failed. They are probably getting quite impatient."

"I expect so," said John. Phryne saw his straight-out-of-bed languor depart and his military bearing return. John was a doctor, not a soldier, but he knew far too much about battles for any enemy's comfort. And he might give up on his own life, but never on Sheffield's.

"I have a trace on Calvi," she told him. "In the choir. It's not a common name. And there are people working on this problem at…well, let us say at all levels. If you get into police trouble, ask them to summon Detective Inspector Robinson. If you get into working-man trouble, mention that you're a comrade of Bert and Cec. In any case, call me. Clear?" she asked.

He nodded. "Clear."

"Then I'll see you…oh, I forgot."

She leaned over him, running a finger down his neck. "Yes, the line should be about here," she said, and then, without warning, bit. She sucked in a mouthful of flesh and he distinctly felt the mark of her teeth. It was curiously unerotic. Moreover, it hurt. He flinched. Phryne let him go and inspected her mark.

"That ought to do it," she said, kissed him on the cheek, and breezed away.

Dressing, John saw what she meant. The round, indented love bite was placed so that it just showed above his shirt collar. Not enough to be evident to all. Just to someone who was looking closely.

Wondering if he had strayed into a production of *Les Liaisons Dangereuses*, John found his shoes. His knee was quite recovered. He must tell young Jane what a good doctor she was going to make. And take his leave of her charming household. After he had shown Tinker how to tie a salmon fly.

Phryne picked up the telephone. She was plotting.

John went into the bathroom to finish dressing. He felt like part of the family. They knew John was an invert and no one had raised so much as an eyebrow, not even the highly respectable Dot Williams. And she was a Good Girl if ever he saw one.

Phryne had gone out by the time he had shaved, limped downstairs, and seated himself in the garden with Dot, who was embroidering; Jane, who was asking him medical questions; Tinker, who wanted to hunt fish on their own terms; and Ruth, who was feeding the family her newly compounded orange cake. Made with real orange juice. It was her own recipe and she was very proud of it. She had also got flour on her plaits again. John demonstrated the knot, watched Tinker loop and tie, and tasted the cake, even though he had hardly any room after all that breakfast. But he would not want to disappoint Ruth, who reminded him of his little sister, dead of tuberculosis so long ago. He bit into a slice.

It was delicious. Molly contributed some fur, a passing bird a feather, and John showed Tinker how to make his favourite salmon fly. Tinker asked and John told him about the roiling toffee-coloured waters on the River Dee at Minnigaff in the Borders, where the salmon schooled, diving upstream, and did not eat, so only the most cunning angler could snare them. Tinker swapped him stories of wrangling huge snapper on a four-pound line.

John considered his state of mind. He was contented. For the first time in a very, very long count of years. Living with his adored Arthur had made him feel like this. Not excited, not surprised. There was tea and gentle conversation about uncontroversial subjects. He was not violently engaged, though he liked his present company very much. He was, in a word, happy. Content.

"Miss Phryne's asking everywhere about who's trying to kill your Mr. Sheffield," Jane told him.

"Yes," said John, wondering how much he ought to tell these children, or indeed how much they already knew.

"Everyone's looking," Jane informed him. "Mr. Bert and Mr. Cec, Detective Inspector Robinson, that man who sends telegrams. I'm sure it will be all right."

"Are you?" he asked.

"Of course," Ruth assured him, patting him

on the arm with a floury hand. "We've seen Miss Phryne do things you wouldn't believe."

"Oh?" asked John.

"She held up a boat almost on her own," said Tinker. He had really liked the adventure with the boats.

"She solved a mystery and rescued a captive maiden," said Ruth, who adored romances.

"She broke a chair over a man who was attacking her," said Jane. She wondered about the tensile strength of the chair, and how much force would have been needed to smash it. Also about the density of the head of the victim, who had been silly enough to attack Miss Phryne. Really, the criminal classes needed remedial education. The Chinese had picked it up very fast, but they were intelligent people.

"She talked a man with a gun out of his weapon under the Eastern Market," said Ruth. "She found a treasure in Castlemaine."

"She's on the side of justice," Tinker reassured him.

"Luckily," said Dot. "I always knew she would come and get me. I was kidnapped," she explained. "They thought they had Miss Phryne but they only got me. Silly of them."

"Indeed," gasped John. And he had thought

that Phryne had retired to Australia for a quiet life. He said so.

"Most of the time it's quiet," said Dot with profound thankfulness.

"Except when it isn't," agreed Tinker, who liked action.

"And then we all have to combine together, obey orders, and it all works out all right," said Jane, with perfect faith.

"How did she meet all you useful people?"

"She collected us," said Dot. "I was out of work and desperate, Tinker wanted to come to the city, Jane was a mystery, and Ruth came with Jane."

"Together always," said Ruth sentimentally. "Eh, Janey?"

"Always," said Jane with unwonted emotion, taking Ruth's floury hand.

"She met Detective Inspector Robinson when she broke a cocaine ring run through a Turkish bath, before we met her," Jane told him. "And Mr. Bert and Mr. Cec carried her to the Windsor from the docks and she brought an abortionist to justice for them. Also Mr. Cec got to hit him. So they're in, whatever she wants to do. And they're wharfies, so they know everyone in the underworld."

"And she helps the police?"

"If they ask nice," said Tinker with a grin. "She's like Sexton. She takes what cases she likes and she does as she thinks fit. That's his motto. I reckon it's Miss Phryne's too."

"But what about…what about her…house guests?" John floundered.

"She likes you, she wants to make you feel better," Dot told him. "Mr. Lines' away, and in any case she's his concubine, not his wife. I don't reckon she'll marry anyone, ever. Mr. Lin won't mind. It's not his place to mind. Miss Phryne does as she likes. And you look better, since she's been comforting you."

"I am," said John quickly. "I am better. She's a wonderful woman."

"Good, so tell us about what she did during the war," urged Ruth. "She won't talk about it."

"It was so awful that she doesn't want to give you bad dreams," said John slowly. "It was like hell."

Dot gave him a speaking look and crossed herself.

John took her hand. "I mean that literally. If I think about hell, I think about Passchendaele. Smoke, stink, blood, mud, horror, high explosives. And into that came Phryne with her ambulance, outrunning the creeping barrage. She never left anyone to die in no-man's-land alone. Sometimes all she could do was lie down in the mud with them and hold their hands. Yet she shot a trench raider dead—with *my* gun—and never turned a hair. She was remarkable. And she was so young. Not much older than you, young feller-me-lad."

"Gosh," said Tinker. "So, knowing her, how did you end up with this Sheffield bloke?"

"My...lover...died," said John, reasoning it out. How *had* he ended up with Sheffield? "I was slowly dying of boredom. And grief. My friend said he knew I was looking for an apartment to share and this Rupert Sheffield, a mathematician, was looking for a roommate. They were very nice rooms, we have a housekeeper, and he warned me that he played the piano all night long, and didn't speak for days on end, and writes equations on the wall, and I didn't mind those things, because I was moody and still so sad, and angry, because Arthur had left me after only a few years."

"He couldn't help it," Ruth pointed out.

"No, but sorrow is not reasonable."

John Wilson could see Jane filing away the statement for further consideration.

"All right, but you're best mates, not just sharing," objected Tinker.

"He is...eccentric," admitted John. "I never know what he is going to do next. He fascinates me."

"And he is extremely beautiful," said Jane dispassionately. "You probably like looking at him."

"Er..." said John wildly. "Er, yes, I do."

"And listening to that lovely velvety voice," she added.

"Yes, it is a lovely voice," agreed John, far out of his depth and still sinking.

"Miss Phryne will fix it," Ruth told him. "But you have to stay alive. I don't want to think about what she'd do to your Mr. Sheffield if he gets you killed. She'll feed him to the sharks."

"Really?" asked John, now ready to believe anything about Phryne.

All of them, including the sober and respectable Dot, nodded.

"Oh," said John. "Well, I'd better stay alive then, eh?"

"That'd be a bonzer idea," Tinker told him. "Have a look at this knot, will you, Dr. Wilson? I've made a blue somewhere."

John untangled the knot, wishing that he felt less disconcerted.

◇◇◇

Phryne Fisher was about to start a fight. In a pub. In a boners pub. Boners were known for the sharpness of their knives and the touchiness of their tempers. They spent their days cleaving animal flesh from bones, and knew a lot of practical anatomy. This made her contemplated action really unwise. But she was there with the full knowledge and almost approval of both the Victoria Police and the local representative of the Communist Party. Bert had come up with a name. The woman who knew all about Ratcliffe owned the Prospect Hotel, known locally as the Bucket of Blood. Slaughterhouse workers drank there. Few other men would dare. A bar full of people who stropped their knives on anything wooden and who were used to carving mammalian tissue, eight hours a shift, made uncomfortable company.

Mother Higgins was a harridan. Her daughter Margery was a pretty, graceful, modest slip of a girl who had apparently attracted Ratcliffe's regard. Mother Higgins disapproved of Ratcliffe, but could do nothing about him. Her most passionate desire was to get her daughter away from him.

Bert had spoken to Mrs. Higgins, and made a deal. If Phryne could get Margery safely away, Mrs. Higgins would tell everything she knew about Ratcliffe. The difficulty was Ratcliffe's watchers, who never took their eyes off the pub. If Margery left, she would be followed, and if she went too far away, she would be snatched. Mr. Ratcliffe was a man who did not take refusal lightly. Therefore a little legerdemain was essential, and therefore the need to start a fight in the Bucket of Blood.

She almost managed it by walking in the door. Visions of loveliness like Phryne did not happen in the Prospect. She allowed the door to swing shut behind her, waiting until her eyes adjusted to the gloom. Right. The bar was a long dirty length of what had been polished mahogany, now irregular in shape because the clientele had tested their knives on its edge. The air was thick with smoke. The stench of exhaled beer was almost palpable. The sawdust had not been changed for years. She refused to think about what she might be walking on as she advanced down the pub. Some things crunched and rolled under her soles and she hoped they weren't fingers.

In the end it was very easy. She blew a kiss to one brutish countenance, choosing the face most resembling something on a police noticeboard. Then she moved out of reach of his grab and blew a kiss at the next candidate for a Wanted poster.

They instantly collided. Someone threw a punch. In seconds it was on for young and old and the barman was ensconced below the bar, clutching the valuable bottles.

Phryne sailed through the resulting riot and walked to the kitchen, where a frazzled girl was crouched next to the stove.

"Up," said Phryne, stripping off her shawl and then her purple dress. Margery tore off her overall and put on Phryne's clothes. Phryne tucked the girl's hair up under her shady hat, draped her in the parrot shawl, and Mrs. Higgins shoved her daughter into the backyard.

"The car's waiting," said Phryne. "Chin up, back straight. Walk like you own the world. Mr. Butler will take you to a safe place."

"Mum?" quavered Margery. She was a pale, doe-eyed, gentle creature. She was shivering.

"You go on, girl. I'll see you soon," said Mrs. Higgins, giving her daughter a fast, fierce hug. "Now, off you go, here come the cops."

The clanging of a police bell announced the arrival of a car full of policemen. At the exact moment that Mr. Ratcliffe's men would be most distracted, Margery Higgins walked out to Phryne's car and was driven away.

"I reckon you better put on Margery's dress," said Mrs. Higgins, surveying Phryne's silk underwear and stockings. "You started a real good barney when you had all your clothes on. If they sees yer now they'll wreck the joint."

"Good point," conceded Phryne, and not only put on Margery's sad grey wrapper, but her cook's mob cap, which hid Phryne's trademark shiny black hair. Then she tied on a stained apron.

"Good-o," approved Mrs. Higgins. "But how are you gonna get outa here? They'll think you're her, they'll follow yer."

"By prior arrangement, I'm going to be

arrested," Phryne told her. "And when I get out I won't be as you see me. Double bluff."

Mother Higgins thought about it.

"That Bert, he said you was real smart."

"That was kind of him."

"You promise my Marge'll be safe?" Mrs. Higgins gripped Phryne's arm with a gnarled hand. She was a hag, raddled and damaged, red-eyed, filthy and tough as nails, but she loved her daughter. Phryne patted the hand.

"I promise," said Phryne. Even now, Margery was on her way to a certain fruit-growing cooperative in Bacchus Marsh, protected by strong-minded women, heavily toothed dogs, and the approval of the whole community. The minions of a city crook like Ratcliffe would stand out in that apple-rich area like a series of badly wounded thumbs. If they caused any trouble, they would be compost. "However, what is Ratcliffe going to do to you when he realises you have smuggled your daughter out from under his nose?"

Mother Higgins barked a short laugh. "I'm not afraid of 'im," she snarled, showing teeth yellowed by a lifetime's pipe smoke. "I got enough knives in this pub to gut 'im like a steer. Yair, and skin 'im and quarter 'im and bone 'im. And I bloody will, if 'e gives me any lip. He knew I couldn't do nothin' while Marge was still 'ere."

"Right. Now, tell me all. We've got about fifteen minutes until they come to arrest me." Phryne took a notebook out of her bag.

Mother Higgins lit her pipe and took a long drink from a bottle of red wine. She wiped her lips.

"Three years ago that bastard comes 'ere, and old Grogan's men started to die. Accidents. Then Grogan was found dead, drowned, caught up in an anchor chain. Ratcliffe took over. I seen bad bastards before, and 'e's no worse. Until 'e set eyes on my Margie I could live with 'im bein' boss cocky. There's always a boss."

"Too true," said Phryne.

"Him and his lah-di-dah voice and 'is Pommy ways," sneered Mother Higgins.

"He was on his own, then? He didn't bring an Italian associate with him?"

"Eyties? Nah, no dagos. Just 'im. And that's enough. He took over all old man Grogan's lurks."

"Which are?"

"Rum, sly grog, smuggling," mumbled Mother Higgins. It went entirely against her grain to tell anyone anything.

"Girls?" asked Phryne.

"Nah," she said. "Not to sell. He takes 'em to keep. He just wanted one more girl. My girl. Fuckin' bastard."

"Right," said Phryne. "And what's he been doing lately?"

"Eyein' off Maginnis' mob and tryin' to take over Willi. Followin' a bloke called Rupert Sheffield. I never heard of 'im. I dunno why 'e's lookin' for 'im, neither. And if I was that bloke I bloody wouldn't want to be found."

"Indeed. Any idea that Mr. Ratcliffe might have been called by another name once?"

"Funny you should say that," said Mother Higgins, gulping more cheap red wine and spilling some down her corded throat to soak into her stained bombazine bosom. "One Pommy sailor called him Mitch and Ratcliffe backhanded him across the deck."

"Where does he live and what does he look like?"

"Medium everythin'," said Mother Higgins. "Brown hair, Pommy skin, bit taller than me—maybe five-eight—close-shaven. Poncy sort of bloke. Brown eyes like rocks. Lives in that big house in Port. Bert knows. Oh, 'e's gonna be sorry 'e ever tried to steal my girl."

"Yes," said Phryne. "He will be sorry."

Mother Higgins, well oiled by red wine and relief, looked up muzzily at Phryne wearing her daughter's clothes, and saw another pair of stony eyes. These shone like emeralds. Ratcliffe's were the Mohr hardness of chocolate fudge by comparison.

"Reckon 'e might be," she conceded.

◇◇◇

Phryne smiled charmingly on the arresting officers, was led into a police car, driven to the station and shown into Detective Inspector Robinson's office. She sank down into his office chair, tearing off her mob cap. An overnight bag was sitting on the desk.

"How did it go?" she asked, eyes gleaming.

"Very good. We broke the Russell Street record. Fifteen outstanding warrants in one pub."

"Mother Higgins must be collecting felons," said Phryne. "Any sign of the watchers?"

Robinson grinned.

"They were three of the warrants. Shop-breaking, burglary and assault occasioning grievous bodily harm. The Magistrates' Court has had to call in reinforcement off-duty beaks. Nicely done, Miss Fisher!"

"I'm so glad you're pleased. Now, before I get out of these revolting garments, let me tell you all I have learned about Mr. Ratcliffe."

She talked. Robinson frowned.

"I knew there was something wrong with Grogan's death. He was an old sailor, never would have got caught in an anchor chain. So this is the new boss, then. Oh, good. And he's moving into Williamstown, where that—" he paused "—unpleasant person Maginnis rules supreme. Therefore, trouble and corpses and my own chief going crook. Oh, joy."

"You can thank me another time," grinned Phryne. "Now, get some lowly constable to show me to the ladies so I can change into the clothes which Dot sent for me, and I shall be taking myself home. I really need a bath."

"And this Margery's all right? You've got her stashed somewhere safe?"

"Safe as houses," promised Phryne, picking up her bag. Jack Robinson didn't notice that she hadn't told him where Margery Higgins was, because she had kissed him very chastely on the cheek as she swept past. Contriving to sweep, even when wearing a skivvy's disgraceful wrapper and grease-spotted apron.

Jack Robinson smiled.

◇◇◇

Phryne caught the train home. No one appeared to be following her, or even noticing her. Dot had sent Phryne some of Dot's own clothes. They were too large for Phryne and she looked suitably dowdy in them. She slipped in through the back gate and found Tinker tying salmon flies at the wrought-iron table. Molly sat at his feet, waiting for stray bits of sandwich. Tinker's fingers moved nimbly. The line was almost invisible in the sunlight.

"That's clever," she commented.

"Dr. Wilson taught me," said Tinker. "He's a real nice bloke, Guv."

"I know," said Phryne.

"But yer not goin' ter keep 'im," said Tinker, reverting to his original accent.

"No," said Phryne. "It's not kind to hang on to someone who wants to be with someone else."

"Why ain't yer jealous?" asked Tinker.

"I don't know," Phryne told him truthfully. "I must have missed out on jealousy lessons. Do not let this worry you, Tink. Now, I'm going to have a bath, and then some lunch. Stay alert. I might have been followed home."

"Right you are, Guv."

Tinker flicked a finger at Molly, who padded to the gate, sniffed all around it, and then returned to the boy, sitting down at his feet.

"No one there," said Tinker. "Me and Molly will be watching, Guv'nor."

"I trust you," said Phryne and went inside, wondering what that conversation had been about. And when had he trained Molly to seek in that admirably silent fashion? Tinker was a very clever boy.

Now for that bath. When she arrived at the top of the stairs, it was all ready for her. The scent of chestnut blossoms hung in the air like a hot afternoon in Paris in spring.

"Dot, you are a gem," said Phryne, stripping off her borrowed clothes and padding barefoot into the bathroom. She stepped down into the green water and lay back. "Divine."

"Did the girl get away all right, Miss?" asked Dot, gathering up her discarded garments.

"Clean as a whistle," said Phryne. "Old prison escape trick dating back to the twelfth century, with a hundred previous users. Worked like a charm. Oh, that is so nice. That pub, Dot, it was dreadful. This ought to take away the smell of blood and smoke and beer. But the licensee of said hostelry is a formidable woman. She hasn't acted against this Ratcliffe because of the threat to her daughter. With Margery out of the way, things ought to become quite uncomfortable for him."

"How nice," said Dot. "He sounds like a nasty man. Mr. Bert and Mr. Cec are coming to lunch, Miss Phryne. Do you have rehearsal tonight?"

"No, thank God. One dose of that conductor is enough for the present. Another unpleasant man. We seem to be specialising in them lately. What's wrong with Tinker?"

"Oh," said Dot. "You noticed."

"I did," said Phryne, stirring the eau-de-Nil water with one hand.

"Jane," explained Dot.

"He's fallen in love with Jane?"

"I think so," said Dot. "She hasn't noticed."

"Of course she hasn't," said Phryne, chuckling. "Can't do any harm, Dot. She's the first female who's ever been interested in him. It will wear off, hopefully before Jane does notice, because I don't think she'd be interested."

"Not in him, or not in any boy?" asked Dot.

"The latter, I think. She's all intellect. But you never know. He'll be good," Phryne assured Dot. "So that's why he was asking me about jealousy. All is now clear."

"All right, Miss," said Dot. She laid out Phryne's most sumptuous house gown, of blue and green watered silk, and went downstairs considerably relieved.

Dried, slicked, powdered and scented and brushed, Phryne floated downstairs, a vision in aquamarine robes, and phoned Fanshawe's number. She told the comfortable female voice on the other end everything she had learned about Ratcliffe. She suspected that the telephonist was knitting while listening. She concluded with an account of the police action at the Prospect, was told to "be careful, dear" and hung up chuckling.

Now for lunch, Bert and Cec, and—aha—an unexpected telegram. Phryne ripped open the envelope and gave the boy a penny from the jar on the hallstand.

"Stay out of my way." No signature. Of course, she had been seen entering and leaving the Prospect, and Ratcliffe knew that she was somehow involved in the vanishing of Margery. A mouse had been spirited away from under the cat's paw. Even calm placid moggies got upset if someone stole their lawful prey. Good. A frustrated Ratcliffe might easily make mistakes. Must double the guard, restock the crocodile swamp, and take the safety catches off the spring-guns, Phryne thought. She was now a target. In her own right.

She drew in a deep breath of contentment. Like Tinker, Phryne liked action. The household ought to be safe enough, with Tinker and Molly guarding the back gate and Mr. Butler the front door. Kidnapping did not seem to be Mr. Ratcliffe's modus operandi. He preferred assassination to solve any of his little difficulties. All she had to do was keep an ear tuned for that gasping "potato-potato" of the Harley. And remember that a Hispano-Suiza, suitably steered, was a match for any motorcycle.

Lunch. Bert and Cec had arrived. She sat down for a conference which might easily turn into a council of war. Beer was provided. There must theoretically be an hour of the day or night when Bert and Cec didn't drink beer, but Phryne had never deduced it.

"You stirred up a real ants' nest," said Bert admiringly. "Blokes runnin' round like headless chooks. Maginnis' men belting Ratcliffe's men. Ratcliffe's blokes necking Maginnis' blokes. Mother Higgins geein' up her knife-men and barrin' the door of the Prospect to any of 'em. She let it be known that any standover bludgers come into her pub they get killed, skinned, gutted, jointed, trimmed, and served for dinner."

"Roasted," said Cec.

"With Yorkshire pudding," said Bert. "And she could do it, too. She's not a bad cook, considerin'."

"Too right," said Cec.

They drank more beer. Phryne showed them her telegram.

Bert sucked in a breath. "Told yer he's rattled," he said.

"Yes," Phryne agreed. "What's his household like?"

"Posh," said Bert, and drank the rest of the beer. He seemed to think he had said all that was necessary. Phryne needed more information.

"Posh, yes, good, but who lives with him?"

"His girls," said Bert. "Poor cows. No better than slaves. That's why Missus Higgins was so scared for Margery. He don't…behave nice with women."

"If I rescue one, can she steal something for me?"

"What d'ya want?" asked Bert.

"A blank sheet of his stationery and a sample of his handwriting."

Bert gave her a very narrow, considering look. "I reckon you're planning something very nasty for Mr. Ratcliffe," he said slowly.

"I am, yes," said Phryne. "What about it?"

"My cousin Siegfried's niece Hildegard works in the house," said Cec. "My cousin's been after her to quit, but she's too scared. If you can give her the ticket to go visit her old grandma in Bundaberg, I reckon she'll do it."

"Good. Count on me for a ticket to absolutely anywhere. It shouldn't be too dangerous, if she dusts the study or the library and empties the wastepaper basket anyway."

"Yair, Hildy's a housemaid. All right, Miss. What else?"

"Who would take over Ratcliffe's gang, if Ratcliffe was removed?"

"That's a problem for another bottle," said Bert, opening it. "I got no notion. Cec, what d'you reckon?"

"Dunno," said Cec. "He's got rid of any bugger

who could challenge him. Real cock on a dung-hill, that bloke. If Ratcliffe's not there, I reckon Maginnis'd just mop up whatever's left."

"Nice," said Phryne. "And the girls?"

"Dunno," said Cec. "You could get your sister on to them."

"Good plan." Phryne's sister Eliza ran a mission for almost any good cause available. She would be able to cope with unshackling the slaves. This Ratcliffe was sounding even more like an excrescence on the fair face of Melbourne than ever.

"And where does Ratcliffe have his working headquarters?" asked Phryne. "In Port?"

"Yair, there's a couple of warehouses, empty, and an old sheet-metal shop. End of Bay Street. They're s'posed to be pullin' 'em down. Till then, that's where Ratcliffe keeps 'is court."

"Right," said Phryne. "I don't want any of us going there—" she raised her voice "—especially you, Tinker. Come in and join us," she invited, and Tinker and Molly slunk into the parlour. "If you want to know what's going on, you can always ask," said Phryne.

"Yes, Guv'nor, but will you tell me?" asked Tinker.

Cec grinned at him. "She's your command-ing officer, son," he said. "She'll tell you what you need to know."

"S'pose," said Tinker.

"I promise, Tink," said Phryne. "When it all gets exciting, you will be there."

"All right," said Tinker, and smiled.

Chapter Twelve

How doth the little busy bee
Improve each shining hour,
And gather honey all the day
From every opening flower!

Isaac Watts,
"Against Idleness and Mischief"

Phryne lunched with Bert and Cec, then went for a fast thinking walk on the beach. She was rather counting on no Harley being able to sneak up on her, as she understood that motorbikes did not do well in deep sand. Then again, if they were like dispatch riders' bikes, which continued to operate even in Somme mud, this might be optimistic. However, no riders careered across the dunes, and she and Molly had a pleasant walk, except for the moment that Molly sighted Mr. Brown, she snarled and he ran away.

Which was rather invigorating than otherwise.

She returned to a light afternoon tea and the news that Dot was going to a dance with Hugh Collins, Tinker and Jane had started a marathon chess tournament, and Ruth was cooking dinner. Mrs. Butler had allowed her free rein of her precious kitchen. Mrs. Butler had a *tendresse* for Ronald Colman, and there was a new film.

So it was going to be a very quiet, studious sort of night. Phryne knew that she had to stay out of the kitchen, where Ruth would be touchy about visitors. She also knew that she had to stay out of the parlour, because Tinker needed to concentrate. Many skills have been acquired by men for love of woman, and chess looked to be Tinker's love-offering.

Couldn't hurt. But that left Phryne with her own rooms or the garden for the perusal of her plan to bring down Ratcliffe. She did not feel entirely secure from being seen in the garden, so she retired to her rooms until Jane should trounce Tinker and Ruth should announce dinner. Molly was on guard by the back gate and the front door was locked.

Phryne sat on her sofa, rolling a bullet round and round in her fingers. It had been extracted from the coachwork of the Hispano-Suiza. A .45, definitely. She wished there was some way to tell which gun a bullet had been fired from. She stared at the bullet. It remained uninformative.

She tossed it into a dish of hatpins and went down to the drawing room for a drink.

◇◇◇

She had not heard from John Wilson all day. Phryne wondered if Rupert was keeping him close, or at least away from Phryne. A promising development, if so, but it left Phryne at rather a loose end.

She was just trying to decide on whether a gin and tonic—which would mean going into the kitchen for ice—or a glass of wine—which would mean going down to the cellar—would improve her mood more, when the doorbell rang and Phryne went to answer it, pistol in hand.

John Wilson seemed a little surprised by his reception. He put up both hands and dropped his stick with a clatter.

"I surrender," he told her.

"Come in," said Phryne, grabbing the cane and allowing him to lean on her shoulder. "And let me listen for a moment."

No sound of "potato-potato." No sign of a motorcyclist.

"Motorcycle?" asked John.

"You really are very quick on the uptake, John dear," said Phryne. She took his hat and placed it on the hatstand.

"Not if you listen to Sheffield," he answered glumly.

"Yes, but I don't," said Phryne sweetly. "Come in, have a drink."

"Excellent notion," said John, accompanying her into the parlour. "Sheffield's dining with the University of Melbourne, and I begged off for the night. I really don't have anything to say to these mathematical chaps, you know. They're far more intelligent than me."

"But you could diagnose beri beri?" asked Jane, looking up from her chessboard. "Check, Tinker."

"Of course," said John.

"Know how many bones there are in a human skeleton?"

"Yes, two hundred and six," said John. This girl disconcerted him.

"And you could name them?" asked Jane, touching a pawn and then biting the end of that finger.

"If I had to," John agreed.

"Well, then," said Jane. "I bet they couldn't."

"Er, no, perhaps not," said John. "Anyway, the scholars picked Sheffield up in a closed car and they'll deliver him back, so he doesn't need me for the night."

"Good, I do. I have a mission of great peril for you," Phryne told him.

He smiled. "And that is?"

"Go into the kitchen and ask Ruth to fill the ice bucket," said Phryne.

Jane was impressed. Ruth wouldn't throw anything really heavy at nice Dr. Wilson. Miss Phryne was really adroit with people, a skill which Jane admitted she did not possess.

Tinker tapped her hand.

"Check," he said triumphantly.

"So it is, how clever of you," she murmured. "I see I shall have to pay attention."

Tinker glowed.

Ruth did not throw anything at nice Dr. Wilson, because her preparations for the cold buffet were all complete and chilling nicely, her salad leaves were washed and her salad dressings made. The mayonnaise crisis had been averted with a timely ice cube, and she was about to offer the company drinks anyway.

So Dr. Wilson carried the ice bucket and Ruth carried the jug of lemonade into the parlour. Phryne compounded a gin and lemon, tinkling with ice, and led her guest into the other room, so as not to disrupt the chess players. Ruth would be taking her romance novel into the garden, as was her wont, until the light failed.

"So, what developments on the assassin?" asked John.

"It does seem that Ratcliffe is Mitchell, and it does seem that he is after Rupert specifically. No sign of Calvi; he does not seem to have stayed with Mitchell. He may not be here at all. I just like to be thorough," said Phryne, sipping. "Ratcliffe is trying to take over in Williamstown, and the warlord in charge of it will not give up easily. Their minions have taken to killing one another. This will keep him suitably nervous and distracted."

"God, Phryne, by coming here I've precipitated a war," said John, looking thunderstruck.

"Not you," Phryne told him, patting his cheek. "This was happening before you and Sheffield even landed in Australia. There's a strike on the waterfront, so a lot of the cargo is going out through Williamstown. Ratcliffe rules Port Melbourne, which is now idle. Therefore…"

"Oh, I see, we have warring tribes."

"Exactly. It's all getting a little intense. How Rupert is involved with all of this I cannot imagine. Except, of course, that Mitchell wants to kill him."

"That is a rather exceptional exception, Phryne," said John.

"Yes, it is. Has he said anything at all about what he has done since he got here? Where have you been apart from Melbourne?"

"Brisbane and Sydney. We were going to go to Canberra but it isn't really set up for visitors yet. Nothing at all untoward happened in either city. Sydney University was delighted to see Rupert and he spent his time talking about mathematics. I did wander around a little. It's interesting, with that half-built bridge like claws across the harbour. It will probably be very impressive when it's finished. I went to the gallery; you know, traveller's pastimes."

Phryne put down her glass and laid a hand on his good knee.

"Did you…sorry, I really need to ask this… did you find any agreeable company in either city? Someone who might, for example, have decided that they wanted to keep you and…"

"Followed me all this way in order to kill Sheffield and take his place?" John laughed. "You give me too much credit, Phryne dear! I'm no pretty boy. I'm a crippled ex-army doctor with a broken heart and a hopeless infatuation. Definitely not the object of anyone's passion. And definitely not worth keeping, much less pursuing. And, no, to answer your question, I didn't go looking for agreeable company. I didn't meet anyone I wanted until I came to Melbourne and saw you coming up the steps. Never was more amazed and delighted in my life."

"Or me," said Phryne. "Are we still friends? I had to ask, you know."

"Of course," said John.

"All right, so we can scrub a personal motive for assassinating Sheffield, unless he really got on someone's quince in Sydney or Brisbane."

John sighed. "He always does, but I can't think of anyone specific."

"Right, then Mitchell/Ratcliffe it is, and we need to make a plan."

"Are you going to use my irreplaceable Rupert as bait?" asked John in a rising tone. "I forbid it!"

"Calm," suggested Phryne. "He only becomes bait if he offers himself up for sacrifice, and I promise it will not go that far. I have made arrangements. All you have to do if he goes out in response to a letter or a telephone call, refusing to explain and forbidding you to follow, is to first phone me—just with the word "go" if you haven't time—and then follow him. Take your service revolver and stick to him like glue. Can you do that?"

"Yes," said John. "Do I let him know that I am there?"

"As you like. I am pretty sure I know where he will be going, the dolt. Bay Street, Port Melbourne—right into the dragon's den. Then we shall conclude this and you can get on with your life without fear of imminent assassination."

"That would be nice," said John.

"Good. Are we agreed?" asked Phryne. "What are your instructions?"

"On his departure in mysterious circs, I phone you, then follow him. I can do that," said John. He leaned forward and put his hands on the chair back either side of Phryne's head, bringing his face down to hers. "Try to keep him alive," he said softly. "I don't care about me, but I care most deeply about him."

"I know," said Phryne gently, and kissed his mouth.

Ruth announced dinner. All this high emotion had made Phryne very hungry.

◇◇◇

John and Phryne sat in her parlour as, until Mr. Butler got back, Phryne intended to guard the door. Not a bark had been heard from Molly in the garden, watching the back gate. Phryne was of the opinion that Ratcliffe was only slightly interested in her. He would suspect that it had been Phryne who had engineered Margery's escape. He would have a lot on his plate, what with Maginnis and now Mother Higgins and her slaughtermen. That telegram had just been an indication to Phryne that he knew who she was and where she lived. A warning. One she intended to heed.

She had coaxed John into talking about his life with Rupert and, as Rupert was always his favourite subject, John had been pleased to comply. She was listening with half an ear, because she had heard the back gate open. Molly gave a short, soft "wuff" and Tinker left his chess game at a fast scramble.

He returned escorting Cec. The tall blond wharfie looked worried.

"I been hearin' your name," he told Phryne. "I been hearin' it from blokes who didn't ought ter know it."

"Yes," said Phryne. "Mr. Ratcliffe is not pleased with me."

"Bastard," said Cec. He held out a paper bag. "What's this?"

"Handwriting and a piece of his own writing paper," said Cec, grinning. "Compliments of Sieg's niece Hildy. I just put her on the train to Queensland. You owe me three quid. She pinched a few sheets in case you want to practise, she said. She's a bright sheila, Hildy. I'm real glad she's out of it, but. That's not a nice house for a good girl. She says to tell you he uses dark blue ink, like a bank."

"Take five pounds," said Phryne, handing over a banknote. "Thank you very much. Are you and Bert out of this firing line?"

"Yair," said Cec, accepting a bottle of beer from Ruth. "Thanks, Ruthie. You know the way to a man's heart. We never belonged to any gang but a stevedores' gang. Maginnis and Ratcliffe don't have nothin' on us."

"I might need you, for the matters I described today," said Phryne. "Are you on?"

"Against Ratcliffe? "Course," said Cec. He drained the bottle, tipped his cap, and went away. Molly wuffed him out of the back gate.

"I just need to make a phone call," Phryne told John, and went out into the hall. She riffled through the paper bag. Sieg's niece Hildy had done Phryne proud, and she hoped that the girl enjoyed her holiday in Queensland. Phryne held five untouched sheets of cream laid stationery with Ratcliffe's name and address on them, and a bundle of scrawled notes and drafts. Excellent exemplars.

She called the number again, and Fanshawe answered. Phryne heard children's voices in the background. This section of MI6 was charmingly domestic.

"Phryne here," said Phryne, running through her identifying phrases. "I need a forger."

"Anything complicated?" asked Mr. Fanshawe. "Yes, yes, Daddy will be back directly. Isn't it time for you to go to bed? It's getting dark."

"Suicide note," said Phryne. "I have the victim's stationery and handwriting samples."

"Right. I shall send someone over in the

morning to pick up the details—no, I'll come myself."

"Listen out for Harleys," Phryne warned him.

"I shall," said Peter Fanshawe, and rang off.

Phryne went back to John. Their only shared memories besides were of the war, and she did not want to talk about that tonight. She wanted to look at John Wilson, with his greying hair and his limp and his shining righteousness, who did not think that, of Sheffield and Wilson, he was the one worth saving. And he did not need to go back to the Windsor tonight.

◇◇◇

After breakfast, John left, and shortly afterwards Peter Fanshawe arrived. He was wearing a workman's dustcoat and had arrived in a plumber's van, requesting entrance at the back gate. It took Phryne's intervention to get him admitted to the house, over Molly and Tinker's strong exceptions. Molly especially didn't like the look of him. He smelt of a strange dog. A strange male dog.

"No, let him in, he's a friend of mine," ordered Phryne.

"You sure, Guv?" asked Tinker, grabbing Molly's collar and hauling her back onto her hind legs.

"Sure," said Phryne. "But you are very good guards. Back to your posts, darlings. Come in, Peter."

"You are doing a very good job," Fanshawe told Tinker. "No one's going to get past you. I'm glad Miss Phryne has sentinels."

"That's us," said Tinker.

Phryne led Peter into the parlour and offered him tea, which he did not accept. She showed him the exemplars and the blank sheets.

"All right, very good. Tell me about the man who is writing this suicide note."

"No friends, no lovers. Uses dark blue ink like banks use. He hasn't any relatives here, or people he loves. This note ought to convey: 'I've lost, I'm beaten, I'm not going to watch Maginnis take over my operation, so goodbye and I'll see you all in hell.'"

"Ah, that sort of note," said Peter Fanshawe.

"Can you do it?" asked Phryne.

"Me, no, but I know someone who can. I'll take those—" he put the papers carefully into his pocket "—and I'll be back before the end of the day. I have quite a journey ahead of me."

"Bon voyage," said Phryne.

"And if you're lucky, I'll bring you back some honey," said Peter.

◇◇◇

"That was odd," said Dot.

"Yes, I know. One does not associate forgers with honey. But there we are. How was the movie?"

"Really good," said Dot, blushing. Phryne surmised that she had spent most of the movie romancing a certain policeman and would not, if challenged, be able to recount the plot. So she didn't ask. She got on with checking the household accounts with Dot. Dot could add up pounds, shillings, and pence in her head. Phryne was impressed.

◇◇◇

Peter Fanshawe took the road for Eltham with a light heart. Matters had transpired on which he could do with advice, and in any case it had been ages since he had seen his mentor, retired MI6 Major Aloysius Tobit, who came to Australia because his asthma was so bad. Arrived, he found Australian asthma just as debilitating, but was cured by a folk remedy: the measured consumption of local apple blossom honey. Thereafter he had retired to the nearest source of apple blossom, Eltham, and indulged himself in innumerable bees.

Fanshawe could take or leave bees, but had a weakness for apple blossom honey. His wife always craved it when she was expecting. And he really wanted to talk to Major Tobit. Fanshawe was worried about Phryne Fisher and the operation she seemed to be running, on his ground, without discernible rules. Or, indeed, ethics. This suicide note for someone who wasn't presently aware of his fate being a case in point. But it was a nice day and the car was running through fields and then through woods. It was very pleasant to be out of the office for a change. He reached the small stone-built house with the green apple trees all around and took a deep breath as he got out of the car. He reminded himself that he must bring the children to visit, now that they were old enough not to grab at the bees.

They circled, lazily, full fed. This house always had bees. He knocked at the green front door.

Major Tobit's wife, Esther, welcomed him with a hug and an offer of scones, clotted cream and—of course—honey.

"He's just out talking to the hives," she told him. "Do sit down; let me look at you." She was a dumpy, comfortable old lady in a pink hand-knitted jumper who had been a premier agent in her time. She still had uncommonly penetrating eyes.

"It's nice to see you, Mrs. T."

"And is all well with the children? Your wife? Good," she said. "What brings you here? If it was just a friendly visit you would have brought your family."

"Phryne Fisher," said Peter, and Esther Tobit laughed out loud.

"Oh, indeed," she said. "I wondered when Phryne would do something to shake earth's foundations! She's been confining herself to crime—how has she dragged you into her whirlpool?"

"You know her?" asked Peter Fanshawe hopefully.

"Certainly, and so does Tobit. I believe she seduced him at some point. She does that. Before I met him and she doesn't mean any harm, you know."

"No?" he squeaked.

"No, and you're in no danger. You're married. Phryne does have some standards. Ah, Ally, darling, guess who's been driving poor Peter round the bend?"

Major Tobit came in, having shed his beekeeper's overall. He only wore it because Esther objected to the sticky patches which amorous bees left on his clothes. Peter had seen him reach into a hive and have the bees crawl and settle all over his arms and face, kissing him and humming. Major Tobit just adored his bees, and the bees returned the sentiment.

"Peter, m'dear fellow." Major Tobit shook hands. He was a chubby, rounded sort of man, just as Peter remembered him. "How very nice to see you! There are such a large number of people who could be driving you round the bend, I cannot possibly choose between them."

"Female," hinted Esther.

"Lord, really? I wondered when Phryne would do something which would stagger humanity." The Major chuckled. His three chins shook. "What has she done to you?"

"Exacerbated a small war between two criminal gangs," said Peter. "Because one of them is an old client of ours."

"Oh?" asked Major Tobit. "Yes, tea, m'dear, and Peter will like scones with honey. She's been experimenting with making clotted cream, just as we used to eat it in Somerset." He still had the remains of a burr in his voice. "It tastes just as I remember it from my grandma's kitchen. Which of our previous clients?"

"Mitchell the gun-runner. Now called Ratcliffe. He's making a spirited attempt to kill Rupert Sheffield."

"I can understand that," commented Esther. "The most insufferable young man I ever met. How Compton put up with him I do not know."

"He was a superb code-breaker, and most of those mathematical chaps are a bit odd, you know," said Major Tobit generously. "Don't tell me Phryne's defending Sheffield? Not her type at all, I would have thought."

"No, Sheffield has a friend of Miss Fisher's with him, one Dr. John Wilson. Miss Fisher is very fond of Dr. Wilson and thinks that Ratcliffe's attempt to remove Sheffield will invariably lead to Dr. Wilson getting killed while trying to protect him."

"That makes sense," said Major Tobit. "Phryne will go to extraordinary lengths to defend her friends. Tell me, you've seen her lately—how does she look now?"

"Small, thin, black hair cut in a cap, bright green eyes, very fashionable," said Fanshawe. "Reckless, I would have said, except she seems to make a lot of plans. Takes precautions. Intelligent. Flexible. She must have been a very good agent."

"She was, until she got bored. Could go any-where and be anyone. The stage lost a great actress in Phryne," said Esther. "However, she left us, went to stay at her father's house, arranging flowers and so on. Then she took off for Australia. We've been keeping a bit of an eye on her, of course. She knows a lot of secrets."

"So, tell me, was she really a Mata Hari?" asked Fanshawe.

Major Tobit snorted. "No! Not at all! Peter, for shame!"

"Sorry," Peter mumbled.

Esther leaned forward and put a hand on his arm. "Mata Hari got caught," she said, and grinned a wicked grin. It looked very out of place on her soft, elderly, female face.

"Ah," said Peter.

"And now for some tea and scones and you can tell me all about Phryne's plans," said Major Tobit comfortably.

Mrs. Tobit brought in the tray. The scones were fresh out of the oven. The clotted cream was remarkable. The honey was golden and scented. Peter loaded and consumed one scone before he started to talk, to give him courage. He had no idea whether Major Tobit would reprove him for his actions.

Then Peter told him everything he knew about Phryne, Sheffield, Dr. Wilson, the Ratcliffe/Maginnis contretemps and the vanishing of Margery from the Prospect Hotel.

Major Tobit chuckled. "She's pulled that one before," he said. "Got it out of a medieval romance, she told me. Only works when there are a few uncontrolled entrances, or she can impersonate someone who is allowed in and out. Having herself arrested is a new twist. Very prettily done."

"But it drew Ratcliffe's attention," Peter protested.

"That wouldn't worry our Phryne. I bet you a jar of my best honey to a brick that her house is well secured."

"Boy and dog at the back gate, Phryne herself at the front."

"Indeed. Armed?"

"I expect so," said Peter. He was feeling better, and it wasn't just the scones and the admirable honey. Major Tobit approved of Phryne. So did Esther. "I asked Central, and they said every assistance. But it might get a bit…tricky."

"You mean that she might kill Ratcliffe," said Major Tobit.

"I know she is going to kill him," said Peter. "I have the means with me for you to forge his suicide note."

"Ah," said the Major. "Well, we can do that. I trust her, and you can too. She will do as much damage as she feels necessary, and no more. And since Mitchell is Ratcliffe, he will be no loss. I'd love to get her a medal, but it really wouldn't do, you know."

"Designing it would be a real challenge to the artist," murmured Esther. "Make sure you wash your hands before you begin, Ally. It won't do to have honey smears on a suicide note."

"Right you are. What sort of ink does the fellow use?"

"Informant said dark blue, like a bank's."

"And the tenor of the note?"

"To hell with all of you, I'm conquered," said Peter.

"I'm not staying to watch your triumph," said the Major.

"Quite."

"No farewell to favourite wife or doggie?"

"No, he hasn't any of them," said Peter.

"As I remember, Mitchell was an Englishman, went to university. So, educated English," said Major Tobit.

"I suppose so," said Peter.

"Right, I'll just go and wash my hands as my colleague suggests, and get on with it. You have another scone. Esther will get you some honey and some cream to take home with you. By the way," said the Major, taking the brown paper bag in his clean hand, "what happened to the other chap? Calvi, was it?"

"No sign of him. He isn't with Ratcliffe. Miss Fisher thinks she may have a line on him, too."

"Admirable girl," said the Major. "Always thought so."

"More tea?" asked Mrs. Tobit.

◇◇◇

An hour later, as Peter was being instructed in the making of clotted cream, the Major called them back into the parlour.

Mrs. Tobit put down her ladle and wiped her hands on her apron. "Yes, dear? How did you go?"

"I think this will do," said Major Tobit, laying out a crumpled draft of a letter on the table, and showing a newly written suicide note. Peter gasped. The writing was not a perfect match, because that would be suspicious. It was a very close match. The handwriting was bold and had flourishes. The draft was a letter about coal supplies for a laundry. The suicide note said:

> *Vicisti, Galilaee! You've won. I'm not staying to watch you take over my concerns. I'll see you all in Hell. Soon.*

It was signed with the full Ratcliffe flourish.

"Beautiful," breathed Peter.

"You do such nice work, dear," agreed Mrs. Tobit.

The Major flexed his fingers. "I've never got arthritis, though my old dad had it something cruel. I put it down to the healing powers of—"

"Honey," said Peter.

"Precisely!" said the Major, beaming and clapping him on the back.

Peter Fanshawe drove home with several pots of clotted cream and a dozen jars of honey. And a forged suicide note.

He delivered the note and one pot of honey to Miss Fisher's house and drove back to the garage to change clothes and vehicles, feeling profoundly pleased that he was in good favour, doing the right thing, and not an enemy of the Hon. Miss Phryne Fisher.

Chapter Thirteen

Since I am coming to that Holy room,
Where, with Thy quire of saints for evermore,
I shall be made Thy music; as I come
I tune the instrument here at the door
And what I must do then, think here before.

John Donne
"Hymn to God, My God, in My Sickness"

Rehearsal was frightful.

Not only was the conductor cruel, partial, and doing unpleasant things to Mendelssohn, wrestling him into the box marked HANDEL and chopping off the bits which didn't fit, the evening had started with a mad rummage to find the orchestral score.

"Sheer swank," snapped Matthew, flushed and irritated. "He doesn't need the full score to rehearse the choir. He just likes to show off."

"Yes, but we still have to find it," said Tabitha, practical as ever. "Where did anyone see it last?"

"Conductor's room," said Isabelle, fanning herself.

"It's not there now?"

"He says not," replied Chloe.

"I'll go and have another look," offered Phryne, as Mr. James was working himself up to a full-dress snit. She took Matthew with her to the comically secured room, unlocked it, and found the score lying on the floor behind the desk, invisible from the door. It seemed a little damp; perhaps the roof leaked. But it was the score and Matthew bore it triumphantly back to the music stand.

The rehearsal started. The choir got through "Baal, We Cry to Thee" without attracting too much criticism. Then they tried "And Then Shall Your Light Break Forth" and were scorned.

"I will have to find a semi-chorus to sing this," sneered Mr. James. "You can't manage it."

"Not only does he push his revolting greasy hair back all the time, he licks his fingers every time he turns a page," said Oliver. "It's disgusting."

"Répétiteur! You're off-tempo. Faster, if you can manage it," ordered Mr. James.

"It says *andante moderato*," said Professor Szabo.

"You will do as I say or you will leave," yelled James, and there was a pause. The choir looked wildly at each other. Where were they going to get another good pianist at this late date? Willing to play for ruby-port money? Finally, the melody was played again, at the tempo which Henry James preferred.

"Again, from B," said James, and they sang again.

It was a relief all round when he finished the rehearsal early, scowled himself out, and the choir wound down by singing a folk song.

"*Oh the summer time is coming*," sang the tenors.

"*And the leaves are sweetly blooming*," sang the altos in answer.

"*And the wild mountain thyme*," sang the sopranos.

"*Blooms amongst the blooming heather*," sang the basses.

"*Will you go*," asked the choir of each other, "*lassie/laddie, go? And we'll all go together, to pluck wild mountain thyme, all amongst the blooming heather, will ye go, laddie, go?*"

Phryne had never sung this before, but the tune was simple. It was also, overwhelmingly, suggestive. Each choir member had nailed down the object of his or her regard and was moving toward them.

"*I will build my love a bower, near the pure and crystal fountain*," sang the sopranos.

"*And about it I will pile all the flowers of the mountain*," sang the basses, "*will ye go, lassie, go?*"

Phryne felt eyes upon her. She turned, singing, and encountered the beautiful trout-stream eyes of Matthew the tenor, aflame with desire. "*And we'll all go together*," she sang, "*and pluck wild mountain thyme, all amongst the blooming heather, will ye go, laddie, go?*" she asked.

He took her hand.

"Not yet," Phryne told him.

"When?" he asked, pressing her palm to his lips. His mouth was open and hot.

"Soon," said Phryne, and took her hand away.

"*If my true love cannot come, I will surely find another*," sang the choir, "*to pluck wild mountain thyme, all amongst the blooming heather, will ye go, laddie, go?*"

Singing, they swept themselves out. They were heading for Aunty Mark's perpetual party. Phryne was intending to follow when she was stopped at the door by John Wilson. He looked worried.

"I say, Phryne, can we come to dinner tonight? Frightful cheek, short notice and all that."

"Yes, of course—you mean both you *and* Sheffield?" she asked.

"His idea," said John, clearly at a loss.

"Really? Very well. I shall just phone my house and warn them that there will be two extra for supper. The household dines early. We can take a taxi. I gave Mr. Butler the night off. And yell if you hear a Harley-Davidson."

"I will," he promised.

Phryne went into the conductor's room and called Mrs. Butler. Two more for one of her lavish suppers wouldn't strain the resources of her admirably well-stocked kitchen, but it was always a good idea to be polite to someone who could poison you, if they felt the need. She also arranged for Bert and Cec to pick her up. No sense in giving Ratcliffe a free hit. She then spoke to Dot.

Phryne occupied the rest of the lecture time in reading the notes to her Mendelssohn score. It sounded like her informants had been correct. Henry James' method was exactly the wrong way to conduct Mendelssohn. No wonder the old professor had gone out scowling. Poor old man. He would be climbing into a bottle tonight. Preferably one provided by Aunty Mark, who only served good wine.

Carried home with her guests without incident, Phryne showed them into the large parlour where Tinker, Jane, and Ruth waited with Dot to greet them. Jane spent a considerable time staring at Sheffield. So much so that after a luxurious little supper and a few glasses of wine, John asked her how her chess was coming along and Rupert offered her a game. Jane looked at Phryne, who shrugged.

"Now, my dear fellow, be civil," urged John.

Sheffield shrugged in his turn. Jane set up the board and held out her closed hands, a piece in each. Rupert did not touch her hand, as was the custom, but indicated the right fist, which Jane opened to reveal the black pawn.

"I'm black," said Rupert.

"But comely," said John.

Rupert flashed him a violet glance. Ruth and Dot returned to their discussion of meringues. Phryne sat near John and murmured, "How have you been getting on?"

"Wouldn't let me out of his sight all day," responded John. "If he was a different person I'd say he was jealous. But he can't possibly be."

"No?" said Phryne. "His next ploy will tell you how he feels about you."

"It will?"

"Watch," said Phryne. "And wait."

Jane pushed forward a pawn in front of her king. Sheffield pushed out his own pawn opposite. Out came Jane's bishop three spaces. Sheffield's mouth turned down at the corners and he brought out his knight. Jane's knight came out to mirror his, and Sheffield's knight swept away Jane's pawn. Out came her other knight, and the black knight took that as well. A pawn in front of her queen captured the knight, and Sheffield, now actually frowning, pushed out his queen's pawn one square. Jane's face erupted into a delighted grin and her remaining knight took the pawn anyway. Now impassive, Sheffield calmly took the knight with his pawn. Straight away, Jane swept her slender arm across the board, grasped her bishop and took the pawn next to the black king. "Check!" she said triumphantly. The ghost of a smile illuminated Sheffield's features, and he moved his king forward a square. Out came the other bishop. "Check again!" Jane crowed, and Sheffield gently laid his king on one side.

"Very good," he commented. "Did you work that out for yourself, or did you read it somewhere?"

Jane looked affronted. "I thought it up myself! Why, has somebody else thought of it too?"

Sheffield smiled again. Twice in one night, thought Phryne, looking on from a safe distance. Why, Mr. Sheffield! Are you certain your face won't crack with the unaccustomed exercise? Better to keep this subversive thought unvoiced, she decided. Sheffield's long, elegant fingers began to reset the board. "It is called the Boden Gambit," he said softly. "It is so rarely played I had quite forgotten it. Of course I should have moved my knight back at move four. If you thought of that yourself, you show promise." He smiled for an unprecedented third time. "And now you should give me a chance to play white." He turned the board around and placed his queen's pawn forward two squares.

Fifteen minutes later, Jane turned over her king.

"I resign," said Jane. "Thank you for an instructive game."

"You are…quite a promising player," said Sheffield reluctantly.

"Thank you," said Jane. "I heard your lecture on the science of deduction. Would you perhaps explain the basis of your mathematical method to me?"

"Do you understand calculus?" asked Rupert. He was so pretty, Phryne thought, with his hand-tailored suit and tousled black curls. Pity he was such a cold-hearted monster. A mannequin. An automaton. All mind, no body.

Beautiful, though.

"No, I haven't done calculus yet," confessed Jane.

Sheffield took out a sheet of plain paper and traced three straight lines without apparent effort using a thin pencil. He scorned such things as rulers. "See this oblique line here? I want you to tell me the slope of this line."

Jane glanced at the line. "I'd say it was around two. It rises twice as high as it goes across."

"Very well." Now he leaned over the page

again and traced a curve. "What about this? It's a parabola now. What's the slope of this?"

Jane stared at the page. "Wouldn't it depend on where you applied a tangent?"

"It would. Try here, where the x coordinate is two. This is a graph of the simplest quadratic, where the height is the square of the horizontal."

Jane took up a hardcover book from the side table and laid it against the curve. She drew two or three tangents with the pencil and frowned. "Is it a whole number?" she asked hopefully. Sheffield inclined his chin without speaking. "I'd guess I was four. Is that right?"

"It is. Now try it where x is three." He leaned over the page again and placed a small, decisive dot on the curve. He watched impassively while Jane drew a couple more tangents before finding one which satisfied her. "Is it six?" she enquired.

"Yes. Now, what would you say if I asked for the gradient at one?"

Jane thought about it for a moment and put the pencil down. "Two?" A short, decisive nod. "Does that mean it's always twice the x coordinate?"

"Yes. Now you have the beginnings of calculus. I can prove it for you, if you wish?"

Sheffield took another sheet of blank paper and wrote a series of equations on it. "As we make the width of our tangent smaller and smaller, the slope is equal to twice x plus the width of the line. As the width approaches zero, the slope approaches two x. Just be careful when dividing by very small numbers. It would never do to attempt division by zero."

"So we're sneaking up on the answer?" Jane gave him a dazzling smile.

"We are."

"I see," said Jane. "I will think about this."

"If you can," Rupert told her.

"Bedtime, darlings," said Dot. "Say good-night to Mr. Sheffield. Doctor. Miss Phryne." She smiled on all three, and led the younger members of the party away. Jane paused at the door to rake Sheffield with a long, analytical stare before Ruth drew her away by the arm. Dot returned after a few moments and took up an unobtrusive place by the lamp, where her embroidery waited.

"That girl," said John, "scares me."

"Indeed?" asked Sheffield. "Why?"

"She's very clever, and completely unsympathetic. You saw her when she was massaging my leg. She could have caused me pain. The reason she didn't was not because she likes me, though I think she does. Or that causing pain is wrong. It was because she wanted those tendons and muscles back in the right order."

"Also because I told her not to hurt you," put in Phryne.

"Yes, that too, but mostly it was a rage for propriety. The muscles ought not to spasm, the bruise ought not be allowed to form. Therefore, arnica, and therefore, massage. I'm not explaining this well. But I am sure that she's a good girl, Phryne," said John apologetically. "And she'll make a very good doctor."

"She wants to go in for forensic medicine. Professor Glaister's book has inspired her." Phryne smiled at John. She was aware of Rupert bridling as she patted John on the arm.

"Well, that means she doesn't have to develop a bedside manner," said John, grinning. "Her patients will never complain of lack of sympathy."

"Fortunately," responded Phryne. "Jane had a very isolated and horrible childhood. She will learn love."

"Is it something you can learn?" asked Sheffield abruptly.

"Of course," Phryne said, pouring herself another glass of wine. "We learn love from the people who love us."

"John." Rupert summoned him with an imperious wave. "A word."

John got up, with difficulty, and limped to where Rupert stood, staring out the window at the windy St. Kilda night. There was a fast whispered exchange. John limped back to Phryne and delivered his message in a tone of absolute astonishment.

"I see," said Phryne to Sheffield. "You wish to wholly and intimately examine a woman. Surely you could hire one for the usual sum?"

The violet eyes shut briefly in pained distaste. Sheffield conveyed that satisfying his curiosity with a whore would induce instant nausea. Phryne was intrigued and not a little annoyed. That always made her reckless. "Very well," she said. Sheffield blinked. She had surprised him. Excellent. "On two conditions," she concluded.

"Of course there would be conditions," drawled Sheffield. That drawl was beginning to really rasp on her nerves.

"Of course," she replied, smiling sunnily into the beautiful face. "One—" she held up her hand "—John comes too."

"Phryne," John began, deeply suspicious.

Sheffield cut him off with a wave of his long fingers. "Agreed."

"You strip as naked as you want me to be."

This time he blinked and also paused.

"Why would you make a condition like that?" he asked. Phryne knew to the iota exactly how much he hated asking a question to which he did not know the answer.

"Power," she said. "The clothed have power over the naked. And while I have always had a soft spot for honest curiosity, I have no intention of allowing you to have power over me. Ever," she added. "You examine me, I examine you."

"Sheffield," said John, who had seen that sweet smile and heard that buoyant tone in Phryne's voice before, notably when she had shot that German trench raider. In the heart. To protect her wounded. "I don't think—"

"Yes, I know," said Sheffield offhandedly. "And in that event, you shouldn't talk."

Right, thought Phryne, that settles your fate, my boy. She had seen the slightly wounded but perfectly resigned look on her old friend's face. Ravishing this creature senseless so that he cried for mercy was probably a tad unfair, but it remained an option. The insult had caused John to cease protesting, which was all to the good. Phryne was about to take a risk to which the term Suicidal Insanity would be appropriate, and she didn't want John upsetting the razor-edge balance.

"Are we agreed?" she asked. Sweetly. John bit a fingernail. Rupert Sheffield accepted Phryne's hand and shook it.

"Agreed," he said.

"Good, bring your magnifying glass and follow me. Dot, dear, no one is to come to my suite after Mr. Butler brings a bottle of the good whisky, the usual accompaniments, and a bottle of cognac for me. Would you like a drink, Mr. Sheffield?"

"I don't drink," he said loftily.

"Of course you don't," she said in a tone reserved by nursemaids for children who have just dropped their rattle out of their cot for the fifth time. "A jug of lemonade as well, if you would be so good, Dot."

John Wilson's sense of unease was growing exponentially. But Phryne was fond of him and a woman of remarkable intelligence and courage. And Sheffield wanted to examine a clean and beautiful woman, which Phryne was, and he had accepted the conditions, and if it took watching Phryne seduce his dearest friend to see that dearest friend naked, then John could pay the price without regret.

Probably.

Phryne's boudoir, by the time they arrived there, had an elaborate drinks tray. John immediately poured himself a slug of the Glen Sporran, which was, he found as he glugged it down, just as good as he remembered it, an excellent single malt.

It did not seem to have an appreciable relaxing effect, so he poured another. Phryne was beginning to undress. She was beautiful, he thought, watching her sit down gracefully on her bed to remove her stockings, then standing to slide off the evening gown, the camisole and the lace-trimmed French knickers. She slipped the bandeau off her head and skimmed it across the room to her dressing table, where the peacock feather waved valiantly.

Then she went to her bathroom and came back with a hand mirror, and a selection of swatches of coloured silk. As Rupert Sheffield shed his clothes she flipped through them, trying to match the hue against his pale skin. As he removed his shirt she found the right colour.

"Ivory," she said. "Do you agree that this is a match for your skin tone?"

Sheffield took the mirror and considered the silk and his own bare chest.

"Yes," he said indifferently. "What is the value of the comparison?"

"That, I believe, you will perceive later," said Phryne. She had the unselfconscious nudity of a cat, clad in its own skin. It is aware that its unadorned pelt is more beautiful than any clothing. She sat down cross-legged on her huge bed, stark white against the green silk sheets, and waited for her examiner to remove his undergarments.

And that made two cats, thought John Wilson, gulping down another whisky, a white tiger and a black cat. Sheffield was interested in Phryne, but there was no sign of any sexual arousal. He merely

bent the whole of his attention on her, something
which could reduce John to incoherence, but which
was wasted on Phryne, who could outstare any
feline. She smiled amiably and asked him where
he would like to start.

"If you could lie down?" he asked, quite
politely. Phryne obliged. Because of the width of
the bed, Sheffield was obliged to stretch his length
alongside her, on the green sheets, and the contrast
between the man's porcelain skin and the verdant
linen was almost too much for John. He dared not
drink any more, and he wanted to look away, but
he could not.

Sheffield was slim, with long bones and long
muscles, supple and untouched. Not a scar on him,
thought John. How could I think that he might
want a battered old veteran like me? God, we're the
same age. He looks so beautiful, lying alongside the
decorative Phryne, the only woman I ever desired.
Naturally they would desire each other. But why
bring me along to watch? Haven't I been tortured
enough?

Apparently not. Sheffield started at Phryne's
feet, picking up each one, pressing the toenails,
flexing them, running a finger along the arch of
her foot. He noted a wince and said uninterestedly,
"Oh, yes, the dancing," and put her foot down.

"Sheffield, you're not going to hurt her," said John firmly.

"No," said Phryne, "really he's not. Because you won't let him. Not dancing. You are pressing too hard. My bones are, as you might have noticed, gracile, being female. Continue, if you please," she told Sheffield, and he did. He worked his way up to her knees, occasionally laying his cheek almost down on her skin, his dark curls sweeping and tickling. Phryne sighted down over her hip and reflected that of all the most gorgeous men she had ever been naked with, this was probably the most strangely undesirable. He was cold, even his fingers were cool on her body, and his lavender eyes might have belonged to an angel, or a demon, a creature unaware of earthly desires. Therefore, of course, unlikely to arouse her, which was to the purpose for what she had in mind.

Botticelli, she thought idly, would have adored him. He was definitely in the Mannerist tradition.

He reached the patch of dark coarse pubic hair, felt the quality of it between his fingers, then asked her to part her legs. Phryne did so. He did not caress her or react at all, leaving Phryne feeling vaguely insulted. Most people, reaching that goal, were at least conscious of the honour. She caught John's appalled gaze and winked at him.

John poured another glass of Glen Sporran.

The dark curls were tickling her inside thighs now, and a cautious finger was parting the labia minora and majora with scientific curiosity. He identified, and unhooded, her clitoris. Phryne suppressed a giggle. Sheffield's head appeared above her belly, noted the giggle, and returned to his scrutiny.

He was kneeling up a little, and Phryne could see the sweet male slopes of his chest, belly and the scribble of hair around his entirely unaroused genitalia. Excellent.

He moved up again, examining her belly, tracing a scar which marked her smooth side.

"Shrapnel," said Phryne. "John and I were in the same raid and we all copped it. He saved my life," she added.

"He saved *my* life," said Sheffield, sounding affronted. He took a breast in his hand, weighed it meditatively, noted that the other breast was slightly smaller, then worked his way up, from breast to shoulder to neck, and then felt and even sniffed over her face.

"Floris Stephanotis," she informed him. "Coconut shampoo…"

"Champagne, Virginia tobacco, raspberries," he told her. "La Rose de Gueldy soap. Cognac."

"Very good," Phryne told him.

"Another scar," he said. "Here, under your hair. Not shrapnel."

"Knife," said Phryne.

He jolted a little, but did not comment. He ran a finger over her lower lip and tasted her lipstick. He made a face.

"John, a little lemonade for your friend," Phryne ordered. "He does not like the taste of lipstick."

"Different if you taste it on her mouth," advised John, entirely against his better judgment, which he seemed to have left downstairs. Sheffield made an interested noise, almost like a snort, then pressed his lips to Phryne's—entirely in the furtherance of science—which felt very strange.

Phryne was beginning to find this examination trying. His mouth was soft, his lips inviting, and she might have been kissing a doll. She took firm hold on her instincts and did not drag him into a bone-shattering embrace. John came to the bedside with the lemonade just in time. He had seen her fingers twitch.

"No, no, like this," he told Sheffield, and leaned down to kiss Phryne. She curled her fingers around his collar and dragged him closer. Now that was a kiss, she thought, releasing him, and intercepting a violet-coloured Very light, full-on glare from the scientist.

Interesting indeed. John, as always, tasted of pipe smoke, his own flavour, and rather too much

Glen Sporran. He had better knock it off or this really wasn't going to work.

"Why not light your pipe?" she asked him. "You must be dying for a smoke."

He retreated to the chaise longue. Phryne propped herself up on one elbow.

"What my learned colleague meant, Mr. Sheffield, is that lipstick by itself is not pleasant. Kissing someone means that you also get their tastes and scent, as you must have got mine."

"Yes," said Sheffield. "You taste of raspberries and cognac and, for some reason, smell like violets and cold water."

"That is my signature scent," Phryne told him. "All humans have a scent and a taste. You taste of cream and a sharp herb: tarragon, perhaps, cut grass or rosemary. Something very green. Refreshing."

"I was aware of the importance of scent," said Sheffield, and continued his examination. He murmured over the strength of her hands and the calluses on her fingers, noted a small scar on her wrist, then asked her civilly to turn over. This time he began at her head, ruffling through her hair, rubbing a strand between thumb and forefinger as though he was classing wool. As soon as he had passed over her ears to her shoulder blades, Phryne asked John for a large cognac, with water and ice, and leaned up on her elbows to drink it.

The Byronic curls were brushing the small of her back—he appeared to be counting vertebrae—and she shivered. In the mirror she caught the concerned glance which Rupert Sheffield sent toward John, who was now sitting at her side.

"Did I hurt you?" he asked.

"No," said Phryne. "Do go on. Fairly soon you will run out of me, and then it is my turn."

Was it her imagination, or was the young man spending an inordinate amount of time palpating her buttocks and sniffing the inside of her knees?

Privately, Phryne grinned such an evil grin that John decided to stop looking into the mirror and go and light his pipe, as ordered. Phryne sipped her very good brandy until her last little toe pad had been closely scrutinised, then sat up cross-legged again.

"Have you all the information you require?" she asked politely.

"Thank you, that was adequate," he said in that Irish coffee voice which ought to be used for charming John Wilson out of his undergarments. Adequate, eh? Phryne gestured, and Rupert Sheffield, displaying his first reluctance, laid himself out, flat on his back.

My Lord, he is so beautiful, thought Phryne, as John puffed out a cloud of smoke and tried to conceal a gasp. She began as he had done, picking up a long foot, aware of the bones in perfect order, close-cut toenails—he had been wearing well-fitting boots since childhood—and decided that she would state her deductions out loud. She considered calling John to sit beside her but there was a limit to anyone's endurance and he might be nearing it, what with this vision of loveliness laid out like a sacrifice. Agnus Dei, thought Phryne. Behold the Lamb.

That was such an odd notion that she shelved it for later consideration and began to speak in a dispassionate, vaguely pedantic tone, guaranteed to annoy her subject as much as possible.

"Here we see that the subject has been well fed and tended since infancy," she intoned. "There are no signs that he has ever run barefoot, no thickening of the sole, and no bunions or deformities of the toes to suggest ill-fitting footwear. No scars from stones or frostbite as one finds on the feet of the poor. Nails professionally cut."

"As are yours," said the subject.

"Indeed," agreed Phryne. "Be so good as to be silent, sir, unless you wish to disagree with my observations. I did you that courtesy."

Rupert Sheffield snorted, but did not reply. John puffed another cloud which almost sounded like a chuckle. Phryne compared the feet, found a thickening in one which showed that a bone had been broken fairly recently, probably by having something heavy dropped on it. She said so. Rupert did not speak. But John said, "Oh, yes, Phryne, that was on Dartmoor, a boulder. I had to haul him quite half a mile before we found some help."

"Right. You, as my dear friend, on the other hand, are welcome to comment." Phryne felt Rupert quiver under her hand. That "dear friend" comment had got in among this pillar of rectitude. She grinned again. This was proving to be most entertaining, and she was mildly shocked to find that she had such a taste for torment. Ah, well. In a good cause, which made it more delicious.

"Strong calf muscles, he is a good walker and runner, lightly pitted kneecaps—gravel, I think, probably from the playing grounds of Winchester. Long bones, long thigh muscles, quite unscarred."

Phryne leaned down and sniffed the porcelain skin of his upper thigh. "Uses honeysuckle soap." She allowed her falling hair to tickle the skin, and Rupert Sheffield shivered, but not with desire. He was dreading where her examination would next take her, but she switched her attention to his hands, examining them carefully.

"Telegraphs," she said. "I knew you were a code-breaker but you also sent telegrams. Look, John, telegrapher's thumb if ever I saw it. Otherwise, clean, well-kept hand, nails cut by the same professional, ink stain on this finger, pen callus on this, a writer's hands. And, of course, you play… what? Quite impressive musculature. No marks of overuse, no longer fingernails on the left hand—" she reached over his body to take the other hand "—so it must be piano. Keyboard of some sort."

"He is a very good pianist," said John dotingly. Rupert shifted uneasily under Phryne's touch. Her breast was pressing against his side. She seemed blithely unaware of this. John Wilson was not the only person who had never met anyone like Phryne Fisher.

And yet, and yet, she seemed unattracted by him. He was offended. Everyone said that he was beautiful. The fact that he did not indulge in foolish affections and desires meant only that he was superior to weak humans, who kissed and wept. This—all right, yes, facts are facts—beautiful, sweet-scented woman was touching him with hands as dispassionate as a surgeon's, and possibly with the same potential to maim.

It was not that he hadn't tried sex. People were lining up to educate him in his Intelligence days. The closest he had come to a lover was a Greek fisherman called Yanni. Yanni had laughed and kissed him and rumpled his hair and slept with him all one long cold night in a fishing boat off Piraeus. But Yanni had gone with the U-boat that killed him, and they never even found his boat, much less his body. And though he had felt pleasure, it seemed like too much trouble, when he could manage his infrequent uprisings of lust all on his own.

Now he did not know how he felt, and was fighting down the urge to look to John. John wouldn't let anything irreparable happen to him. John was always there. John was his friend. He shut his eyes but Phryne was moving again, this time paying attention to his chest, noting the lack of hair on it, until she leaned down over his belly and breathed on his genitalia. Her hair tickled him. She touched very lightly, said, "Circumcised," and moved on. Rupert released his held breath.

Now her gaze moved up to his face. She tilted his head to inspect his jaw, spent some time looking at his ears—"Long lobes, short cavum, quite the right proportion"—and then gazed down into his eyes as she ran a hand through his curls. He tried to look away but she had a firm grip on his hair.

"Most interesting eyes," she said. "Really, violet eyes. And in some lights—would you look to the left, please?—yes, see, almost silver. Remarkable."

"They are," rumbled John's blessedly familiar voice. "I have never seen such beautiful eyes." There, see, Rupert did not say aloud, John thinks my eyes are beautiful. I wish I had never agreed to this. I could have bought any whore's time, and

I could have made her take a bath first. But this woman is so…

Phryne asked him politely to turn over, so he did, feeling less vulnerable. She had been right. The clothed have power over the unclothed. And those that do not care if they are naked or not have power over those who do. John, on the other hand, was there, fully dressed, and smoking his pipe (Robinson's Navy Cut as usual) and Rupert could smell his signature scent—thank you, the Hon. Miss Fisher, now I have a term for it—which at the moment was overlaid with Scots whisky, probably a single malt. Knowing Miss Fisher, fabulously expensive and only made to order in a small glen in the Highlands to some secret clan recipe. Cooked up in a *poit dhubh*. Which means "black pot" in Scots Gaelic.

His mind was wandering. He was shocked. His mind never wandered! Rupert Sheffield's mind never lost its focus! What was happening to him? Concentrate. I am lying prone, a naked (!) woman is making observations about my spine, and John is watching. She's right about those scars, too. Curse her. Now John has seen them. I never meant him to see them.

"A flogging," said Phryne, rather shocked and schooling her voice. "Serious. Was he in battle?"

"Intelligence," said John, sounding concerned. "Never mentioned this. Contemporary with that time, at least. Ten strokes with a cane, I think, rather than a lash."

John's hand, larger, warmer than the woman's, smoothed the shameful scars as though he wished he could erase them with his touch.

"Torture?" asked Phryne. "You may speak, Mr. Sheffield."

"Landed on the wrong island," he said into her pillow. "Turned out to be Turkish, not Greek. Beat me on general principle, really. Then dumped me into the sea, from which I was rescued. When I got back Compton told me not to be such a bloody fool again or he'd send me back to England on a tramp steamer, tied in a sack. Which had previously held fish heads. He would have, too."

"The salt made an instant scar," said John, stroking the marks again. "Must have hurt like hell."

"I believe that I screamed, yes," drawled Rupert. "But I was lucky. If they'd kept me for another day…"

"Rape," said Phryne with unacceptable bluntness. "The Turks usually raped prisoners."

John winced. Rupert merely agreed.

"That was on tomorrow's agenda. But they got bored with me, so I escaped a dreadful fate."

"You never told me," said John.

"Why would you want to know?" asked Sheffield, genuinely curious. "It wasn't too bad," he added, trying for some reason to comfort John, who sounded upset. "Not after school. My fifth form Latin master could strike a good deal more shrewdly than that." He expected to hear John laugh, but he did not.

Phryne's inspection moved downwards, stating that his buttocks were solidly muscular, confirming her views on his ability to walk and run. She worked her way down to his feet again and bade him sit up and drink his lemonade, as he must be thirsty. He did so and she sat facing him on the big bed, her female parts shamelessly displayed, looking at him very carefully. He had previously noted her very bright, very shrewd, very green eyes.

"Another experiment?" she asked. "Since we are here?"

Rupert Sheffield had trained as a spy. He was constitutionally suspicious. But he knew that there was no one in the world more intelligent than he was. Phryne simply could not out-think him. It was impossible.

"Does it involve you touching me?" he drawled. Poor woman must desire him after all.

"No," she said, surprising him again.

"Or me touching you?"

"No," she said, with a hint of a smile.

"Very well," he said. "It may provide more data."

"So it may," she said softly. "John?"

"My dear?"

Rupert disliked the way his John called her "my dear" so effortlessly. John was not her dear. John was his. But John wasn't his in the same way as he belonged to her…

"You are overdressed," said Phryne. "Take off your coat and your shirt, please."

"Phryne, do you know what you are doing?" he asked, even as his hands moved to his buttons.

"I do," she said.

"If this does not work, you will break my heart, you know," he said quietly, hanging his coat over the chair, removing his tie and taking out his cufflinks.

Phryne looked back at him with a steady gaze. "I know. Trust me."

"I do," sighed John, and stripped off his shirt, turning to display his bare, muscular chest.

In a flash, Phryne had whipped the hand mirror out from under the pillow and shoved it in Rupert Sheffield's face.

"Look at your eyes," she ordered. He looked.

"Four signs of sexual attraction," she said relentlessly. "Havelock Ellis' discovery. Dilated pupils. Are your eyes dilated?"

"Yes," he said.

"Shortness of breath. Is your breath short?"

"Yes," he gasped.

"Increased heartbeat." Her cool fingers pressed on his pulse. "Right. And finally—" she held up the silk sample against his chest and reflected them in the mirror "—arousal flush. You are now, at a guess, musk rose."

"Yes," whispered Rupert. He did not move. Phryne took the lemonade glass out of his hand. Rupert still did not move. Phryne sighed and walked to John, who knelt at the end of her bed, naked to the waist. She put a hand on his chest and bent to kiss him.

She was shoved out of the way by a flying Renaissance angel, who grabbed John Wilson, dragged him into his arms and kissed him fiercely, mashing their mouths together, until John's hand came up to run through the black curls and they slid down into a full body embrace. Interesting. Sheffield appeared to be trying to burrow inside John and nest inside his bones, like a worm in an apple. Phryne had never seen such a ferocious first kiss. Perhaps among tigers, say. The larger predators. Something with a lot of teeth.

Rupert's fingers were digging into John's shoulders, his long thighs were wrapped around John's waist, and he freed his mouth long enough to say, "You are mine—mine! And I never thought I'd have a lover but I choose you. John? Now. Forever. John? Say yes, John."

John was too stunned and overcome to speak. He breathed in the scent of Sheffield's hair and skin and almost wept with relief. His warm hand splayed out across the scars, obliterating them and their importance. He did not realise that he hadn't answered a question until a soft desperate whisper next to his collarbone said, "Please?"

Phryne found her clothes and gown and collected the drinks tray and waited until she heard John Wilson say gently, "Yes, my dear, yes, my love, yes, yes, yes."

Then she withdrew into her boudoir, settled down on her couch, and poured herself a large drink. She felt that she deserved it. That had been, as the Duke of Wellington had remarked about a minor military engagement by comparison, a damn close-run thing. If she had not practically flung them into each other's arms, they would have spent the rest of their lives as they had been, Sheffield not noticing John's devotion but shamelessly relying on it, and John going down unkissed into his lonely grave.

A situation which could not be allowed to continue, but she had taken an enormous risk. Even now she was listening for a cry of horror or disgust from next door when Sheffield realised how entirely he had lost control.

If he came storming out, Phryne swore, she would trip him, tie him, sit on his chest, and deliver him a scathing lecture on ingratitude, and proceed with the "ravishing him senseless" which had been on her original agenda. And he would deserve it.

She took another sip. Really, she was shocked at herself. But she wasn't going to get dressed and see what was left of supper, though she was suddenly ravenous. These tentative lovers needed a guard, and in lieu of Cerberus, they had Phryne.

Which didn't mean she couldn't call Mr. Butler for a tray of tidbits, so she did that. Razor-edge diplomacy made you hungry. No wonder all those ambassadors were so rotund.

◇◇◇

John kissed Sheffield again, because he could, and felt the long-imagined soft lips yield beneath his own, the untaught mouth open, the tip of his tongue just tasting, withdrawing, returning. He was flooded with gratitude and lust in roughly equal proportions. He probably shouldn't do this, but he was bloody well going to, because Sheffield had leapt on him and kissed his mouth, Sheffield wanted him. And John hadn't said a word or made a move. Sheffield, astoundingly, marvellously, had seduced John. He might never get over this.

He wasn't sure that he wanted to get over it.

Amazement could go no further. If Phryne had ridden in on a unicorn he would merely have remarked on its elegant hocks and golden horn and suggested that she enter it weight for age at Flemington. Well, no, not a unicorn. Not Phryne. A dragon, perhaps. He was sure that she could tame a dragon. Look what she had done to Sheffield. His beautiful man, lying in his arms, squirming to get closer, closer. They were lying chest to chest, and he could feel the soft, smooth skin which he had often imagined kissing. Wonderful. If only this, utterly wonderful. But it appeared it was not going to be only this.

Rupert pulled at his belt.

"Too many clothes," he complained.

"Quite right," John agreed. He unlatched as much of Rupert as he could to allow him to remove his shoes and socks and garments, then allowed himself to be pulled back into the octopus embrace. Naked skin slid against his own nakedness. John wondered if he was actually going to swoon like a Victorian maiden. Excess of sensation was bringing him terribly fast toward a climax he did not yet want to have, in case, God forbid, this should be the only time Rupert Sheffield lay in his arms. He would have to talk to him. He would have to talk about whether Sheffield really wanted to do this.

Presently. After he kissed down that entrancing

neck to the hollow of his throat, where a fast pulse beat. Later. After he sucked lightly at an earlobe and felt Rupert shudder. Any moment now. After Rupert had slid his hands down their joined bodies to his lower back and slammed them together. After which it was a confusion of kisses, caresses, and touches of such excruciating sweetness that he entirely forgot everything; except Rupert's mouth, his silky skin, the blaze of his lambent violet eyes.

When he recovered a little, he was lying in a tangle of limbs on green silk sheets with the most beautiful man in the world wrapped around him, as though John was a teddy bear. Rupert had fallen asleep. His sweet breath stirred across John's shoulder, cooling and drying his sweaty skin. Relaxed, he was a solid weight, not the ever-moving dragonfly he was when awake. John adjusted the position of his injured leg and Rupert murmured a protest in his sleep and dragged him back again, pinning him down with those long legs.

He resigned himself. Sheffield was quite determined that John wasn't going to go anywhere, and that was that.

John Wilson smiled. He firmly rearranged Sheffield so that he was not lying on the scarred leg, and gathered him close. Rupert gave a small broken sigh and settled down again. It was so unbearably touching that John felt tears track, silently, down his face, and drip into the curly black hair.

He had the impression that the door had opened gently. Then it closed again, just as gently. Then he fell asleep, or possibly swooned. Like a Victorian maiden.

When John Wilson woke, he was so blissfully comfortable—more comfortable than he had ever been in his life—that he was disinclined to move. He allowed his eyes to rove. Nice room, lady's bedroom; of course, Phryne. Warm body next to him, for some reason lying heavily on his belly. Not Phryne. Black curls. A finger tracing the starburst of scar on his thigh, and moving up to touch the curved shrapnel fragments in his side.

"I want to know all of you," said the Irish coffee voice of Rupert Sheffield. "Every bit of you. John." He said the name as though it was an endearment.

"Sheffield," replied John. "How do you feel?"

"Are you asking after my health, my state of mind, or whether I regret leaping upon you and claiming you as my lover?" he said clearly, still tracing shrapnel scars.

"All of those," replied John. Sheffield was not going to stop being Sheffield just because he had dived headfirst into the lusts of the flesh. "I want to know if you are going to push me away, scream that you have been violated, denounce me as a seducer, or say that this was some obscure experiment and we must never speak of it again."

Rupert's face appeared above John's hip, eyes wide, mouth open.

"I hadn't even *thought* of some of those," he said admiringly. "But to answer the question, I am healthy, I feel wonderful, and I will never regret, never, taking you as my lover. Forever. You said forever," he whispered in John's ear, throwing himself into the doctor's arms. "You said yes."

"I did," John reassured him. "You are everything that I want."

"And I suppose I have to share you," Rupert said, thinking about it. "I don't want to share you."

"Why would you have to share me?" asked John, puzzled.

"With her," said Rupert. "This is her bed."

"But she won't expect me to lie in it again. With her, I mean. She's an old friend. She was comforting me...." John began to chuckle. Rupert felt his laughter through his cheek, which was pressed to John's chest. It tickled. He had not known that laughter tickled before.

"Why are you laughing? It feels strange," complained Rupert.

"She was comforting me because of my hopeless unrequited and unrequitable love for a heedless asexual curly-haired genius with a talent for getting himself into trouble," John said.

"Oh," said Rupert.

"Yes," said John encouragingly.

"That would be me," he concluded.

"Indeed. You need a guardian. People keep trying to kill you. For some reason."

"I know who it is," said Rupert, silencing John's exclamation with another kiss. This lasted for some time.

When John reclaimed his mouth and his breath, he said, "Who?"

"Oh, I broke up a rather promising arms-smuggling ring when I was in Greece with Compton. He told me there would be trouble about it. But I never expected it to follow me here."

"Sheffield…" John's patience was wearing thin. Rupert slid a hand down his thigh, which distracted him. Really, this lovemaking was wonderful. Endless possibilities. There was so much of John which he did not know. If he had laid John out naked and examined him inch by inch he would have been lying in his arms a good deal earlier. A shameful failure in scientific method.

"We'll have to send a telegram tomorrow and ask what happened to the principals. I know that two were shot by the Albanians and one by the Turks and the rest should still be in jail in Greece.

But there was an Englishman we never caught. Mitchell. He must have seen me here and thought I was coming for him—that the Science of Deduction was just a cover story. It's very funny," said Rupert, and laughed in his turn.

"Sheffield, he's been trying to kill you!" protested John, sitting up. Rupert examined his face and put out one finger to soothe away the crease between his brows. His very own John whom he did not have to share with anyone.

"Yes, but he won't succeed, not while I have you with me. Isn't it time that you kissed me again?" asked Rupert, and John found that it was.

The kiss turned into lots of kisses, languorous, sleepy kisses, until Sheffield announced, "I'm hungry."

"So am I. I wonder what the time is? I had a watch somewhere."

There was a knock at the door. Rupert dived beneath the green sheets. He had no intention of being seen naked by Miss Fisher ever again. John got up.

"Phryne," Rupert heard him say, with that detestable note of familiarity. "We ought to give you back your room."

Rupert didn't hear the reply but he heard the laugh and a kiss. Then the door closed again.

"She kissed you!" he protested.

"Be charming," John advised. "Not only do we not have to move, she's sending up supper. A lady does not give up her bedchamber lightly. Mind your manners, my dear."

Rupert glowed. That "my dear" was the same easy affectionate "my dear" he used to Miss Fisher. He resolved to be exceedingly charming. Especially since he was hungry, needed a wash, and never wanted to let John Wilson out of immediate grabbing distance ever again. He seemed to be magnetically attracted to his body. Some sort of electricity? He experimented with moving away, rolling over to the cool side of the bed, and was struck with a very unpleasant isolated sensation, so he rolled back and embraced John again. That was right. Close. John chuckled and kissed his neck.

Presently Miss Fisher came in with the supper trolley. She was presented with a memorable sight.

Rupert Sheffield, smiling like a minor deity, was wrapped around her old friend John as though he never meant to let him go. The contrast of John's stocky muscularity with the porcelain skin and the violet eyes was striking. They would make a very good painting, quite in the art deco style, of a soldier and his guardian angel. Rupert would look lovely with rainbow-coloured wings. Though guardian angels probably didn't have that glutted, sated, utterly debauched, smug smile. At least, not since Botticelli got so involved with Savonarola. She had never seen John Wilson look so dazedly content.

"Supper," she said. "Do eat, darlings. You need to keep up your strength. The bathroom and WC are through that door. Breakfast downstairs at eight, when I need to reclaim my room."

Rupert let go of John and leaned out of his embrace to take Phryne's hand and kiss it. Phryne smiled at him. He was softened by love, violet eyes glowing, lips swollen with kisses. He looked like Canova's Eros.

"Thank you," he said. "For giving me my John."

How much did that overactive mind actually deduce about what Phryne had done? Who was the player, and who had been played? Impossible to tell. Phryne leaned down and kissed his cheek, told him it was her pleasure, and went out.

Mrs. Beeton always advised that any hostess who wanted to run a comfortable house should spend a night in her own guestroom. Phryne always kept an overnight bag in a spare room, in case of eventualities. And the narrow little bed was very comfortable, considering. Ember, shut out of her boudoir, joined her for the remainder of the night, sleeping decoratively on her pillow. As males in her bed went, he was undemanding and very, very pretty.

Chapter Fourteen

Poison grows in this dark.
It is in the water of tears
Its black blooms rise.

Wallace Stevens
"Another Weeping Woman"

Breakfast, Phryne considered, might easily be sticky. She had ordered the lovers to come down by eight, and by eight they were indeed ensconced at the breakfast table. They were freshly rinsed and looked chipper. John was tucking into a variety of things and Sheffield was eating scrambled eggs with slow relish.

"There is a *cuisine de famille,*" he told Ruth. "And this is part of it. These are really quite adequate eggs."

Ruth was about to bristle when Jane put a hand on her shoulder. From Rupert, that was a compliment. The two of them were warm and easy together. Phryne was pleased. She did not feel up to delivering blistering lectures this early in the morning.

"Have some of this honey for your toast," she advised John. "Apple blossom, it's really delightful."

"Excellent," agreed John. Phryne was looking at the side of his neck. Where her own delicate love bite had been was another, covering and obliterating it. Someone with a bigger mouth and a lot more suck had bruised John Wilson afresh over that token which Phryne had put there. The extra bruising meant, quite unequivocally, Mine.

They ate, drank tea, and farewelled their hostess. John kissed her on the mouth for the last time. It was a sweet kiss. She leaned a little into his stocky body, his warmth. Then she released him into other custody. Rupert, to her astonishment, also gathered her into his arms. He was slim and muscular and his body was almost vibrating under her hands.

"*Je vous en prie*, Madame," he whispered into her hair, "em*brasse-moi?*"

"*Avec plaisir*," Phryne told him. She kissed him. He tasted of green herbs and sex.

They smiled at her and left, John leaning on Rupert's arm. That limp was going to be a great advantage when they wanted to touch in public.

Fortunately today was laundry day, and Phryne went up to gather her sheets before they shocked

Dot. Who would, indeed, have been horrified by their state. Phryne smiled. Goodbye, then, to Dr. Wilson. It had been so nice while it had lasted.

But there were other options available. Though before she could choose one, she needed to solve the murder of the conductor. Which was proving difficult.

Oh, and bring down the loathsome Ratcliffe, of course.

For that she needed another cafe au lait. And perhaps a nibble of that scrambled egg dish of which Rupert Sheffield had condescended to approve. She tasted.

For *cuisine de famille*, it really was something special.

◇◇◇

In an attempt to protect the choir from their conductor, Matthew had called an informal rehearsal, quite voluntary, no need to tell Henry James about it at all, for which Phryne had offered to pay. She had received a phone call that informed her that the Guido Calvi in question was indeed her Luigi Calvi's uncle. He had not emigrated to Australia with his brother in 1919, and no trace of him could be found. Phryne thought it would be easier just to ask Luigi.

The assembly hall was noisier during the day,

but the choir had relaxed. Matthew was conducting from an ordinary choral score. The prof had not woken from his daily port-induced swoon, so the notes were being picked out by Daniel the giraffe boy, with Josephine to turn pages for him. Phryne had hopes that he might notice her, now that she was standing so very close to him that if he turned his head he would be nose-to-breast. He was an adequate pianist for note-bashing and the choir was getting the gist of the chorus "*Baal, We Cry to Thee!*".

"*Heed the sacrifice*," they sang. "*Heed the sacrifice we offer!*"

Just as Baal's attention should have been well and truly caught, the altos got lost and the sopranos, using the wrong note for their cue, went flat.

"Try again," urged Matthew. "This is sounding really quite good now."

Baal was supplicated again, this time with more accuracy. Had there been a Baal, Phryne thought, he would have at least heard them. Whether he replied was always problematical, with gods. Elijah was defying them, saying there are a lot of you, calling on your god, there is only one of me, but I'm calling on the real God. The one with a capital letter.

"*Let thy flames fall and extirpate the foe!*" the people implored.

Now that had never worked. Any extirpating was going to have to be done by the people themselves. They had got themselves into this.

"*Hear us!*" cried the choir. "*Hear us!*"

From the door, Elijah replied, "*Call him louder! For he is a god. He talketh, or he is pursuing, or he is on a journey, or peradventure, he sleepeth. So awaken him, call him louder!*"

"Go on!" said Matthew, and the chorus ventured on the quartet, gathering confidence from Aunty Mark's presence.

"*Hear our cry, O Baal!*" rumbled the basses. "*Hear our cry, O Baal!*" sang the tenors, "*Hear our cry, O Baal!*" added the altos. "*Hear our cry, O Baal!*" the sopranos came in, with heavy emphasis on their G entry. "*Baal, now arise! Wherefore slumber?*"

"*Call him louder,*" sang Elijah scornfully. "*He heareth not! With knives and hatchets cut thyselves after your manner; leap upon the altar ye have made: call him and prophesy. Not a voice will answer you. None will listen. None heed you!*"

"*Baal!*" the bass voices burst out. "*Baal!*"

The chorus surged on. They knew this one, and it was coming together seamlessly now that the recit had been added in. They were singing for Aunty, who was now leaning on the conductor's podium, concentrating. Phryne thought him very handsome. But she always found intellectual processes intriguing. This was an expert singer listening to the chorus like a mechanic listening to an engine, trying to locate the (metaphorical) knocking noise which interrupted the smooth operation of the motor. And he himself was part of that operation. Who is the singer, and who the song?

Singing in a choir feels good, Phryne thought. The voices, the deep breathing, the exhilaration of listening to the parts fitting together, like a musical puzzle, like the music of the spheres (which would have to be four-part harmony). *"Mark how the scorner derideth us!"* sang the people, seconds before they had to change sides and become Israelites.

"Draw near all ye people," sang Mark. *"Come to me!"*

As Elijah sang his prayer, Phryne examined all the faces she could see. None were angry. Even Leonard was listening to Aunty with admiration. Aunty Mark was a universal favourite. Then why did Phryne feel uneasy? Everyone loved Mr. Henty, the celebrated baritone. She shook herself and paid attention to her score.

"Lord God of Abraham," sang Mark, *"Isaac and Israel, O hear me, O hear me and answer me—"* He coughed. He stopped. He waved at Matthew. "Sorry. You go on: 'Cast Thy Burden.'"

The one chorus in this oratorio which everyone

liked and everyone knew was "Cast Thy Burden" and the choir segued into it easily. "*Cast thy burden upon the Lord, and he shall sustain thee,*" they sang, almost note-perfect. Phryne thought of all her soldiers, and hoped that they too were sustained: all the lost and injured and shell-shocked and mad. After all, if you have to cast a burden on someone, why not the Lord? Wasn't that what he was for?

"*He never will suffer for the righteous to fall: he is at thy right hand.*"

She hoped this was true. Things were about to become rather perilous, what with a sadistic warlord attempting to kill people of whom she was fond. *And me, of course,* she added to herself. This really was beautiful music.

"*Let none be made ashamed that wait upon thee!*" declaimed the choir.

Matthew let his hands fall and the choir relaxed, grinned, laughed with relief.

"That was really good!" said Tommy, sounding amazed. "Of course, we aren't supposed to be singing it, it's a quartet, but that sounded really good! Maybe he'll let us sing it."

"We've got it," said Calliope.

"Tea break," announced Matthew. "That was good, friends. If we can manage the rest of the work as well as that, we will have done a very good thing."

"Tea," said Mark. "I never drink the stuff.

Ruins the voice. A good working champagne is what a singer needs. I didn't know you were rehearsing—why didn't you tell me?" He sounded a little hurt.

Matthew hastened to explain. "We were just note-bashing. James is so—"

"Much of a bastard," put in Tommy.

"That we thought we'd better be prepared for him."

"I'd use an axe, myself," commented Mark. "Or you could think about stoning him to death. That ought to add an edge to the work. "*Take all the prophets of Baal…*"" he sang and the choir joined in with fervour.

"*Let none of them escape you!*"

"See?" He grinned. He did not accept tea but drank hot water.

Phryne noticed that Daniel had taken Josephine's hand and kissed it. Nice. Really, she could choir-watch for hours. They were so volatile.

Someone pressed against her from behind. Ah, her constant ithyphallic admirer.

"*Ciao,* Luigi," she said, without turning her head.

"*Ciao, bella!*" he replied into her neck.

"*Dove é Zio Guido?*" she asked.

"*Zio Guido é morte,*" he replied. He was surprised, but he did not remove his hot hand from her hip. Phryne wriggled a little to dislodge it. She turned and looked into his face and saw nothing but relatively uncomplicated lust in those liquid brown eyes.

He was just about to ask how she knew Zio Guido when they were back onstage and Mark led into the next chorus.

"*O Thou, who makest thine angels spirits, thou whose ministers are flaming fires, let them now descend!*"

The choir answered with such force that Phryne expected to see the score burst into flames. Another fugue: alto and soprano together, bass and tenor. They were the faithful people witnessing a miracle which would save their prophet's head. They put the *fuoco* into *allegro con fuoco*.

"*The fire descends from heaven!*"

Phryne wouldn't have been more than half surprised if it had. And wouldn't the Scots Church be annoyed. What would their insurance company say? Act of God?

◇◇◇

Phryne went home for a little rest, some honey and lemon, to which she added a judicious quantity of whisky, and a round-up of the day's news. Nothing out of the way had happened, which was pleasant. She felt at a loss. Her lover had moved on, Lin

Chung wasn't back from Hong Kong for another fortnight, and she felt vaguely restless. Her body had become accustomed to a pleasant and engrossing lover every night. Now her bed was empty. She almost wished that Ratcliffe would make his move.

"Drat it all," said Phryne, and took Molly out for a walk. She was passing peaceably along the footpath, trailing her sunshade, the picture of innocence. A picture that positively cried out "Shoot me now!"

She was quite pleased when she heard the "potato-potato" of the Harley. As the assassin approached, slowing markedly—she surmised that he had a pistol and thus needed to get quite close—she stepped aside, thrust the steel-shafted umbrella into the spokes and gave him a strong push. The bike shuddered and the engine screamed. The rider fell hard. Phryne pounced. She dragged him off the road and dropped onto his chest with both knees. Molly stood next to his head, snarling.

She ripped off the flying helmet and goggles and stared down into a pair of terrified eyes. Male, spotty, young.

"Are you going to tell me why you were trying to kill me, or am I going to let Molly tear out your throat?" she asked affably.

Obligingly, Molly snarled again. She really did have excellent teeth. Primal terror transfixed the assassin. Mammalian ancestors shrieked at him to run, climb, hide from the dire wolf. He did not even think of grabbing for the pistol on the lanyard round his neck.

"You…you can't…"

"Oh, but I can," Phryne assured him warmly.

"You wouldn't…"

"Ah, but I would," she said.

"No!" he wailed.

Phryne thought that she had better conclude this before he collapsed from terror.

"I'm going to let you up," she said, climbing off his body and souveniring the pistol, which she levelled at his head. "You're going to pick up your bike and go away. And you're going to tell Mr. Ratcliffe, from me, that if he comes near any of my household—or me—again, I will destroy him. Repeat the message."

After a few false starts, the assassin managed to repeat it, word for word.

"Off you go," said Phryne. "Oh, and tell him he owes me three pounds. That was a very good sunshade."

He pulled his bike back onto its misshapen wheels, removed the mangled sunshade, and limped away, pushing the machine. Molly barked him out of sight.

"That was instructive," Phryne told her. "Good dog!"

She felt much better.

◇◇◇

Rehearsal that night was worse than the night before. Phryne was impressed. She hadn't thought he could get any worse. But there was Henry James the conductor, shoving back his black hair, licking his forefinger, snarling at the choir. Even the chorus that they had got right during the day lost focus and died under his ferocious baton.

"You're useless, every one of you!" he yelled finally. Phryne thought he looked rather green— surely they hadn't been that bad? And again he finished the rehearsal early. He rushed out into the street, leaving the choir to finish their tea in disconsolate silence.

"Perhaps we should just abandon the concert," suggested Julia, clasping her hands. "And it was my chance at singing in the quartet!"

"No, dammit, we're not going to allow that bastard to upset us like this," stated Matthew. "Come on, let's sing something to cheer ourselves up, and then we can go on to Aunty Mark's. '*Come again!*'" he sang.

The others looked at each other, but the gravitational pull of the song was too strong.

"*Come again! Sweet love doth now invite! Thy graces that refrain, to do thee due delight…*"

Phryne loved this one. The voices chiming in exactly on time and in key made her shiver with a sensual pleasure which also belonged to scented hot bath water, a lover's mouth, or green chartreuse.

"*To see,*" sang the sopranos.

"*To feel,*" sang the altos.

"*To touch,*" sang the tenors.

"*To kiss,*" thundered the basses.

"*To die!*" they sang, a musical orgasm. "*With thee again, in sweetest sympathy.*"

"*Come again! That I may cease to mourn, at thy unkind disdain, for now lost and forlorn…*"

"*I sit,*" sang Julia.

"*I sigh,*" sang Calliope.

"*I weep,*" sang Josephine, looking at Daniel.

"*I faint,*" sang Luigi, staring at Phryne.

"*I die, in deadly pain, and endless misery,*" sang LobeliaandDavid, to each other.

"*Gentle love! Draw forth thy wounding dart. Thou canst not pierce her heart. For I that do approve…*"

"*By sighs,*" sang Tommy to Caterina.

"*And tears,*" sang Millicent to Luke.

"*More hot,*" sang Geneva to Luigi, who was distracted from Phryne for a moment.

"*Than are,*" sang Oliver to Chloe.

"*Thy shafts,*" sang Jenny to Bones.

"*Do tempt, while she, while she for triumphs, laughs.*"

On cue, Caterina laughed.

There was a moment's silence, and then they all joined in. God bless Dowland, thought Phryne. She hoped he was very happy, swapping tunes with Mozart in heaven.

She was following the choir out of the hall, en route to one of Aunty Mark's little soirees, when she found the score on a bench. That score. It had the requisite pages torn out. It was not marked with a name. The cover would never take fingerprints and, in any case, any member of the choir would have a right to handle it. Another dead end. Drat again.

She put it back where she found it.

Just ahead of her, Leonard was arguing with Professor Szabo.

"He's the conductor, he rules the choir," he said. "Unhappily."

"He is a butcher," said the old man. "He has no respect for the music. Neither does your Elijah."

"No, really, Prof, he's singing it beautifully," protested Calliope. "You didn't hear him sing the recit in "Baal, We Cry to Thee" today. Scornful. Perfect."

"He interrupted the music to sing the Pirate King," said the old man stubbornly. "No respect."

"Have it your way," said Calliope. "Are you coming with us to the party?"

"No," said the old man. "I go home." And he went.

"Not like him to turn down free booze," commented Tommy.

"Never mind," said Calliope comfortably. "He's upset. Come along," she said, and the choristers went down the steps.

Phryne was in two minds. Party? Singing? Go home and spend a blameless evening and a chaste and pure night?

Only one mind, really. She set off after them.

◇◇◇

Aunty Mark had the best parties. She was briefly drawn into a consultation with Gawain.

"I worry about him," said Gawain. His plain face was concerned.

"Why?" asked Phryne. Aunty Mark was singing, glass in hand, the picture of Dionysian splendour.

"He's so bold." Gawain shivered. "He takes risks."

"Only in trusted company," said Phryne. "But, look, here's my card. If he gets into any trouble, ring. I'll come right away."

"Oh thanks," said Gawain with real gratitude. "Thanks. That's very kind of you."

"Pleasure," said Phryne, and went to get another glass of wine.

Now that Luigi was staying away from her he was unwearying in his pursuit of Geneva—such a relief—she had time to sip excellent champagne and appreciate caviar and sing rude songs. Not that they were all rude. Some, of course, detailed the adventures of the young apprentice in the chandler's shop, the regrettable hirsuteness of the Mayor of Bayswater's charming little daughter or spoke of remarkable engineering achievements involving reciprocating wheels, but others were just songs, sung with the heartiness of people who knew how to sing and had abolished any shyness with alcohol and good company in about equal quantities.

"*Fine knacks for ladies! Cheap, choice, brave and new! Good penny worths, but money cannot move,*" sang Aunty Mark, a creditable falsetto.

"*I keep a fair but for the fair to view,*" replied the choir. "*A beggar may be liberal of love.*"

Then, all together, they sang, "*Though all my wares be trash, the heart is true, the heart is true, the heart is true.*"

"*Great gifts are guiles, and look for gifts again,*" sang Luigi to Geneva. "*My trifles come, as treasures from my mind.*"

The song went on. Aunty Mark had a fair soprano and was enjoying the song immensely. When they reached the last verse, Phryne found herself standing near Matthew. His face was slightly flushed, his lips soft and red, his eyes trout pools where sensual fishes lurked.

"*But in this heart, where Beauty serves and loves,*" sang Matthew to Phryne.

"*Turtles and twins, courts brood a heavenly pair,*" sang Phryne to Matthew.

Dowland was doing a lot of the talking in this gathering.

"*Happy the man who thinks of no remove, of no remove, of no remove.*"

He really couldn't be a murderer, Phryne was telling herself, shifting closer. Just as she had decided to kiss now and think about it later, the door banged open and Leonard ran into the room. He was manic, dishevelled, and panting.

"Henry James is dead!" he cried. "Now I get to be conductor!"

◇◇◇

After that there was not a lot of point to continuing the song. They gathered around Leonard, glasses in hand, firing questions at him.

"Dead? Are you sure?" asked Calliope.

"Yes," said Leonard. "I went to his hotel room

to…to have a discussion about what he was doing to poor Mendelssohn, and the door was open and he was there on the floor."

"Dead?" asked Chloe.

"Really dead?" squeaked Julia. Phryne noted that Tommy had stationed himself behind her in case she fainted. He was the Harmony Choir designated Julia-catcher. She was far too interested to faint.

"Henry James dead?" demanded Mark, in his booming Elijah voice.

"Yes. I saw him," babbled Leonard. "Now I have to be conductor."

They all looked at him.

"I have to be," he insisted, his voice taking on an hysterical edge. "It's my turn!"

"Be that as it may," said Phryne, pushing to the front of the group, "what have you done?"

"Me?" asked Leonard, quailing a little.

"Yes. About this death. Have you called the police? An ambulance? Told the management?"

"No, I came straight here to tell you that I have to be—"

"Right," said Phryne. She exchanged exasperated glances with Matthew and Aunty Mark. "Mark, you keep him here. Give him another drink. Bones, Tabitha, come with me. What is his room number?"

Leonard told her. Someone thrust him down into a chair and shoved a drink into his hands. They were trembling.

"I understand why you're taking him, he's a medical student, but why me?" asked Tabitha, nevertheless putting down her drink and her young man and joining Phryne at the door.

"You're a vet," said Phryne. "You're not squeamish. And I want a couple of irreproachable witnesses if matters are…as I think they might be."

"What do you think?"

"I don't know, I haven't thought it yet," said Phryne. "Come along. He might only be terribly ill, and that idiot left him on the floor."

But when they reached the conductor's room, it was clear that Leonard might be an idiot in many ways, but he knew dead when he saw it. Dead, horribly. The floor bore witness to the violence of his vomiting. The room stank. Tabitha and Bones watched from the door as Phryne tiptoed in and touched the dead throat.

"Newly dead," she said. "He's still warm. But definitely deceased. Let's shut this door, and we'll tell the management and get them to ring the police."

"Why do we need the police?" asked the medical student. "That death could have had many causes."

"And the most obvious one?" asked Phryne, raising her eyebrows.

"Poisoning," said Tabitha. "Do keep up, Bones! A strong poison, at that. Not strychnine. Perhaps digitalin? Most poisons produce vomiting and purging; the system tries to rid itself of the agent. That's why they're so bad in horses, who can't vomit."

"Right," said Bones faintly.

"You go back to the party and sit down," said Tabitha kindly. "We can do the rest."

Tabitha was so sensible and bracing and she was excellent company when one had to go and advise the management of a very prestigious hotel that one of their guests was (probably) the victim of either a homicide or a suicide.

They took it as well as could be expected.

Tabitha and Phryne went back to the party, which had toned down a lot. Aunty Mark consulted Phryne with a look as she returned and shut the door. She nodded. He immediately announced, "Now is the time for a good solid lament. 'Weep, O Mine Eyes.'"

Matthew took up a spoon and began to conduct.

"*Weep, o mine eyes, weep, o mine eyes, and cease not*," they sang.

That John Bennet must have been really cheerful company, thought Phryne, mind racing. Who had killed Henry James? The trouble was there were so many possibilities. If possible, he was even more hated than Hedley Tregennis. Even Phryne had forced her homicidal feelings down, though she would never have resorted to poison. She just wanted to shoot him where he stood, abusing the répétiteur. That would have been nice.

No one stood out, except the loon presently getting stuck into his second glass of gin and grinning. Would Leonard kill Henry James for the chance to conduct? It did appear likely.

The song moved into Mozart's *Ave verum corpus*, one of the most agonisingly beautiful laments he ever wrote.

"*Ave verum corpus*," sang Tabitha at her ear, "*natum de Maria Virgine…*"

Phryne kept thinking, singing without concentration, until the music swelled into the "*in cruce pro homine.*" Then she stopped thinking at all.

◇◇◇

It was to a grave and solemn *Requiem aeternam* that Detective Inspector Robinson arrived at the crime scene, though he was by no means sure that it was even a crime. But the initial search of the room had found no poison, and no box, bottle, paper, or glass which could have held poison. And when he saw Phryne Fisher emerging from the musical room his heart sank.

"So it is a murder, then," he said to her.

"Yes, I expect so," she replied. "I suggest you have a very serious word with Leonard Match. He really, really wants to be conductor."

"Seems like a minor motive for two murders," demurred the detective inspector.

"It's not," said Phryne. "And we've known murders done over tuppence and a funny look."

"So we have," he said heavily. "Right. Let them keep singing, and I'll interview them one by one. Don't want your Leonard to bolt."

"Any idea how long he's been dead?"

"Only hours," said Jack Robinson.

"Because he was looking a bit green at rehearsal and he finished it early," said Phryne.

"So he might have eaten or drunk it at your rehearsal?" asked Robinson. Singers. He hated talking to singers.

"We didn't see him eat or drink anything, and he rushed off before tea. So if it was there, he must have brought it with him."

"Well, well, maybe he's a suicide—but we haven't found a note."

"He would have left one," Phryne was certain. "Something like 'what an artist is lost in me.'"

"Nero," returned Jack. "Last words."

"You never cease to surprise me, Jack," Phryne told him.

Chapter Fifteen

Like a rose rabbi, later, I pursued,
And still pursue, the origin and course
Of love, but until now I never knew
That fluttering things have so distinct a shade.

Wallace Stevens
"Le Monocle de Mon Oncle"

Phryne had returned home late and alone. Questioning choristers had been as fruitless as Robinson knew it would be, but he had grimly done it anyway. The result was a lot of people who alibied each other in a vague way—There were five tenor voices in the semi-chorus of "He Spoke the Word"—which added up to a large amount of nothing much.

The police were searching the Scots Church hall and the hotel room for anything which might have contained poison, and so far were not finding it. Leonard Match had voluntarily, for a strict sense of the word, emptied his pockets and revealed hand-kerchiefs and loose Dr. McKenzie's Menthoids and some paper which might have contained a white powder, which he could not currently explain, being drunker than several skunks. Robinson had filed him in the holding cells for the night, until he became a little more lucid.

Would anyone really kill two conductors to take over a choir?

It seemed unlikely. But Miss Fisher was involved, and that always saw the Unlikeliness Quotient rocket sky high.

Robinson took himself home for four hours' sleep, Mark calmed the choristers and sent them away, and Phryne went home by herself. There were places she could have gone, things she could have done. But she wasn't in the mood for indelicate delights. What she really wanted was a cup of cocoa, a bath and a soft bed.

When she came in all the household was fast asleep. Only Molly gave a formal "wuff" of greeting and then lay down again with her head on her paws. Phryne walked slowly upstairs, forgot the cocoa in favour of a tot of brandy, and put herself to bed. She was exhausted.

And so, she did not sleep immediately, but allowed her mind to rove freely over the available evidence. She considered the death of Tregennis:

his mistress had drugged him, but an adventitious passer-by had stifled him with that torn-out music from a choral score. An unmarked choral score. Not one of the two that were missing. Then Henry James: a cruel and stupid man with no manners or mercy and a list of enemies that must far outweigh his friends. Both men were such very good candidates for murder, and—what did one make of Leonard Match? Did he want to be conductor so badly that he would kill for it? The murder of Tregennis had been a matter of seizing an opportunity, but the murder of James had required planning. Arsenic, for example, might have been the poison, and that had to be signed for in the Poisons Book. This was a legal requirement for any poison sale. The medical examiner was doing an analysis. Soon Robinson would know what had caused James' demise. And he would tell Phryne.

So all Phryne had to do was go to sleep, and the morning would bring answers. She embraced a pillow, hugging it to her body, and snuggled into her clean sheets. She fell asleep at last, and dreamed of music.

◇◇◇

She was awoken by Dot bringing coffee and her croissant and the news that Detective Inspector Robinson wanted a quick word.

"I'm staying in bed this morning, Dot; I promised myself a lie-in. If he just wants a quick word, he can come up here."

"Well, you're decent enough, Miss," agreed Dot. Phryne had donned an extravagant red silk gentleman's dressing gown over her nightgown. It was rather too large for her, but it presently smelt of John Wilson, and Phryne liked the scent. Dot liked the golden dragons.

Dot relayed the message via the house phone, and poured Phryne another cup of coffee. Presently Jack Robinson plodded up the stairs.

"How goes it?" Phryne asked.

"Examiner reckons an acute dose of an irritant poison, probably arsenic," he told her. He slumped down into an armchair and Dot poured him coffee, too. He looked as though he needed it.

Jack Robinson was only familiar with coffee from a Bushell's Coffee and Chicory Essence bottle with a genie on it. The real thing came as something of a shock to his tastebuds. Then he gulped.

"So, antimony, arsenic, rat poison, something like that?" asked Phryne.

"Yair," agreed Robinson. "You sure he didn't eat or drink while he was with the choir?"

"Yes," said Phryne. "He was in my direct line of sight the whole time. He was unusually unpleasant to the sopranos—usually he has it in for the altos—and I'm a soprano, so I was watching him closely. For my cue. Also, trying to work out where to stick a stiletto for maximum efficiency," she admitted. "Another murder victim who has been positively begging for an unpleasant death, though possibly not this unpleasant."

"Yair, it was nasty, all right," said Robinson. He leaned back in the soft chair and closed his eyes. Just for a moment.

"Dot, ring down for another pot of coffee. Jack, you're falling asleep, and you don't want to do that until you can sleep for more than a few minutes."

Dot obeyed. Phryne let him drift until the fresh pot of coffee came. "Dot, would you pour the detective inspector a cup of black coffee with a lot of sugar? Drink it down, Jack dear, and your eyes will just pop open."

"Jeez," observed Jack Robinson, having absorbed the black, bitter, oversweet liquid. "You're right. Now, where was I?"

"Asking if I was sure that he didn't eat or drink while with the choir."

"Yair, I remember." Robinson was dealing with a rush of caffeine into his bloodstream. It felt very strange. But good. He'd have to find out how to make this sort of coffee. It was only a matter of time until it became an illegal drug. "You're sure?"

"Certain. But he did begin to get sick while I was watching him. He turned green, finished the rehearsal early with curses all round, and ran out."

"Then where did he get the stuff?"

"Perhaps he wasn't feeling well from natural causes. He looked like a man who liked good food and wine. He might have lunched too well, felt ill, and rushed back to his hotel to take some patent remedy—which had the poison in it."

"Yair, except there's no sign of it in the room."

"Then the murderer took it away. He hadn't been dead long when I saw him, Jack. He was still warm. But no pulse, no respiration."

"You don't think he could have still been alive?"

"No," said Phryne, wrapping the dressing gown closer around her thin frame. "I know death when I see it."

Jack Robinson believed her.

"All right. Any bets on who did it?"

"If it wasn't Leonard, I can't imagine who did it. They all hated him. But poison's difficult. The murderer can be miles away when the actual murder happens."

"Yair, it's a bastard all right. Anything on the… other front?" he asked.

"I warned off a young thug on a Harley yesterday. Since then I haven't heard a thing."

"You didn't injure him?" asked Jack, getting up.

"No, I just threatened to allow Molly to tear out his throat. I must say she played up to it splendidly. Some dogs do have a sense of theatre, I find. Why?"

"Harley and rider found in the river this morning," Jack told her. "Fouled a chain-link ferry. Cut throat."

"Not me," promised Phryne, crossing her gold-embroidered dragon with a wet forefinger.

"Right. Just asking," said Jack.

"But here," said Phryne, reaching into a drawer, "is his gun. It was on a lanyard round his neck. British Army-issue Webley Mark VI. I borrowed one during the war."

"There must be thousands of 'em kicking around," observed Jack.

"I expect so," said Phryne. "You'll let me know about the autopsy?"

"Yair," said Jack and went away, slightly dizzy with caffeine.

◇◇◇

Phryne lay back in her bed and sipped her own coffee. Mr. Ratcliffe was a stringent employer, and clearly had never been told that it was unwise to shoot the messenger. Fewer people would now be willing to bring him bad news, and warlords needed to know what was happening.

She had ensured that young man's death as surely as if she had shot him herself.

As she was willing to do that, she did not allow the notion to upset her. Instead, she found her copy of *Bleak House*, adjusted her pillows, and read herself back to sleep, until Dot woke her at noon with the news that her bath was run and she had a visitation of choristers.

"Which ones?" she asked sleepily.

"They gave their names as Matthew, Calliope, Bones, Caterina, Tommy, Tabitha, and Oliver," said Dot, consulting her list.

"Right, well, they are welcome, and they can wait until I've finished my bath. Offer them some refreshments, Dot, and I shall be down directly. I don't feel like doing anything energetic today so I shan't dress. And tell Mrs. B that was very good coffee. Her coffee would raise Lazarus."

Dot looked pained at the blasphemy. "Miss," she protested.

"All right, tell her that it raised a partially unconscious policeman," Phryne offered. "Poor Jack. Nothing but problems. Tell me, Dot, any sign of watchers? Any trouble?"

"No, nothing," said Dot, crossing herself. "Thank the Lord."

"And what is everyone doing?"

"Tinker and Jane are playing chess in the

garden, Molly is keeping an eye on the back gate, Ruth is in the parlour making a scrapbook of recipes, and I'm here," said Dot. "Ember is in the kitchen, because Mrs. Butler is making fish pie."

"I love that fish pie," said Phryne, shedding her dressing gown. The scent would fade within a few days, and that would be the end of John Wilson in Phryne's life. She would miss him.

"So does Ember," said Dot meaningfully. Ember was an expert snatch-and-run bandit. Mrs. Butler had better keep a heavy pot lid over her cooling fish.

Phryne bathed in a leisurely fashion, dressed in her aquamarine gown, and went down the stairs to find a knot of choristers too excited to sing, which was an index of how excited they were.

"The cops think Leonard did it!" exclaimed Matthew.

"And what do you think?" asked Phryne, sitting down. Her blue-green dress flowed around her. Matthew found her distracting.

"We…" He faltered. "We don't know."

"You mean, 'I don't know,'" snapped Tabitha. "It's a silly idea. Even though he has got one of those French things about conducting…"

"An *idée fixe*?" asked Phryne.

"Yes, one of those. About being a great conductor."

"Is he a good conductor?" asked Phryne.

They all exchanged glances.

"No," said Tommy.

"In a word, no," agreed Calliope. "He cares about it too much. He has to examine the history of every note and why it is where it is. Nothing ever gets done and he can't forgive the slightest error."

"So, not destined to be a great conductor?" asked Phryne again.

"Never," said Matthew sadly. "It's a pity."

"But, as I was saying, he isn't a murderer," insisted Tabitha.

"How do you know, Tab?" asked Oliver, rubbing a hand through his unruly red hair.

"I just do," she stated.

"That isn't actually evidence, you know," observed Bones. "People with an obsession will do anything to get what they want. I haven't done psychiatric practice yet, but that's what the textbook says. I looked it up," he added.

"Yes, but really! The two murders aren't the same. One was just because someone walked past and found Tregennis dying. The other must have needed planning," argued Tabitha.

"Precisely what I told Detective Inspector Robinson this morning," said Phryne. "There are two explanations. One is that there are two murderers."

"There are enough people who would want James gone, if not actually dead and gone," agreed Caterina.

"But that means there are two murderers in the one choir!" protested Oliver. "That's really unlikely!"

"The whole situation is really unlikely," said Matthew. "Unlikely doesn't mean impossible."

"True. Use the Sherlock Holmes maxim and what do you get?" asked Phryne. "Either two murderers with entirely different motives in the one choir, or one murderer who might have just found Tregennis lying on the floor, probably with his mouth open, and stuffed music into it on impulse. And then, he knew he could kill. So the same murderer planned the death of James. When my policeman comes back I shall know what sort of poison was employed. Which thesis do you consider most probable?"

"One killer," conceded Matthew. "Two really is pushing probability further than it will go."

"All right, now if it isn't Leonard, then who is it?" Phryne paused as Mr. Butler brought in the tea trolley. The choir poured tea and milked and sugared and tasted the petits fours and thought.

"Who hated James the most?" asked Tommy.

"Everyone, really," answered Calliope. "He nagged and cursed all of us. He usually played favourites, which was always embarrassing, especially for the favourite. You know, call as it might be Caterina out of the choir, tell everyone they ought to be able to sing as prettily as she can, make her sing the soprano part, abuse the sopranos for not being Caterina."

"And make Caterina wish she wasn't there," said Caterina feelingly. "But he hasn't had time to pick out the favourites with this choir."

"He's just been sticking to generalised abuse," said Bones. "He doesn't like altos. Maybe an alto killed him."

"Very funny," replied both the altos present.

"We really don't know," confessed Bones. "I still think that it could be Leonard. In which case he really isn't fit to plead, and will spend the rest of his life in a nice comfortable bin, conducting the lunatics' choir."

"You really are a cold-hearted bastard, aren't you?" asked Calliope.

"He's a medical student," explained Phryne. "He'll get his compassion back once he's dealing with people."

"Or?" asked Matthew, who was quick.

"Or he'll become a surgeon," said Phryne. "Let us consider anyone with medical expertise. How about you, Bones? Could you lay hands on anything like antimony?"

"God, yes, there's a jar of it in the lab," replied the student. "Arsenic, too. Strychnine. On the open shelves. But, as it happened, I didn't."

"And you?" Phryne looked at Tabitha.

"It's in rat poison," she replied. "So I know how to treat animals that have been poisoned. But I didn't, and I wouldn't. Thanks for asking," she added, and took another petit four.

"Matthew?"

"No, it wasn't me. I don't know anything about poisons." He looked quite unmoved by the accusation.

"Calliope?"

Calliope flushed red with anger. "No! How can you ask? I don't even use rat poison. I just acquired a serviceable cat. He's called Orion, the mighty hunter. Oh, and here's another…I bet you're a great big dangerous rat killer, eh, beautiful boy?"

Ember, foiled of his attempts to get at the fish, had hopped up onto the garden table to see if anyone had a little milk or possibly even cream to spare. He nosed agreeably at Calliope's cheek as she leaned down to talk to him. He knew that tone. It meant food and devotion. He liked both.

Calliope could not possibly have poisoned James, thought Phryne, watching her carefully scooping the cream off her apple tart and feeding it to Ember, lick by lick.

"Tommy?" continued Phryne.

"I don't know nothing about poisons, and if I wanted to kill James, I would have thumped him." This was self-evident, and in the event James would have stayed thumped.

"Oliver?"

"God, no," he said.

"Caterina?"

"It wasn't her," said Tommy instantly.

"Let me speak for myself," said Caterina, pushing Tommy's protective hand from her shoulder. "No, it wasn't me. I'm Italian but my name is Caterina, not Lucrezia."

"Indeed. And it wasn't me," Phryne told them. "Are you going on with the concert?"

"Probably," said Matthew. "We really need the money. I can carry on as rehearsal master until we get a new conductor. We're getting quite good," he added hopefully. "And Aunty Mark has come down from Sydney specially for this concert, as well."

"And your new conductor isn't going to be Leonard? I mean, even if he didn't kill the previous conductors?"

"No," said Matthew. "Poor chap. He'll be so disappointed."

"Well, keep me informed," Phryne told him. "And, listen, Matthew—be careful. Someone doesn't like your conductors. I think you are…

charming—" her voice held a world of promise "—and I don't want harm to come to you."

"All right," Matthew told her. "I'll be careful."

"Good," said Phryne, and had them ushered out. Something was itching at a corner of her mind, and she wanted to think.

◇◇◇

Twenty minutes' hard thinking just got her a memory of a Renaissance portrait of a pale, sad lady. Bugger, thought Phryne, and decided that she needed distraction.

Unfortunately there was no one around who seemed likely to provide it. She was not good enough at chess to understand the game Tinker and Jane were playing. Mrs. Butler was busy. Finally she joined Ruth in the parlour, cutting out the recipes which she had saved from newspapers and magazines as Ruth glued them into her scrapbook and spoke excitedly of feasts to come. Phryne found her company soothing.

◇◇◇

John Wilson sat in his own room, trying to gather his wits. It had been a fascinating but shattering couple of days and he felt as though he had been broken into small pieces, pieces which had then been jumped up and down upon by elephants and then reconstructed with strong glue in an unexpected form. He had lost a lover, Phryne, and found a lover, Rupert Sheffield. He felt honoured and terrified in about equal proportions. Now Sheffield had him, John Wilson, what would he do with him (John Wilson)? Had Sheffield ever had a lover, of either gender, before? If so, what had he done to them? Were bits of them scattered in some foreign field? How could he ask? He didn't have the words. But he really needed to know. When Sheffield said—insisted on—forever, how long was that? Next week? Next year? Until Rupert got bored? Until Rupert got them killed?

More likely to be until Rupert got him, John, killed. But that didn't matter. He still needed to know. He had told Phryne that if she calculated incorrectly and Rupert rejected him, she would break his heart. He wasn't at all sure that it might not now be exploded into a thousand pieces, now that he knew what lying all night in Sheffield's arms felt like.

It felt like he had died and gone to heaven.

But John reminded himself that he was a doctor and had survived the Battle of the Somme and was supposed to fall with his face to the foe, and all that. Humming "Land of Hope and Glory," not entirely ironically, he stood up to open the communicating door between their rooms and found

Sheffield standing on the other side, hand out to grasp the handle.

"Ah," said John, taking the hand in both of his own.

"Come in," said Sheffield. "Are you having second thoughts? This isn't going to be easy. We are an illegal relationship. We will have to watch every public move."

"I know," said John. "No, I have no second thoughts."

"But you have questions," said Rupert. The violet eyes flicked over his face. "Ask, and I'll answer."

"I think I'd like to sit down," said John. His injured leg was threatening to collapse under him. Sheffield locked the communicating door and the room door and lay down on his bed. He extended his arms. "Come here," he said quietly.

John lay down. He arranged their limbs so that he could look into Rupert's face.

"Ask," said Rupert.

"When you say 'forever,' my dear, what do you mean?"

Rupert arched an eyebrow. "Really, John, I thought English was your native tongue..." he began. "I mean forever, until we both die, until the end of time," he said calmly. "You are mine, I am yours."

"What if you get bored?" asked John, frantically trying not to exult.

"I won't," Rupert assured him. "You are endlessly fascinating."

"But, Rupert, have you ever had a lover before?"

"There were people who wanted me," he answered slowly. "But I did not want them. A girl kissed me, a French kiss, her *tongue* was in my *mouth*—and I felt sick. In fact I seem to remember I *was* sick. I was sixteen. I never tried that again. Women are…squelchy. Swampy."

"So, not girls. What about boys?" asked John.

"Several people in Athens tried to seduce me," said Rupert coldly. John felt instantly very sorry for them. They probably swore off sex for life. Nunneries. Monasteries. That response would have sent me straight off to Mount Athos as soon as I could get a ticket, John thought. "Then I was captured," he said. For the first time his voice broke. John embraced him and Rupert buried his face in John's shirt front for a moment. "They talked about what they were going to do to me. I realised that I had never had a lover, and after they had finished with me, I never would have. So when they got bored…"

"There was more to it than that, wasn't there?" asked John, stroking the curly hair.

"Yes, all right, yes," said Rupert, his voice ragged. "I fought. I bit and clawed and shrieked curses; I fought like a mad thing, like an animal, and I got loose and I ran straight into the ocean. I didn't care if I drowned. I swam out to sea. My back hurt, I was cold, I was weak, I started to sink. I remember looking up at the stars. Cold, distant, beautiful. Then a Greek fisherman called Yanni picked me up. He pulled me out of the sea into his little boat. He called me a merman, *thallasandros*. He dried me and put olive oil on my back and gave me wine and when he put a hand on my thigh and said, *parakalo*, please, I said, *ne*, yes. Because I could still die and I didn't want to die without finding out what love felt like."

"And what did it feel like?" asked John, very gently.

"It was cold and I was in pain but it felt… pleasant. He ruffled my hair and called me *thespoinis*. Maiden. He only had one blanket and we lay all night off Piraeus, waiting for the tide to turn. He kept me warm. I was shocked and shaking. Yanni liked me. He called me *adelphemou*, my brother. In the morning he took us into harbour, and Compton was very cross with me."

"What happened to Yanni?" asked John, filled with tenderness.

"He was killed. A U-boat. I never saw him again." And Rupert Sheffield laid down his head and wept for Yanni the fisherman, while John stroked his hair. "And I felt so sad that I thought, never again. If this is love, the pain is much greater than the pleasure. So I decided not to do it again. Until I met you. And until I saw you with your Miss Fisher."

"Did she make you jealous?" teased John.

"Hopelessly," agreed Rupert. "You're mine."

"And I have a big bruise on my neck to prove it," said John.

Rupert loosened his collar and exposed his throat, a gesture strangely like a wolf signalling submission.

"You can bite me, if you wish," he said in his cut-glass accent.

"That won't be necessary," John told him.

Rupert opened his violet eyes wide. "If I ask politely?" he said. "Please will you bite me?"

Overcome by primitive emotion, John grappled him. John pinned Rupert flat on his back, knelt over him, growled, "And you're mine!" and bit.

Rupert Sheffield laughed out loud. Marked. John, unlike Miss Fisher, was biting his throat at the junction with his shoulder. This token of possession was not meant to be generally seen. Only John would see the marks of his teeth on Sheffield and know that he was his.

John thought of everything. He must be protected at all costs. Mitchell remained a threat to John because John would die to protect Sheffield, and Sheffield could not allow that situation to continue. Mitchell thought that Sheffield had recognised him and was about to seize him and turn him over to the authorities for treason.

Surely when Sheffield offered him a deal—his silence for John's safety—then he would agree. It would be a rational outcome.

And John must not know. He would worry. He would interfere. Sheffield could handle this small matter of negotiation all on his own.

Chapter Sixteen

I help myself to material and immaterial
No guard can shut me off, no law prevent me.

Walt Whitman
"Song of Myself"

Since no one had actually died on the premises, the Scots Church allowed that night's rehearsal to go ahead. Matthew was conducting. Leonard was still in police custody. Fortunately, he had lost his temper with the arresting officer and punched him. That meant he could be charged with assaulting an officer of the law, and his lack of bail money meant that he was staying where he was.

The choir were trying to show decent regret, and not doing very well. So they were singing, instead. "He Shall Give His Angels Charge Over Thee." It was even beginning to sound beautiful.

Mendelssohn did a really good angel, Phryne considered. That was Tinker's opinion, too. Angel music. "That they should protect thee in all the ways thou goest." This was usually sung as a double quartet but the Harmony Choir had, by tradition, always sung it as a chorus. "So everyone gets to sing the pretty bits," Matthew had explained it to Phryne.

"Nice," said Matthew. "Now, we need to get 'Yet Doth the Lord See It Not' right. Just take it slow and watch the dynamic, it ought to flow, gently."

"It's *allegro vivace*," said Professor Szabo.

"Quite right," said Matthew. "But let's try it slowly to start with, all right? Then we can speed it up. We've got to put in all the notes."

"Mendelssohn," grumbled Caterina. "Too many notes."

"At bass entry—from the top," ordered Matthew, and the basses growled, "*Yet doth the Lord see it not!*"

No wonder Leonard wanted to be a conductor. The power. Raise hands and everyone sings. Make the cut-off gesture and everyone falls silent.

Matthew, however, was not at all interested in power or dominance. Phryne found that very attractive. Matthew just wanted the music to sound beautiful. And his devotion was catching. The choir, disrupted, grumpy and scratchy, began to calm and to sing out. Music did have charms to soothe the savage breast, thought Phryne, puzzling over the soprano entry, and then deciding just to go along with Chloe. She had a strong, sweet voice and she never missed a note.

Chloe, as the widow, led into the soprano solo, *"O man of God, what have I to do with you?"* singing while buffing her nails, easily, her voice creamy and accurate. When she finally donned her breastplate and mounted her horse, her Valkyrie would summon heroes into her arms before they could ask, "What hit me? Oh," which were most heroes' last words.

The widow implored Elijah for the life of her only son. Then Chloe realised that she was singing alone. Elijah was still sleeping off his hangover, probably in very tasty company.

"Sorry," she said, breaking off and flipping through her score.

"No, that was lovely," said Matthew. "Really. But if we could get on with 'Blessed Are the Men—'"

"Hear, hear," murmured Phryne. Tabitha chuckled.

"'—Who Fear Him,'" concluded Matthew firmly. "Right?"

He raised his hands. They sang. After an hour's hard work, they could sing *allegro* quite enough to be going on with *vivace* for "Yet Doth the Lord," and even Professor Szabo was pleased. The choir went to get tea and the professor began to play.

He was wonderful. Phryne forgot about tea and sat where she could see him, the hunched, elderly, drunken gnome, his miraculously undamaged fingers flowing over the keys, a Liszt piece of hideous difficulty. Even on the rehearsal piano, a cranky old grid, the music was remarkable.

"He's such a good player," murmured Matthew at Phryne's ear, offering tea. "Such a pity."

"What drove him to drink, when he had music like that in him?" asked Phryne, accepting the cup. Milk and one sugar. Just as she liked it. How lucky, or observant, of Matthew. Both qualities were useful.

"The grog got him," said Tommy sadly. "Poor old bloke. Orchestras need pianists who come to rehearsal sober. I think he got sacked a few times, then he got a job "tinkling the ivories" on a cruise ship, came to Australia, and liked it here. He can't stand the cold. That's what he said, anyway."

"You like him," said Caterina.

"Yair," said Tommy, blushing and shuffling his feet.

"I think that's very kind of you," Caterina told him.

Tommy stammered but Caterina caught the cup before he could spill hot tea all over his trousers.

Calliope smiled. "He only plays when he's happy," she told Phryne. "And that isn't very often, poor old man. We must have pleased him."

"Well, Matthew is just conducting Mendelssohn to the written tempo and dynamics," said Oliver. "That's how Mendelssohn wrote it. The prof's a Mendelssohn purist."

"And a good thing, too," observed Tabitha. "I hate all these experiments. The composer knew what he was doing."

"Hear, hear," said Tommy.

The professor finished the Liszt and began on a Chopin étude. He played for the whole break, and when the choir were again in place and Matthew announced "Open the Heavens and Send Us Relief," he segued into it without pause.

This occupied the rest of the time allowed. When they finally got it right and sang it through not only without a mistake but *andante sostenuto*, there was a loud crash overhead, and it began to rain.

And the choir began to laugh helplessly, leaning on each other, sobbing with mirth, and Professor Szabo sat at the keyboard and laughed until he wept.

◇◇◇

It was a cheerful party who stood at the door and

looked at the rain pouring down without cease. Behind her, someone began to sing the boy's solo. It was Caterina, and to the sound of the rain it was startlingly effective, the last word rising to a high surprised squeak.

"Behold! A little cloud ariseth now from the waters. It is like a man's hand. The Heavens are black with cloud and with wind: the storm rusheth louder and louder!"

And the choir sang, *"Thanks be to God for all his mercies,"* beginning with the awed whisper of those who had seen a miracle, then swelling to a triumphant shout. *"Thanks be to God, he laveth the thirsty land!"*

"The waters gather, they rush along!" sang Phryne, as the gutters filled and pedestrians ran for cover. *"The stormy billows are high, their fury is mighty!"*

They sang through to the end.

"Thanks be to God," said Matthew. "He laveth a thirsty land, you know. Now, who's got an umbrella? And are we all going to Aunty Mark's party?"

There were five umbrellas in all. The choristers ferried one another to the Windsor Hotel, singing an ironic, damp, but entirely cheerful round called "Sumer Is I-cumen' In."

Phryne still didn't know who had suffocated Tregennis, and she definitely didn't know who had poisoned Henry James (though choristers did seem like the obvious suspects), but for the moment she didn't care. If it had been Leonard, as seemed likely, he was in safe custody and that meant Matthew was safe. Phryne wondered if the Harmony Choir would find it difficult to persuade another conductor to risk this performance of *Elijah*, which seemed to be comprehensively cursed.

Still, she had sung in a scratch production of *The Gondoliers* in France, where the theatre had been shelled just when the Duke of Plaza-Toro had entered into his patter song. He had kept singing. Bits of roof had rained down on the audience. This was not a possibility in Australia. Thanks be to God.

Exhilarated by racing through the rain, they were singing silly songs. It was a silly song sort of evening.

Aunty Mark, enthroned on a large armchair probably meant for a visiting monarch, began, "*Be kind to your web-footed friends…*"

"*For a duck may be somebody's mother,*" rejoined many voices.

"*Be kind to your friends in the swamp, where the weather is always domp (to rhyme with swamp)*" explained the tenors.

"*You may think it's the end of my song, well it is, but to prove that I'm a liar,*" sang the altos.

"*I'm going to sing it again, and this time I'm going to sing it even higher*," boasted the sopranos.

Phryne enjoyed the resultant cacophony. Fortunately the Royal Suite had no floors above it. Even the Windsor might find this level of noise a little hard to tolerate in a lower room.

Finally the song reached its logical conclusion. "*You may think it's the end of my song, well it is.*"

Complete unison, absolute silence. Then they laughed and started talking again. Aunty Mark announced that tomorrow night he would have a quiet night in, with just a few drinkies and a good book. Phryne cynically doubted that he would be reading much. His friend Gawain blushed.

Phryne walked out to get a taxi not terribly late, kissed Matthew goodbye, and took herself home. When she arrived there was a message which asked her to ring Fanshawe's number.

The soothing voice of Mrs. Thomas greeted her. "Ah, yes, Miss Fisher, have you had a nice sing? Ratcliffe is preparing his warehouse for something. One of his men bought ammunition today: .455."

"A Webley," said Phryne.

"In all probability. Now, you take care, dear. Ratcliffe has eight thugs always with him. And he killed one of his motorcycle assassins because—"

"Yes, I heard," said Phryne. "Pulled out of the river. With the bike, which seems wasteful."

There was a sigh. "These criminals," said Mrs. Thomas. "Mr. Fanshawe says, anything you want, whenever you need it. Any idea what you'll need, or when?"

"I will probably need a couple of armed men, probably near that warehouse, and knowing this sort of power-mad lunatic, probably soon."

"No, they don't generally have a lot of patience, those bad sorts. I'll station two men near that warehouse, dear. Your identifying phrase is Black Cat. They can help, and they can also clean up a bit if things become messy."

"Thanks. I'll try to keep the scene as clean as I can."

"You do that, dear. Someone on this line all the time—you call if you need us. Take care of yourself, my dear."

"I shall, thank you. Happy knitting," said Phryne, and rang off.

Among the mail, there was a note from John Wilson, asking her to lunch at the Windsor on the morrow. Phryne grinned. She would certainly go. She was very tempted to take Jane, who had beaten Sheffield at chess, or Ruth, who would love the food, or Dot for the decor or Tinker for the shock value. But only her name was mentioned, so she would be lunching without domestic support.

This gave her an agreeable freedom of action. And the Windsor's food was always worth eating.

Bed, thought Phryne. Bathed and changed, she rootled out Lambie from the bottom of her wardrobe, and took him to bed with her. But when she dreamed, she dreamed not of John Wilson, now irretrievably lost (but gone to a good home). She dreamed of Matthew. And woke feeling that the day was full of promise.

This feeling persisted through the morning. Dot reported that no watchers had been seen and no suspiciously vegetable-sounding motorcycles had been heard. Tinker said that Molly had slept through the night on the foot of his bed without twitching an ear. Dot was taking the young persons to the zoo. Phryne declined to accompany them. As she paused at the door, Dot looked at Phryne and said, "You will be careful, Miss?"

And Phryne embraced her and told her, with not a single qualm, that she would.

"You go to hell for lyin'," observed Bert, who had come in through the kitchen as was his wont. He had slightly startled Phryne.

"I'll save you a seat," she snapped.

"Deal, Comrade. Oughta be real cosy down there. Meet all our old mates again," said Cec. "We brung them plans."

Phryne repented her rudeness. "Good, have

a seat, the family has all gone to the zoo. Dot likes the monkeys, Tinker loves big cats, Ruth loves feeding the bears and the elephant ride and Jane adores snakes."

"I mighta guessed it," grunted Bert. "I hope that Sailor ain't up to his antics, or Dot won't know where to look."

Phryne had once attracted the attention of the infamous Masturbating Monkey, and giggled a little at the thought of what poor Dot would do. Sailor was a mandrill who reserved his most impressive performances for when there were women in the audience. One either admired his brightly painted behind or his…well, yes, the less said the better about what you could see in his fist when he turned around. Still, it was a patriotic behind. Red, white, and blue, as Phryne remembered. PG Wodehouse had commented when he saw one, "That chap's wearing his school colours in the wrong place."

"Show me the plans," requested Phryne, as Mr. Butler brought in the beer.

"Bay Street," said Bert, running the hand not holding his bottle down the street. "Here's the warehouse. Something's been happenin' in the second one. Far as anyone knew, it was empty. Now he's moving there—men, or maybe cargo. No one's talking, and they're all jumpy."

"This gate, it's wire?" asked Phryne.

"Yair, cyclone wire. Padlock. This one's wood. Old wood, you could bash through it—though not in that pretty car of yours."

"Nice idea, but I forgot to order a tank," responded Phryne. "Guards on the gates?"

"Couple of 'em, all the time. Guns. When the local Ds see 'em, there's gonna be trouble," prophesied Bert.

"Did you see anyone watching this factory?" asked Phryne.

"One bloke with a pair of binoculars. I caught the flash from the lens," said Cec. "Dunno who he's working for."

"Me," said Phryne. "There should be two of them. If you encounter them, use my name. It's Black Cat."

"Suits yer," said Bert, holding out a hand without looking for another beer. Cec put one into his grip. They really had the most remarkable partnership. She was pretty sure they could read each other's minds. Meeting on the hot cliffs at Gallipoli had that effect. Herodotus' Spartans, fighting to the last man at the Hot Gates, Thermopylae, must have been much the same. *At first they resisted with their weapons, and when they were broken, with their hands and their teeth, until they were overcome by a new army coming from behind, and they fell and left a name that will not be forgotten.*

Phryne swallowed down a sob. The Great War never really went away, however much she tried to forget it. She hoped that she was better at strategy, in this little tiny war, than General Haig had been in his great big one. Then she snorted. The veriest schoolchild would be better at strategy than General Haig. And Phryne had left school a very long time ago.

"All right," she said. "This is what we will do."

Bert and Cec listened and approved.

When her household came home, full of buns and artificial lemonade, telling of bears and taipans and extremely rude monkeys, Phryne knew what to tell all of them. They had parts to play. They knew them. And Tinker, particularly, was very pleased at being included.

John Wilson should have his lover. And his life. Phryne had made up her mind.

◇ ◇ ◇

Phryne and Lambie slept the sleep of the entirely innocent, which was hardly fair.

The morning might have dawned fair and bright, as it tended to do in Australia in summer, but Phryne did not see it. She was in a languid mood. She bathed sumptuously, lay about impersonating an odalisque all morning, and then dressed and went to lunch at the Windsor. Her life did seem to be concentrating about this part of the city, these days.

One glance at Rupert and John revealed that they were one. At last, Phryne thought. John was glowing. He looked like the John Wilson Phryne had met on the Somme, when she had dragged him into her ambulance, though cleaner and less shell-shocked. Younger, in some senses. Happier. Some sort of *éclaircissement* must have been reached about what Rupert meant when he said "forever" and "mine." And if she had not been able to deduce that just from looking at Rupert, there was the bruise on John's neck.

Rupert looked exactly like Ember who had just polished from his whiskers the very last of the crème Chantilly. A bowl of crème Chantilly, moreover, which had been carefully placed on a high shelf out of the reach of the most athletic of cats. He had something he wanted, he had consumed it, and it was too late for anyone to demand its return.

Phryne made a point of leaning down and kissing Rupert. His skin was as white as porcelain and strangely cool under her lips.

"My dears," she said, and beamed at them.

John beamed back; Rupert looked away.

"Lunch," said John.

A waiter appeared with menus and advice about wine. Phryne ordered briskly. Rupert ordered for John.

"I say, Phryne, is it your choir that's been singing in the Royal Suite? Lovely voices," said John.

"That's my choir, and we have been plagued with murders, the latest being a poisoning death—arsenic—on your floor. Henry James. A man who had so many enemies that finding who killed him is going to be testing for the local police. There are so many candidates, including me. Horrible man."

"Aren't you going to help them?" asked John. "When I first met you again, after so many years, you said—"

"My small talents are at their disposal," said Phryne, and Rupert Sheffield actually smiled. He looked like an angel approving of Good Deeds Amongst Mankind.

"Your talents, Miss Fisher, are not small." Rupert had won the perceived contest, and felt magnanimous. Phryne thought that was nice of him. She supposed.

"Arsenic?" said John. "Silly poison to use in these modern times. We can test for it, you know."

"Marsh's test," said Phryne.

"Indeed. And we can tell from the deposit in the hair shaft how long the person has been poisoned. I gather this was a bit sudden?"

"Yes, he was ill one hour and dead the next."

"So, acute arsenical poisoning. It dissolves quite easily in a weak acid—lemon juice, say, or hot tea."

"I know, but there was no bottle or flask, no means of delivery that anyone can find. I can only assume that the murderer brought it with him and took it away when he—or, of course, she—left. But this is not a nice topic for a luncheon table. Are you enjoying your stay at the Windsor?" asked Phryne.

"I think it will always be one of my favourite hotels," responded Rupert. "Despite the singing. Then again," he added, as John frowned at him, "I have seldom heard 'The Sexual Life of the Camel' sung with such skill and fervour."

"It is one of our favourites," admitted Phryne.

Lunch proceeded through tomato soup, a rather good *boeuf en croute*, and an Australian delicacy, a pavlova, for dessert. During which Sheffield was called away to the phone.

"I think this might be it," said Phryne. "Don't take your eyes off him tonight. That isn't too harsh a task," she added.

John leaned over and grabbed her forearm. His knuckles turned white. Phryne knew that she would have a bruise on that arm. She did not move but instead took his free hand in her own. He knew that clasp. It meant safety. The dying lads in no-man's-land had felt that grasp. "Don't let him get killed," he said fiercely. "Promise!"

"I promise," said Phryne. "Remember your instructions. Don't let him out of your sight, and call me. I have it all arranged."

"All right," said John.

"Now let me go, he's coming back, and you're creasing my sleeve," said Phryne, and John laughed. He dug into the confection of meringue, fruit and cream and he and Phryne were discussing tropical fruits amicably when Sheffield came back from the telephone. He was tight-lipped. Lunch concluded shortly afterwards.

When Phryne got home, she stayed within hearing of the phone. She was waiting for trouble. Which didn't meant that she allowed anyone to miss dinner. Dot, who was not formed for combat, was given the code words and the phone number to call Fanshawe if Phryne was not home before morning. She resolved to sit up and sew. What with Mrs. Thomas knitting and Dot sewing, they ought to have the matter stitched up in no time.

Because everyone was nervous and no one could concentrate, Phryne played a noisy game of snakes and ladders with her household until, at about eight o'clock, the phone rang.

It was John Wilson, and all he said was: "Go."

"Right," said Phryne. "Minions, it is time to

don your disguises. I have to ring Bert and Cec and Fanshawe and Dr. MacMillan. Now, darlings, stay calm, stay detached, and stay out of the way of any stray ordnance. Clear?"

"Yes, Guv," said Tinker.

"Yes, Miss Phryne," chorused Ruth and Jane.

Phryne made her calls. Then she went upstairs and changed her clothes. Bert drew up outside in the taxi. Cec drew up in a battered van which had once belonged to Jno Clarke General Carrier. Or possibly still did. Cec might have borrowed it. Phryne kissed Dot and got into the van. The minions got into Bert's taxi. And they drove away.

Dot sat down in the comfortable armchair, found her embroidery and moved the light. It was going to be a long night. Before she started sewing, she took out her rosary, and began praying for Miss Phryne's intention.

Chapter Seventeen

The TRUMPET's loud Clangour
Excites us to Arms,
With shrill Notes of Anger,
And mortal Alarms.
The double double double beat
Of the thund'ring DRUM
Cryes, "Hark the FOES come;
Charge, Charge, 'tis too late to retreat."

John Dryden
"A Song for St. Cecilia's Day"

Rupert Sheffield had left John asleep in their mutual bed; an after-dinner snooze. He had kissed him goodbye and was sure that he would see him again soon. Mitchell had called and requested a meeting. Rupert could tell him that he didn't know who Mitchell was, that Mitchell was perfectly safe, and to call off his dogs before Rupert went to the local authorities. Mitchell would then do so, and

Rupert would come back. He was sure that he would be home before John woke up.

As soon as the door clicked shut, John leapt up, dragged on his clothes, found his service revolver and cracked open the door. He could see Sheffield just ahead of him. He followed, as silent as a famished wolf who had been short of fresh lamb for a very long season of winter.

He lurked until he heard Sheffield tell the doorman, "Bay Street, Port Melbourne." Then he telephoned Phryne with the code word from the lobby telephone, and was soon in his own taxi, in pursuit.

The taxi driver was chatty. He might not have entirely believed the reasons that John gave for his visit to the most dire portion of Bay Street, but money was money, and the fare was an affable bloke and very sound on cricket. And he was very nice about Bradman, considering he was a Pom.

Arrived, John saw the last flick of Sheffield's coat as he rounded a shabby warehouse, and caught up with him.

"What are you doing here?" hissed Rupert.

"I'll always be here," said John. "At your back. Bare is man's back that is brotherless."

"I'm just going to talk to the man," said Rupert. "You shouldn't be here."

"Oh, yes," said John, sliding a hand around

Rupert's jaw and holding him so that he had to look into John's eyes. "This is what 'forever' means, my dear. You don't walk into danger on your own. Not anymore."

"Oh," said Sheffield. "I hadn't thought of that."

"Think of it now," said John.

"My aim was to keep you safe," said Rupert.

"And if you get killed doing so, I shall follow," said John. "Promptly."

Rupert ran a finger down John's neck to the love bite. One flesh.

"All right. Let's go," said Rupert, and John followed, his Webley in his hand, hoping frantically that Phryne's plans were sounder than those of General Haig.

The warehouse, when they forced the rusted doors open, was dark and quiet. But some sort of noise—shouts and thuds—was happening at the other side of the building. John was alert for sentries and spies and danger, but couldn't see much in the dim light. Of course, this Mitchell bloke—Phryne had called him Ratcliffe—would give orders that Rupert should pass unmolested. That didn't mean that marksmen weren't hidden in this infernal gloom.

"Mr. Sheffield," said the man from the darkness of the warehouse.

"Mr. Mitchell," said Sheffield. "I do not know

you and I do not need to know you. What you are doing here is no concern of mine. You can forget about me. You do know that I have never seen your face?"

"Let's keep it that way," said Mr. Mitchell. A very educated English voice.

Sheffield's mind raced. "Born in Leeds, probably a working man's child, went to a local school, won a scholarship to a public school—Eton, I think—and thence to Cambridge. Sciences," drawled Rupert. "Main motivation: money."

"Money is power," said Mitchell.

"A certain sort of power, yes," agreed Sheffield. "Well, here I am. What do you want with me?"

"I'm going to kill you," said Mr. Mitchell.

"I rather thought it might be that," responded Sheffield.

"Would you like to know why?"

"I rather think I know," said Rupert. "The arms business—not a lot left of your organisation after Compton and I finished. Your chiefs are all dead or in jail. And I've heard that Greek jails are really quite uncomfortable."

"That, yes," agreed Mr. Mitchell. "But the reason why I am not just going to shoot you cleanly, but spend some time on your demise, is a man called Andreas Katzis. Do you remember Andreas?"

"Yes," said Rupert, who never forgot people

who tried to strangle him with a fishing net. Anyway, so far, Andreas occupied a set of one element.

"You killed him," said Mr. Mitchell, his Cambridge accent fraying back to its roots.

"I might point out that he was trying to kill me at the time," said Rupert evenly.

"Doesn't matter!" yelled Mr. Mitchell. "He was my son!"

Rupert did not reply.

"Aren't you going to lie, and say you're sorry, to save your miserable life?" screamed Mr. Mitchell.

"If you like," said Sheffield calmly. "But since there's just you and just me, as you promised, there doesn't seem to be a lot of point."

"I didn't come alone," said Mitchell.

"Oddly enough, neither did I," said Rupert. He stepped swiftly into the shadows. "Are we going to re-enact the Gunfight at the OK Corral?" he asked. He sounded only mildly interested. He was listening for the other men breathing. To his left, he knew, it was John. There, to the right—high up—a sniper? Surely not. But someone had shifted his feet. This was beginning to look like a major miscalculation. He should have enlisted some soldiers of his own. But that would have meant asking either the loathsome Fanshawe or Miss Fisher. He had not reasoned that he would need help.

"First, Sheffield, I will shoot your friend John

Wilson. He knows your mind. He is an honourable man and I can't imagine how he tolerates you. It's always good business practice to exterminate any potential avengers. Then, you. It will be such a pleasure. You killed my son and you drove me out of my business. I retired to Australia, as far away as I could get, and what did I see? You." Mitchell's voice was gluey with passion.

"And the cream of the joke," Rupert replied, "is that I was not looking for you and I don't know you by sight. But you do not need to shoot Dr. Wilson. He knows nothing at all about my Intelligence days. I only met him after I retired and went back to pure maths. You could still walk away from this."

"No," said Mitchell slowly. "It is just unfortunate about Dr. Wilson. You ruined me, and I am going to kill you. Slowly. Beginning with the gut," he said consideringly. "That will take ever so long to kill you and every moment will be agony."

He lifted and aimed the gun.

"No," shouted John Wilson. Too late to shoot and stop that finger on that hair trigger. He leapt for Sheffield and threw himself between his lover and the gun just as it went off. Rupert Sheffield caught John's body full in his arms. Then he looked up into a face he had never seen before and waited to die.

He heard an exasperated snort above him.

Then a boy in trousers, unravelling jumper and cap, dropped down from above and kicked the semi-invisible Mr. Mitchell very hard in the testicles.

"These megalomaniacs are *so* boring," the boy said. He grabbed the gun and shot the man in the temple. He was speaking as the boom and crash died away to echoes. "If you'd just shut up and killed Sheffield, this could all be over now," he told the corpse. "But you just had to gloat. Now you are dead and it serves you right."

Sheffield, frantically investigating John for injuries, felt a small hand grab him by the hair, compelling his attention. Green eyes burned into violet eyes.

"Get up!" said Phryne Fisher. "Pick up John—I think he's fainted. He really hates being shot. You idiot. This is all your fault. And I shall expect you to be grateful for your rescue."

Grief and horror had not derailed Sheffield's mind. He stood up, gathering John into his arms. John was moaning. He was bleeding!

"How…?"

"Tell you later, darling." She dropped a folded white paper on the dead man's lap. Then she wiped the gun and placed it carefully in his hand, closing the fingers around it. "Grab John and let's go. I have some friends distracting the others but that can't last forever. This way."

Rupert slung John's unconscious weight over his shoulders into a fireman's lift, holding on to one leg and one arm, and ran after the boy in the cap into a yard, through a tall gate and into the back of a tradesman's van, which instantly began to drive. Rupert sat down with John's body in his arms and lolling head supported by his shoulder while Phryne opened his coat. There was some blood, but not enough to indicate a serious wound.

"All right," said Phryne. "For a blithering idiot, a pair of blithering idiots, both of you have got off very lightly. He will live to blither again. Press here. You might as well have his blood on your hands literally as well as figuratively."

"Why did you intervene?" asked Sheffield, feeling blood well up hot from the much-loved flesh, aching with the idea that John would be in agony when he woke. The sensation was strange. And novel. And extremely painful. He bit his lip on something that might have been a sob. Phryne took off the boy's cap and shook out her hair. She lit a gasper, which filled the van with the sweet scent of Virginia tobacco, overlaying wool, sugar and rubber, which had been its previous cargos. And, dreadful, the coppery butcher's shop scent of John's blood. On his hands.

Phryne's voice was incisive, as though she needed to get some information to Sheffield before

John recovered consciousness. "Because John is my friend and for some reason he adores you, and you are so pretty together, and you were going to get him killed," she said, blowing a smoke ring. "You walked open-eyed and alone into a trap, you madman."

"I didn't know John was there until later," said Rupert.

"Where else would John be? You said 'forever,' I heard you."

"With me," whispered Rupert Sheffield, pressing his cheek against John's forehead.

"Right. And instead of asking for help, you march into a warehouse in a city which you do not know without telling anyone, offering yourself up for…sacrifice…" Phryne remembered her vision of that alabaster body laid out on her bed. Agnus Dei. She sucked some more smoke and wished she had thought to bring a flask. "Who do you think you are—Sexton Blake?"

Rupert Sheffield stiffened and was about to take offence when John moaned and reached for his free hand, and he kissed the fevered cheek.

Phryne Fisher, clad in boy's clothes, one hand flourishing her cigarette and the other tapping Sheffield's knee for emphasis, was unforgettable. And impossible to ignore. He knew every inch of that body. And he knew nothing at all about her. A valuable lesson. Stay away from women in future. They were incalculable. She was talking. He was listening.

"You can't leave John behind ever again; he's part of you now, and however much I might want to slap you until you weep, he can't live without you, and if he dies, how long are you going to survive him?"

"Oh! Yes," said Sheffield, who hadn't thought about this before. "I don't believe…I would want to live without him. In fact, it was a relief, looking into that gun barrel. If John was dead, I wanted to die with him. Most illogical."

Phryne snorted and clipped him lightly across the ear.

"Idiot! Right. So I needed to make sure that your Mr. Mitchell, who is my Mr. Ratcliffe, set his ambush, then spring it before he killed anyone valuable, and then I had to take care of his future threatening behaviour."

"By?" asked Sheffield, feeling John begin to shiver. He was going to need warmth and treatment soon. Phryne stubbed out her gasper and lit another.

"Making sure he didn't have any future. Though I may have to review my previously scornful opinions on the Sexton Blake sort of villain. That man really did spout the same sort of twaddle;

he really did delay your death until he could get through his speech, giving me time to shoot him."

"Nature and art," said Sheffield.

"Which you need not tell John. He already thinks I'm some sort of monster."

"No," said John as he swam into consciousness, lifting his head from Sheffield's chest. "No, I really don't, Phryne." He sat up a little, wreathing an arm around Sheffield's neck with perfect trust. "Did you kill him?"

"Certainly I killed him. Did you want to spend the rest of your honeymoon being hunted by a not-quite-retired-enough arms dealer?" said Phryne waspishly. "Good. We're here. Dr. MacMillan will be waiting. I'll just scout a little…"

Rupert saw her jump lightly out of the van, and look right and left. In both cases she caught some sort of signal. Then she waved them out, Rupert supporting John, and hustled them into a nice little garden. The van took off. The garden gate closed. There was a strong scent of cut grass, full-blown roses, water and blood. John was taking some of his own weight and asked Phryne as she opened the door of a small, tidy house, "Where are we?"

"This is where Dr. MacMillan grows her roses and lays her blameless head. Come in, sit John down. Here's a chair. John, don't bleed on the carpet."

Dr. MacMillan came in calmly, ordered Sheffield to bring John into the back garden, and laid him out on a scrubbed, draped table in the summerhouse. It was overgrown with the dark red roses called Black Boy after King Charles the Second, and the scented petals dropped all around as the mannish woman—the best kind, Sheffield decided—laid the wound bare, cleaned it with gentle hands, put in a lot of iodoform powder and stitched it shut. Eleven stitches, and everyone felt as if it had gone through Sheffield's flesh as well. Then she sat John up to wind a bandage around his body, pressing a pad against the wound. She watched for a moment. No staining was evident. She administered morphine by injection. She began to scold him in her soothing Scots voice as she directed Sheffield to carry him again, into the house and into a nest of soft blankets on a couch.

"The shirt is for the fireback," she told him. "You daft great gowk, puttin' yerself in the way of harm after all this time out of a war. Pining for the battlefields, is that it? Now, your friend will go into my bathroom there and wash his hands, he will be back directly, and I shall see about tea."

Rupert Sheffield, scrubbing John's blood from his hands with a nailbrush and hospital soap, swore that this was the last time, the very last time, that he would have to do this. John's blood was on his shirt. He ripped it off and threw it to the floor.

When he came back Phryne was perched on a chair in the parlour, sipping whisky and combing her hair with her fingers. He sat down bare-chested on the couch, wrapping himself and John in the blankets, and felt his friend lean gratefully on his chest as Rupert's arms closed around him. Then Rupert raised his head and stared into Phryne Fisher's eyes.

"I promise," he said, "that I will never endanger John again."

"Or yourself…" she prompted.

"Or myself. And I have to thank you," he added. "For our lives."

"Pleasure," said Phryne. "On the understanding that if you do this again I will personally shoot you in the head."

He did not doubt her sincerity. Or her marksmanship.

"If this happens again and it's my fault, I will let you. Indeed, I will beg you."

"Deal," said Phryne. "And if you break his heart, I will cut you into bits. No one will ever find them. Because they will be such very *small* bits."

"That, too," agreed Sheffield.

"The local sharks see my wharfie friends as good providers," she elaborated.

"Agreed. But what if he leaves me?"

"He won't," Phryne replied. "He has a true and faithful heart. Or, rather, he had it. He gave it to you. If you die, he'll die."

Sheffield felt John shift and snuggle in his embrace and acknowledged the truth of this remark. He could not imagine his John ever leaving him, except in death. He suddenly and desperately sought for something else to think about.

"Will you tell me how it was arranged?" asked Rupert. "You seem to have a very efficient organisation."

"I borrowed a couple of men from Fanshawe," Phryne told him.

"Fanshawe is a fool," said Rupert.

"He's really not," Phryne commented. "He's useful. About time you learned the difference, my boy. Shall I go on?"

"Please," said Rupert.

"I wanted them in case we needed to have official sanction. They were my reserve; I didn't need them, as it happened. My wharfie mates staged a scene at the gate, refusing to let Mr. Ratcliffe's minions in. Backed up with a shotgun. A sobering weapon at close range. My adoptive children were my lookouts. Cec drove the van. Bert was in the warehouse, ready to carry anyone who was hurt. He was also armed. We had at least three alternative plans. Luckily Plan One worked well and here we are."

"And that fetching jumper?" asked John, surfacing on a cushion of morphine, chuckling.

Phryne stood up with one elegant hand on her hip, turning to the audience like a mannequin exhibiting a striking new gown.

"Isn't it just the peak of the mode? I borrowed it from Tinker. He'll be cross, it's got a bit more unravelled." She pulled at a sad, grey-blue thread. "Do you think I can I call them in, Elizabeth?"

"Indeed, any danger of pursuit should be over. If they followed, they will have gone haring after that van, and Cec is very good at losing followers," said Dr. MacMillan.

"And, in any case, their chief has killed himself," observed Rupert.

"As you say," said Phryne.

"That takes the impetus and ambition out of most gangs," observed Rupert.

"That is true," said Phryne.

"And the suicide note is right there in his hand."

"Yes, I saw it," said Phryne.

"And naturally the handwriting will match any samples available," insinuated Rupert.

"Of course it will," said Phryne.

"Shot through the temple. The right temple," mused Rupert. "So he must have been right-handed.

And his fingerprints are on the gun, still clutched in his hand."

"Right again," said Phryne.

"And if it was expedient that he should disappear, that would have been managed also?"

"Concrete pour tomorrow morning two factories away," Phryne told him.

"I asked Compton about you," said Sheffield.

Phryne grinned. "Did you now? What did he say?"

"The most dangerous woman in the world," quoted Rupert. "And what did he say when you asked about me?"

"Idiot savant," said Phryne. "Emphasis idiot. Emphasis savant."

"That sounds like Compton," said Rupert.

"Was he wrong?" asked Phryne.

Rupert looked down at John lying on his chest, injured because of him, smelt a faint afterscent of copper, swallowed, and said, "No, he was right. On both points. And about you."

"So kind," said Phryne, and went to the front door to call in her family. There was a scatter of feet and Rupert stared at the lookouts.

Boy, one, ragged, evident source of that disgraceful jumper as he was wearing a beige version of same. Bright eyes, filthy tweed cap. Two, female, long legs in a too-short, too-small dress, crammed on sun bonnet which concealed her face, plaits. Basket. Three, also female, hauling a large sugar bag, overlarge dress and apron, scarf. The third put down her sack and Phryne dived on it, extracting some garments and a pair of sandals. She bent to take off the heavy boots and winced from her bruises. Instantly the boy knelt to undo the knotted laces. Miss Fisher's minions served her, thought Rupert, out of love. He could understand that now. Phryne patted Tinker's cheek as the boots and ragged socks were removed, and wriggled her toes as if she was glad to see them again.

"Nail down those filthy socks, Tink," she told him. "God knows what they'd do if they escaped."

"Right you are, Guv'nor," said Tinker, grinning up at her. Phryne shucked her trousers and went into the bathroom, tossing aside her jumper as she went.

Rupert noticed that her undergarments were of her usual silk. Anyone undressing that particular boy would have been in for a surprise.

And a bullet in the head, of course. Or at the least a boot in the testicles.

"She is, you know," murmured John sleepily into Rupert's collarbone.

"She is?" asked Rupert.

"The most dangerous woman in the world," said John, and fell asleep again.

"That's true," said the girl in the candle-snuffer bonnet, bending so her friend could haul it off her head. It gave with a ripping of seams. "We're just lucky that she's on our side."

"Which side would that be?" asked Rupert.

Jane looked at him as she found her own and Ruth's clothes in the sack and handed the rest over to Tinker.

"Miss Dot says she's on the side of the Light," she replied. "A religious concept."

"I am familiar with it," Rupert told her.

"Otherwise you could say that she is ethical," Jane said, removing her scarf and fluffing out short blonde hair. "For instance, when she rescued me from a mesmerist, we told her she couldn't take me and leave Ruthie in a terrible place, so she took the two of us."

"And she got me from Queenscliff on approval," Tinker told him, stripping unaffectedly and putting on respectable shorts and a shirt with no holes in it. Suddenly he had become a nice public school boy home for the holidays. Rupert blinked.

"I have seen you before," he told Tinker.

"Yes, you have," said Tinker in his best "polite" voice. "Too right, mate," he added, in his original accent.

"And you," he told Jane. "I played chess with you. You were quite promising."

"Thank you," said Jane. "You seem different."

"How?" asked Rupert.

"Softer," said Jane, before her sister elbowed her in the ribs. "No, I'm not being rude, Ruthie," she protested. "Look for yourself. You know Miss Phryne says we should observe carefully."

"Only if it isn't impolite," said Ruth primly.

"He won't mind," said Jane. "He's been observing us. Fair's fair."

"So it is," said Sheffield. In Jane he had met a nature as direct as his own, though she had learned manners much earlier. "Well? What are your deductions?"

"I can't use a mathematical proof," said Jane. "But when we saw you before you were arrogant, and you didn't like people. Not just us. You were jealous of Miss Phryne. You were unhappy, and you tried to make everyone else unhappy as well. And you needed us to know how much more intelligent you were than anyone in the world."

"Jane!" cried Ruth.

"He asked me for my deductions," said Jane mulishly.

"And I bet he's sorry he did," said Ruth.

A tender heart, thought Rupert. I used to

think that was a contemptible weakness. What an idiot. Compton was right.

"Go on," he told Jane.

"Now, you're not snarling, you're not telling us how clever you are. You never touched anyone before. You wouldn't even touch my hand when I held out the chess pieces. You're touching Dr. Wilson, you're embracing him, skin to skin. As though you love him."

"And he's snuggling into your arms as though he loves you," said Ruth, clasping her hands. "It's just like a romance except it's men."

"Jeez," said Tinker, who had a limited tolerance for romance.

"Dr. MacMillan has tea in the kitchen," said Rupert out of a merciful impulse, and Tinker left. Sheffield recoiled a little as Jane approached and stared straight into his eyes. Her own were blue and very sharp.

"Yes," she said coolly. "Softer. The underlying musculature has relaxed a little, the overall definition of flesh over bone is more—"

"Sculptural," said Phryne, coming back wearing a green linen shift dress which might indeed have been at the peak of the mode. "What are you doing to Mr. Sheffield, Jane?"

"He *asked*," said Jane, wounded by all these

people who misunderstood her motives. "He asked for my deductions."

"I did," affirmed Rupert.

"More, Jane?" asked Phryne, smiling. That pitiless, uninvolved gaze scanned him again. It was like staring into a searchlight.

"There's a blue shade under his eyes; he's had a shock. His hand has just the remains of a tremor, and he's scrubbed that hand very hard. Did it have blood on it? Not his blood, he's not hurt. Dr. Wilson's blood. An enemy's blood wouldn't worry him. No gunsmoke on his arm, either, so the person who did the shooting was Miss Phryne." Jane took Phryne's hand. "And not your usual Beretta, it must have been a bigger handgun. You've pinched the webbing between thumb and forefinger."

"And can you guess who I shot?" asked Phryne.

"The bad man," said Jane, smiling up at Phryne with perfect faith. "Of course."

"And that will do," said Dr. MacMillan, allowing Tinker to wheel in a tea trolley. "Tea. You will make a great diagnostician, nae doot, my hinny, but you need tae improve your bedside manner."

John woke and drank extremely sweet tea in a room which contained Phryne and her family and, of all the most unlikely and wonderful things in the world, Rupert Sheffield holding the cup for him to drink. He drank all of it, not objecting to the sweetness. Rupert took the cup away and kissed him gently.

He closed his eyes.

◇◇◇

When he awoke again he was disoriented and in pain.

"The morphine has worn off," observed Rupert. "John? Do you know where you are?"

"You're here," said John with vast relief. "I thought I was dreaming."

"No, you're in Dr. MacMillan's house. You've been—"

"Shot," groaned John. "I know how that feels. It feels bloody awful, in case you are still collecting information. I remember. The warehouse. You're unhurt?"

"Entirely. If I put my arm behind your shoulders can you sip some water and take these pills? The doctor left them for you. She said you'd wake in pain."

"She was right. How long have I been asleep?"

"Four hours. It's early morning. You should sleep again."

"It was worth a wound," said John, groping for Rupert's hand, "to have you with me."

"No," said Rupert sharply. "Nothing is worth your being wounded. How can you say such a thing? There's a slice out of your side; I felt your blood pulse under my hand. Never say that again."

"All right, my dear," John agreed. He drank the water and swallowed the pills. Morphine, he knew that bitter taste. "These pills will take half an hour or so to work," he told Rupert. "Until then, would you…would you lie down beside me? The thing about pain," he went on, "is that it makes you feel rather lonely."

Sheffield removed his shoes and his outer garments and crept into bed beside him, wincingly careful not to jolt or touch the bandage. John lay on his side and Sheffield embraced him very gently. John, who had been chilled, relaxed into his warmth. The wound burned. But he had endured worse, and not in such precious company.

"Talk to me?" he asked, for distraction and the pleasure of hearing Rupert's beautiful voice. Irish coffee, Phryne had called it. Now, only when speaking to John, it was Irish coffee made with pure whisky and dark chocolate and cream.

"What would you like me to talk about?" asked Rupert, close to John's ear.

"What did you make of Phryne's children?"

"Remarkable. The boy is just a boy. Fisherman. Has a black and white dog. Poor parents, missing father. Wants to be a policeman, I think, and is a devotee of Sexton Blake, which is why he calls Miss Fisher "Guv'nor" and why he's called Tinker. I doubt that's the name with which he was christened, if he was christened. Ruth, the girl with plaits, has a gentle heart and is probably a good cook. Flour on one of her plaits. Strong hands from kneading and whisking. Reads a lot of romances. She thought we were a pretty sight. And the one called Jane is going to rule the world someday. She deduced your injury from the way that I had scrubbed my hands."

"Clever," admired John. He caught his breath at a minor movement, then said, "You liked her?"

"Scared me to death," confessed Rupert.

"She has that effect on me, too." John tried not to chuckle.

"Not one of them thought there was anything wrong or even strange about us being together," said Rupert. "Well, Tinker went out to the kitchen, but that was dislike of sentiment, not…not…loathing."

"Any child who lives in Phryne's house," said John, "is guaranteed a very liberal education. If their brains don't explode in the first couple of weeks, then they're probably immune to any surprise."

"Pity mine was not so liberal," observed Sheffield. "I thought all sexual desire was both wrong and sinful and love was a sign of weakness."

There was a pause in which John winced again. The house was quite silent. John could hear a clock ticking two rooms away. He was never going to be reconciled to the idea of being shot. But it was just a furrow in his flesh. No ribs had been broken. He would heal, with another scar for Rupert to memorise. And the splendid Rupert, who loved him, John, forever, he was untouched. His mind was wandering away. Rupert took his hand.

"I am so sorry," said Rupert desolately. "I have made major errors and I nearly got you killed."

"Yes," said John. "Yet here we are." He grunted a laugh and regretted it instantly. He squeezed Rupert's hand.

"Isn't the drug working yet?" asked Rupert anxiously. "Shall I fetch the doctor?"

"It will work soon, and I'm not going to arouse our Lisbet from her lawful bed. She gets very sarcastic when woken without cause. I'm wounded already. I'll be all right in a little while," said John, leaning back into Rupert's arms, feeling his lover's body heat saturating every cell. "Stay with me. Be here when I wake again?"

"So, you forgive me?" asked Rupert into John's hair.

"Yes, my love, yes, my dear," said John, sliding into sleep. "Yes, yes, yes."

Chapter Eighteen

Was this the face that launched a thousand ships?
And burnt the topless towers of Ilium?
Sweet Helen, make me immortal with a kiss!
Her lips suck forth my soul: see where it flies!

Christopher Marlowe,
Doctor Faustus

Phryne and her minions did not get home until a scandalous three o'clock in the morning. While Tinker, Ruth and Jane told Dot all about it, rummaging for provender in the American Refrigerating Machine, Phryne reported to the imperturbable Mrs. Thomas the whole story. She tutted, wondered what the world was coming to, reported that the carefully arranged suicide had been just the thing, and that Maginnis' men were now battling the disheartened remains of Ratcliffe's in the warehouse in Bay Street, whence they had been summoned by a Mysterious Message through—possibly—communist channels. Local police had been alerted and were on their way.

"Nice, neat operation, Miss Fisher," said Mrs. Thomas. "I think the stories I've heard about you might be true."

"Please," said Phryne, who felt that some informality was called for, "call me Phryne. Convey my best wishes to Mr. Fanshawe in the morning. Goodnight," she said.

"Goodnight, dear, sleep well," said Mrs. Thomas cheerily.

When Phryne got to the kitchen there was really quite a lot of egg and bacon pie left. She ate two pieces before Tinker scoffed it all.

◇◇◇

The whole household slept in. Breakfast was a merry meal more akin to lunch. When the doorbell rang, they all stopped and waited until Mr. Butler returned with an enormous box of Haigh's superfine chocolates and a huge bouquet of orchids. They were blooming, varicoloured, strangely scented, and rare. Phryne arranged them in a glass bowl.

Ruth read the card. "*To the Fisher family. From John and Rupert. Heartfelt thanks.*"

"Very proper," said Phryne, and awarded everyone the chocolate of their choice.

The household scattered to their usual tasks.

Phryne, who had just remembered the portrait of the sad Renaissance lady from her cogitations before Sexton Blake had taken over her life, took down the *Encyclopaedia Britannica* and turned to B. She read while she ate her cherry liqueur chocolate.

Half an hour later she was ringing Jack Robinson. An hour after that she had alighted from the police car sent to fetch her, at the Medical Examiner's office.

"What gave you the idea?" he asked.

"You couldn't find the container for the arsenic. All the cups and glasses in both places tested clean. And you're thorough, Jack, you wouldn't have missed anything. That seemed odd. Then a member of the choir," said Phryne, "told me her name was Caterina, not Lucrezia. In connection with me asking them about poisons. Arsenic was very popular in the old days, when there was no forensic science and no Professor Glaister. Inheritance powder, they called it. Pure, deadly, white, dissolves in any weak acid."

"What's a weak acid when it's at home?" asked Jack Robinson.

"Tea is tannic acid, vinegar is acetic acid, orange juice is citric acid; there are a lot of acids about in general use. Lucrezia Borgia, of whom I am sure you have heard, had a hollow ring which she could use to deposit arsenic into a drink.

It could be mixed with, say, lard as a base, and rubbed into leather to make poisoned gloves. It's an adaptable poison, and in the old days people died quite frequently of typhoid and cholera. Same symptoms. Can be used long term to produce a chronic toxicity…"

"And you're doing my work for me again, Phryne?" asked the spry and elderly Dr. McLaren. He was an emeritus chemistry professor at Melbourne University and called in when forensic problems were beyond ordinary knowledge. In person he was another gnome, small, shrunken and bald. But Professor McLaren was vibrant with purpose and bright of eye. As a hobby, he bred Siamese cats.

"No, no," said Phryne, who had great respect for the old man. "Just a few preliminary notes."

"Fine puzzle you've set me," said the old man, with relish. "Though I believe Lucrezia Borgia to be a much maligned woman. What could she be but what her father and brothers made her? They married her off at the ripe old age of thirteen—the first time. Poor girl. However, as my learned colleague Miss Fisher was saying—" he led the way into his laboratory "—arsenic use was widespread. Now that we have a reliable test for it, it is not so much used, homicidally. But it's reliable and, of course, the fact that there is a test for it doesn't mean that the death will be seen as suspicious. If no one tests, it might as well be one of those Sherlock Holmes colourless, odourless, undetectable South American poisons."

"Granted," agreed Jack. Laboratories made him nervous. He always felt that sooner or later they would blow up. His experience at school—where an overenthusiastic application of sodium metal to a sink full of water had taken out the sink and the ceiling—had confirmed this view.

The full orchestral score lay on the metal bench. Professor McLaren put a hand on it.

"Now, you say this vanished?"

"Yes," said Phryne. "For up to twenty-four hours."

"And when you found it again, it was a little damp?"

"Indeed."

"And your conductor used to lick his finger before turning the page?"

"That was his disgusting and invariable habit," she confirmed.

"Right. I suppose I can't just cut up the score?" he asked hopefully.

"Not yet, but you can cut the ends off a few pages. They wouldn't have had to poison the whole score. Just the top right-hand corners. That was where his wet finger landed."

"Well, we'll see," said the professor, taking out a scalpel and slicing a number of corners off the score.

"What is this all about, Miss Fisher?" asked Robinson.

"Borgias," said Phryne, watching the little bits of paper bubble away in an Erlenmeyer flask with an attached glass condenser. The professor had placed it in a fume cupboard. "They rather specialised in poison. Drinks, knives, gloves, and books. One nasty method was to send someone a pornographic book, and poison the pages so that when the reader, aroused and careless, licked his finger to get to the next page to find out what happened to the lovers, he would get a small dose of poison. Depending on his libido, he would either be slowly poisoned or would get an acute dose. In either case, he would be dead. Arsenic is cumulative. It stays in the system. This is Marsh's test for arsenic."

"All I can see is bits of paper in clear fluid," said Robinson.

"Oh, but wait, my dear sir. The distilled water is free of all contaminants. Look at that glass surface," said Professor McLaren excitedly.

"It's clear," said Jack. "Or, no, wait, it's going smoky. Like a stain."

"Indeed, dear boy," said McLaren, who had never really left the lecture theatre.

The thin smoky stain deepened and widened. It was a brownish charcoal colour with a shining metallic disc in the middle.

"There is the mirror," said Phryne.

"That is arsenic?" asked Jack.

"Arsenic or antimony, they are both Group Five semi-metals. Both are inimical to life. But with the addition of a weak solution of chlorinated lime, we shall see."

He poured in another clear fluid. Jack was going to steer clear of transparent fluids for a while. Beer seemed a good substitute.

The blackish mirror cleared as if by magic.

"Arsenic trioxide, without a doubt," crowed Professor McLaren. "Thank you so much for this, my dear." He kissed Phryne on the cheek. "I haven't been so amused for ages. I had no idea we had such inventive murderers in these parlous days."

"How much arsenic is in that score?" asked Jack.

"Oh, grains and grains, my dear sir—enough to kill an elephant. Several elephants. Though where your murderer got pure arsenic I don't know. Commercial arsenic is coloured with either soot or indigo. There's no trace of any colouring agent. And no trace of any admixture, either."

"Not rat poison, then?" asked Jack.

"No," said Professor McLaren. "Now, it's been

such fun, but I must get on. Princess the Lady Regina of Alphington is about to kitten. I must be there to support her."

"Right," said Jack.

They went back to the police car. Phryne made a note that the choir needed a new orchestral score. Allen's would provide.

"So, how did he do it?" asked Jack.

Phryne waved a hand. "Oh, simple enough. Nasty, though. Shows a very vindictive spirit. One would take the score home, dilute your arsenic in hot water and lemon juice, then just paint it onto the tops of the pages. Might take a while because you'd have to wait for each page to dry. That probably explains why it was a little damp when I found it."

"Who could have done it?" asked Jack. "You know these people."

"The whole choir," replied Phryne. "I think your best bet is to find the arsenic. Pure arsenic is used in a lot of industrial applications—paints and dyes and glass-making. Someone must be missing an oz or two."

"Blimey," said Robinson, and slumped in his seat.

◇ ◇ ◇

Phryne was conveyed home. That was inventive, she considered, and Jane was most impressed when

Phryne told her about the Borgia feast and how it should be avoided.

"But what does it taste like?" asked Jane.

"It's pretty tasteless, or so I have been told," answered Phryne. "I direct your attention to the encyclopedia. And I utterly you forbid you to try rat poison. That wouldn't be a good test, anyway, as it's a combination of poisons."

"And we don't have any," Jane told her, sounding disappointed. "Mrs. Butler won't have poison in the house. Ember catches the rats and mice, and she keeps out the black beetles with bicarb and flies with oil of mint and mosquitoes with citronella."

"Never mind," said Phryne, and went to lie down. She needed to think. If this was Leonard's doing, he had displayed a breadth of imagination which she did not think he had. Were there history students who might have read about this method and decided to try it on James? If he stopped licking his fingers and turning pages, if he abandoned this repulsive habit, then he would not be poisoned. If he persisted in it, he would die.

As a lesson in manners, it seemed a little extreme.

◇◇◇

Rehearsal was pleasant, without Henry James. His ghost was not heard as the choir worked on their full-dress choruses. "Then Did the Prophet Elijah Break Forth Like a Fire.. It was a little scrappy, but adequately *moderato maestoso*. Matthew was pleased and Professor Szabo played minuets for the tea break. Most of the choir began to dance.

Phryne felt someone take her hand. It was Matthew.

"May I have this dance, beautiful lady?" he asked. "Less energetic than the Charleston."

"Certainly," said Phryne and walked, moved, dipped, through the set piece, which was clearly designed to allow everyone in the room to see who was dancing with whom and what they were wearing. It was soothing. Various versions of an actual minuet were being danced. But they were all decorative, even if they were not canonical. Phryne saw that Caterina was coaxing Tommy through the steps with admirable patience. They were very sweet together. Daniel was dancing with Josephine. Both of them were concentrating hard, which made the disparity in their height less ridiculous. DavidandLobelia, however, were dancing the wreathed-together, swaying embrace known as "the nightclub shuffle", usually only seen when both parties needed to lean on someone because they were too drunk to stand up on their own.

They went back to rehearsal, and managed the final chorus, "And Then Shall Your Light Break

Forth," with the last words of the oratorio: "*Lord, our Creator, how excellent thy name in all nations! Thou fillest Heaven with glory*," and then an Amen noticeable for its brevity. They stopped and drew breath. They were pleased with themselves.

"Good!" said Matthew. "Right, it's Aunty Mark's night in, so everyone go home and do the same. We are really improving, friends. And the good news is, Pat Bell's Ballarat engagement is finished, and he's coming Wednesday to take over."

"Oh, wonderful," said Calliope. "He's such a nice man. But you've been very good too," she told Matthew.

The choir applauded as he left the dais for the last time. He gave them a graceful bow.

"Are you sorry?" asked Phryne.

"Me? God, no," he said, transparently honest relief washing over his broad face. "It's a huge responsibility, getting it right. Hearing all the parts, trying to slot them together. Finding out where the mistakes are. I'm handing us over with a reasonable chance of getting up to concert pitch by the time of the performance. That's enough for me!"

"So it is," said Phryne. "What a very nice man you are."

"Er…thanks?" he said.

"I'm so sorry that I can't take you home with me and ravish you," Phryne told him. "But I still have to find out who murdered two conductors. You should be safe now; you're out of the spotlight."

And she went away, leaving Matthew feeling as though someone had carelessly nailed him to a wall. With hot, gold nails. *What* had she said?

Phryne had already gone. He would ask her to elaborate on Wednesday. Or maybe not. That was a lady who knew her own mind. And they still didn't know who had killed Tregennis and then killed Henry James. General opinion was that it was Leonard. But he had not been arrested. And that policeman was still making enquiries.

Matthew reminded himself that Gran would be cross if he was late in cooking her dinner. When she was cross, she was very unpleasant. And he had his pets to feed.

So he took the tram to Carlton, very agreeably confused.

◇◇◇

When Phryne arrived home to a light supper, more tributes had arrived. There was a modest but expensive bunch of gardenias from Peter Fanshawe. A fiendishly valuable flask of Attar of Roses, without its import/customs duty stamp, directed to Officer, Commanding. An obviously hand-picked sheaf of garden roses tied up with a bandage from Dr. MacMillan—she really did grow beautiful roses.

They were Black Boy, the roses which covered the bower in which she had operated on John Wilson. They smelt intoxicating. The note said *such pretty boys* and probably didn't refer to the roses. Now, unless Rupert had utterly gone back on his word and somehow damaged John, in which case she would shoot him in the head, however beautiful, things ought to work out well between those two. It still worried Phryne that Rupert did not appreciate what an altogether excellent person John was, but that would come in time.

It had better.

Supper was delicious, and she and Lambie slept well. The morning brought a host of household tasks, which Phryne managed; a hairdresser's appointment, a sister alight with indignation and a worried policeman.

"Phryne!" exclaimed Eliza. "Comrades Bert and Cec brought me three women they said came from a man called Ratcliffe's house."

"Yes," said Phryne. Eliza was her opposite. Phryne was small, thin, dark and heterosexual. Her sister was tall, bosomy, fair and a devout Sapphic. Despite which they got on very well.

"Yes, I told them you might be able to look after the freed slaves."

"Do you know what that beast did to them?" demanded Eliza furiously.

"No," said Phryne. "And you don't need to tell me, I can guess. My memory is already well-stocked with horrors. Can you find someone to care for them?"

"Yes," said Eliza.

"And a small donation might be acceptable?" added Phryne, reaching for her purse.

"Of course," said Eliza. She eyed Phryne narrowly. "Comrade Bert said that Ratcliffe is dead. Is that true? These girls need to know. I've never seen…slaves really is the best word…so terrified. They are sure he is going to recapture and punish them."

"He's dead," said Phryne, pressing a banknote into her sister's hand.

"How do you know he's dead?" demanded Eliza.

"I killed him," replied Phryne.

Eliza did not even blink. "Jolly good," she rejoined. "Well done. I only wish that you could bring him back."

"Why?" asked Phryne, startled.

"So you could kill him again."

◇◇◇

The policeman was exhausted and discouraged.

"This case has got me stumped," he confessed.

"Me, too," said Phryne. "We know "how",

which ought to mean we know "who", but I really can't think that Leonard Match thought out that Borgia trick. I doubt he reads anything but music. And the history student who might know about it, Caterina, is the one who used the name Lucrezia. She didn't particularly have it in for Henry James. And I suppose the two murders are connected."

"Maybe they aren't," offered Jack accepting a tea cup. "Thanks, Mr.. What if the Tregennis smothering was some passing chorister who just hated him for a moment, and then sort of forgot about doing it? Pure spur of the moment thing? And the James murderer had been planning it for months?"

"Can't have been; we didn't know we'd get James until after Tregennis was killed. But, all right, what if James had a deep and passionate enemy amongst the choir, who, once James was actually in his power, decided that his long-nurtured plan could now be carried out? I'm saying "his" for convenience. Poison does tend to be a female weapon."

"That could happen," agreed Jack. "Still too many people who hated the nasty coot."

"Yes," said Phryne. "What about the source of the arsenic?"

"We've been looking," Jack told her. "But almost everyone in paint or dye uses it, and they're real careless with it. Couple of foundries, you could walk in and help yourself to a pocketful of the stuff and no one would notice. They use it so commonly they forget the blasted stuff is lethal. And that's just the white powder, the arsenic trioxide. Chemists keep a poisons book for the commercial arsenic. No names we know, so far."

"I'm still watching," said Phryne. "Something will break. I'm going to sing in this *Elijah*; it is going to be very good. And we've got a new conductor coming tomorrow. His name is Patrick Bell and apparently he is well known as a sweetie. That will be a nice change."

"I bet," said Jack. "Be careful," he added, and took his leave. "By the way," he said at the door, "you didn't have anything to do with that riot in Bay Street last night, did you? Where Ratcliffe killed himself and Maginnis got cut up by Mother Higgins' slaughtermen? The riot squad is still finding bodies—the fight spread out into a sheet-metal shop as well."

"Me?" asked Phryne, clasping both hands to her breast.

Jack Robinson smiled grimly. "I thought as much," he said, and Phryne closed the door.

Phryne decided that she would attend Aunty Mark's party. She might also have a word with Rupert Sheffield, if she saw him, about the immense value of his lover. Rupert had not seen John as Phryne had seen him: courageous, exhausted, gentle with the injuries which he could not treat, swift and skilled with scalpel and needle.

He was not, however, with any luck, likely to see anything like that.

Phryne decided to have a nap. Tonight she needed to watch everyone in the choir, and that would prove tiring. Lambie was waiting for her faithfully in her bed. Wrapped around him was Ember. Phryne snuggled up to them both.

◇◇◇

The Windsor really was coping with Aunty Mark's perennial party very well. On her magnificent way up the main staircase, she encountered John Wilson.

"How are you, my dear?" she asked, not touching him.

He took her hand. "I'm not really damaged, Phryne, it was just a bit of a scrape. Scared poor Rupert, though."

"So it did," said Phryne. She hoped it had scared him into a suitably humble frame of mind.

"He's hardly let me out of his sight. I just needed a little air. Going for a walk in that park over there. I left him asleep. You look gorgeous," he told her. Phryne posed. She was wearing a trailing dark-blue and gold brocade gown. Her fillet held a peacock feather. It just about suited her, thought John.

"I'm going to Aunty Mark's," she told him.

"Have a lovely time. We're almost underneath, in seventeen, as you know. Try to sing some madrigals. Rupert likes madrigals."

"All right," said Phryne, and watched him limp away. He was favouring his side, but not too much. Those stitches must be pulling. But he was healthy. He would heal. And now he had his lover. A good result all round, thought Phryne, and continued up the stairs.

She was intercepted and offered an arm by Tommy, who had Caterina on his other arm.

"Between two beauties," he said joyfully. "A thorn between two roses."

Phryne and Caterina smiled at one another. They knew they were beautiful. And Tommy was a thoroughly nice chap. If Caterina wanted him, she could have him.

At the second staircase they met Rupert Sheffield, who had woken up without his John. He looked worried and almost dishevelled.

"He's gone for a walk in the park," Phryne told him. "Just across the road."

It was a measure of Rupert's improvement in manners that he stopped, took Phryne's hand, kissed it, and murmured, "*Madame est magnifique*," before he hurried in pursuit.

Aunty Mark had decided on an Ancient Greek theme, and was draped in a very revealing tunic and a chlamys made of a bedsheet. He sat on his throne and ordered his "slaves" to sing songs for his amusement. The slaves were delighted to comply as long as the champagne held out. Someone had leaned out of the window and hauled in a rope of ivy to crown the participants. A bacchanal. How delicious.

"Marcus, I am feeling overdressed," she said to him.

"That can be remedied." He grinned wolfishly. "You would have no shortage of volunteers to assist you in disrobing."

"Perhaps later," promised Phryne. "Can we have some madrigals, Your Majesty?"

"Mad wriggles? Indeed!" he agreed. "Come along, slaves, it is the month for Maying."

While they started to sing, "*Now 'tis the month of maying, when merry lads are playing…*" Phryne got herself a drink and sat down by the window. She looked out into the well-lit street. And there, coming past the statue of General Gordon, were John and Sheffield. John was leaning on Sheffield's arm. They were well dressed and polite and obviously gentlemen, and no policeman would ever think that the reason John was holding on so tightly to his friend's arm was that he adored him immeasurably with a totally illegal passion. "You see, but you do not observe," murmured Phryne to herself.

"Hmm? What are you looking at?" asked Mark, manifesting himself beside her.

"Lovebirds," said Phryne.

"Oh," he said. His mobile mouth formed a perfect O. "Well, isn't that the haughty piece and his shadow? They've come together, haven't they? How very agreeable."

◇◇◇

The party went on. Phryne spoke to all of the choristers in turn, even Julia, and gleaned no useful information. Professor Szabo told her that Matthew had been quite a good conductor, and he didn't know about this Patrick Bell. Several voices put in that Pat Bell was an excellent musician, and a good fellow besides, but the professor seemed unconvinced, and reminded them of the almost godlike conducting of Thomas Beecham. At which point, they stopped listening, as usual.

Phryne was about to finish her gin and tonic and take her leave, pleased but not enlightened, when there was a hubbub. She was grabbed bruisingly tight by the arm. It was Gawain and he was beside himself.

"Quick!" he shouted at her. "It's Mark!"

He dragged Phryne through a throng of discomfited singers to the magnificent bathroom, where Mark, in his tunic, lay in the huge tub. His ivy-leaf crown was still on his head. He seemed to be asleep. But his face was under the water.

Phryne took charge. "Tommy, Oliver, get him out. Shoulders and feet, hurry up! Gawain, run down to room seventeen, it's almost under this one, and bring John Wilson here. Tell him I sent you. Go. Run!" she ordered, and he ran. "Everyone else, please get back. We need some room."

"Shouldn't we put him on the couch?" asked Tommy, who was bearing the weight without any strain.

"No, floor—he's got water in his lungs. We need to get it out."

They laid him down.

Phryne touched his neck. A pulse throbbed beneath her fingers, thready but present. "He's still alive. Where is Gawain with that doctor?" She dropped to her knees beside Mark and opened his mouth with her finger. A little fluid trickled out.

She leaned forward and locked her mouth on his, breathing some life into him.

Nothing happened. His chest rose and fell and was still again. Why couldn't she remember what to do? She breathed for him again. Rise, fall, stop. Rise, fall, stop.

Then someone thudded down beside her and said, "Keep going, Phryne dear, good work. You two boys, take his arms. Now move them out and up, then in and down. One, two, one, two. Good lads. Keep going."

John, thank God. Gawain, jealous and frantic, shoved her aside and took over the breathing. Phryne blindly put out a hand for someone to help her to her feet and found that she was being embraced by Rupert Sheffield, who was watching John work with absolute fascination. Phryne was breathless and dizzy. Rupert held her with perfect sureness, but all his attention was fixed on the lifesaving scene at his feet. John was exhorting, encouraging, dragging everyone in his orbit into the rescue.

He had always been able to do that. Phryne remembered him in a battle, rallying the less injured to care for the more gravely injured. And he had persuaded them, too, while the sky exploded overhead.

Rupert asked, "Was he like that in his casualty clearing station?" and she answered, "Just so. Sorry to lean on you, I'm feeling a little unsteady," and he said absently, "Not at all. I had not realised that he was so…charismatic."

"Only when saving lives," said Phryne. She could have straightened up but she was also fascinated, and she liked embracing Rupert Sheffield. He was quite strong, though so slim. He was only wearing a loose shirt and trousers, not his usual suit. He and John must have been interrupted in preparation for bed.

"I can see why you dragged him into your ambulance," he murmured.

"He told you about that?" she asked, surprised.

"No secrets," said Sheffield. "Not anymore."

"There, that's a good lad," said John with satisfaction.

Mark dragged in a breath all on his own, was turned on his side, and water gushed out of his mouth, staining the carpet. He heaved and choked.

"You're all right, my dear," John told him. "You passed out in the bath. But Phryne was here and she saved you."

"Actually, it was Gawain, Tommy, Oliver, and mostly John," said Phryne.

Rupert gave her an absent-minded squeeze of approval.

"Now let's get you cleaned up a bit, my dear chap. You'll be all right, I promise. Someone phone down for some hot tea, honey, and lemon." John sat Mark up against his arm. He put his ear to the wet tunic and listened. "Good. No nasty sounds. You can't have been under long. Where's his bedroom?"

Oliver and Tommy made a chair and carried Mark to his bedroom. He was already recovering, giving a little royal wave as he was borne from the room. Gawain, Phryne and Rupert followed. John excluded the others.

"Strip off that rag, rub him dry and warm," ordered John, and Gawain obeyed.

When Mark was re-clad in startling purple silk pyjamas, sitting up against a pile of pillows and sipping hot tea, John said, taking his wrist and feeling for his pulse, "You really shouldn't bathe when you're too tiddly, you know. That could have been serious, if Phryne hadn't got you out."

"I didn't," protested Mark. "I seldom bathe in my clothes."

"Then what happened?" asked John. "You had a lot of water in your lungs."

"I don't know. One minute I was ducking into the bathroom for a quick pee, the next I was kissing Gawain with a couple of louts hauling on my arms. Felt like an elephant was sitting on my chest, too," answered Mark querulously.

"Ah," said Phryne.

Rupert exchanged a glance with her. Green eyes met violet eyes.

"John, have a look at the back of his head," said Rupert.

John felt through the curly hair. His fingers stilled. There was a lump.

"A nasty little blow?" hazarded Phryne. "Just hard enough to knock him out for as long as it took to load him into the tub and run a bath?"

"How did you know?" asked John. "How did you *both* know?" he clarified.

"Observation," said Rupert. "He says he doesn't bathe in his clothes. His eyes are a little unfocused. He's a big strong man, it wouldn't be easy to persuade him to lie down and be drowned."

"Thank you, precious," said Mark. He was definitely recovering. "And it's true. I would not like being drowned at all. And only select persons gain admittance to the royal bathing chamber."

Gawain giggled, mostly from relief.

"But he wasn't drowned just in water," said Phryne.

"Indeed?" asked Rupert.

"Extra data," she told him, apologetically. "I started the breathing process, so I kissed him first. Sorry," she said to Gawain. "And the taste in my mouth was champagne."

"You had been drinking it," said Rupert, testing the hypothesis.

"No, I was drinking gin and tonic. Quite a

distinct taste. Not only champagne but the Pol Roget. An unforgettable wine."

"Which I'm rapidly going off," murmured Mark.

"Which means," said John, "that someone dotted him a good one, shoved him into the bathtub, ran the water, then opened his mouth and poured champagne into it until he drowned."

"That's it," said Rupert. "Any idea who might want you dead?" he asked Mark.

"I really can't think of anyone," he said sadly. "I thought I was among friends."

"You'll have a headache," said John. "But you aren't concussed. Take some aspirin. Rest for the night. If you don't feel better by morning, call me. I'm in room seventeen."

"Take two aspirin and call me in the morning?" said Mark, and began to laugh helplessly. Gawain joined in, wobbly giggles.

"Just so," said Rupert, and escorted John from the room. He was already whispering into John's ear as they left the gathering.

"That's it for the night, darlings," Phryne told the party. "Aunty Mark needs her beauty sleep. Why not take a bottle home? And package up all this food, it's too good to waste."

"You can all come back to my place," offered Tommy. "Just down the street. My dad's away."

Slowly, gossiping, the choir scavenged the feast with the thoroughness of ants at an unguarded picnic and went away. Phryne saw them all leave. None of them had the wet arms and shirtfront which the murderer must have had. Phryne made sure that the rooms were empty and saw herself out.

That had been interesting. Someone had tried to kill Mark, who had no enemies. And wasn't a conductor. And Leonard was still in jail.

But she had been privileged to see John Wilson at work again. And so had Rupert. He would never look at his lover in that dismissive way again.

On the whole, a good night. Everyone, at least, was still alive.

Chapter Nineteen

Is death in hell more death than death in heaven?

Wallace Stevens,
"For an Old Woman in a Wig"

"So," said Robinson, "the murderer must have left early. None of the people you saw were or had been wet."

"No. It was early in the night so they were all clothed…no, I am not going to elaborate. Clothed in what they had worn to the party."

"Right," said Jack, grinning at what Phryne was not going to elaborate on.

"Only Mark was wearing a costume. A tunic and a sheet. He was still wearing the tunic when he was in the bath. He had been hit over the head, then rolled into the tub. The assailant needn't even have had to be very tall. Or very strong. There's a knack to moving an inert body. I have it myself."

Jack Robinson suppressed another smile.

"I can see how that might be handy," he told her. "But I don't reckon you could manhandle a hundred and fifty-odd pounds of bloke that far all by yourself."

"Lie on the floor," ordered Phryne.

He looked at her. She was serious. He did as she ordered, lying flat on his back. He hoped that Phryne's family would not come in.

They came in, of course—Dot, Jane, Ruth and Tinker. They stopped. They stared. Jack tried to sit up.

"Stay still," said Phryne sternly. "You have just been hit on the head and rendered momentarily unconscious. I have to move fast, so I can drown you before you start to wake up. Imagine that sofa is the bathtub. Are you imagining it?"

"Yes," said Jack, aware of four sets of fascinated eyes riveted on the scene.

"I can't dead-lift you; you're too heavy and I'm not strong enough. So I use your own body to move you. Here is a rigid lever, knee to hip. So I use that…" She forced his knee down and to one side, and pushed. His body rolled with it. "Then I use your shoulder and spine—they're all attached, see, your skeleton is a frame—and do this."

Another shove, and he rolled onto the sofa. The minions applauded.

Jack sat up. "All right, I was wrong. Where on earth did you learn to do that?"

"Loading stretchers on the Western Front," said Phryne. "It's called a *point d'appui*. A point of balance. So, as you see, the murderer might be anyone. I just need to find out who left that party early. They must have been wet. Someone might have noticed, though choirs do tend to be wrapped up in each other."

"How did you do that, Miss Phryne?" asked Jane. "Can you show me?"

"With your knowledge of anatomy it should be a cinch," Phryne told her. "But not now, and not with poor Detective Inspector Robinson. He's embarrassed enough to be going on with."

"No, really," said Jack, blushing to show that he wasn't embarrassed at all. "Do you think this attempted murder might be…might be because Mr. Henty is…"

"An invert?" asked Phryne. "Surely not. Anyone meeting him for more than seven seconds would know that. If they objected they wouldn't go to his party. Probably wouldn't be in the choir, either. It's well known that he is a general favourite."

"But that method, that opening his mouth and pouring champagne down his throat, that's…"

"Personal?" asked Phryne. "Yes, it is. And he

hasn't any rejected lovers floating around. I asked specially."

"What if he approached some bloke who doesn't bat for that team, and the other bloke took…"

"Belated, elaborate, vicious revenge?" asked Phryne. "It's possible. Just not very likely. Aunty Mark's usually pretty specific in his tastes. He wants someone who wants him in return. He wouldn't ask anyone of whom he wasn't pretty sure. He'd be too easy to blackmail. Look what happened to Oscar Wilde. They all walk a knife's edge every day. Anyway, the evening hadn't got to the invitation-only part. But I shall think about it."

"Good," said Jack. "Can I get up now?"

"Of course, my dear," said Phryne, extending a hand. "We may now consider you thoroughly drowned."

Ruth, at this statement, threw herself into Robinson's arms. "Just don't drown for real," she sobbed.

Jack patted her. "What's the matter with you, now, Ruthie?" he asked gently. "What's come to my good girl?"

"I just saw you drowned when Miss Phryne said that. I could see how it might happen. And I like you," said Ruth.

Jack hugged her. "I like you too," he told her,

offering her his handkerchief. "Wipe your eyes now. I promise not to get drowned."

"Never?" she demanded blurrily.

"As far as I can manage it," he assured her.

Jane, rigid with disapproval, had withdrawn to the parlour. Tinker didn't know where to look so sent Molly over to lick Ruth better. Molly obeyed and Ruth laughed as the warm tongue washed her face. Then Dot took Ruth away for some tea and iron tonic.

Jack let her go. Phryne fanned herself.

"What was that about?" asked Robinson. "Poor little thing!"

"She has a gentle tender heart, poor girl, and she imagined you drowned rather too vividly," explained Phryne. "And she likes you, so she was upset. You reacted correctly, Jack dear. But I and my family are really putting our backs into embarrassing you today, aren't we? Need I apologise?"

"For you manhandling me and then having a pretty girl cry over my corpse?" asked Robinson. "No fear!"

"Nice," said Phryne. "Tea or beer?"

"Better be tea," said Robinson. "Or maybe some of that coffee?"

"Coffee it is," said Phryne. "I'll have some too." And Mr. Butler withdrew.

"Thing is," remarked Robinson, "that this is

the third murderous assault connected with that choir. Shouldn't they just abandon this concert?"

"If they do that, we will never find out who is doing this." Phryne sipped her drink. Homemade lemonade and ice, lovely. "We have a new conductor tonight. Patrick Bell. I shall arrange a guard for him."

"But you can't trust any of the choristers!" objected Jack.

"I know two who are completely innocent," said Phryne. "And one more who probably is. None of them would have attacked Aunty Mark. And they are the requisite Big Blokes. If they shadow him at all times, he should be safe enough, and we might catch the killer. Otherwise they will have to disband, and that would be a pity. Besides, I want to sing this oratorio."

"Have it your own way," sighed Robinson. "Keep me posted."

"I will," said Phryne.

Robinson drank his coffee. It was real good stuff. And it was nice to know that someone would weep at his funeral.

◇◇◇

"Right, let's get started," said Patrick Bell. He was a middle-sized, rangy welterweight with cropped brown hair and an easy manner. Phryne was disposed to approve of him. He was conducting from the choral score, for a start. He had no floppy hair to push back and so far he had shown no signs of licking his fingers.

His deep blue eyes flashed briefly over the choir. "I don't know what you've been doing with this work so far, but here's how it looks from where I'm standing. You're a small choir, and I'm told you are really good singers. So while we don't have the forces to do a huge Sir Thomas Beecham production number out of this, that doesn't matter." His thin lips curved in a momentary grin. "Because I don't think that's what Mendelssohn wanted. This is a work of light and shade. You may have noticed, for instance, that the recitatives are very spare and filled with silences. If he'd wanted to do Handel-style recits with first inversion chords with the left hand, he would have written them. He knew how to. He just didn't want that. I've had some of the soloists clenching their fingers in mock anguish while they sang them, and that's not good. You have to sing the silences in Mendelssohn. There are moments of comedy, there are moments of savagery, and there are choruses of angelic bliss. I want you to sing "He Shall Give His Angels," and "He That Shall Endure to the End" as if you were little angels flapping your heavenly wings.

Barely any vibrato, please: just a little bit of colour on top. And if you can sing them the way I think Mendelssohn wanted, then I'll consider giving you "Cast Thy Burden" as well. That's usually done as a bravura quartet, but I'd like to see it as another angelic chorus. So let's hear you sing "He That Shall Endure", please."

Fair enough. Another Mendelssohn purist. The chorus picked up their scores, took a deep breath, and began to sing.

Matthew had done well to take them over the lumpy bits over and over again. The entries were still a little ragged, but the bulk of the notes were there and in the right place. The conductor stopped them seldom, always to go back over a large chunk of music, so that the alterations merged into the whole and made sense. He did not swear. He did not abuse them. He did not yell. At most, he winced occasionally. His beat was as clear and regular as a metronome. He knew exactly what he wanted, and meant to get it.

Yes, Phryne approved of Patrick Bell. So did the professor. He played Schubert lieder for the soloists to sing during tea break. Tabitha and Caterina sang "The Brook" to general applause.

"Hello," said Patrick Bell to Phryne. "You're the famous Miss Fisher, aren't you? Pleased to meet you."

"Delighted," said Phryne. She was, too.

Phryne shook hands. Tommy and Oliver flanked the conductor, who was beginning to look a little beset, even overshadowed.

"You chaps couldn't find something else to do for a moment, could you?" he asked.

"Miss Fisher said to stay with you," said Tommy. "So I'm staying."

"And me," said Oliver. "We always do what Miss Fisher tells us."

"I did," Phryne told Patrick Bell. "Because you are a very good conductor and we don't want you to go the way of the other two."

"I heard about that," said Patrick.

"So," Phryne rejoined, "you have a bodyguard. They are responsible for your body, and not for anyone else's, and while you're with us, you aren't going anywhere without them."

"Oh," said Patrick. "That's very kind of you, Miss Fisher, but I can take—"

"Care of yourself?" she finished. "So could Tregennis and James. And Mark Henty."

"God, don't say anything's happened to Aunty Mark?" gasped Bell. "Best voice in Australia. Nice chap, too. Even though he's "so". I was looking forward to his Elijah, it ought to be tremendous. He's a treasure. That baritone with a tenor, almost clarinet quality!"

"He's all right," soothed Phryne. "But someone tried to kill him last night. And he's another big strong man who can take care of himself."

"I get the point, Miss Fisher," conceded Bell.

"Good, because the next time I was having to say "big strong man" it was going to be "big stwong man" and no one wants me to do that," she told him. "Scorn is not good for the voice."

"Neither is getting murdered," observed Tommy.

"Too right," said Oliver.

Together they constituted a wall of muscle and it might take a siege engine to get through them to Bell. And Phryne doubted her murderer had brought a ballista with him. She noted that Leonard was back, looking nervous. No one was talking to him. He bustled up to Patrick with a sheaf of notes about Mendelssohn and entered into a ferocious discussion. Discussions raised no welts. Leonard was unarmed and either Tommy or Oliver could flatten him like a bedsheet with one blow of a mighty fist.

Rehearsal began again. Bell stopped the choir.

"No, no," he said. "You want to sound round, round vowels. Not back-country Australian," he drawled. "You must have respect for the language you are singing."

"Then why aren't we singing it in German?" sniped Leonard. "It was written in German."

"Because we want the audience to understand the message," replied Bell. Leonard didn't seem to have any effect on him at all, though Leonard drove Phryne up the wall. "The message is faith and love and truth and peace shall conquer. No one who lived through the last war would associate peace, truth and love with German."

There was a clash of notes as someone slammed both hands down on the piano keys. Then Professor Szabo staggered out from behind his instrument. A long, sharp dart fell from a blowpipe in his grasp. He shuffled forward, fell on his knees at Patrick's feet, and took his hand. Oliver and Tommy moved closer. Phryne broke ranks to kick aside the weapon and draw her little gun.

"I couldn't kill you," wept Professor Szabo. "You understand Mendelssohn."

Rehearsal, after that, was abandoned. Patrick Bell, rather shaken, sat down with Professor Szabo while several choristers went to find a telephone to summon Detective Inspector Robinson from his cosy home, where he was doubtless enquiring after the state of health of his orchids. He would want to be in on this. Phryne kept the little gun to hand. Professor Szabo might be peaceable enough at present, but if he had managed to kill both Tregennis and brought down the "big stwong" men all by himself, then he had to be closely watched. Phryne would back her Beretta against anything, however big or strong.

The old man was so unthreatening. He was shrunken and drunken and running out of years as fast as a mayfly runs out of days.

"Tell me, Professor," she said, patting his hand. "You found Tregennis already dying—I understand that; the man was a pig."

"I just stuff the music down his throat. He never bother to learn it properly. I take the pages out of my own score. I know this music in my bones. I don't need a score," said the old man.

"Right, and I am sure that Henry James was a cruel and stupid man, which is a bad combination, I agree."

"He butchered the music," snarled the professor. Some of the choir stepped back onto the toes of those behind. Suddenly, they were beginning to believe that the old prof might be a murderer after all.

"Yes, he did," said Phryne in a voice as smooth as cream. "Where did you get the arsenic?"

"I work a while in a glass factory when I came here," he replied, still holding Bell's hand. Tommy was watching him very closely. If he produced a knife or something, Tommy could stop him.

Tommy liked feeling brave. "I keep a little arsenic, in case things get too bad for me. They tell me all about how dangerous it is. So I borrow orchestral score, and I paint it on pages. If he stopped licking, then he goes free. Until I think of something else. But he didn't, he was a pig, and—"

"All right," Phryne commented. "I understand. But what had Mr. Henty done to you? He's a great singer."

"Pervert," snarled the old man. "He made fun of the oratorio with his Pirate King. And he was going to sing the prophet, the holy man! Elijah is a prophet of God! This is holy music. And he had his parties and his friends and his…his…"

"Success," prompted Phryne. "His admirers."

Professor Szabo showed the stumps of yellowing teeth.

"What right had a pervert to admirers? People love him! And he would corrupt the music, the divine music!"

"So you knocked him out, stuck him in the tub, and poured champagne down his throat?" asked Phryne. Patrick Bell was beginning to feel beset again. The old man's clasp on his hand was hot and his pianist's fingers were very strong.

"I did!" said the old man. "I did it and I am proud—proud! But you," he said to Bell, "you understand. I was going to fire that dart into you.

No one would have known where it came from. Then the concert would be cancelled. No one would be able to lay filthy hands on my Elijah."

"But you liked my conducting," said Patrick Bell.

"Yes! You understand Mendelssohn. The silences. The angels."

"So you couldn't kill me," said Patrick steadily.

"No," confessed Professor Szabo. He burst into tears.

◇◇◇

Jack Robinson arrived, was apprised of the situation, and took the professor away. The choir sat in the hall and sang rounds and madrigals. "*Aprille is in my mistress' face,*" sang Tommy to Caterina. "*But in her heart, but in her heart a cold December.*"

They smiled at each other.

Singers, thought Phryne. Well, that concludes that puzzle, and neither Rupert nor I could solve it. The prof had left Mark's party, covering his wet shirt with his coat, before the alarm had been raised. And everyone was so used to his unexpected arrivals and abrupt departures that they didn't even notice him.

Calliope was weeping. She was being consoled by Bones.

"It's all right," said the young man. "It's like I told you. He isn't fit to plead."

"That's not why I'm crying," she informed him. "But never mind. I would like a hug anyway."

Bones obliged.

"Oh, Lord," sighed Matthew, burying his head in his hands.

"What seems to be the problem?" asked Phryne.

"Now we don't have a pianist," said Matthew. "We can manage all right for the rehearsals, but who's going to play the piano in the concert?"

"There is," Phryne told him, "a concert-level pianist presently in Melbourne who owes me rather a large favour."

"Will he need to be paid?" asked Matthew.

"He already has been," Phryne told him.

◇◇◇

Phryne telephoned the Windsor and told John Wilson that she had to see him and Rupert at once.

"Very well, my dear. Is this another medical emergency?"

"No, it's the solution to the murders, and Rupert didn't deduce it, and neither did I. You will want to see his face as I tell him and I want to ask him for a favour."

"I do and you shall," replied John. "Would you like to come up to our room?"

So quickly had it become "our" room.

"I'll be right there," said Phryne. "Order me a very large gin. And maybe a little tonic. If you insist. The choir will be flocking over soon, so prepare for a noisy night."

"I'm prepared," chuckled John.

◇◇◇

"Before we go to Aunty Mark's—" Patrick halted the general movement to the door with the conductor's raised hands; obediently, everyone stopped "—we have to decide what to tell him. About the murders."

"What should we tell him?" asked Tabitha.

"That a mad man tried to kill him because he mocked Mendelssohn with his Pirate King," said Bell, looking at them all in turn. Heads nodded. Tutts were tutted. No one wanted to flay Aunty Mark with Professor Szabo's blistering hatred.

"But…" Leonard started. The entire chorus turned as one and glared at him. He struggled. "The truth…"

"Leave the truth to Mendelssohn and God," said Bell.

"But…" Leonard was wriggling.

Tommy dropped a meaty hand on his

shoulder. "We aren't going to hurt Aunty Mark's feelings," he told Leonard. "Because if we do, he won't sing for us. And we want him to sing for us. Also, we really like him. Am I making myself clear?"

"But…" Leonard's voice was a whisper. Holding in a piece of information this juicy would give him an ulcer, he knew it.

Tommy leaned down so that he could speak into Leonard's ear.

"If," he whispered, "Aunty Mark learns about this from you, I will pound you into putty."

"And I will help him," whispered Oliver into his other ear.

"Really smooth putty," elaborated Tommy. "Like they use to fill cracks between floorboards."

"All right!" squeaked Leonard.

"Not a word, gesture, lifted eyebrow, pursed lips, grimace, knowing smirk, hint, allusion or written communication?" demanded Isabelle, who worked in a lawyer's office.

"No!" squealed Leonard.

"Good," said Patrick. "You know, I could really do with a drink. Several drinks. Big ones. Are your rehearsals always this exciting?"

◇ ◇ ◇

When she reached their door, John let Phryne in, Rupert handed her a very large gin to which a little tonic had been added, and both escorted her to a chair.

"You solved it?" asked Rupert. His voice was quite even, but a little rancour was leaking out at the edges.

"No," confessed Phryne, who had much less invested in always being right. "I didn't have a clue, it was a complete surprise."

Rupert relaxed a little. "Not enough data?" he asked.

"Precisely, and a very interesting series of misdirections, the first of which was, of course, that in Tregennis' case there were two murderers."

"*Novus actus interveniens*," said Rupert. He looked like a large, well-fed cat, lounging on this untouched bed—this must be the room they weren't sleeping in—and plumping a pillow for John, who needed to rest his leg. Without being asked. It would be strange having a lover who could anticipate one's every wish. Intoxicating, in fact. Like this drink. She felt she had to translate.

"Which, learned colleague, is Latin for "a new act intervening." If the violinist had been the only murderer, then we would have found Tregennis on the floor, an obvious victim of a heart attack from chronic ingrained bad temper, and it would not have been investigated," said Phryne. "He might not even have been examined."

"Possibly," murmured Rupert. "If the medical examiner was busy."

"Indeed," agreed Phryne. "Then there was James. A noxious individual. Plethora of enemies. Hosts of them. It would be hard to find anyone who *didn't* want to kill him. But then there was Mr. Henty. A darling. Everyone loved him. And that attempted murder seemed more personal, more vicious, more—"

"Manic," supplied John. "An outburst of crazy hatred."

"Exactly. The act of a fanatic. I could not imagine who it was; and neither could you, Rupert?"

"No," he admitted abruptly. "I could not deduce. Too many variables."

"Quite. So all I could think of was to provide my new conductor with bodyguards, Tommy and Oliver, both huge, as a wall between him and the killer. It would take time to dig a hole through either of them and someone was bound to notice."

"A good notion," agreed John. "So what happened?"

"I shall a tale unfold," said Phryne with relish, and unfolded it.

She was pleased with the result. John and Rupert gradually, perhaps without noticing, drew closer and closer together, until they were actually embracing, shoulder to shoulder, backs against the headboard. John had commented as she spoke, calling upon his God repeatedly, but Sheffield had not said a word. Phryne finished her drink.

"You could not have found him," said John. "You didn't have enough clues. Either of you."

"Insufficient data," agreed Rupert. "They hate us," he added flatly.

"Some of them," agreed Phryne. "Especially if you limit your search to deranged Hungarian maniacs with an obsession for Mendelssohn. This is a small set," she told him, smiling.

"I suppose so," he replied, and smiled in return. He was more beautiful, now. More present. The Sons of God, she recalled, who descended to earth and fell in love with humans. Rupert was definitely one of them.

"And now, I have a favour to ask," she told him.

"Ask," he said.

Phryne asked.

◇◇◇

In the morning Phryne woke with a headache and a sense of a job well done. Or at least, done. And neatly packaged in brown paper, tied with a ribbon, and posted to the correct address. Dot brought her coffee and croissant and she sipped and nibbled with pleasure.

"Detective Inspector Robinson, a huge bloke

who said to call him Tommy, and Hugh are downstairs," she told her employer.

"Not a new problem, Dot? I'm out of solutions and I have a headache," said Phryne.

"Here's your aspirin, Miss, and they're just sitting down to breakfast. You've got time to recover a bit. You must have got home late," said Dot.

"Yes, it was a rather wild party. Did you hear the end of the mystery?" asked Phryne, taking the powders and drinking down a large glass of water.

"Yes, Miss, Hugh told me. That Mr. Sheffield didn't work it out, either, Miss."

"As long as it was resolved, Dot, I don't care who worked it out. At least it's over."

"Yes, Miss, it's over. The prisoner killed himself last night in the holding cells. He had arsenic concealed in a coat button. He's dead."

"That's that, then. Poor old man. A Borgia plot and a Borgia death. I think I had better have a coolish shower. That ought to set me up for the day. Wait, Dot—if Szabo is dead, why are Jack and Hugh here with Tommy? Apart from the pleasure of our company, of course."

Dot blushed. "The old man's room. He's left all his property to this Tommy. And Hugh says that Detective Inspector Robinson wants a stickybeak."

"So do I," replied Phryne. "Back in a tick. Find me some easily washed clothes suitable for poking around sordid places," she added as she vanished, naked, into the bathroom.

When she came back Dot gave her a cotton skirt and loose coat in dark blue, which Phryne had never much liked, and a faded blush-pink blouse.

"Good," said Phryne, flinging on her garments. "If this ensemble gets destroyed, it will be no loss. See you later, Dot dear."

◇◇◇

Collins Street, thought Phryne; my life has lately revolved around this bit of Collins Street. The room was, as she had predicted, sordid. The landlord of number eighty-eight was lounging in the doorway, eyes alert for easily abstracted valuables. Robinson ordered Hugh to go downstairs with him and pick up anything he might have taken from this room "for safekeeping." The landlord sighed. Cops. He had better hand over the engraved watch, the two pounds ten and the cufflinks. But he was keeping the odd seven and threepence. A man had his pride.

The room stank of old alcohol and perpetual misery and unwashed socks. Tommy, exerting his strength, broke through eight layers of paint and hauled the window open. The clanging of trams drifted in with the smell of ozone.

The floor of the room was largely carpeted with bottles. Tommy, a tidy soul, was packing them into a box so that no one turned an ankle. The bed was indescribable. Professor Szabo had not gone in for laundry. Phryne found a clear space in the nook which held clothes and dropped into it the sheets, a filthy shirt, some appalling underwear, threadbare socks, dreadful trousers. The only thing actually hung up in this wardrobe were his concert clothes, safely enclosed in the cleaner's paper bag. The only pair of shoes on the floor were concert shoes, polished shiny and worn through, their soles complemented with cardboard.

Otherwise there were bottles. Jack took the drawers of the dressing table out and laid them on the stained, denuded mattress.

"Hello, hello," he said. He had found a small shagreen case.

"A medal?" asked Phryne. Jack opened it. The hinge broke. This hadn't been opened in a long time.

"I don't know that one," said Tommy.

"*Eisernes Kreuz*. It's an Iron Cross," whispered Phryne. "And here's his citation." She puzzled through the German which described the feat for which the honour had been awarded. "He was a doctor," she told Tommy. "He rescued the wounded under fire. On the Western Front. That's how he knew how to move unconscious bodies. His name was Maximilian Schneider."

"Tailor," said Robinson. "That's what Schneider means."

"And so does Szabo," said Phryne. "He ran away from the Great War. He had been a concert pianist with Beecham and then he joined up. And we know what that war did to people."

"Poor old bugger," said Tommy. "I should send this back to his people. Any letters or anything? Did he have any people?"

"I can't see anything else. Here are concert programs, more concert programs—yes, see, here's his name. He did play with Beecham. Maximilian Schneider. I think he's kept every one."

"Put them in this bag," said Tommy. "I'll look after them."

Phryne packed the carefully preserved paper into the cloth bag. "And here's a letter. Read a lot; look at the wearing in the folds. A love letter, perhaps, to be so treasured. Oh," she said.

"To a very fine pianist, with thanks for a superb performance," Tommy read over Phryne's shoulder.

"It must have been with this," said Hugh, who had retrieved the landlord's loot. He opened the back of a gold watch. "*To Maximilian Schneider, a fine pianist, Beecham.* Gosh," added Hugh.

Phryne was flooded with a sense of the

limitless tragedies of the world, which was soaked in bitter tears. She shook herself.

"Right, nothing else here but razor and tooth-brush and cheap soap. You?" she asked Robinson.

"No, just some newspapers—no letters, no passport. He must have jumped ship. Left his old life behind."

"But he couldn't leave music," said Tommy. "You can never leave music behind."

This was such a profound comment from someone whom Phryne had considered simple that she stared at him.

"I can understand what Caterina sees in you," she told him.

"Yes, well, anyone got time for a drink?" he asked, blushing. "I've got two pounds ten."

"And I'll get the rest of the money from that landlord on the way out," said Jack.

Chapter Twenty

Just as my fingers on these keys
Make music, so the selfsame sounds
On my spirit make a music, too.
Music is feeling, then, not sound;
And thus it is that what I feel
Here in this room, desiring you,
Thinking of your blue-shadowed silk,
Is music.

Wallace Stevens
"Peter Quince at the Clavier"

John knew that the task would be hard, but he was resolved to go through with it anyway. Whatever Sheffield might say about the matter, Phryne had given them each other, and therefore her favour must be repaid. He was firm. He was determined. Rupert had never seen him like that before. He agreed.

But that didn't mean he had to like it.

"The creaky old heap of strings will be

miserably out of tune," he protested, as they went in the front door at the Town Hall. The piano was on stage. It was a highly polished Bechstein Grand. And the piano tuner was just playing a brisk Irish jig to test the tuning.

"Wrong," said John, with relish. He so seldom got to say that to Sheffield.

The piano tuner, led by his little daughter, tapped his way down the aisle. He stopped near Rupert. The little girl whispered something. The piano tuner said, "'Scuse me, mate," took Rupert's hand, spread it over his own, and pinched the base of the thumb. Rupert, unused to Australians, was at a loss and did not move, frozen with outrage. "Yair," said the old man. "You'll be bonzer. Beaut piano. Nice hands."

The little girl smiled shyly at John and led her father away. Rupert scrubbed his right hand down the side of his trousers to wipe off the contaminating touch.

"He was just being friendly," John told him. "He's blind, he couldn't just look at your hands. Come along. Play me a song."

"I am sadly out of practice," protested Rupert. "I probably won't be able to remember how to play."

"Try," insisted John. "I'm not critical."

He knew that was exactly the wrong things to say, which was why he said it. Rupert bridled, pulled up his cuffs, and laid hands on the keys. He played a C chord. Then he played all the notes on the keyboard, one after another, a long ordered tumble of sharps and flats.

"Adequate," said Rupert.

He closed his eyes and instead of the loud, flashy thing with a lot of chords which John expected, he played a little music box tune by Couperin. It was charming.

"Nice," said John. "Play some more, love?"

"Requests?" asked Rupert. He flexed his hands. Nice hands, the blind man had said. It had been far too long since he had touched a keyboard. And now he could play for John. That was an unexpected pleasure.

"You're one with culture," said John. "Mozart? That Russian feller?"

"Mozart is the king," said Rupert, and began to play, from memory, the piano concerto he loved the most, K 595. The last movement. He found the fact that he loved Mozart and now loved John interesting. Loving John did not mean that he loved Mozart less. Curious. He was not, however, intending to add anyone else to his portfolio. Mozart and John would do nicely.

John listened. No such decorative creature had sat down at the piano since Liszt died, he thought.

Tall, slim, tumble of raven curls, pale skin, elegant profile. Rupert was completely focused on the music. His violet eyes were open and tranced. His hands flew. The music built all around him, like the golden ladder which took Jacob to heaven.

Other people had drifted into the auditorium, attracted by the music. Cleaners docked their brooms, the ticket seller left her box, the carpenter put down his tools. Twenty musicians left their backstage rehearsal to lurk in the wings and listen with appreciation.

"This bloke, who is he?" asked French Horn of Trumpet. "Why haven't we heard of him before?"

"He's that mathematician the Harmony hired to do their *Elijah*," said First Violin, unconsciously straightening her skirt and combing back her hair. First violins are always well informed. "He's come to try out the piano. The door keeper told me."

"Jeez, he's bloody good," said Percussion. "How do Harmony rate him? He's concert level."

"Lucky," said First Violin. "I suppose. We'd better get this *Elijah* right."

"Yair," agreed First Clarinet. "I don't think he'd like it if we messed it up. Someone go and get Greg. P'raps we ought to have a bit of a rehearse with this bloke. What's his name?"

"Sheffield," said First Violin. "Rupert Sheffield. Gosh, isn't he gorgeous?"

"Good player," agreed First Clarinet.

First Violin whispered, "That wasn't what I meant, Jimmy," as the concerto came to an end. Rupert shook his hands and wiped his hair out of his eyes, and became aware that he was being applauded.

He scowled. Then he stood up and bowed to the cleaners and the carpenters. And John. John returned the bow.

"God, that was marvellous," he enthused.

"I'm a little rusty. Eleven wrong notes and one transposed phrase."

"I never heard one note out of place," said John enthusiastically.

"And neither did we," said First Violin, who had ventured out onto the broad expanse of empty stage, unsupported. "Hello," she added, quailing a little under the violet gaze. "We're the orchestra."

Seventeen, if that, female, violinist (callus under jaw), nervous, Australian, prodigy, lonely, poor, orchestra is her family, thought Rupert.

"Only one of you?" asked Rupert. He smiled. John exhaled the breath he had been holding. Being loved had had a wonderful effect on Rupert's manners.

"There's twenty of us," she explained as the others came onto the stage.

"So I see," said Rupert.

"And this is our conductor, Mr. Kale."

"Mr. Kale," said Rupert politely.

"Heard you playing," said Greg Kale, a short, perspiring, plump man with sandy hair. "Lovely. You played with an orchestra much?"

"No," said Rupert, concealing the fact that he had never played with an orchestra at all.

"Right, right, you were recital, weren't you? Suppose we do a run-through of *Elijah* now, and we get the feel of playing with you."

"I don't have the piano score," said Rupert.

"No worries, mate, here she is," said Mr. Kale briskly, plucking the score from a pile of them. "Now, Pat Bell will be conducting the actual performance, due to me losing to him when we cut cards for it—I reckon he's got a dodgy pack; I always lose to him. But my boys and girls are good. Some of 'em are bloody good. And I won't have 'em forgotten for a lot of bloody screechers hogging the limelight. So we need to get this one right."

Rupert sat down again. John rose and stood beside him. He couldn't read enough music to know when to turn a page, but he and Rupert had devised a system of nods so they worked very well together. The only real difference in their partnership, John thought, as he propped his stick so that he could easily lean on it and turned to the first movement of *Elijah*, was that now I can tell him how much I love him, and he can tell me.

"Sheffield?" he asked, under cover of the orchestra dropping music stands, swearing, and accusing each other of stealing their favourite chair. (The mystery of how the timpani sticks ended up in the cello case never did get solved.)

"John?" breathed Sheffield.

"I don't think I've ever been so happy in my life."

"Nor me," said Rupert, and very gently laid his hand on John's thigh.

First Violin saw this gesture, as she came to the piano for her tuning notes, and sighed.

John heard her, and looked up into her eyes. "What's your name, my dear?" he asked.

"Jasmine," she replied, tightening a string.

"There'll be someone for you, Jasmine," he told her.

"How do you know?" she demanded in a fierce undertone.

"Because there was someone for me," said John. "When I never thought there would be."

She smiled. Rupert murmured an agreement.

Jasmine took her bow and played a long, clear, heartfelt A.

From "As God the Lord of Israel Liveth" through "He Shall Give His Angels Charge Over Thee", from "Baal, We Cry to Thee" through "Them That Shall Endure" all the way to "And Then Shall Your Light Break Forth," everyone agreed that the concert was a triumph.

It had been sold out, as news like Rupert Sheffield and Mark Henty got around in musical circles. Jack Robinson had quite enjoyed it, especially since his killer was caught, the murders all explained, and the poor old man who had done them was safely in the morgue and had no need to worry about being hanged. No doubt he was now explaining his actions to Satan, who was reputed to enjoy a good tune.

Dot liked the sacred quality of the libretto, and Tinker loved angel music. Ruth liked the way that they all looked, the ladies in long black skirts and white shirts, the gentlemen in black trousers and white shirts. The soloists in liturgical colours: Chloe (soprano) in green, Caterina (soprano) also in green, but darker, Tabitha (alto) in purple, the bass Oliver with a gold rosette, and the tenor Matthew with a white one.

Jane was uninterested in music. She wondered if Dr. Wilson was straining his stitches and over-exerting his injured leg by standing so long next to Sheffield, turning the pages. Why turn pages? Couldn't someone invent a device like a piano roll, which scrolled the music past the player's eyes? That would mean no one would have to stand there and turn pages. They could sit down and not hurt their sore leg.

Wasted effort made Jane cross. On the other hand, her chess opponent looked very handsome in his beautiful black suit. Savile Row again, she assumed. Jane could hear the ladies around her, discussing not the music or the execution of it, but how very delectable Sheffield was. Jane rolled her eyes. Sheffield was spoken for. Couldn't they see how his eyes were resting on his page-turner? No one else's approval mattered to Rupert Sheffield.

The choir and the orchestra grinned at each other, light-headed. "We got away with it" could have summed up their mood. "We just sang way above our usual ability! Where did *that* come from?"

The orchestra felt the same. No one had lost their place, those tricky entries were always marked with a good downbeat from this Bell bloke, who wasn't a half-bad conductor, and the choir had mostly kept up. The piano had been close to fault-less and Jasmine had played as though possessed by the spirit of Paganini.

Everyone bowed. The applause went on. The soloists walked off. The clapping continued. The soloists came back. Phryne heard Mark say, "Three curtain calls, darlings, then I'm off to the party."

He was right. Three curtain calls, and the soloists walked off and did not come back. Followed by the orchestra. The conductor bowed one last time and stepped off the stage. Followed by the choir.

"That ought to keep us for the winter," Matthew remarked to Oliver. "We sold out the Town Hall!"

"Some of it's down to that Pommy bloke," conceded Tommy. "And that little girl with the violin."

"And some of it is down to us!" cheered Calliope, embracing Oliver. "And Pat!" She embraced him, too. It was an embracing sort of night. John, who felt the need to sit down for a bit, fended off questions from Jane as to how badly his leg hurt.

"Nothing at all, I'm just a bit tired. Wasn't that a marvellous concert? Haven't heard better in London."

"John, are you all right?" asked Rupert anxiously.

"I'm just sitting down for a bit, my dear chap. You played very well."

"I have never played with an orchestra before," confessed Rupert. Jane noted that his curls were damp. It was hot under the lights. "Exhilarating! I kept expecting something hideous to happen."

"But it didn't. It sounded fine!" said Phryne. "Rupert, John, your taxi is waiting to carry us to the hotel in style. Jane, Ruth, Tink and Dot, your taxi is waiting to ferry you to St. Kilda. I shall be home late. Come along, darlings," she said, ushering them effortlessly out of the Town Hall and into the street. "Good night." She waved and her family was driven away. Cec opened the car door and allowed Rupert to help John in. Somehow he didn't mind as much as he had used to that Rupert knew how crippled he was. Phryne planted herself in the front seat next to the driver.

"Windsor, Cec dear. Did you enjoy the music?"

"Beaut," commented Cec, the hand-rolled cigarette never moving from the corner of his mouth. "They did real good in that tricky chorus, where if you ain't careful it sort of sounds like a waltz. "Thanks Be to God, He Laveth the Thirsty Land." Mendelssohn ain't sugary. Bloody good work. And the orchestra was first rate, especially that little girl and her fiddle and your mate on the piano."

"Thank you," said Rupert faintly. He would never get used to Australia.

"And this ride's on me," said Cec, stopping outside the Windsor. "Thanks for the ticket."

"My pleasure," said Phryne. Cec let John alight at his own pace, then slammed the door and took off. Rupert took John's arm.

"You'll want to wash and change," said Phryne.

"I will, this suit's like a sponge," said Rupert. He had become human.

"But will you come up to the party later?"

"Certainly," said John.

"Indeed," replied Sheffield. "I would like to congratulate Mr. Henty on his noble performance."

"See you then," said Phryne and ran up the stairs, moving through groups of choristers, alight with success, and probably a bit short of oxygen. Phryne had a party in prospect, a drink and a few of the Windsor's celebrated cocktail canapés, and then she would be taking Matthew home with her. The murderer was dead, the case closed, John had his Rupert and all was gas and gaiters.

◇◇◇

Aunty Mark was enthroned again. The choir milled about, intoxicated with their performance. The only sign of tension was in Gawain, who had nearly lost Mark and didn't intend to let him out of his sight ever again. He certainly would never bathe alone in the future, though that would not worry either of them.

Phryne collected a drink. She noticed that Mark had changed his brand of champagne to Veuve Clicquot, quite Phryne's own favourite. Understandably, he had lost his taste for the Pol Roget '97. Excellent wine though it was. Caterina was elated, climbing onto Tommy's shoulders and singing, "*Free from wards in Chancery, up in the air so high, so high,*" while Tommy hung onto her legs with an expression of baffled devotion which simultaneously brought tears to Phryne's eyes and made her giggle. Free indeed! Free to find another lover, free of anxiety, free of care altogether.

Which called for another drink. She turned in her concert white and black, anonymous in the crowd, and someone offered her a frosted glass.

Matthew. Oh, he was good-looking. Snub nose, broad face, golden hair which begged to be tousled—so she tousled it. Trout-pool eyes, warming into hope. Red mouth begging to be kissed.

So Phryne kissed it. Then she kissed it again. Then she drank the drink.

"Will you go home with me?" she asked.

"I would go anywhere with you," he answered.

"A very good reply," said Phryne. "Agreeably unconditional." She patted his chest and grinned at him.

A stir at the door announced the entry of Sheffield and John Wilson. There was a cheer. Rupert slid through the well-wishers to congratulate Mark. Aunty put his head on one side, suppressed a laugh, and congratulated Sheffield on his "performance."

John laughed and found a seat. He was instantly supplied with drinks and food by elated choristers. Here was an audience member who could tell them how good they had been.

And John did. It was his honest opinion, which warmed their hearts.

"*Tu as joué du piano comme un ange.*" You played like an angel, said Phryne to Rupert.

"*Et tu as chanté comme une ange.*" You sang like an angel, he rejoined, violet eyes glowing.

"*Qu'en est-il de Jean?*" And what of John? asked Phryne.

He laid a hand on her shoulder, a voluntary touch. "*Tout ira bien pour Jean,*" he said. All will be well with John.

"*Pourquoi?*" asked Phryne, mesmerised.

"*Parce que John est un ange incarné.*" Because John really is an angel.

"*Tu l'as remarqué?*" Oh, you noticed? asked Phryne, patting the hand.

"*On me l'a signalé.*" It was drawn to my attention, said Rupert, and smiled a conspiratorial smile.

◇◇◇

"Sing for me," John suggested. "I would like that."

He was running out of compliments. They ringed him. Phryne, Matthew, Calliope, Caterina still mounted on Tommy, Oliver, Miriam, Lydia, Chloe, DavidandLobelia, Isabelle, Irene, Bones and Tabitha, Alison, Millicent, Annie, Mary, Geneva, Luke, Ophelia, Aaron, Emmeline, Maisie, Daniel Smith, and Josephine, Leonard, Luigi, and Julia (that's going to be an explosive mixture, thought Phryne; light the blue touch paper and retire immediately), Helen and Jenny.

"What shall we sing?" asked Matthew.

"Whatever you sing when you're happy," said John desperately.

Sheffield rescued him. "I heard you sing Laudate last night," he suggested. "Christopher Tye."

"*Laudate nomen Domini, vos servi Domini,*" they sang, the four parts meeting and melting and joining in an entrancing way. "*Ab ortu solis usque ad occasum ejus. Decreta Dei iusta sunt, et cor exhilarant! Laudate Deum, principes, et omnes populi!*"

So they did. Praise the Lord, princes and all people. John and Rupert smiled, drank a final toast, and went back to number seventeen and their shared rhapsodies.

Thereafter the party slipped into rude songs, ruder songs, and positively obscene songs. There seemed to be no end to their repertoire.

All of which, Matthew noticed, Phryne knew. Even the one about the wheel. Even the one about the protected status of the hedgehog on shipboard. He had edged closer to her and was standing at her side when she put out a hand and asked, "Coming?"

And he followed her, as he had said he would.

If Phryne had a plan, she always carried it out unless it was a really unwise plan, when she might think about it again. This was a good idea that needed no further consideration. Matthew was whisked through the night, admitted, and conducted through the silent house, up a flight of stairs, and into a lady's boudoir such as he had never seen.

She turned his shoulder so that he saw his face in the mirror. The reflection was crowned with ivy leaves.

"Are you a bacchante?" he asked. She kissed him in reply.

All previous, fumbling, not really sure which way to turn his head to fit that mouth, nose-banging episodes in his past were forgotten. Phryne knew exactly what she wanted. So did Matthew.

"Buttons," she said, both hands at the front of his shirt. He tried to undo the ones on her concert shirt. They were dressed exactly alike. They resisted his fingers. Phryne flicked them open, shedding the shirt and the camisole under it. Breasts.

He had never got enough of breasts. These were perfect; they fitted into the palms of his hands. They felt indescribably lovely.

"Matt," she breathed. "Just remember this. I don't belong to you. I don't belong to anyone. And you don't belong to me. I just want to make love with you. Agreed?"

"Agreed," he whispered. Of course she didn't

belong to him. No one this…divine could belong to anyone but herself. But, oh, she was dropping the skirt, kicking off her shoes, rolling down her stockings. He grappled with his obdurate garments. Why did anyone put so many buttons on trousers? What use were they? Had he ever *asked* for buttons? Finally, he managed to divest himself of every impediment, and flung himself down on Phryne's bed, where she was waiting for him.

Naked, she was beautiful and curious. She rolled him over and studied his back, licked a line down his spine, turned him back again and threw herself onto him, like an amorous cat, sliding and purring. He grabbed a thigh and a handful of buttock and ground himself closer to her soft flesh, her smooth skin. Then he found himself engulfed in warmth, and stifled a groan in her kiss. Nipples scraped his chest. Fingers caught in his hair. He felt the strangest internal series of muscles clutch and close like a hot, wet, velvet-gloved hand. He cried out.

He found himself flat on his back, wet, panting, astounded, while Phryne nibbled meditatively on his earlobe.

"That was good," she drawled.

"Yes!" he said.

"For a beginning," she told him. "*Baise-moi!*"

◇◇◇

When Matthew woke in the morning to the censorious glare of a black cat, which wasn't one of his black cats, his world had utterly changed. For the better.

Phryne liked happy endings.

Glossary and Notes

"SO" accompanied by a gesture, the hand held bent from the wrist with the little finger crooked, was a universally recognised sign for a homosexual man. As was the term "playing for the other team." Before the useful phrase "Are you a friend of Dorothy?" which allowed gay men to safely identify each other. There were, of course, other markers <g>, but these ones seem to have been in use since Oscar Wilde's time. Male homosexuality was illegal and punishable by imprisonment until very recently. Practitioners of the "love that dare not speak its name" walked the edge of a razor every day, and had to be careful. Contemporary documents use both the term "queen" and "quean," which seems to have been pronounced differently, perhaps "quaine." An incomplete limerick I found in some collected letters—the first lines of which are "There once was a pretty young quean / his suitors were often in pain'—leads me to this conclusion, though I wish the irritating person who scribbled it in a margin had scribbled the rest. How did it end? Gain, Main, Deign, Fain, Again, Vain? Rats. I have ventured to finish it in the "naughty" style of many 1920s limericks:

> *There once was a pretty young quean*
> *His lovers were often in pain*
> *He demanded they kiss*
> *Some of that, some of this*
> *Again and again and again.*

But it isn't history, of course. Quean was a word in the Guid Scots Tongue for a flaunting woman. One sees the attraction of the term. I would give a lot for a tape of the '20s equivalent of the "Omi Palone" homosexual dialect of Soho, but until someone invents a reliable time machine, I am not going to get one (and the same goes for dropping in at the Library of Alexandria with a large skip)—sigh.

VERY LIGHT: a very bright starshell, sent up to guide the gun-aimers to their target. Accounts say it was a bright, bluish, very hot light, similar to lightning. Thunderstorms would later trigger shell-shock episodes in returned soldiers who had been exposed to it. Some of them were my relatives, so I am sure about this. I can't understand how anyone on the frontline got through the Great War even passingly sane.

TRENCH RAIDERS crept across no-man's-land to kill soldiers in the opposing trenches. They did not use firearms, but clubs and knives, aiming to strike silently and slide back without being detected.

PRIVATE EYE is not a modern term; see Pinkertons' emblem, the open eye, with their motto "We never sleep." This dates to the nineteenth century and was in common use. A common phrase for a private detective in the 1920s was private dick, which I don't like for many reasons, and "tec," which sounds too much like "tech" to modern readers. Just saying.

LEVITICUS AND SCRIPTURE I refer you to Luke 7 for the story of Longinus, and to Galatians chapter three for the statement that Old Testament Law is no longer applicable to those of the new Faith (ie, Christians). I too sat for long hours in church and read the Bible, and came to some of these conclusions all on my own (and for the others thank Professor Dennis Pryor, who spoke fluent Ancient Greek). The soldier who thrust a spear into Christ's side might have been called Gaius

Cassius Longinus, but "Longinus" just means "the tall bloke," so it might have been a common name. He isn't a saint in the Catholic church but he is in the Eastern Orthodox, though there he might be spelled "loginus," which resembles the Greek word for "the word," "logos." Or the man whose lover had been healed by Christ might have found himself promptly martyred for saying that Jesus was indeed the son of God. It is now impossible to tell whether he existed or what his name was if he did.

Paul went on to make severe remarks about homosexuality, but that was flesh-hating Paul of the "better marry than burn." I prefer him in Galatians.

PHIZZ-GIG: an informer.

FURPHY: a rumour. In the Great War, water was carried in tanks marked Furphy and Co. They were naturally centres of gossip.

COMPTON MACKENZIE was head of British Intelligence for the Mediterranean during the Great War. He has left extensive memoirs, for one of which he was prosecuted in 1934 for breaching the Official Secrets Act. He says that British Intelligence Melbourne had an office in Collins Street but doesn't tell me where, which considering what he does impart, is annoying. I've put it at the Parliament end, rather than the legal end, for no other reason than it fitted nicely with the Scots Church Assembly Hall and the Windsor Hotel, and I have always loved those unassuming, delightful, brass-plate-decorated shops. (When I was a child I met an apricot poodle called Andre there and had orange crush at a white-painted outside table while wearing a new dress. A highlight of my youth.) First Athenian Memories and Gallipoli Memories are still valuable insights into that part of the Great War. Anyone who picks up a sly ref to a TV show on which I doted in my youth is not wrong.

Sherlock Holmes and me (a love/hate relationship)

I read all of the works of Arthur Conan Doyle as a child, including *The Lost World* and Professor Challenger, his appearances in the cross-correspondences after death, the Brigadier Gerard stories, and all of the Sherlock Holmes stories. I was mildly annoyed while I was fascinated, because what Holmes was doing—his Science of Deduction—was a common female skill and, like all female skills, was awarded no applause and even sneered at as "women's intuition." Picture the scene: my mother and I are working in the kitchen when my brother staggers in, white as a sheet where he isn't green, and collapses to the floor doing a very good imitation of a dying child. My mother gave him one raking, comprehensive look and said, "I told you not to eat those apricots." When he started throwing up it was clear that he had, indeed, climbed the apricot tree and eaten a lot of green ones, which he had been strictly forbidden to do. I was relieved. I am fond of my brother. And I was also impressed. I demanded to know how my mother knew that he hadn't been stabbed in the stomach or was dying of beri beri or the Black Death (you can imagine my reading at the time). She had to think about it, then she rattled off, all in one breath, "Scuffs on his shoes, bark in his hair, juice stains on his T-shirt, sap on his front, bark in his fingernails, drying juice around his mouth. And he was guilty."

That is Sherlock Holmes' deduction at its best. The basis of Holmes' method is exceedingly close observation. He needs to use deduction on criminals because they won't tell him the truth. Had my mother demanded of my brother what he had been eating, he would have denied eating anything, for the same reason as any other law-breaker. Women have deductive method because they need it. As the gatherers in hunter/gatherer societies, and the providers of the bulk of the food, they have to be able to keep an eye on everything, while grabbing the straying toddler and trying not to walk on thorns.

It's an unfocused, all-encompassing, panoramic attention. It's special.

Which is why Sherlock annoyed me. As the Duchess says in Dorothy Sayer's novel *Clouds of Witness* (at page 106), "My dear child, you may give it a long name if you like, but I'm an old-fashioned woman and I call it mother wit, and it's so rare for a man to have it that if he does you write a book about him and call him Sherlock Holmes."

I actually wrote a Sherlock Holmes homage and pastiche story for a collection of food-related mysteries which I wrote with Jenny Pausacker, *Recipes For Crime*. It was called "The Baroness" Companion", and was a fair working Sherlock Holmes story. Conan Doyle plots very well, but he writes not very brilliant Victorian prose, not hard to imitate if you leash the adverbs and severely limit the use of adjectives. And employ occasional Victorian metaphors like "the wind cried like a child in the chimney." The experience of writing it was illuminating. I knew his methods, (Watson). I employed them.

Then people started making movies. Basil Rathbone was good, but his Watson was too bumbling—not like the man of action in the books. Jeremy Brett was a marvellous canonical Sherlock, the best there will ever be. His Watson was a very Conan Doyle Watson. Then a movie was made which emphasised the almost homoerotic edge of Sherlock and Watson. I had already thought about this because of a novel called *My Dearest Holmes* by Rohase Piercy, where they finally got together after the Reichenbach Falls. Touching. The original allows such an interpretation. "It was worth a wound; it was worth many wounds; to know the depth of loyalty and love which lay behind that cold mask." "I am here to be used."

The BBC then decided to rethink Sherlock Holmes for a modern technological age and it is mind-boggling (though I'm not altogether sure that I wanted my mind to be boggled this much). BBC Sherlock is a borderline Asperger's prodigy, amazingly rude to everyone (which the original Sherlock never is), his PTSD army doctor Watson is beyond excellent, and his Moriarty is not the Victorian Capitalist Villain of the original but a genuine psychopath. "I'll burn the heart out of you." I've met murderous psychopaths in my legal practice and BBC Moriarty is exact. Also, Benedict Cumberbatch is astoundingly, strangely, beautiful. I still haven't been able to watch him fling himself off the top of St Bart's Hospital.

I saw half of one episode of *Elementary*, where Sherlock is in America and his Watson is a woman, and it's silly. The BBC Sherlock possesses the imagination.

But I can't write a psychopath. I have to get inside a character to put them in a novel and I have enough nightmares as it is. Really. Those uninterested eyes—the same if they are looking at an apple, a chair or a dying woman—frighten me even in retrospect. So my villain at least has reasons for doing what he does, and my Sherlock-type character is a mathematician. His companion is a Great War doctor. During that obscenity of a conflict, the British Army did drag students out of the medical schools to run casualty clearing stations. Even for wars, that is unbelievably cruel. What they were doing is now called triage. God knows what that experience did to them. Actually, I have a pretty good idea. So, me and Sherlock. I naturally own no rights in any of the incarnations of the divine detective. And if I met the original, I would be hard pressed as to whether I would kiss him, or belt him over the head with a brick.

Possibly both.

On choirs

Music has always been important to me. Everyone in my extended family could sing, and one was a singer with the D'Oyly Carte Opera Company and sang *Invictus* before King George. That was my great Uncle Gwilym, who had that "baritone voice with a tenor quality" shared by my Mr. Henty. I was a singer as soon as I could speak. So naturally I joined choirs, and became a very part-time amateur folkie for a while. Choirs are important. Even mediocre singers manage university choirs, because everything they sing is note-bashed until the veriest tone-deaf tyro can sing it. I love singing in choirs. Listening to the way the music builds, diminishes, folds, where the parts slot into the whole, is fascinating. And when a choir actually performs the piece they've been rehearsing, and it works—and for some reason such things always work, even when the choir doesn't deserve it—it is magical. A fine natural high. I met most of my enduring friends by singing with them. Anyone who thinks they recognise themselves in this work probably does, though some people are compilations. And my conductors are definitely not portraits, but rather a vicious and spiteful combination of everything that has annoyed me about conductors over the last forty years. So there. A soprano's revenge may be long in coming, but when it arrives, let the wicked tremble.

Bibliography

Songbooks and music

Mendelssohn, Felix, *Elijah* (recording) Bryn Terfel with Renée Fleming, the Edinburgh Festival Chorus and the Orchestra of the Age of Enlightenment, conducted by Paul Daniel, Decca, 1997.

Mendelssohn, Felix, *Elijah* (vocal score), New Novello Choral Edition, Novello & Co. Ltd.

The F4 Compendium (songs) (ed. David Greagg).

The Monash University Choral Society Songbook (compiled by Alistair Evans, Gudrun Arnold and Ximena Inglesias, with Carolyn Edwards, Andrew Scott, Anneliese Wilson, David Young and Winston Todd; illus Bill Collopy), 1996.

Books

Abrahams, Gerald, *The Chess Mind*, Penguin Books, London, 1960.

Doyle, Sir Arthur Conan, *The Casebook of Sherlock Holmes*, Penguin Books, London, 1927.

The Epic of Gilgamesh (trans. Herbert Mason), New American Library, New York, 1970.

Glaister, (Professor) John, *The Power of Poison*, Christopher Johnson, London, 1954.

Hoffnung, Gerald, *The Symphony Orchestra*, Souvenir Press, London, 1955.

Homer, *The Iliad* (trans. EV Rieu), Penguin Classics, London, 1950.

The King James Bible

Mackenzie, Compton, *My Life and Times* (series), Chatto & Windus, London, 1964.

——*Gallipoli Memories*, Panther, London, 1965.

——*First Athenian Memories*, Cassel & Co., London, 1931.

Pausacker, Jenny and Greenwood, Kerry, *Recipes For Crime*, McPhee Gribble, Melbourne, 1995.

Piercy, Rohase, *My Dearest Holmes*, Gay Men's Press, New York, 1985.

Sayers, Dorothy, *Clouds of Witness*, New English Library, London, 1962.

Willet, Graham, Murdoch, Wayne and Marshall, Daniel (eds), *Secret Histories of Queer Melbourne*, Australian Lesbian and Gay Archives, Parkville Vic., 2011.

To receive a free catalog of Poisoned Pen Press titles, please contact us in one of the following ways:

Phone: 1-800-421-3976
Facsimile: 1-480-949-1707
Email: info@poisonedpenpress.com
Website: www.poisonedpenpress.com

Poisoned Pen Press
6962 E. First Ave. Ste. 103
Scottsdale, AZ 85251